ULTIMATUM

ULTIMATUM

Matthew Glass

Atlantic Monthly Press
New York

Printed in the United States of America

FIRST EDITION

ISBN-10: 0-8021-1888-7
ISBN-13: 978-0-8021-1888-2

Atlantic Monthly Press
an imprint of Grove/Atlantic, Inc.
841 Broadway
New York, NY 10003

Distributed by Publishers Group West

www.groveatlantic.com

09 10 11 12   10 9 8 7 6 5 4 3 2 1

ULTIMATUM

Tuesday, November 2

Wright Convention Center, Phoenix, Arizona

He came onto the stage just before eleven o'clock. In studios across the country, analysts and pundits were cut off as producers switched to the stream from Phoenix. By now the outcome wasn't in question, only the margin of victory. Vermont, the first state to be called, had kicked off a landslide rout that was roaring south and west as the evening progressed. One swing state after another came in. Ohio, where it was now one a.m., had been called for him almost as soon as the polls closed. Florida had joined his column a bare half hour later.

Dick Moberly, Arizona state chair of the Democratic Party, was onstage to introduce him. Dick was a short, round guy and every time he tried to start talking, the crowd whooped louder. He personally knew just about everyone in the hall. An excitable character at the best of times, he wasn't exactly helping his cause. Instinctively, as the crowd yelled, his arm went up and he punched the air.

"Okay, okay," said Moberly eventually. A few more stray yells came from the floor. Dick grinned but managed to keep his arm down. Finally there was silence. "Ladies and gentlemen, I give you the senior senator of the fine state of Arizona. I give you the president-elect of the United States of America . . . Joseph Emerson Benton!"

On cue, into an explosion of light and noise, he came out with his wife, Heather, and his two grown-up children, Amy and Greg. Joe Benton was a tall man, lean, with a handsome head of silvering hair, a fine straight nose, and deepset brown eyes that gave him an expression of seriousness and focus until his twinkling smile cracked it open like the top off a can. The smile cracked open now.

For two minutes solid, the crowd yelled. It wasn't words, it was just noise, sheer exuberance made into sound. The senator held up his hands. Then he turned to Heather, and Heather smiled, and then he held up his hands again, thumbs up. Still the noise went on. He dropped his arms and somehow, somehow, managed to bring it to an end.

"Friends," he said, "today the American people have made a bold choice. They have chosen to face our shared challenges with a strong heart and a brave will. They have chosen to create a new foundation. I can tell you that I have just received a call from President Gartner, who has graciously—"

Joe Benton had to stop as the noise rose in the hall. He smiled again, nodding.

"I have just received a call from President Gartner who has graciously conceded defeat in this election. I thanked him for putting up a fine, fair fight, which was a credit to our democracy."

There were sardonic cries from the crowd. The tactics of the Gartner campaign had turned as dirty as any in living memory when the true threat of Joe Benton's challenge became apparent. But it was too late by then. Nothing Gartner's people could invent came near enough to stop him.

A total of forty-six men and one woman in history had preceded Joe Benton in reaching this point, the announcement of election to the presidency of the United States. Like each one of them, he had followed his own individual, personal path to this moment. Each progress to the presidency is an odyssey, and each odyssey is unique, an unpredictable combination of circumstance, personality, timing and luck. Joe Benton was a three-term senator from Arizona. In his first term he was already being spoken of as a potential Democratic presidential contender, and speculation about him had gone on so long people had begun to believe he would never run. Too upright, too principled. Straight Joe Benton, as he was known in Arizona. But Benton knew there was only one way he could present himself as a candidate, he couldn't offer anything but the policies and the programs he knew to be right. Four years earlier, under extreme pressure to run against Mike Gartner's first bid for the presidency, he had reluctantly judged that the American people wasn't ready for the message he would give. In the end he declined to join the race, and the general view was that his moment had passed.

A lot had changed in those four years. Back then, Joe Benton was one of the few politicians of national stature talking seriously about Relocation. Not now. With two consecutive years of extreme floods on the Gulf Coast, Relocation had surged onto the mainstream agenda like a storm wave out of the Caribbean and Gartner had been forced to go to Congress for a funding package to move people out of areas that had become patently unin-habitable. Miserly and inadequate as the package was, it established Relo-cation as a central issue for the upcoming election. How had the situation reached such a dire state? Why were millions of people now to be uprooted and moved, and why had so little—nothing meaningful, in reality—been done to prevent this? Mike Gartner, as president for four years and vice president before that for eight, found it difficult to put daylight between himself and the answers to those questions. The electorate was growing disenchanted with other aspects of Gartner's administration. Unilateralism in foreign policy. Disengagement from the Kyoto process. The long U.S. military presence in Colombia and Pakistan. At home, a little too much of caring for the rich and letting the poor find their own way. This time around, as people began urging him to run, Joe Benton could feel a difference. Maybe there was an audience for his message, and maybe it was big enough not only to send him to the White House but to send enough Democrats to Congress to let him get on with the job. As the fall turned to winter, a support base coalesced for him out of the left, the center right, middle-class women, and ethnic minorities who wanted that message to be heard.

And so he hammered it home. No fancy sales pitch, no window dress-ing, just the simple things in simple language. Health. Education. Reloca-tion. Jobs. A four-part package, New Foundation, as he called it. He hammered the message home, unwavering, undeviating, while Gartner's people tried their tricks. And the more they tried, the more it looked as if Mike Gartner from Virginia didn't have an answer to Straight Joe Benton out of Arizona, the more tired Gartner looked, the more oily, the more un-trustworthy. Circumstance, personality, timing and luck. Through the spring and on into the summer, support for the Benton juggernaut kept on growing. After successive Republican administrations, this one was com-ing to an end.

"I want to thank everyone who worked so hard for the Benton-Chavez ticket. I recognize so many faces as I look around here tonight. Arnie . . . Margaret . . ." Joe Benton pointed to a couple of longtime party workers whose faces he saw, and cheering erupted in the hall around them. "Too many to name. I thank each one of you, in this room, in the country, wher-ever you are tonight. I don't know if you realize what an awesome job you did. It was a long road. I remember New Hampshire. Do you remember New Hampshire? That was cold." Benton's face cracked in his trademark smile. "Almost too cold for a Phoenix boy."

The crowd roared.

"Almost. But not quite."

The crowd roared again.

"But we made it. You know what? We're here!"

He nodded, and the roof almost came off the hall. He glanced at Heather and the children, and they smiled back at him.

"I won't keep you long. I know you've got a lot of partying to do. Enjoy it. You deserve to. This is a good night for the Democratic Party. I believe we already have six new senators, four governors, and a whole clutch of fine new representatives. And the night is young. This is a good night. Not only for our party, but for our country."

There were cheers.

"For our country. Because whatever our differences, whatever has been said and done over the past months in the spirit of a free and fair election— an election that has been contested hard, and strong, which is exactly how it should be contested—whatever is past, is past, and my job now, the thing I have been asked to do, is to work for all Americans, to make life better for all Americans. And from this moment, that is what I intend to do."

The noise had died away. Everyone in the hall knew something more serious was coming.

"Friends, we have work to do. If we have achieved anything in this election today, it's only a prelude, it's only so that we can start to achieve more, much more tomorrow." He gazed around the room. "The challenges we face are great. But we can face them with confidence, because if we have the courage truly to face them, to measure up, we will overcome them. Not only overcome them, but build on them to create a better country for ourselves, for the ones we love, and for everyone with whom we share this land."

An absolute hush had fallen in the ballroom. Every eye was on the senator, every face absorbed. Joe Benton knew that at this moment, all over the country, all over the world, on home screens, on their handhelds, people were watching him. These words, he knew, these images, would be restreamed for days to come. Right here, right now, his presidency began.

He had thought long and hard about the words he would utter next. They had been carefully crafted. Benton didn't want to be triumphalist. There was too much work ahead for that. But he didn't want to dampen the exuberance his people deserved to feel on this night. Yet he wanted everyone to know that even in the midst of celebration, the work, for him, had already started. The size of the task awaiting him, he knew, was extraordinary. Even with a majority in both houses of Congress—which now looked within reach—there was no certainty he would be able to do all that needed to be done. Everything would have to go right. And Joe Benton had been in politics long enough, had watched enough presidents and seen their support shrink and their pledged programs unravel under the pressure of events, to know that it never did.

But he also knew he would never get people even to make a beginning unless they believed he would get them all the way to the end. More than anything, he wanted these words to make people eager to start, to make them trust that if they went with him now, if only they took the first steps that he was asking of them, they would find a good, solid path ahead.

He spoke calmly, matter-of-factly.

"We must take care of each other. This has been the spirit of our republic since its founding days. If we have lost a little of this spirit, we must regain it. In the next years, we will face a great migration. Together, we can make this a time of renewal and growth. Here is the promise that I ask you to make with me. Each one of our fellow Americans who must uproot themselves will find a better life among us—not a worse. They will find the warm hand of friendship—not the cold shoulder of hostility. Communities that welcome them—not shun them. Rarely does a country have the opportunity to remake itself for the better. Those who live at such a time are blessed. My friends, we have this opportunity. It isn't something to be feared, but to be welcomed. It won't be easy, but I ask you, if any country can do it, surely it's these United States of America, this republic that has grown, endured, and prospered through more than a quarter millennium in human history, that is the one that can. Today, the American people have given me the responsibility to make sure that we do not miss this opportunity. From this moment, I will do everything in my power to make sure we succeed. Tonight, I ask each one of you—Democrat and Republican, black and white, Christian, Jew, Muslim, Buddhist or atheist, gay or straight, anyone and everyone in this great community of our republic—join me."

The senator stopped speaking. For a moment, his words hung silently in the hall. Then applause began, and it swelled, and soon the room was a thundering chamber of noise.

In network studios, on screens around the world, people saw Joe Benton reach for his wife and put his arm around her. They saw her whisper something into his ear, and he looked down at her and nodded. They saw him look around for his two children, who came closer, and he put his other arm around his daughter. The images zoomed in, and people saw his fine, lean face—a face they knew would become increasingly familiar to them over the coming four years—and they saw a slight furrowing of the brow, a slight clenching of the jaw, as he contemplated the hall before him, contemplated the responsibility he had just taken upon himself.

Joe Benton leaned toward the microphone. His face cracked in a smile.

"Goodnight," he said. "God bless you. God bless the United States of America."

Benton Transition Headquarters, Lafayette Towers, Washington, D.C.

He was going to be nothing if not ambitious. The morning after the election, at a press conference in Phoenix, Joe Benton declared that he would complete his cabinet nominations by Christmas. He also announced that Benjamin D. Hoffman would serve as director of the Transition Board and would come to the White House as his chief of staff.

Ben Hoffman was a forty-three-year-old Bostonian who had served on Benton's senatorial staff in his first term and had since gone on to hold cabinet posts in successive Massachusetts state administrations. He was a natural conciliator, amiable and attentive, but his mild exterior and chubby frame belied a powerful combination of organizational talent, political insight and fierce commitment to objectives. Hoffman was going to need all these skills from day one. There were eleven weeks until the inauguration and they would be a frenzy of staffing. His first task was to get the transition organization staffed and the process for nominating key White House and government appointments under way.

Hoffman immediately confirmed a number of key people from the campaign for roles on the transition team and brought in other personnel who had been lined up discreetly prior to the election. One of these was Steve Naylor, a well-networked, thirty-eight-year-old Los Angeles lawyer who had served as the California Democratic campaign finance director. Naylor's role was to oversee the vetting of candidates for key posts. This enormous job involved drawing on a diverse range of sources to gather names, finalize short lists, collate background research and put together briefing notes for the senator and others involved in the appointments. Naylor would soon have his own vetting team of five.

Joe Benton's first priorities were economic and domestic appointments. He wanted to keep the momentum of his campaign going all the way to the inauguration and into the first hundred days. At a Veterans Day speech that he would be making in Williamsburg later in the week, after paying due homage to the sacrifice of past veterans, he was going to draw an analogy between the collective national effort required in time of war and the collective effort required of the nation now. He was then going to announce that he would be upgrading the post of director of the National Relocation Commission to cabinet level, and that he would be creating a National Relocation Council, along the lines of the National Security and National Economic councils, to coordinate policy among the relevant departments and agencies. He would also announce a Relocation summit of experts and community leaders to be held within a month.

He was back in Washington by the weekend after the election. Monday morning, he was at his campaign headquarters at Lafayette Towers, which had now morphed into the transition headquarters, for his first meeting with Naylor. He arrived at the entrance five minutes before the meeting was due to start and didn't make it to the meeting room until a half hour later. This was the first time he had been at the headquarters since the election. The mood was elated. Staffers who had given every waking moment of the last six months of their lives to the campaign wanted to shake the senator's hand. And he wanted to shake theirs. Joe Benton climbed on a chair and made an impromptu speech, interrupted by exuberance and applause. He got down off the chair and kept shaking hands all the way to the meeting room door.

Ben Hoffman and Steve Naylor were waiting for him. Three other people were present as well. Jodie Ames had been the campaign communications director and the senator had already asked her to stay on and come to the White House. John Eales was a big, hard-hitting Chicagoan who was Joe Benton's closest political advisor and strategist, and he would be coming to the White House as well. And Angela Chavez was the vice president–elect, a two-time governor of New York State who had helped bring the women's and Latino votes to the Benton ticket. As a New Yorker, she also represented a state that would be both a relocation and reception state as people were moved out of threatened areas around New York City and into upstate reception zones. This would give her credibility in the hard lobbying that was sure to be needed over the coming months to get the legislation required for the Relocation package through Congress. In inviting her onto the ticket, Benton had promised to involve her strongly in the work of the administration, and he had every intention of doing that.

Everyone was in high spirits. It took a little time before they settled down to the business of the day. Naylor talked through the state of play of the vetting operation and then began to walk the senator through the names he had already pulled together. Benton wanted to offer the directorship of the Office of Management and Budget to Jackie Rubin, a Texas congresswoman who served on the House Budget Committee and had impressed him on a number of occasions when they had met. He wanted to hear if Naylor had found any reason to decide otherwise. He hadn't. Ben Hoffman said he'd set up a meeting.

They went through the other key economic roles, secretary of treasury, labor secretary, commerce secretary, chair of the National Economic Council, chair of the Council of Economic Advisors. Benton was determined to avoid the pitfall of stuffing his cabinet and administration with friends and former colleagues out of the Arizona party machine. Even when he had a preference, he wanted Naylor and his team to give him alternatives so he was sure to get the most competent performer.

"And we're looking for at least one Republican here," said John Eales. "Don't forget that. That's critical for credibility on the economic team if we're going to get support for our programs."

Naylor glanced questioningly at the senator. Benton nodded. Then he grimaced for effect, and there was laughter around the table.

"I guess there must be one Republican out there who doesn't turn our stomachs," said Hoffman.

Steve Naylor raised an eyebrow.

They went through the domestic roles. Benton spoke about the position of director of the National Relocation Commission, outlining his vision for the role, and Angela Chavez added some thoughts.

"I want an A-one person in this post," said Benton. "This is all about delivery. We're going to put the legislation in place and get a serious budget, and then this person's job is to take that and go out there and build an organization and get stuff done."

"And let's not forget," added Eales, "we're going to be trampling on about every special interest group in the country. This person's going to need to kick butt. This is going to have to be one thick-skinned son of a bitch who eats nails for breakfast."

The senator glanced at him. "Sounds like we ought to get you doing it, John."

"If only we could clone me."

"God help us," said Ben Hoffman.

The senator laughed.

"Maybe we should think about looking at industry for this one," said Naylor. "Senator, would you be comfortable for me to do that?"

Benton liked the idea.

"We're aiming to announce the director of the commission before the Relocation summit, right?" said Jodie Ames.

Eales nodded. "And the economic team too."

Jodie Ames glanced at Steve Naylor, who made a note.

They went through the state of play on the remainder of the domestic posts and then turned to the security roles. Joe Benton had earmarked Alan Ball, an ex–assistant director of National Intelligence and his closest campaign advisor on security and foreign affairs, for the position of national security advisor. For secretary of state he favored Al Graham, a New York lawyer who had served as undersecretary of state for Latin American affairs in the last administration but one, and had been another source of foreign policy advice during the campaign. John Eales wasn't sure about Graham and wanted the senator to keep an open mind. Ben Hoffman thought Graham was banking on secretary of state. All the more reason, in Eales's opinion, to look at other candidates.

"Al might do well at the UN," said Angela Chavez.

Benton thought about that. "Possibly. Who else is in the picture for State? I'd consider Sandy Murdoch."

"Henry Gonzalez?" said Hoffman.

"How about Larry Olsen?" said Naylor.

Benton smiled at that.

"No? Thought I'd try something from left field."

Angela Chavez laughed. "Larry Olsen? That *would* add an interesting complexion to the administration."

"Steve," said Benton, "draw up a short list for State. Keep Al Graham on it, please. I'm definitely not ruling him out. And let's have Sandy Murdoch on it as well."

John Eales glanced at his handheld. He got up and left the room. When he came back he caught Benton's eye and tilted his head meaningfully to the door.

"So, we're done?" said Benton as soon as the last cabinet post was discussed. "Steve? Okay. Good work. Anything you want to clear up, and Ben can't help you, give me a call."

"Thank you, Senator."

"Jodie?"

"We're fine, Senator."

"Angela, I'll catch you later."

Chavez nodded. She was staying on with Hoffman to talk through details of the Relocation summit.

Benton left the room.

"There's someone who wants to talk to you," said Eales when they were in the corridor. "I just got a call."

Benton glanced at him questioningly.

"Mike Gartner."

Joe Benton smiled.

"I'm serious."

Eales took the senator to the small office he used at the headquarters and gave him his handheld.

"Gartner wants to talk to you personally. That's the number . . . right there."

Eales watched as Benton made the call. After the opening pleasantry, the senator said little, mostly listening. His brow furrowed. "Certainly," said Benton. "I'll get him to do that." Then the call was over. It had lasted about a minute.

He gave the handheld back to Eales. "He wants to meet."

"We're setting up a meeting for a couple of weeks from now. Ben knows about it. You want me to get Ben?"

"Not that kind of meeting. Just him and one or two of his guys. No press, he doesn't want anyone else to know about it. Ed Steinhouser's going to call you to set things up. He'll tell you how we're going to do it. You and Ed talk directly so no one knows."

"When does he want to do it?"

"Soon. Ed'll call you today." Benton saw Eales open his mouth to ask the obvious question. "He didn't say what it's about. Just said it's something we need to talk about and when we do I'll understand why he wants to do it like this."

Eales nodded. Neither Joe Benton nor John Eales had ever been through the transition to the presidency before. Anyone who does it, does it only once, and it isn't the custom to leave instructions behind. Neither man knew what the rules were. They didn't know if there were any rules.

"John," said Benton. "You think this is normal? A secret meeting like this?"

Eales shook his head. "I was just about to ask you the same thing."

Monday, November 15

Canoustie House, Virginia

The Virginia countryside was wintry. Gartner was waiting inside when they arrived, along with Ed Steinhouser, the White House chief of staff, and Art Riedl, a special advisor who had been the man closest to Gartner during his presidency.

Mike Gartner was a Virginia Republican who had served two terms as vice president under Bill Shawcross before moving into the White House on his own account. Thanks to Joe Benton, he was going down in history as a one-term chief executive.

"Sit down, Joe," he said as he sat himself down in a big armchair upholstered in some kind of a floral fabric

It was the first time the two men had come face-to-face since the last debate before the election. Benton was generally considered to have wiped the floor with Gartner during that encounter. He had forced the president into defending his record, his long list of tax cuts and reductions to federal programs. The more Gartner defended it, the more hard-hearted he seemed.

"You ran a good campaign, Joe," said Gartner.

"Thanks," replied Benton. "I think I was saying what the American people wanted to hear."

"What they want to hear ain't necessarily what they need to hear," said the president.

Joe Benton didn't respond to that. The American people had given their own answer two weeks earlier.

Gartner shook his head. "One-term president." He looked up at Benton. "That's not something I recommend."

Joe Benton didn't say anything to that either. There was nothing to say he wouldn't be in the same situation, he knew, four years hence.

"Your son might run next time round, Mr. President," said Art Riedl.

"And give these boys another Gartner to wallop?" muttered the president sourly. "I don't think so." Gartner's oldest son had been elected junior senator for Florida four years earlier. "Remember what happened the last time we did that? What a fuckup! Twelve years in Iraq. What a goddamned fuckup."

There was silence.

"And now we're stuck in Colombia. Another godforsaken shit hole. You know, the funny thing is, people think I was one of the people who wanted to take us in there. But you ask anyone who knows." Gartner slapped his hand forcefully on the armrest of his chair. "I told Bill Shawcross. I said we'll never get out of that place. It's a fucking swamp. But he took us on in. Said there's only one way to stop the drugs coming out. Just a limited intervention. Pressured the Colombian government to invite us in to help beat the insurgency and the limited intervention expands and before you know it you're dropping bombs on housefuls of villagers and the whole goddamned cycle begins again. I'll tell you this. There's no such thing as a limited intervention. You start it, you never know when it's going to end." Gartner laughed disgustedly and ran his hand through his thinning dark hair. "There's some advice I hope I didn't need to give you. Well . . . You boys want coffee?" he asked suddenly. He motioned to a sideboard where there was coffee and juice and water.

Ed Steinhouser got up and started pouring. He gave a coffee to each of the men in the room.

The president slurped a couple of times, then put his cup down.

"Okay, we should get down to business," he said. "I apologize about the secrecy and all."

Benton smiled. "I thought you normally left a sealed letter on the desk."

"Yeah, I guess that's one way of doing it. It'd have to be a damn big letter."

There wasn't even a flicker of a smile on Gartner's face as he said it. Suddenly Joe Benton thought the other man looked weary. He had known Gartner for years, known him as a fellow senator even before he became Bill Shawcross's vice president, always ebullient, usually overbearing. He didn't think he had ever seen him look so down.

"What is it, Mike?"

"There's some stuff you've got to know about. I wanted this meeting secret because I don't want the press asking what we talked about. Pretty soon it's going to be your problem. Believe me, Joe, you don't want the press asking."

"What is it?" said Benton.

"I'm sorry to have to spring it on you like this. But you wanted the job, right?" The president picked up his cup and slurped again. "Okay. Tell me; you spoken to President Wen since the election?"

Benton nodded. About half the world's leaders had called him in the days following the election, including President Wen of China.

"What'd he say? You don't mind me asking, right?"

"He congratulated me. Said he hoped we'd work together. The world has big issues and we have to solve them as partners."

"What big issues? Anything specific?"

"It was a general conversation." Benton couldn't say much more without checking his notes. To his recollection it was pretty much the same conversation he'd had with most of the other leaders who had called, part congratulation, part platitudes about working together.

Gartner nodded. "Nothing else?"

"Like what?"

"Like we've been holding negotiations with the Chinese."

"What about?"

"Emissions. Bilateral negotiations, Joe. Strictly bilateral and strictly secret."

Benton stared at Gartner. Then he glanced at Eales, who had stopped, coffee in hand, and was staring at the president as well.

As president, Gartner's stance toward the Chinese had been one of perfect intransigence. That was one of the reasons the country had dumped him. The crucial swing vote—the Latino community and women between the ages of thirty and fifty-five—found him excessively belligerent and unilateralist in international affairs. Fully seventy percent of them, for instance, believed he was more likely than not to expand the U.S. military presence in Colombia. The percentage that believed Joe Benton would do that was so low it was essentially unmeasurable.

Gartner's line on China had always been that the Chinese government would have to show they were genuinely doing something on carbon emissions before the United States could sit down with them again. They had broken too many promises on emissions reduction in the past. Action first, was Gartner's line, often repeated. Action first, words later.

"How long have these negotiations been going on?" asked Benton.

The president glanced at Art Riedl.

"Seven months," said Riedl.

Benton nodded. It was starting to make sense. Gartner had been hoping to keep it secret, then announce some kind of a deal with China just before the election. Pull a rabbit out of a hat, steal the show, and ride triumphantly back into the White House.

He glanced at Eales.

"Now, I know what you're thinking, Joe," said Gartner. "But you're wrong. I'm not denying it would have been nice. Would have. But there were other reasons for keeping it secret. I'd like you to meet somebody." The president looked at Ed Steinhouser, who got up and left the room. "One of the fun things about this job," said Gartner as they waited for Steinhouser to come back, "is you get to find out about all kinds of stuff you never even knew existed. Stuff I had no idea about even as vice president. I'll tell you, if I had known there was all this stuff I didn't know when I was vice president, I'd have been frustrated as hell. And it was frustrating enough, that's for sure. You're lucky, Joe, you never had to do the job. That running mate of yours, Chavez, I pity what she's going to go through."

"Angela's going to be involved," said Benton.

"Sure," said Gartner, and he smiled knowingly.

Ed Steinhouser came back. A woman in uniform came with him. She was small, slim, with tightly coiffed blond hair.

"This is Dr. Richards," said the president. "Dr. Richards, Senator Benton."

Benton stood up and shook her hand.

"Dr. Richards heads a navy unit that's responsible for environmental surveillance," said Riedl. "I should add that the information Dr. Richards's unit gathers is not released publicly nor is it shared with any other government."

"Combining this with the data available in the wider scientific community, Senator," explained Richards, "we have the most complete data set available. That means we have a far more precise and accurate picture of environmental trends than any other government in the world. This puts us at a significant advantage in the quality of our scenario generation."

"In't that great?" quipped the president.

"What kind of data is this?" asked Benton.

"Deep ocean salinity, deep ice sheet temperature and thickness variations, ocean current velocities, ionosphere particulates and a number of other critical variables. Few institutions have the ability to track these variables even sporadically, and none have the ability to track them constantly, which is what we're able to do at the Environmental Surveillance Unit."

"They have a whole fleet of vessels," said Riedl.

"Fourteen," said Dr. Richards, "including support ships. And we have a number of ESU land stations. The unit was established nineteen years ago, Senator, after Kyoto 2 in the Copenhagen round, and with the quantity of historical data we now have we're reaching a point where our predictive accuracy is quite high."

"How high?" asked Eales.

"We feel in general we're now in excess of ninety percent accuracy."

"And what have you found?" asked Benton.

"We believe our previous predictions were incorrect. We're finding that the rate of change across a range of variables is fifteen to twenty percent higher than we had projected."

"Because no one's in compliance with Kyoto 3," said Benton.

"No, sir. That's factored into our assumptions. The increase appears to be largely due to carbon feedback effects. Principally we're talking about release of trapped carbon dioxide as ocean temperature rises and areas of permafrost thaw, and reduced reflection of sunlight as the Greenland ice pack melts and sea ice generally disappears. The Amazon fire is also having an effect, and a number of more minor feedback effects are in play as well."

Benton frowned. "None of this is new, right?" The senator was aware that feedback effects in climate change had been under discussion for decades, and if he knew about them, he assumed there must be deep understanding of the phenomena in the scientific community.

"No, sir. As you say, the existence of these effects isn't new, but the implications are. Let me explain. A feedback effect is a cycle. The more you have, the more it happens. It ramps itself up, if you will. For example, the more sea ice melts, the less sea ice there is to reflect sunlight, so the warmer the temperature becomes, so now even more sea ice melts, so now even less sunlight is reflected. And so on from year to year. That's easy. As you said yourself, we've all known these effects have been happening for many years. What's harder to determine, until you actually see it, is the rate at which the cycle ramps up. A huge number of variables can have an effect. Previous models had to guess, they were built on assumptions about the rate of increase. They tended to assume a fairly moderate rate."

"You mean to be on the safe side they should have assumed a faster rate?"

"It's not my place to comment on what others should have done, sir. I'm just pointing out that the models assumed a certain range of rates. The Relocation plan you outlined during your campaign, for example, would be based partly on these assumptions, because the models on which it was based had these assumptions built in. What's new is that we now have sufficient data to actually tell what the rate is with a high degree of confidence, and what these data are telling us, Senator, is that the cycle appears to be ramping up quicker than the previous models assumed."

"But if this is happening," said Eales, "other scientists will be picking it up."

"Oh, it's happening, Mr. Eales. And other scientists will pick it up. I would say, in a matter of two to three years, the trends will be more broadly obvious. We just have the ability to pick it up earlier because of our superior data gathering and monitoring capabilities."

"Dr. Richards," said Benton, "you said your projections were mistaken before. How do we know they're not mistaken again?"

"We've learned, sir."

"So you're confident of what you're saying?"

"We're confident that we're seeing effects happening at a rate fifteen to twenty percent faster than our models predicted. We can be ninety-nine percent certain that the increase is more than ten percent. Or to put it another way, there's less than a one percent chance that the trends we're seeing reflect less than a ten percent increase in the actual rate of change."

"In other words, you're sure."

"I never say I'm sure, sir."

Benton looked for a hint of a smile on Dr. Richards's lips, but didn't see one.

"Now, do you want to hear the bad news?" said the president. "Dr. Richards?"

"As I said, Senator, this is a feedback loop. That means the longer it goes on, the more it accelerates itself. To put it simply, the longer it goes on, the worse it gets. Not in a linear fashion, but exponentially." Dr. Richards paused. "With respect, do you understand the terminology, Senator, and its implications, or would you like me to explain?"

Benton nodded. "I understand."

"It's only in the last year that the trends have become this clear."

Benton watched Dr. Richards. She looked back at him with a clear, assertive gaze in her blue eyes. For a moment he wondered what she felt under that crisp exterior, if the numbers she cited so efficiently, the percentages, the degrees of certainty, found their way under her skin in terms of what they were going to mean to people. To millions of people, probably, if he had understood what she was saying.

"Can you outline what the chief effects of this will be?"

"Exacerbation of the phenomena we're already projecting. Sea level rise, enhanced storm activity, altered rainfall patterns, altered growth patterns, alteration in disease ranges, and desertification. The whole panoply of effects, Senator."

"More specifically?"

"Dr. Richards," said the president before she could answer. "Thank you. That's fine for now. Perhaps you could wait outside in case we have any further questions."

Richards nodded.

"Thank you," said Benton.

She turned to go. Ed Steinhouser led her out.

"Don't want to get too technical," remarked the president. "You'll have numbers coming out your ears if you let her go on. Believe me, I've seen it. It ain't pretty."

"We can get the detailed projections from her?" said Eales.

"Sure. Art'll set it up."

"Mike, you haven't made any of this public," said Benton.

"Would you have?"

"But you thought you could do a deal on this with the Chinese government?"

"Listen, Joe," said Gartner, "this is bigger than partisan politics. Way bigger. You heard what Richards said. This process accelerates itself. If we're going to do anything about it, we have to put an end to it right now."

"And the Chinese? What's the angle with them?"

"China hasn't honored a single agreement on emissions it's signed up to. Not a single clause. Not Kyoto 3, not Kyoto 2."

"We haven't been much better," said Eales.

"That may be true, Mr. Eales," replied the president sharply. "But China is worse. They overtook us as the world's biggest polluter in absolute terms twenty-five years ago. That's a whole quarter century, but they speak and behave as if they're still a developing country. They have to take some responsibility."

"Mike," said Benton, "I accept that. But if it's not for partisan reasons, I don't understand the secrecy here. We've got Kyoto 4 coming up. Surely that's the forum for this."

"You may choose to make it the forum, Joe. That's your decision now."

"I said all through my campaign we have to engage internationally, and I meant it. With respect, Mike, I think failure to engage in multilateral forums was one of the mistakes of your administration and of Bill Shawcross's, and I think the American people have just shown that they agree."

"With respect, Joe, that's just so much horseshit. The campaign's over, it's time to govern. You can say what you like when you don't have to deliver. Go ahead, deal with it through Kyoto 4 if you want. But you listen to me. I signed Kyoto 3. Bill sent me. Remember? I was the one in Santiago with the pen in my hand." Mike Gartner sat forward in his chair and stretched out his arm. "This hand right here. Now let me tell you something. There were a hundred and fifty-three other leaders there that day in the Palazzo whatever-the-hell-it-was, and they all signed, every last one, and I swear to you, as they signed those papers, not one of them intended to stick to the obligations they were signing up to. And not one of them did. And that includes the Chinese, and the Indians, and the Brits, and the EuroCore, and whoever the hell else was there. And us as well, I'm not saying it doesn't. And Kyoto 3 was *weak*. Remember? We were coming off the back of the recession and it looked like the global economy was doing half the work of emissions control for us. But when the global expansion started up, no one remembered that, and we all just went for growth like we always do. Held the line that new technologies would make everything better without any pain. Voluntary measures were enough, we'd all act honorably, no need for sanctions. The usual Kyoto crap, we'll all just wait ten years and see where we've got to." Gartner sat back in his chair and shook his head in disgust. "The pace never gets any quicker. A chunk of ice the size of Maine floats off some ice shelf in the Antarctic . . . Art, where was that again?"

"The Ronne Ice Shelf, Mr. President. And it was the size of New Hampshire."

"Right. And when was that? Eight years ago?"

"Nine, Mr. President."

"Right, nine. The size of New Hampshire. Splash! And what do we do? Same process, same speed. Like a fucking snail that's only got one gear. So you can listen to me, Joe, and take it from someone who knows, or you can learn it the hard way. Try to do it through Kyoto 4 if you want, just like you promised in your campaign. Spend another two years negotiating while this feedback cycle keeps ramping up, and then spend another five years monitoring until it's obvious everyone's in breach, and then it'll be time to start negotiating Kyoto 5 and see where we are then. Go ahead. It's your show now. You're the boss."

"China's not the only emitter," said Benton. "Even if you did a bilateral deal with them, what happens next?"

"Senator," said Art Riedl, "what has to happen is for the world's leading emitters to agree to sharp cuts, even savage cuts, and to show they're doing it. Action, not words. You get us doing it, you get China doing it, and then you've got the leverage to bring the rest of the world on board. No one's going to believe it's going to happen if the United States isn't involved, but you can't sell this to the American people if the Chinese aren't on board as well. So that was our strategy. Us and China first, then use that to bring the rest of the world into line. We believe the American people will take the pain if they can see China doing it as well and if there's a genuine verification mechanism with penalties to back it up. We don't believe they'll take the pain for the sake of yet another Kyoto that's going to turn out to have been ignored by everyone else in ten years time."

"How deep were the cuts?" asked Eales.

Riedl and the president looked at him.

"The emissions cuts you offered the Chinese, Mr. President. What did you offer them?"

"We showed them the data," said Gartner. "They knew why it's necessary to do something. When it came to the bottom line, we offered an immediate freeze, and a matched point for point emissions reduction over the next seven years. Mutually verified."

"How much?"

"Eighteen percent," said Gartner.

Benton didn't react. Not outwardly. Eighteen percent over such a short time frame was a massive reduction. And all the painless steps to cut emissions had been taken long ago. The economic impact of this would be . . . considerable.

"The time when we could do this easily is long gone," said Gartner quietly. "That was thirty years ago. There's no way to do it easy anymore."

"Mike," said Benton, almost not wanting to hear the answer to the question he was about to ask, "this accelerated rate of change we've been talking about—what's the impact? How bad is it?"

"The Relocation plan I took to Congress envisaged the abandonment of the majority of the Gulf Coast, parts of southern Florida, the Chesapeake Bay area, parts of the San Francisco Bay area, and sectors of New York and other coastal cities. That was a total of a little over six million people and the congressional requisition was 4.2 trillion over the next ten years."

There was silence in the room. Everyone waited for what was coming next. They all knew the numbers Gartner had just listed. Joe Benton had fiercely opposed Gartner's plan. The estimate of the total population to be relocated, he knew, was too small, and the financial allocation, six percent of the budget projection, was way too low to do anything but condemn those people to poverty. Benton expected to have to double it.

Gartner took a deep breath. "Magnify it fivefold. And while you're at it, say good-bye to Miami. The tri-county area will take a category four or better hurricane every two years and the storm surge will drown every living thing all the way to Orlando. And in case you're wondering, the drought in southern California, its never going to end. We're talking desert. All up, we're talking maybe thirty million people, and a cost of twenty-five trillion over the ten year period."

Joe Benton stared at him.

"Art can show you the math."

Benton didn't need to see it. Whatever Gartner said about the cost, he'd have to double it at least. "Is this done, or does it only happen if we don't get a deal for the emissions cuts you mentioned?"

"Most of it's done," replied Gartner. "Art's got the exact breakdown. You go spending another five years messing around with Kyoto 4 and it's all this and then you can add some more."

Riedl nodded. "I've got those numbers as well."

The magnitude of what he was facing left Benton groping for something, anything, to get a handle on it.

"I'm sorry to dump this in your lap, Joe. Truly I am."

Benton didn't reply. Whatever Gartner said, Benton knew that the chance of cutting a secret deal and announcing it just before the election would have been to the fore in his mind.

"Mr. President," said Eales, "can you tell us what the current status of the talks with the Chinese government is?"

"At the moment we have no talks, Mr. Eales. The latest word out of Beijing is they see no point continuing negotiations with my administration since it's effectively no longer in power."

"Who was in your team?" asked Eales.

"Art here. Art was the team. No one outside this room even knows we were talking with them."

Eales turned to Riedl. "You'll give me a full briefing?"

Riedl nodded.

"Joe," said the president, "I'm convinced now the Chinese never intended to cut a deal. They were stringing me along. They're conniving, deceitful bastards, and you can't trust them further than you can throw 'em."

A perfect match, thought Benton.

"They figured they'd buy time by letting me think they'd cut a deal before the election. But we had nothing back from them, all right? I want you to understand that. I'm telling you the truth here. Nothing."

Benton knew what that meant. Gartner had given the Chinese a proposal for the cuts he had outlined without receiving even a counterproposal in return, so chances were the Chinese would hold on to anything they considered favorable in Gartner's proposal and demand that as a starting position in further talks.

"I don't know how you're going to play it, Joe. I'm stepping back. I've got nine weeks left. I'll go along with whatever way you want to do it."

"Do you think they'll restart talks now?"

"With you?"

Benton nodded.

"Maybe," said Gartner, "but they'll be playing for time. They'll see if they can get anything out of you. If you ask for anything back, they'll say you're not in power yet."

Joe Benton thought that was probably right. "What about our allies internationally? Do any of them know about this?"

Gartner's lip curled. "Let me give you a word of warning, Joe. Whenever the Europeans say they'll do something, halve it. That's how much you'll get. And you'll get it about half as fast as they promise it. You want to act quick, you've got to go it alone. That's why we did it like we did. I want you to believe that, Joe. I can only tell you again, you can take this into Kyoto, but that would be a disaster for our country."

"Anything else?" said Benton.

"Isn't that enough?"

"More than enough."

"Then we're done," said the president. "Art'll give Mr. Eales the details. We can talk again if you want after that. Just let me know. Anything else happens, I'll keep you informed." He stood up.

Benton stood as well.

"We have a meeting in a couple of weeks with our staffs. Pretty pictures. I guess you can understand now why I wanted to do this one a little more quietly."

* * *

Outside, a cold fog had descended with the dusk. The limo headed off past bare, sticklike trees.

Joe Benton thought over what he had been told. "Usually the Republicans just tell you the budget deficit's going to be twice what they said in the campaign," he murmured. "But you've got to hand it to Mike Gartner. He always goes one better."

"He's been president for four years and vice president for eight," said Eales. "And he's got the nerve to tell us now, after the election, that everything's five times as fucked-up as he admitted. He was vice president when the Ronne Ice Shelf collapsed! What the fuck did he try to do differently afterwards?" Eales turned and looked back. The house where they had met the president had long disappeared from view. "What a piece of shit."

Benton didn't disagree.

"He never had a chance with the Chinese," said Eales in the same disgusted tone. "They would have played him like a cat with a mouse. But that's Mike Gartner for you. Hold the whole country to ransom for seven months just to try to keep his sick butt in the White House."

Benton nodded. That was exactly what he thought. That was exactly why Gartner had kept everything secret.

They rode on in silence.

Or was it? Benton saw the image of Mike Gartner thrusting out his hand toward him, the same hand with which he had signed the Kyoto 3 treaty in Santiago. He heard him saying that it was easy to talk from the sidelines, when you didn't have to get things done. And Art Riedl, explaining their strategy. It *was* a strategy, Benton had to give them that. And he could almost have believed their reasoning if everything in their past didn't show they were as much a pair of lying, deceitful, conniving bastards as anyone they could possibly have come up against on the Chinese side.

No, it was a strategy that just happened to fit the unilateralist prejudices of Mike Gartner and his entire administration. And one which conveniently might have allowed him to pull off a miracle win in an election he had all but lost.

"Get the details," said Benton.

Eales nodded. "I'll get with Riedl for a briefing. I want to see exactly what they offered."

"And talk to the navy woman as well. Directly. Don't trust Riedl."

There was silence again. Joe Benton tried to come to grips with the numbers he had heard, what it would mean for his presidency. Most of the damage was inevitable, even if rapid cuts in emissions could be negotiated. Gartner had mentioned a fivefold increase in the impact. If Benton had thought he was facing a challenge with the scale of relocation he had known about, now that looked almost easy.

What would this do to his plans? Day one, behind the desk in the Oval Office, what should he do about it?

Eales's thoughts had gone in the same direction. "Do you want to bring Angela in on this?"

Benton thought for a moment. "No. I don't think so. Not yet, anyway. Not before I figure out where this is going."

"I agree," said Eales. "And we keep Jodie away from it."

That hardly needed an answer. The last person Joe Benton wanted involved at this point was his communications director.

Day one wasn't far away. This would affect everything, his legislative program, the economy, his foreign policy. Benton knew that he urgently needed to start thinking through the implications. But he didn't have a team on board yet, not one to which he could confide information of this sensitivity.

Yet of the people who could help him, there were two, at least, who had already agreed to join his administration.

Thursday, November 18
Georgetown, Washington, D.C.

Jackie Rubin and Alan Ball came in by the front door. The senator wasn't too worried if they were seen arriving at his Georgetown home by press who were watching the street. Although he hadn't made any announcements yet, Rubin had agreed to leave the House of Representatives to become director of the Office of Management and Budget, and Alan Ball was slated to be the national security advisor. They arived at eleven p.m. The Bentons had just returned from a dinner for the Health Advocacy Forum, an activist organization they had supported for years.

Heather showed Ball and Rubin in. The senator was taking a call from Hugo Montera, a New Jersey lawyer he wanted as his Secretary of Labor. When the call was finished he joined them.

Rubin was in her forties, with an earnest, expressive face and short dark hair. Ball was a small, dapper man with a head that seemed too large in proportion to the rest of him. He was currently professor of international relations at the Kennedy School, prior to which he had been chair of the UN commission on viral pandemics and global avoidance. Further back he had served six years as an assistant director of national security.

John Eales joined the group as well. Benton gave a short introduction, stressing that no one outside this group, and an equally small number of people in the Gartner White House, knew what they were about to discuss. Then he asked Eales to give a briefing. Eales had spent a half day with Art Riedl getting full coverage of the negotiations with the Chinese, and another half day with Dr. Richards. He summed up concisely.

"What I want to do tonight," said Benton when Eales had finished, "is get the thinking going on this. I'm not looking for decisions yet, obviously. Let's get some first thoughts on what you see as the implications, any ideas for how we take this forward, and then we can all go away and think about it a little more. Let's start with your initial reactions. First of all, from each of your perspectives, then we can loop back to the bigger picture."

Alan and Jackie looked at each other.

"Go ahead," said Ball.

"Gee, thanks, Alan."

There were smiles for a moment. Then a serious frown came over Jackie's face.

"Speaking off the top of my head . . . The first thing that occurs to me is, I'm not sure where we go with our domestic programs if we have to absorb a hit like this. We've agreed all along that we ought to expect a deficit at least half as big again as the deficit the administration projected in the campaign, but this is a whole nother issue. If we're really looking at thirty or forty trillion more over the next ten years, that's almost . . . we're talking about numbers that are getting up towards half our total budget. Proportionately, that's probably more than we've ever spent even in a war situation." Rubin paused. "I'll check that. Maybe we're going to need to think of ourselves as kind of a war economy. There's going to be a massive transfer of productivity from consumption to capital investment just to replace infrastructure."

"We already anticipated that," said Eales.

"But not on this scale. Without seeing the figures, I'm guessing this is so big you can't expect to manage it within the economy as usual and there's going to have to be a significant restructuring of the allocation of resources. In other words some kind of central involvement in the allocation."

"In the allocation only, or in the investment?" Benton asked.

"I'm guessing both." Rubin frowned. "I have to think about this. And I need to get the numbers and have some work done on them."

Benton nodded. "Anything else?"

"I'm worried about what this does to our programs in the short term. Health and education in particular. If we're looking at something on this scale, are we going to be able to do better than just pick people up and move them and put them in a trailer somewhere like Gartner was proposing?"

"We have to do better than that," said Benton.

Jackie nodded. The frown on her face deepened.

Benton turned to Ball. "Alan?"

"If you're asking from my perspective as potentially a national security advisor, I guess my first thoughts are, Gartner went bilateral to try to deal with this with China, and that's not our style. I don't think anyone here is going to say we shouldn't be putting this into the Kyoto process like you said we'd be doing all through the campaign."

Benton gazed at him. "Go on."

"Even if we had any doubts, what Gartner's told us just demonstrates why that approach won't work."

"Because the Chinese didn't cut a deal?"

"Exactly."

"Why is that, do you think?" asked Benton. "They face the same problems as us. John has just said, the projections show swaths of their southern coast becoming uninhabitable because of inundation and storm activity, and they'll have a considerably greater problem than us with desertification in their central provinces."

"Exactly," said Ball again.

"Then shouldn't they have done a deal?"

"Joe, they're not going to do it bilaterally. Particularly not with a president who's desperate to do it for electoral reasons."

"But they should have figured they'd get a better deal in that situation than they could get any other time," said Eales.

"True. And yet still they didn't do it. Doesn't that prove my point?"

"On the other hand," said Eales, "maybe they figured a president who cut a deal out of desperation wouldn't be able to get the Senate to ratify, and they'd be left exposed. If that's the case, if they wouldn't do one with a president who was desperate for electoral reasons, maybe they'll do one with a president who isn't."

Benton glanced at Eales. He knew that the big Chicagoan often tested ideas to destruction by getting behind them and seeing what arguments came back, even when he didn't agree with the ideas himself.

Ball smiled. "You can't have it both ways, John."

"Sure, but what I'd like to know is which way is the right way."

Ball laughed.

Benton was thinking through the implications of what Ball had said. "What you're suggesting, Alan, is by making this information public, taking it into the Kyoto process, that makes China more likely to cut a deal."

"And everyone else. Not just China. India, the EuroCore, Japan, Brazil, Russia. All the big emitters."

"Plus a hundred and fifty other countries," said Eales.

Benton glanced at Eales again. A hundred and fifty countries. He could imagine the special pleading, the side deals, the concessions, the watering-down that would go on to get a deal between so many parties. Mike Gartner's words came back to him. Spend two years negotiating, another five years verifying and finding out no one's in compliance, then start negotiating again. And all the time, the feedback loop would be ramping itself up. He couldn't help thinking that cutting a simple, straight, sanctions-backed deal with China—if it could be done—and then using that deal as combined leverage with everyone else, really was an attractive alternative.

Throughout the campaign, Joe Benton had been rock solid in support of Kyoto 4, which was scheduled to kick off toward the end of the following year. He had promised that his administration would create a leadership role for the United States within the process so that this Kyoto treaty, unlike its three predecessors, would provide the framework for a truly just and lasting solution to the emissions problem. But Benton knew that his statements about a leadership role in Kyoto were generic, and he and his advisors had done very little thinking about what this would actually translate to, or what could realistically be expected out of the new treaty. He was also sufficiently self-aware to know that, like many incoming presidents, he had little direct experience of foreign affairs, and he felt that this was where he would be most vulnerable when it came to heading the executive. Listening to Gartner had made him feel like a novice, and Benton was pretty sure Mike Gartner was aware of it. Enjoyed making him feel like that. Yet on this question Gartner really did know what he was talking about, a lot better than Joe Benton did. Gartner had been a midwife to Kyoto 3, as much as any American politician had been. It was his signature on the treaty. If he had opted for a bilateral approach with China now, maybe there really was more to it than the hope of pulling a rabbit out of a hat before the election.

"This gives us the chance to truly take leadership on Kyoto," said Alan Ball. "I'll put some thoughts in a paper on how we use this to seize the agenda."

Benton nodded. "Thank you, Alan. That would be good." He paused. "Okay, let me turn this to something else. It's Inauguration Day. Do I make this public? I could announce it and say we're using whatever plan we've come up with to seize the Kyoto agenda. Alternatively, I could keep it quiet like Gartner did, at least for a while, until the timing's right. Hope it doesn't leak. If it leaks, say its speculation, say it's just a scenario, there's no certainty. I want to think about the options politically. John, why don't you kick off?"

Eales was silent for a moment. "My first thought is there's something attractive about announcing it. Just throwing it out there. One, you don't face the risk of leaks, no one's going to turn around and say you've misled the people. Two, it's like you throw down a challenge to the American people. In a way, that's what our whole campaign was about. Here's a challenge, I've got the courage to admit it, now let's rise to it together. That worked. It caught the mood of the American people. So we can ride that mood. Now it's just, okay, the challenge is bigger. If anyone can put that out there, Senator, it's you. You've earned that right. You've earned that credibility. You could throw it out right there at the inauguration— we face this, we have to deal with it, join me, work with me. Together, we'll overcome it."

"Like Roosevelt," murmured Rubin. "We have nothing to fear like fear itself."

Eales nodded. "Exactly right, Jackie. We have nothing to fear but fear itself. And you also dis Gartner's administration. Basically, you're saying, he messed up, I'm going to clean up. You dissociate us from the problem. You associate us with the solution. That's why it's got to be day one. If we don't do it day one, we lose that opportunity. It's got to be absolute silence or complete confession."

"What's Gartner going to do?" said Alan Ball.

"He said he'll go along with however I want to play it," replied Benton.

"No, but if you dis him, what's he going to do then? What are the Republicans going to do?"

"They're a minority in both houses," said Eales.

"But they've still got forty-three senators," said Rubin.

Everyone in the room knew the significance of that number. To mount a filibuster, and cause endless obstruction to a president's legislative program, the opposition party requires only forty senators on the Hill.

"There's a half-dozen Republicans who'll support our program," said Eales. "Just give them the right incentives."

"Not if you dis the party. Not if it turns partisan."

"Everything's partisan."

"Not this partisan. Not like it is if you go out of your way to dis your predecessor."

"Jackie's got a point," said Benton. "I want everyone in the tent that I can get, Democrat or Republican."

"Senator," said Ball, "I know we're looking at this primarily in terms of domestic politics, but we need to think of the Chinese government as well. How does it make them look if we go public like this? It's kind of saying, President Gartner couldn't handle them, but we darn well will."

"I won't be saying that."

"But that's what it might look like. Seen from there, it feels aggressive."

"Maybe we need to be aggressive," said Eales.

"Senator," said Rubin. "I'm going back to John's idea. The Roosevelt idea. When John said it, I liked it. It's bold, imaginative, honest. Like John said, that's why the country elected you. And there's a nice symmetry here. It's exactly a hundred years since Roosevelt came to power. You could do a lot with that in your speech."

"A second Gettysburg Address," said Eales, only half in jest. "Five score years ago, a man stood in this place . . ."

Benton smiled briefly.

"Senator, I'm concerned that if you do that, it'll deal a blow to your presidency you'll never recover from." Jackie frowned. "It's not the same as Roosevelt. When Roosevelt came to power, the problem was clear. Two years of depression and an administration that was utterly unable to deal with it. Roosevelt could pose as being the solution. He didn't put a drastic new problem in front of the people. When you get up on that podium January twentieth, Senator, there is no problem. Not this problem, anyway. Not until you start speaking. You put it there. And even though you didn't make the problem, you become tainted with it. You're the messenger. And the other thing is, Roosevelt had a solution. We don't. All we can say is, if we convince other countries to get on board, *then* we'll have a solution. If that's all we do, if we just go with the problem, my fear is the problem is all anyone's going to think about."

"But we do have a solution," said Ball. "We put it into Kyoto 4."

"With respect, Alan, that's a process, not a solution, and it's not a process most of the American people have a lot of respect for. Senator, as it is now, what you're going to be judged on is New Foundation. That's something we can deliver, that's something we can control. But if you put this out there on Inauguration Day, then that's what the administration is going to be judged on: whether you get a solution out of Kyoto 4. And negotiations over setting up Kyoto 4 are going to take the best part of the next two years, which is when we should be getting your major programs in place. That's the most viable period of your first term. So if your ability to execute New Foundation is hostage to progress on Kyoto 4, I think that's a huge risk to everything we're trying to do. Let's be judged on New Foundation. Kyoto's something you can't control. In fact, the more that other countries see you're being judged on it, the less control you have, and the more they'll hold you hostage on it."

"This is the single biggest problem we face," said Benton. "Isn't it right that I should be judged on it?"

"But there are other things, Senator. There are other things you want to do right away. Even if you can't win on this thing, we can still do them. And like I said, they're things we can control. Education. Health. Jobs. Relocation. Again and again, you've said you're going to be a domestic president. I fear you won't have a chance to do any of those things if you invite people to judge you on Kyoto 4. Senator, look how many years of Republican administration it took to get the chance to do something about these things, and I fear that if you stand up on Inauguration Day and start talking about what John has told us tonight, we're going to lose it in the course of a single speech."

"That's a grim thought," said Benton.

"Yes, sir. It is."

"And if we keep it quiet," said Eales, "and the day after the inauguration some journalist finds out about this—if Gartner decides to leak because he wants to dis us before we can dis him—we look like we've started off by deceiving the American people. Do we ever recover from that?"

"I know," said Rubin. "I know. Senator, can I ask, what's your inclination?"

"My inclination is to do the thing that will best serve the interests of the American people."

"Which is?"

Benton smiled. "I'm not sure yet."

Heather was still awake when Benton went upstairs.

"Problems?" she asked.

Joe shook his head.

Heather watched him for a moment. "Okay."

Joe sat on the edge of the bed. But he didn't do anything. He stared at the rug.

"Looks like Hugo Montera might turn me down for Labor," he said eventually.

"And you want a Latino in the job?"

"He's a good guy."

"Why's he turning it down?"

"He wasn't very clear. Disillusioned, something like that. Disillusioned with government after his last stint."

Heather Benton reached for her husband's hand. "Then you just have to reillusion him, Joe. You can do that."

Joe looked at her and smiled. He could see the way she was watching him. She knew whatever was troubling him, it wasn't Hugo Montera turning down the Department of Labor.

"You know," she said, "I've had a thought. Maybe I won't give up my job when I become first lady."

Joe stared at her. Then he started laughing.

"What? Is it crazy?"

Heather Benton was CEO of YouthMatters, a Washington-based organization that relied on private donations to run programs in inner city neighborhoods.

"I think it's great. It'll give them . . ." Joe hooted with amusement. "I don't know what they'll make of it."

"Do you think it'll make things too difficult for you?"

"Hell, no! You do it!"

"It's just, I can't see why I should leave. I care about this job. I care about these issues. I know there are things I can do as first lady, and I'll cut back my time so I can carry out my functions. I'll ask Walt if we can employ a deputy, and I'll forgo salary so there's no financial issue . . ." She stopped. "What do you think? Really?"

"I think it's groundbreaking. You want to do it, honey, you do it."

"I still need to think about it. I haven't said anything to Walt because I wanted to see what you'd say."

Joe nodded. He laughed again. "Let's give 'em hell!"

"Well, I'm still going to think about it."

The smile lingered on Joe's face. He looked down at the rug again. The smile faded.

"Do you remember the night Al Gore lost to George W. Bush?" he said. "First the concession, then the withdrawal."

Heather looked at him. "Sure."

"I was in my senior year of law school at U of A. That was the first election when I was really active in a campaign." Joe smiled and shook his head, remembering. "That was one hot summer. I saw every dusty square inch of Arizona." He turned to Heather. "Where were you that night? Do you remember?"

"I," said Heather, "was a sophomore at Brown. Dating an incredibly objectionable guy called Will Danforth. I can't believe I did, now that I think about it."

"And on that night . . ."

"Well, that's the point. He was so damn happy that night, I think that's what turned me into a Democrat. And that, my darling, is possibly the reason I was at a certain rally in Boston four years later. Which is where, if I'm not mistaken, I met a certain young staffer on the Kerry campaign called . . . now, who was it? Oh yes. Joseph Benton."

"Hell's bells! You're saying I have George W. Bush beating Al Gore to thank for thirty years of married bliss?"

"And Will Danforth," said Heather, with an exaggerated shudder.

Benton smiled. Then his expression became serious again. "You know, that night, the night Gore lost, I felt the world had just kind of fallen in. Everything was going to get messed up by that goddamn fool George W. Bush and nothing would ever be all right again."

"That wasn't far off the truth."

"The thing is . . . You think, if Gore had got in, we wouldn't be in this mess now?"

Heather ran her fingers over Joe's hand. "Is the mess really so bad, Joe?"

Joe looked at his wife. He hadn't told her what he had learned from Dr. Richards three days earlier. But Heather could sense that something had changed, something disturbing.

"You think Gore would have got us going? You think we would have started doing the things we haven't even started doing now?"

Heather didn't say anything. She watched him.

"Our whole trajectory might have been different. Maybe we wouldn't need Relocation. We'd be in a whole different place. The whole world would. That would be something, wouldn't it?"

Heather nodded. "It would be something," she murmured.

Joe thought about it. Then he shook his head. "You know, I think I was wrong that night. I don't think things would've been too different if Gore had got in. He would have had to work with a Republican Congress. Would he have had the strength and the smarts to push them around?" He shook his head again. "By the time that election came around, I don't think Al Gore knew who he was anymore. Took that defeat for him to find out."

"And win a Nobel Prize."

"For raising awareness. I don't think that says he would have been an effective president. To be effective as a president . . . I realize it's a little early for me to speak, but to be a good president, you need to know who you are. I think you really need to know who you are."

"And do you know who you are, Joe?"

"I hope I do." Joe frowned. "I guess I'm going to find out." He gazed at Heather. Then he smiled. "Where's Amy?" he said. "Wasn't she supposed to be home from Stanford last weekend?"

"That's next weekend, honey."

Friday, November 19

Benton Transition Headquarters,
Lafayette Towers, Washington, D.C.

It was the Pakistani president who had requested the call. The stability of Nabeel Badur's regime depended on the American forces in the country, and his purpose in calling had ostensibly been to outline his plans for reimposing government control over the area along the Afghan border. In reality, Benton knew, Badur was trying to assure himself that a new Democratic president wasn't going to haul the troops out of Pakistan. Benton's line during the campaign had been that once he was elected he would initiate a thorough review of the aims of the U.S. presence. In the call, Badur had given Benton plenty of opportunities to commit himself to ongoing military support. Benton adroitly avoided them. There was no way he was going to commit his administration to anything, even in a private conversation with Badur, before he had a secretary of state and a secretary of defense.

Eales had been listening in and doing the note-taking. When the call finished, they discussed it briefly. Then Eales brought the conversation back to the meeting of the previous night.

"That Roosevelt thing was interesting," he said. "I just wanted to see where the idea might take us. Jackie was right. It ties us to the problem, not the solution. What's interesting is that Jackie and Alan both found reasons to oppose making it public right away. Even though they both think you should take this into the Kyoto process, neither of them thought you should come out with it on day one. Even when I pushed, I couldn't get them to say you should."

Benton had noticed that.

"It's kind of interesting," said Eales. "Anyway, what about Nleki?"

Earlier that morning, at a press conference in Warsaw with the Polish president, the UN secretary-general, Joseph Nleki, had said that he was expecting an early affirmation by Senator Benton of his campaign promise to commit the United States fully to the Kyoto 4 process.

"Nleki's just pushing," said Benton. "He knows my position."

"You don't want to respond, right? Jodie wants us to. I'll talk to her. Your position's well known and it hasn't changed."

Benton nodded. The strength and consistency of his support for Kyoto 4 during the campaign meant he could avoid making a new statement. And he didn't want to make a new statement, not right now.

"I've been thinking about what Gartner and Riedl said the other day. About the logic behind their strategy."

"I've been thinking about it as well," said Eales. "There's a logic there, Joe. I hate to admit it, but there is. As to how they tried to execute what they were doing . . . They're such damn liars, that's the problem. Who knows what to believe?"

That was exactly what Benton thought. There was a logic to what they had said, he couldn't get away from that. He wished he could convince himself there wasn't, but each time he thought about it, the more convincing it seemed.

"Al Graham wants us to respond to Nleki as well," said Eales. "Have you spoken with him?"

"Not yet."

"He's going to call. He thinks he's got State. He's just waiting for you to tell him." Eales paused. "I had a thought last night, on the way home. Joe, I think you should see Larry Olsen."

Benton looked at him in surprise.

"Even if only to get a point of view. I'm not saying you necessarily want him at State. But we're in a whole new scenario. Everyone around you is going to say the same thing—put it out there into Kyoto and go lead the process. You heard Alan. You ask Al Graham, and he'll tell you that more than anyone. Joe, you've got to talk to someone who doesn't say that. You've got to at least hear that point of view."

There was a knock on the door. Ben Hoffman came in to see if the senator was ready for his next meeting.

They headed out of Eales's office.

"How do you know Olsen won't say I should do the same as all the others?" asked Benton.

"Larry Olsen?" Eales laughed. "If he says you should, then you really know there's no alternative."

The meeting was about progress on preparations for the Relocation summit, which was now set for the sixth and seventh of December in Cincinatti. Benton was about to take a three-day tour of cities in the west whose mayors had pledged their towns as lead reception communities, and before he went he wanted to make sure the summit was on track, not only to deliver the right message about his determination to radically upgrade the Relocation program, but to generate substantive discussion among the participants from which real initiatives could develop. A number of Benton's policy aides summarized the papers they were preparing. Afterward, a call came through from Al Graham. Benton took it in the car on the way to a meeting on job creation policy with the leadership of the AFL-CIO.

Graham was as bullish on Nleki's statement as Eales had said he was. He didn't want to stop at issuing a statement. His advice was to set up a meeting with the secretary-general. Benton told him he didn't think that was a good idea.

"Joe, it'll show how strong you are in your commitment to Kyoto."

"People know I'm strong in my commitments," replied Benton. "That's why they elected me."

"I'm not questioning that."

"They don't want to hear me keep saying stuff, they want to see me start doing stuff."

"That's why you should meet him," said Graham. "That's doing something."

"Al, meeting Nleki's not doing something. It's just saying the same thing with a different guy in the room."

"With respect, Joe, Nleki's not just any other guy."

"Al," said Benton, "all I'll be doing is saying the same stuff I've already been saying. Let's leave this, all right?"

It took a little longer for Graham to get the message. Benton glanced at Eales and shook his head impatiently.

Then Graham asked about progress on appointments.

"The economic and domestic teams are my priority at the moment," said the senator.

"Sure. I've got some thoughts for the UN ambassador. Sandy Murdoch could do it. Benny Chopra would be good. Should we meet to talk about it?"

"Send the names to Naylor."

"I think we should meet."

"Al, you know I'm heading out west. I can't do it until I get back. Talk to Ben. And send the names to Naylor."

"Okay. I will. Anything else happening?"

"No."

There was silence on the phone. Benton knew that Al was waiting to hear more, hear him say he was going to nominate him secretary of state.

"Joe, I've been doing some thinking on Colombia, what we can do to get out of there. I think that should be a key goal and if we're smart about it we can be looking to be out in twelve months. I'd like to be able to put that out there as a target early in the first hundred days. What do you think?"

"I think it would be great if we could do that," said Benton.

"I'll put a paper together."

"Okay."

There was silence again.

"Okay," said Al eventually. "Well, I'll try to see if we can meet when you're back from the west."

"Talk to Ben," said Benton.

"I will."

Benton reached forward and ended the call. He glanced at Eales.

"I'll tell Ben to keep him out of your hair."

Benton nodded. His core agenda was domestic. Abroad, he wanted to get American troops out of Colombia, if possible, and to minimize the presence in Pakistan. Getting out of Pakistan entirely was probably going to be impossible until late in his first term, if then. Beyond those objectives, he wanted to repair the damage that twelve years of Bill Shawcross and Mike Gartner had done to foreign relations and to use that credibility to strengthen multilateral institutions, to legitimize American leadership within those institutions, and use that leadership to promote peace and stability. "A secure and prosperous America in a secure and prosperous world." That had been his catchphrase when he was asked about foreign policy during the campaign. His real interests—the specific things he said he would do and which the American people had elected him to do—were domestic.

Eales began tapping on his handheld.

Benton looked at him questioningly.

"I'm going to get Naylor to send you a briefing on Larry Olsen."

Monday, November 29

DeGrave Marriott Hotel, Washington, D.C.

He was waiting in an armchair when Benton walked into the suite on the fourteenth floor. The senator had just hosted a gathering of nationally prominent minority leaders in the hotel's conference center on the ground floor. Ben Hoffman had had the bright idea to get a suite upstairs, allowing Larry Olsen to slip in while the press was distracted by the photo session at the end of the meeting.

"Thanks for coming, Dr. Olsen," said Benton.

Olsen stood up. He had an unruly shock of graying hair and a generally rumpled look to him. "They say you don't turn down an invitation to meet with the president-elect."

"Sit down, please." Benton smiled. "I sense from your tone you don't necessaily think too much of my foreign policy."

"I think it's too early to judge, Senator. But to be honest, I'm not sure you have a foreign policy. I think you have foreign policy values."

"So do you like them?"

"Wait until they're tested. Reality has a habit of doing unpredictable things to values."

"Agreed." Benton looked around. "You want a drink? I'm having a scotch."

"A scotch would be good."

"How do you take it?"

"Water."

Benton went to the bar and poured two scotches. He handed one to Olsen. Then he sat down.

"Cheers."

Olsen raised his glass.

Benton took a sip and savored it contemplatively. According to the briefing he had been given, Larry Olsen was an old State Department hand, fluent in Mandarin, ex–undersecretary of state for China, and with coverage of other Asian desks in the course of his career. For the last four years he had been teaching at Yale.

"You like teaching?" he said to Olsen.

"Not particularly."

Benton smiled. "I had one year at Arizona State. I've had some bad years, but that was a bad one."

"It has its compensations."

"Like what?"

"It's a job."

Benton laughed. "Why'd you leave the State Department?"

"Let's just say I didn't see eye to eye with all the people who mattered."

That's what Joe Benton had heard. And that Olsen had a habit of getting under the skin of his superiors, which Benton could believe after only two minutes in the same room with him. But also that he was very smart, decisive, able to get stuff done and with a peculiar ability to gain the loyalty of the people who reported to him.

Benton liked him. Instinctively. And yet he felt in Olsen's case that was something he needed to guard against.

"You come highly recommended," he said.

"As what?"

"Why don't you tell me?"

"Look, Senator," said Olsen, "I'm flattered to be asked down to talk to you, I really am. But I don't think you really want to hear the kinds of things I have to say. Your position is more, let's say, inward-looking. This country's foreign involvements are a background, if you will."

"I'm not sure that's right," said Benton. "I can see why you might say that. It's a matter of degree. Primarily, I see this country's foreign policy as a means of creating the best conditions for prosperity within the United States. You could say that's pretty limited. But in our global world, I don't underestimate how much influence conditions abroad have on prosperity within this country. I don't underestimate how important—from a domestic perspective—it is to do the right thing in relation to our friends and allies. And our enemies, I might add. So I think you can come at it from one direction or you can come at it from the other, but fundamentally, I don't think it makes too much difference."

"I think there is a difference."

"Perhaps. Some. I'm no expert, Dr. Olsen."

"If we don't lead, Senator, we will be led. Therefore we must lead."

"Again, agreed. There are different ways of leading, though, don't you think?"

"Only if they achieve the necessary effect."

Benton looked at the other man with interest. "Is that important to you? Having an effect?"

"What else is diplomacy for?"

Benton shook his head. "You must sure as hell hate teaching."

For the first time, Olsen smiled. Ruefully.

"Tell me more about yourself," said Benton.

Olsen did. He kept the detail sparse.

"You know Alan Ball?" asked Benton.

"Sure, I know Alan."

"What do you think of him?"

"Alan's got a fine mind. Always makes a good contribution. I don't often agree with him. His outlook is probably more in keeping with where you're coming from. I heard you've got him down for national security advisor."

Benton didn't respond to that.

"I understand you're announcing some nominations tomorrow."

"The economic team. The security posts are taking a little longer."

"Well, I'm sure Alan will do a fine job." Olsen took another sip of his scotch.

"Can I top you up?" said Benton. "Go ahead. Do it yourself."

Olsen got up and poured himself more whiskey. Benton watched him.

"You ever read Machiavelli?" asked the senator.

"Sure," said Olsen, sitting down. "When I was a freshman."

"What happens if I surround myself with people who all think like me?"

"You'll probably have very harmonious meetings."

The senator laughed. "Good answer."

Olsen put down his glass. "Senator, I think the secretary of state you're looking for—if you asked me here to get my opinion, if that's what this is about—is someone who's going to be content to see this country play a largely reactive role. My sense is your administration is going to be highly focused on domestic issues, and your secretary of state is going to have to look at foreign policy through that prism. In other words, I don't think he's going to have a very strong voice within the administration. I'm sorry, I don't mean to be telling you what you're going to be doing, that's just how it looks to me. Personally, I think that's a great mistake, particularly at this time in history. In fact, at any time in history. It also won't make it much fun to be running State. But I'm biased. I'm a State guy. I'm going to say that, aren't I?"

Benton was silent for a moment. "Tell me something," he said.

"What?"

"Anything. Colombia. What do I do with Colombia? How do I get out? How quick do I push?"

"Colombia's not important," replied Olsen.

"Except that we have four House resolutions in the past three years calling for a pullout."

"That's exactly what I mean," said Olsen. "The House passing resolutions is a domestic issue, and the only reason you'd respond to that is if you want the House's support for domestic reasons. If you want to pull out of Colombia because of domestic pressures, that's fine. But that's a different question. That's not a question of foreign policy. That's not what you want State taking into account."

"What do I want State taking into account?"

"State should be considering the geostrategic context and the implications of action, or lack of action, on the ability of the United States to achieve its objectives both in Colombia, the region, and in other parts of the world. Senator, if you want my personal opinion, here it is. Colombia is of no genuine geostrategic interest to anybody except us. We were invited in by their government as a means of dealing with a decades-old insurgency. That may have been a pretext Bill Shawcross chose to exploit, or even helped create, but there it is. Last time I heard, President Lobinas was still asking us to stay. Now, the truth is, Colombia is a failing state, and probably will fail if and when we pull out. In the meantime, our personnel suffer very low attrition—unfortunate, but we can absorb it—and we reduce the flow of cocaine into the United States by three-fourths. This is not an urgent issue for resolution. I wouldn't expend an ounce of our credibility on it."

"Except that every time we talk to anyone about their human rights situation—the Chinese, the Russians—they tell us to get out of Colombia before we come preaching to them."

"But they're not analogous situations. We're not abusing human rights in Colombia the way China and Russia abuse the rights of their own citizens. We're not even an occupying power. We're not there in defiance of the local government. On the contrary, the local government invited us to come in."

"But other countries still use it against us."

"Correct, but the very fact that they use this—which is a nonanalogous situation—just shows that they use it because they need something to use against us. Anything. Pull out of Colombia and it'll be something else.

"So you're saying I do nothing about Colombia?"

"Senator, you asked me for a State Department opinion. You may have domestic reasons to do something about it. That's why you're the president, so you can balance all those things together. If you have domestic reasons, and if those reasons are good enough, you'd have to act."

"But if I don't, I do nothing?"

"On the contrary. Ideally, I don't want American soldiers dying in Colombia any more than you do. Here's what you do. In the first instance, you do stay in Colombia, because the interdiction of supply to cocaine is worth the price we're paying militarily. But you also lean hard on Bolivia and Peru to get them to meet their obligations on ending cocaine production and you impose real sanctions if they fail to do so. That's what finances the insurgency in Colombia, which is what keeps us in there in the first place. We've lost sight of that. We're fighting the snake's tail. We're not doing anything about its head."

Benton was silent for a moment. Then he got up and poured more scotch into his glass. He sat down and took a sip.

Olsen leaned forward in his chair.

"Senator, you want my strategic priorities? One, we need to accept the reality of the Shia alliance and work with its moderate leaders instead of pretending its threat can be dealt with by the relevant states. Two, we need to get Syria and Iraq talking seriously to end their dispute over the Euphrates, and we need to lead a broader water conference in the Middle East. We need to find a way of dealing more effectively with the insurgency in Pakistan and of transitioning from the Badur regime back to a democratic form of government. We also need to give counterinsurgency aid to Indonesia if we want to prevent it becoming the next Pakistan. We need to get the Indians talking with the Bangladeshis, and I believe in the end we will need to provide significant aid for the resettlement of the Bay of Bengal water refugees. Officially, more than eleven million are already in India, and in reality it's probably more than double that. So if we're going to have to help, let's start doing it and not wait for a regional war to break out before we act. We need urgently to strengthen the global quarantine framework. We need to start offering asylum to Russian opposition leaders as a first step to achieving the restoration of meaningful democracy there. And we need to put troops in the Congo and develop a multistate solution to the political breakdown of Central Africa."

"Why the Congo?"

"The civil war in the Congo has gone on for sixty years. Eighteen million people have died."

"Granted. On a humanitarian level, I agree. Where's the U.S. interest?"

"The Congo conflict destabilizes the entire central African region. This sends refugees to North Africa, which destabilizes those countries and adds to environmental migration from them toward Europe. This means more refugees crossing the Mediterranean toward Spain, Italy, and Greece, who try to keep them out. This means these southern European countries are effectively fighting a low intensity naval war against civilian populations. Given the populations we're talking about, this is also a racial war, and the countries prosecuting it are becoming increasingly xenophobic. These countries are our allies. Xenophobic countries do not make good allies for the United States, sir."

Benton was impressed. He didn't want to show it. "That's a wish list," he said.

"It is for you. For me, it's a to-do list."

"Nothing's a to-do list from Yale, Dr. Olsen," said Benton pointedly.

Olsen stared at him for a moment, then silently shook his head.

"Tell me about emissions," said Benton. "You haven't mentioned that."

"Your position's well known on that issue, Senator."

"You said you were going to tell me your strategic priorities. Isn't emissions among them?"

"We need to develop a standing mechanism involving ourselves, the EuroCore, Brazil, Russia, India, Japan, and China to controllably reduce them." Olsen's tone was mechanical, as if he was saying it for form's sake, not expecting the senator to agree with any of it. "That puts ninety percent of the world's emissions on the table."

"You wouldn't use Kyoto?"

"I would pull out of Kyoto. I opposed Kyoto 3. It's no secret. They gave you a briefing about me, didn't they?"

"You said it was too weak. Maybe we can make Kyoto 4 stronger."

Olsen shook his head. "Kyoto's all process. Right now, the illusion that we can solve things through Kyoto is the most dangerous piece of fiction in the world. Someone has to have the courage to kill Kyoto and liberate us from it. I would kill it, day one."

"And how do you envision that we get to the mechanism you mentioned?"

"Bilateral negotiations with the Chinese. Start there. Once an agreement's in place, we apply sanctions to those who don't join. The moral force of the argument will be powerful. The economic force of combined sanctions from the U.S. and China will be irresistible."

"That only leaves the slight problem of how to get the Chinese to agree."

"I wouldn't call it a slight problem, Senator. But they're going to have to agree one way or another, at some point, whether through Kyoto or another mechanism, so there's no way of avoiding it, is there? Kyoto doesn't solve the problem for you—it just puts it into a context that's a thousand times more complicated."

Joe Benton didn't say anything to that. Olsen's point struck him with a strange force. If Chinese agreement was the sticking point—and it had to be, with China being by far the world's biggest polluter—somehow it had to be overcome, whatever the framework.

"Senator, we've had thirty years of Kyoto treaties. Kyoto itself, then the Copenhagen round, then Santiago. How long do you keep going before you admit a process isn't working? The people who negotiated that first Kyoto Protocol would not *believe* the world we live in today. Southern Europe is on its way to becoming a desert. The fire in the Amazon has been burning for the past four years and no one has any idea how to put it out. How much of the Greenland ice pack is left? Every country with a coastline accepts that millions of people are going to have to be moved. Already we're seeing ethnic conflict over this. That's the world we live in, Senator. Do you think when they agreed on the first Kyoto Protocol in 1997 they thought this was what they were going to achieve? If those people were here today, do you think they'd count this a success? Senator, those people, if they were around today, would be the first ones to declare the process dead. They'd tell you, Stop! For God's sake find another way."

Olsen stopped. He shook his head slightly, as if struggling to contain his exasperation.

"Tell me why you think Kyoto's been such a problem," said Benton quietly.

"It gives too much room for cover. Too much diffusion of responsibility. It's too easy to avoid agreeing any kind of meaningful sanctions. It's all promises and no way to enforce execution. Senator, you and I differ in outlook. I think multilateral negotiations rarely work, not when we're talking about something on this scale with so much at stake and so many parties involved."

"I don't know if I agree with that. What about the World Trade Organization?"

Olsen smiled, the kind of smile, Benton imagined, he might use in his seminar room at Yale. The senator didn't much like it.

"The outcomes of the WTO can afford to be imperfect," said Olsen. "And they are. Very imperfect. But the future of the planet doesn't depend on them. The analogy here for me isn't the WTO, it's the SALT and START treaties between us and the Soviets in the later decades of the last century. Bilateral negotiations on limiting nuclear weapons. Senator, let's look at history. Why did they work?"

"We were the only countries involved."

"Not so. A number of other countries possessed nuclear weapons at the time, and had the means to deliver them. The limitation by the two leading exponents created an irresistible pressure on those others to limit proliferation as well, which led to the Comprehensive Nuclear-Test-Ban Treaty. But would there have been a multilateral test ban agreement without the bilateral treaties between the two global arms leaders to create the imperative? I submit that there would not. The lead shown by the dominant nuclear powers—their ability to do a bilateral deal—was the crucial thing."

"This is different," objected Benton. "Every country is affected by climate change."

"Every country would have been affected by an outbreak of full-scale nuclear war between the U.S. and the U.S.S.R., arguably more severely than climate change will affect them. Would you have invited Fiji to participate in the SALT talks? Would you have restricted yourself to conditions they agreed with?"

Benton didn't reply. Olsen could see he was listening.

"Look, Senator, you and I and everyone else on the planet know that if you get the top seven polluters agreeing to what needs to be done, the problem's solved. China, us, India, the EuroCore, Japan, Brazil, and Russia. So why do we go to a conference where we sit down and listen to Malawi tell us what they think we should do? I'm sorry, I've never met a Malawian I didn't like, but that is just not going to work. Now, first thing you do, is you admit the emperor has no clothes. When you see a process that's busted, you kill it. Then, you start with the top two polluters, and you get agreement with them—and that's the top two economies in the world—and that unlocks the rest. And if Malawi doesn't want to play ball, if it won't cut any of its emissions, you know what, it doesn't even matter." Olsen shrugged. "I'm sorry. I know that's not what you want to hear. It's only my opinion, but if you can find anything in the history of Kyoto that tells you otherwise, let me know."

Olsen leaned back. He shook his head again, as if he knew he wasn't going to get anywhere with what he had said.

Joe Benton frowned, gazing at the coffee table that stood between him and Olsen. Then he looked back at the other man. "Have you been working with the White House on this?"

Olsen looked at him in surprise. Then he laughed. "If you can show me a less competent administration in foreign affairs I'd like to see it. Senator, you're insulting me."

Benton smiled. "Unintended."

"Fine."

Benton frowned again. "You make a powerful case, Dr. Olsen."

"Others have been making it."

"Not as eloquently. Not to me."

"So much depends on who you listen to, doesn't it?"

"Yes," said Benton. "Yes." He said it emphatically. "You mistake me, Dr. Olsen."

"How so, Senator?"

"You said I need someone at State who wants our foreign policy to be reactive. You implied that's because that's the role I think we should play. I don't think either of those things is true. What I need at State is someone who does want to see this country take an active leadership role, and doesn't use the domestic prism for foreign policy. I need that counterbalance. You said it yourself, it's my job to make the call between domestic and foreign priorities. So I need that State viewpoint given to me sharp and clear every single time I have to make a decision, and I need it given to me by someone who won't be afraid to stand up and say what he thinks, even if he knows that a majority of the people in the room are instinctively against him. Which they may well be, by the way. And I need that person to know how to work the State Department machine so he can go out and do what he has to do. And by the way, I need that person to have a very, very good grasp of Chinese affairs."

The Senator paused. Olsen was watching him closely.

"But here's the other thing, Dr. Olsen. I need that person to be able to live with decisions he doesn't like. That's what worries me about you. Because after that person makes the case—when we're talking about the major foreign policy issues for this country, the crucial strategic ones— they're going to be my decisions. And if he hasn't persuaded me on one of them, then I'm going to ask him to go out and do something which he may not necessarily want to do. You talked before about having a voice within the administration. Well, that person will have a voice. He'll have his chance in the debate, he'll have his chance to persuade me—he'll always have that chance—but after that, he's going to have to execute the policy I agree with. Now, that may not sound great, but if I was in your shoes, it would seem like a pretty good deal to me. The only way you could get more is if you ran for president yourself. So what you have to ask yourself, Dr. Olsen, is do you want to spend the rest of your life talking about the things on that to-do list you've got in your head—or do you want to actually start doing some of them? Not everything, but something. Do you want to get out on the park, or would you rather stay in the dugout?"

Olsen stared at him. "What are you saying, Senator?"

Joe Benton hesitated. He had agreed to this meeting only because John Eales had pretty much insisted on it. Privately, he had thought it would be a waste of time. He had expected to have a conversation with Larry Olsen and then call up Steve Naylor and tell him he was offering State to Al Graham. Yet in forty-five minutes, Olsen had demonstrated a more crisp and cogent approach to foreign affairs than Benton had had from any other advisor. It was also more challenging, provoking, and demanding of his attention. And that, paradoxically, was the most important reason Joe Benton said what he proceeded to say next.

"Dr. Olsen, let me be clear about this. If you do come in as secretary of state, you come in for at least one term. You don't sit there for six months and decide you don't like it. And on critical issues, you execute the policy I authorize. But I've promised you I'll always hear what you've got to say, and I'll protect your ability within the administration to say it. Now, if I was you, I'd be asking myself whether Yale's a more attractive proposition."

Olsen shook his head slowly.

"If you find this a little hard to believe," said Joe Benton, "that makes two of us."

"Does Alan Ball know about this?"

"No," said Benton. He wondered again if what he was doing was completely insane. Olsen's views and style couldn't have been more opposed to Ball's. It almost made him wince to think what might happen if he brought them together at the same table.

"Can I have some time to think about it?" said Olsen.

"How much do you want?"

"A couple of days."

"Take until Friday."

Olsen nodded. "Senator, you'd better think about this as well."

Thursday, December 9

CBS Webcasting Center, New Jersey

The journalists around the table had fallen silent. They were staring at Ben Lacey, a correspondent who had covered a good portion of the Benton campaign. Lacey couldn't keep the smirk off his face.

"Say that again," said Fran O'Lachlan. She was editor in chief of the CBS politics stream, a sharp, energetic woman in her fifties who had built a reputation as a shrewd political analyst, and it was her daily editorial meeting that Lacey had just brought to a halt with his announcement.

A week previously, President-elect Benton had presented the nominees for his economic team. Paul Sellers, Benton's nominee for secretary of commerce was the only surprise. He was a moderate Republican congressman who had served as deputy U.S. trade representative under Bill Shawcross, and it was widely seen as a smart move by Benton to get a cross-party figure on the team. Hugo Montera, whom Benton had persuaded to join the administration, was named as his choice for labor secretary. And what Lacey had just said was that there was dirt on Montera.

He explained. Two years previously, Montera's law firm, where Hugo Montera was a senior partner, had been sued by an employee who claimed he had been unfairly dismissed. The case had been settled out of court with the usual nondisclosure provisions and nonadmission of guilt. For those two years, the nondisclosure condition had been kept. Now, according to Lacey, the plaintiff in the case wanted to reveal what had happened.

But Fran O'Lachlan was way too experienced to take something like this at face value.

"Why's he talking to us?" she asked.

"He's got an aunt who's a friend of my mom," said Lacey. "She said, go talk to Ben."

"There's a piece of fine investigative journalism," quipped someone at the table.

O'Lachlan ignored the remark. "You don't know him?" she said to Lacey. Lacey shook his head.

"So he's just going to break his nondisclosure?" Eleanor Engers was lead anchor of the CBS politics pod. "How much does he want?"

"Nothing." Lacey grinned. "So here's the cool thing. He's dying. He's got some kind of cancer in his brain and the medical folks say he has maybe six months left."

There were grimaces in the room. On the wall screen, Matt Ruddock, the D.C. correspondent, frowned. "What was that, Ben? I didn't catch it."

"He's dying. Six months max. The agreement means nothing to him. What are they going to do? Sue him? He'll be dead before the case gets near a court. And what does that do to Montera anyway? You think the Senate's going to confirm a secretary of labor who's suing a terminally ill former employee over an unfair dismissal claim? Fran, this guy wants justice. He feels outraged. All this time, he feels justice wasn't done, and now, when he's got nothing to lose, that's what he wants."

"How do you know his brain cancer hasn't done something to his memory?" asked one of the other journalists.

"He's fine. He's sane."

"You've spoken to him?" said O'Lachlan.

Lacey nodded. "He's dying, that's all."

"Guys," said Ruddock. "I've got to leave you now. Benton's press conference is about to start."

"What is it today?" said Engers.

"His national security team. For what it's worth, I say, if the guy with the brain cancer has a story, we tell it. Fran, I'll call later."

Ruddock went offline. Someone switched the screen to the stream that would be showing the press conference. O'Lachlan turned back to Lacey. "So what's he saying?"

Lacey leaned forward conspiratorially. "Montera himself was the one who sacked him. The pretext was insubordination. The truth is, he says, one of the other partners didn't like him."

"Didn't *like* him?"

Lacey grinned. "It gets better. Not only did the partner not like him, he liked one of the other junior associates an awful lot. A female associate.

And this other associate was kind of friendly with our man, if you know what I mean. So the partner goes to Montera, and says, we got to sack this guy. And Montera does it."

"It's like David and Bathsheba," murmured Andrea Bartinevsky, an intern out of Columbia. She saw the way the others were looking at her. "What? I went to Bible class when I was a kid."

"Exactly," said Lacey. "What else do you want, Fran? Sex, deceit, unfair dismissal . . . Like Andy says, it's biblical."

"Did Montera know? Maybe the other guy convinced him there really was insubordination."

"Fran, who cares? Throw sex into it and no one's going to look into the nuances."

"But did he *know*?" repeated O'Lachlan. "He may have been acting in good faith."

"So what?"

"Fran," said Engers, "if he didn't know, he should have checked." Engers didn't much like Lacey, but she was with him on this. "If Montera just took the word of the partner against the word of the other guy, that's negligence, if nothing else."

"Come on, Fran. He's nominated to be secretary of labor. If he's been involved in an unfair dismissal, that's a public interest issue whichever way you look at it. And if we don't run with it, the guy's taking it to Fox. The only thing keeping him alive is the desire to see the truth revealed. Whatever we do, this story's coming out." Lacey grinned. "What are the odds, huh? Getting shot down by some guy who's got six months to live just when the president nominates you to the cabinet. Not even I'd take a bet on that."

"Okay," said O'Lachlan. "Do some checking. See if you can find the other associate who was involved. And the other partner. If they won't go on the record, get them off. I want to be one hundred percent sure this is true before we use it. In the meantime, I'll talk to our legal guys and make sure it's okay for us to go ahead with this. Get me a copy of the settlement agreement."

"That's irrelevant," said Lacey. "The agreement doesn't involve us."

"We'll be abetting someone in breaking a legal agreement."

"I'm not offering an inducement."

"Document that. And get him to sign something."

"I will."

"And get me a copy of the agreement."

Lacey rolled his eyes. "Fran, we're not—"

"Ben, get me a copy of the agreement. Understand? If he won't give you that, tell him we're not interested and he can go to the *National Enquirer*."

"All right. But Montera's dead in the water, I'm telling you."

"Maybe he is. Get it worked up so we can use it. And make sure I see everything. Nothing goes out until it's watertight."

Lacey nodded. He glanced at Engers. He had Montera. He had him like a deer in his sights.

On the screen Benton's press conference was starting. The senator was speaking, with a couple of people standing either side of him. O'Lachlan turned to watch. Ben Lacey looked at the senator as well. He smirked. There stood Straight Joe Benton, with no idea what Lacey was about to unleash on him. He wasn't going to look so straight after that, was he?

"That's Larry Olsen," murmured O'Lachlan.

"Where?" said Engers.

"Him. There."

"Benton just said he's nominating him to State," said one of the other journalists.

"What?"

"That's what Benton just said."

Olsen was stepping forward to the microphone now.

"Turn up the volume," said O'Lachlan.

Olsen made a brief statement. He really was going to be the next secretary of state.

"Look at Graham," said Engers. "Look at his body language. He's pissed."

"What's Graham's job?" said O'Lachlan. "Anyone hear?"

"UN."

O'Lachlan frowned. Her journalistic antennae were tingling. "What's the message here? What's the point of having Olsen in? We're going to demand a tougher Kyoto 4? We're going to walk away?"

"No way Benton's walking away," said Engers.

"So what's he doing with Olsen? What's changed?"

Lacey stood up. "We done? Fran, I've got stuff to do. We done?"

She was still watching the screen.

"I'll get you that agreement," said Lacey. "You'll have it tomorrow."

"Fine."

"Fran, we're going after Montera, right?"

O'Lachlan took her eyes off the screen. She nodded. "Just make sure the story's tight."

The reaction of the right-wing press had been knee-jerk. That morning, Heather Benton had announced that she would continue in her position as CEO of YouthMatters. Ten minutes later, she was being accused of degrading the presidency. The liberal media were less strident, almost uncertain. Joe Benton found it interesting to see how they were reacting. Apart from the lunatic fringe, who wanted to be seen denying a woman the right to her own career? Benton thought it would eventually blow over and in four years no one would understand what the fuss had been about. In that sense, it was a truly groundbreaking step that Heather had taken, and he was all for it.

He had spent most of the day with congressional leaders reviewing the outcomes of the Relocation summit that had taken place the previous week in Cincinatti. Meetings with the Republicans had been cool but cordial. A couple had fired not-so-disguised shots at him over Heather. The Democratic leaders hadn't said much about it. They weren't happy, he could see that, but they were caught in the same dilemma as the liberal media. The meetings with them had been more substantive, going into his legislative requirements in some detail, particularly the key planks of the Budget Reconciliation Act, which would be critical to create the economic underpinnings of New Foundation. A number of Benton's policy aides and cabinet nominees sat in on the discussions, as well as Ben Hoffman and Barb Mukerjee, who was coming to the White House as Benton's chief legislative aide and would be essential in doing the legwork required to get majorities on board.

The Democrat leaders were attentive. At this stage, Benton knew, they were mostly listening. When they kicked back, it wouldn't be in front of a dozen aides, advisors and cabinet secretaries. After they were gone, he had an hour scheduled in his senatorial office to start the process of drafting his inaugural address.

Sam Levy had worked with Benton for years and had been his senior speechwriter throughout the presidential campaign. He was a chubby New Yorker with thin blond hair and in his years working with Joe Benton had developed an intuitive grasp of the senator's turn of phrase and style. No one had a better ability to crystallize ideas into words that would sound natural coming out of Benton's mouth. For this initial meeting, which included Jodie Ames, Ben Hoffman, John Eales and Angela Chavez, Benton had asked Sam not for a draft speech, but to think through possible themes. Sam set these out, together with a number of key points, illustrations, and soundbite phrases that had occurred to him along the way.

Benton let Levy go through to the end before he responded. "First thing, Sam, whichever way we go, I want the speech to be real. When I finish, I want the people who have heard this speech to know what I'm going to do. I want them to know why it's going to make their lives better. I want them to know how they can contribute. I want them to understand why they should support me. Those four things. I'm going to be a real president. I'm going to do real things for real people. I want a real speech."

Levy nodded and tapped some notes into his handheld. So did Jodie.

"Think of Joe Kowalski sitting in a bar somewhere watching this speech."

Sam nodded again. How many times had he heard that? Every campaign speech had been written for Joe Kowalski, Joe Benton's imaginary listener.

"The average length of the past ten inaugurals was 2,188 words," said Levy. "I say we go shorter."

"Agreed," said Benton. "Was anyone awake by the time Mike Gartner finished speaking? I sure as hell wasn't."

"His was 3,423. Jack Kennedy's inaugural was 1,355."

"Let's aim for fifteen hundred. At the outside."

"I'm going to go to Mary Poulakis and Ed Beale for drafts as well," said Jodie Ames.

That was fine with Benton. They talked through the ideas Levy had offered. At an early session like this, for such a critical speech, Joe Benton didn't mind spending some time freely kicking ideas around without trying to put them into a definitive framework.

"What about the theme?" asked Levy, after they had been talking for a while. He had offered a number of possibilities, but only for the sake of completeness. "Let's come back to that. I'm assuming we want to stick with New Foundation."

"We have to," said Ames. "That's what the campaign was about. It's natural to cap it off with this."

"Maybe we want to draw a line," said Eales. "This is different. That was the campaign. This is the presidency. Make that clear, use a different theme."

"There's no line," said Benton. "We stay with New Foundation. But I want to do something new with it. I don't want anyone to be able to say they heard this or that part of it on the stump before."

"We should get Joe Kowalksi to write it," muttered Sam Levy. "He's heard every speech you ever made."

Benton smiled. Then he was serious again. He tapped the armrest of his chair. "New Foundation isn't about running away from something. It's not about making the least worst of a bad situation. It's about turning that into a good situation, like the Founding Fathers. That's core."

"We've used that," said Levy. "About a million times."

"Can't have too much of the Founding Fathers," said Hoffman.

"It's about opportunity," continued Benton, searching for the germ that might grow into a novel variant on the New Foundation theme. "It's about lifting people up, not putting them down. It's about turning challenges into growth. It's about remaking the nation."

"It's about time," said Eales

"What time?" asked Levy.

"Time to remake the nation. Our time. This is our time."

"That's really original," said Jodie Ames.

"No, I like it," said Levy. "I can work with that. Young and old. This is our time. It's your time. We should have used that in the campaign, Senator. How did we not use that?"

"We managed." Benton raised a finger. "No verbiage, Sam. No flights of rhetoric."

"An inaugural's got to have some flights, Senator. People expect it."

"Well, let's keep it real. Nothing ridiculous."

"Where's the fun?" muttered Levy.

"I'll be getting drafts from Mary and Ed as well," Ames reminded him.

"You want more?" asked Hoffman. "I got a pile of drafts from every nut in the country."

Levy shrugged. "You know what? Let me look at them."

"What? You got no ideas of your own anymore?"

"The man who listens to no voice but his own is a man who speaks only to himself. You know who said that, Ben?"

Hoffman laughed. "When you stop making up sayings, Sam, then I'll start guessing who said them."

"Senator?" said Ames. "How do you want to handle foreign issues? We've focused on domestic but you're also sending a message to foreign governments."

"What do you suggest?"

"What you said in the campaign. That you'll work with our partners. That our problems are shared problems, and the solutions have to be shared solutions. In the broader context of the speech, you're saying you're focused on America's domestic issues, but you're not going to neglect the historic leadership role of the United States internationally. But you're not going to use that role coercively. You want a better life for everybody."

"You could lay out some specifics," said Angela Chavez. "On Kyoto, for example, that's the obvious one."

"I want to think about that." Benton glanced at Eales, then looked at Jodie. "We'll need to get thoughts on this from Alan and Larry. Jodie, you want to have a word with them? In the meantime, Sam, let's go with something general to start with on the foreign side, and short, and we'll take it from there."

Levy nodded.

"All right," said the Senator. "Sam? Are you happy? Have you got enough?"

"I think so."

Benton looked around at the others. "Are we done?"

There were murmurs of assent.

"Jodie, Sam, I've got some business here with Angela."

Ames and Levy left. Chavez stayed behind with Eales and Hoffman. They talked through the issues that had come up during their meetings with the congresspeople that day. The sheer scale of the legislative task ahead of them was becoming apparent, and it was even greater than Joe Benton had imagined it. He wanted to explore the possibility of Angela taking hands-on responsibility for driving the legislation through, running a kind of permanent command center. That would mean working closely with Ben Hoffman. Neither of them seemed too comfortable about it. Not because they didn't like each other, but because Angela had her own chief of staff and her own organization, and it wasn't clear how it was going to work.

"Maybe it won't," said Benton. "But we need to be flexible. Let's at least see if we can make it work. If we can, we'll have much stronger firepower."

Angela and Ben nodded. Not entirely convincingly.

"All right, I'll let you two think it through. Ben, where are we on health?"

"Raj and his guys are going to have the packages detailed right after New Year's."

"Costed?"

Ben nodded.

"No later than that?"

"They're on it," said Hoffman.

"Education?"

"Same timescale, Senator. Ewen's on it."

"Keep me involved in the policy. They can have as much of my time as they need before the inauguration. This is when they can get it, I'm not going to have the time later. Take as much as you can get, Ben. Be greedy."

After Chavez and Hoffman had gone, Benton pulled out a bottle of scotch and a couple of glasses. He poured for himself and Eales. Then he sat back in his chair and looked out the window at the winter darkness of a Washington evening.

"You know, if it goes bad," said Eales, "you're hanging Angela out to dry."

Benton sipped at his drink. "That's not why I'm doing it. We need the firepower. She's effective. She can give it to us."

"But you're going to send her out with this program, and then if we come out and say, you know what, this program isn't adequate, and *here's* what we need, there's a risk she'll look like a fool. It'll look like you set her up just so you could step back from it yourself."

"That's not why I'm doing it," repeated Benton softly.

"Joe, I know that."

"We just have to handle it so that doesn't happen."

"And Jackie?" said Eales.

Jackie Rubin had been working intensively, developing options and programs to make New Foundation a reality. At the end of the Relocation summit, Benton had pledged to present New Foundation to a joint session of Congress within a month of his inauguration. But the New Foundation package as it was currently being planned wouldn't be enough to deal with the full scale of the relocation that awaited them, nowhere near enough, and Jackie was one of the few who knew it. In a second discussion Benton had had with Rubin, Ball and Eales, Jackie Rubin came right out with the questions. Were they going to keep planning on the basis of the old projections despite the data Dr. Richards had provided? When Benton went to Congress, was he going to conceal the full extent of the relocation that would be required? Because these were ten-year plans they were presenting. Were they going to come back in six months, twelve months, and tell Congress they had to tear everything up and start again? *When were they going to tell people?*

Benton hadn't had an answer for Jackie. All he knew was that he didn't think he could say it yet. People weren't ready to hear it. And if he said it when the American people wasn't ready to hear it, he would lose them on everything.

He sipped his drink again.

"I will not lose these bills, John!" he said suddenly. He thumped his fist on the chair. "Once in a generation you get the momentum in this country to really *do* something. I won't blow it. Health. Education. Relocation. Jobs. I won't blow those priorities. I will not."

Eales didn't say anything.

"If we can get the program going, if we can get New Foundation established, working, proving itself, then maybe we can move people on to the bigger scale. Then we can talk about the relocation we really face over the long run, and what it actually means in terms of our emissions policy and the additional programs we'll need to fund. But we have to put the elements of fairness in place first. We have to get the principles established, we have to show they work, we have to show it's possible. Give them legitimacy. If we don't get them in place first, if we don't get them working, we never will. I'm convinced of that. Hell's bells, John! All I'm talking about here is the basics. Health, education, jobs. What else is there? Without those, you don't have the foundation of a fair society. If we don't get them in place now, the chance is gone and we're back where we were. It'll be another generation before another president has the chance again. And frankly, if that happens, given the magnitude of what we face, if we don't manage to do it, I don't know what'll be left of our country by then."

"So how long do you wait?" said Eales.

"You tell me. I think we need a year. At least to get the legislation in place. That's the minimum."

"So you're not going to say anything at the inaugural?"

Benton closed his eyes. He let out a long breath. "How do I lie to the American people?"

"It's not a lie. It's just not the whole truth."

"Sophistry," murmured Benton.

Eales didn't reply. He finished his scotch.

Joe Benton could literally feel the pressure bearing down on him. "I can tell you one thing, John. We need to be a hundred and ten percent above board. We're going to need every scrap of support to get New Foundation through. Every hit we take is going to damage our chances. I don't want a single skeleton in anyone's closet. Every appointment we make, every single person we bring in, every one of them needs to be clean as a whistle."

Saturday, December 25

Benton Ranch, Wickenberg, Arizona

The Bentons had been getting together with the Travises for Christmas lunch for close on twenty years. Joe Benton had no intention of changing that now, any more than Heather did. So it was Christmas Day as usual at the Benton ranch outside of Wickenberg—apart from the bevy of Secret Service agents who were taking turns patrolling the grounds and having their own lunch in the kitchen, which Heather insisted on providing for them.

Ray Travis had been elected to Congress for the Arizona fifth district in the same year that Joe Benton first went to Washington, and it had been that experience, two Arizona Democrat freshers on the Hill, that had sealed their bond. And the fact that their wives got on. And the match with their kids. Ray and Emmy Travis had two girls, Penny and June. June, the younger, was almost exactly the age of Amy Benton. And everyone had always joked that some day Greg would marry Penny.

Ray Travis had served two terms in the House before he went back home and settled into a law partnership in Phoenix. Joe Benton stayed on in Washington. Inevitably, their worldviews had diverged somewhat over the years. But the friendship remained strong, and it was never long before the talk turned political when they were together.

"So where do you think your main opposition inside the party's going to come from?" asked Ray, while they were having eggnog before lunch.

"Where I least expect it," said Joe.

Ray laughed.

"Ray," said Emmy, "I'm sure Joe doesn't want to talk politics today." She glanced at Joe, and almost blushed. Although she had known Joe for twenty years, the mantle of president-elect made her somewhat in awe of him.

"Sure he does," said Ray. "That's all he ever wants to talk about."

"That's true," said Heather.

"The House is solid but the Senate's flaky," said Ray.

Joe nodded. "The Senate's always flaky, Ray, you know that."

"Christopher and Bales will come on board," said Amy. "Dad'll get 'em on board."

"You think so?"

Amy nodded. Joe smiled. More often than not, Amy was right.

"Greg, what do you think?"

Greg shrugged. "I don't know anything about politics, Mr. Travis. God invented politics to keep boring people from boring the rest of us. With politics, they just bore each other."

Joe smiled indulgently. He didn't rise to the bait. He had learned to avoid that with Greg.

"So you think that's right?" asked Ray. "Christopher and Bales are going to line up behind you?"

"Of the fifty-six senators we have, there are seven or eight we'll have to treat very carefully. Are Christopher and Bales among them? Yes, I think they are. Can we handle them the right way? I hope so."

"You've just got to increase funding for the Farm Reversion Program, Daddy. Christopher, Bales, right across the Midwest they'll get behind you."

"And what about Montera?" said Ray. "You think you'll get him through?"

The allegation of a scandal in Hugo Montera's past had broken two days before Christmas. Benton had spoken to Montera, who had explained it. Benton couldn't see that he was guilty of any wrongdoing.

"We'll get him through," he said quietly.

Ray Travis sat forward in his seat. "Here's the thing, Joe. The Relocation package, where's it all going to come from? Just how high are you going to put our taxes?"

"Ray, I've got some of the smartest brains in the country working on that right now."

"But you are going to put taxes up?"

"It'll be selective. I've said there'll be a cost. How can there not be?"

"The American people voted for it," said Amy. "I don't think Daddy hid anything."

"Honey, politicians always hide something."

"Amy's right," said Joe. "People knew. They recognize there's a need to do something here. The Gartner Relocation package was a miserly, stingy piece of work that would have condemned millions of people to poverty for generations. And I'm not only talking about the poor souls who have to be moved, I'm also talking about the communities they're moving into."

"Four trillion dollars over ten years, Joe. You could hardly say that's miserly."

"It is. It's not only miserly, it's shortsighted. This movement of people can be a tremendous moment in our history. We can use it as a platform of growth. Or it can be a sinkhole of misery. Make your choice."

"I'm not arguing with that."

"You can't just move them. You can't just give them a bus ticket and put them in a trailer someplace and give them a couple of hundred thousand compensation and say get on with your lives. That's what Gartner's bill did. We can do better. We have to do better. You've got to put in the infrastructure. You've got to prime the pump. Put those people into communities with health care, education, jobs, and within ten years, five years, they'll be flourishing, not languishing. That's why it's a package, Ray. That's why I kept saying it and saying it and saying it. And I'll keep on saying it. Health, education, relocation, jobs. They all come together. And it's our role as government to make sure they do come together."

There was silence. Amy gazed at her father. Even Greg watched him out of the corner of his eye. Emmy, Heather and June, who had started talking about something else, looked around to see what was happening.

"I was just wondering where it's all going to come from," murmured Ray.

"Well, we're working on that. But we're going to have to pay. Our generation is going to have to put in. But it's for our children, Ray, and our children's children. And the way I see it, our generation is only living as good as it does because no one has paid yet. We haven't taken any of the pain. And our parents didn't, and our grandparents didn't, but it's no point complaining to them because they're not here anymore. They figured we could keep growing our economies at the fastest pace and somehow with a nip here and a tuck there the environment would be okay and we could have the best of both worlds. Trading carbon credits would solve the problem. Well, you know what? It just made a bunch of traders rich. Or technology would do it for us. Well, plenty of time and money was spent on technology to get hold of fossil fuels that previously we couldn't even access. Twenty, thirty years ago we should have started taxing fossil fuels at the true cost of the damage they do, like we'd do for any other commodity that causes public damage. We should have taken that money—and it would have been a huge amount of money—and put it right into research for the technologies that would replace those fuels."

"Who?" said Ray. "Government?"

"Why not? Government funds basic health research, and we fund it out of taxes. Isn't this just as important? Sure, at some point, you commercialize it. But if you've got a long-term crisis, and the market isn't dealing with it because market incentives are focused on the short term, it's the role of government to make sure the research gets done. That's exactly what happens in health. Now, if we'd had that money and been putting it into research for the last thirty years, wouldn't we have come up with solutions to replace fossil fuels? You bet we would. But we didn't do that. We didn't make fossil fuels pay their true cost because we were too damn scared it would take a little off our economic growth. And every time we had a slowdown, our fine words about saving the planet went right out the window and all we cared about was getting growth up again, whatever it took. Sure, we had plans. Too many of them. Obama's plan, Currie's plan. Some of them were even good plans, or would have been if we'd carried them through. The problem wasn't not having enough plans, it was actually doing what we planned to do. Always some reason, some special interest group, some industry that needed an exemption. And we gave in to them, over and over and over. Come on, Ray. How much legislation, how many emissions targets have you and I seen go by the wayside because it turned out to be just too damn painful to stick to them and too damn easy to convince ourselves that the market or technology or some other thing would magically solve everything for us? And you want to know something—why not? Why should we have taken any pain, why should anyone, when you could be absolutely sure that no other government in the world was going to live up to the cuts they'd committed to make—not if it meant sacrificing even a single percentage point of growth—and there was no mechanism to make them do it? That's how it's been. We haven't done what we had to do, what we said we'd do. So for a start, we're better off now than we have a right to be. And now the bill for the cost is here. It didn't go away just because we ignored it. Someone's got to pay." Joe raised his hands. "It's us. The buck stops here. It's got to. We don't pay the bill, it's Amy, and it's Greg, and it's June and it's Penny who are going to pay. And the bill will keep getting bigger. And you know what? Things happen when you don't pay the bill. You go back to France in 1789. Hell, you don't have to go to France. Look at 1776."

Ray smiled. "You're saying we're going to have a revolution?"

"I'm asking you. I'm saying you've got ten million people suddenly dispossessed, in poverty, and what are they going to do? Now make that twenty million. Make it forty. I'm just saying we have to be aware of the historical processes we're a part of. We're only seeing the tip of the iceberg. If you think you know everything that's been happening, if you think Gartner's plan was sufficient, even at a minimum, even at the bare miserly, stingy minimum he proposed, then I've got to tell you . . ."

Joe stopped. Suddenly he was aware of the way everyone was looking at him.

"How many people did you say?" asked Heather.

Joe frowned for a moment, wondering how he had let that happen. He hadn't meant to say that, or anything like it. "I was just saying . . . if you don't deal with it, who knows how bad it'll get?"

There was silence.

He forced a smile. "At least there's a saving grace. The American people understood. I can't think of greater evidence of our common sense, of the spirit of our community, the spirit our Founding Fathers would have wanted to see in us, than that they said yes on November second. Because Mike Gartner was offering them the easy way, storing up more trouble for the future. And the American people said no, we're going to face this trouble now." The senator tapped his finger forcefully on the armrest of his chair. "We're going to saddle up and go out and deal with it. They could have chosen the easy way but they didn't. That's what really makes me proud to be the next president of this country."

"God bless America," muttered Greg.

The senator turned to him sharply. "God *bless* America. You better believe it, Greg."

There was silence again.

"Well, it's Christmas," said Heather. She cut the tension with a smile. "I'd say it's about time for lunch."

The Travises didn't leave until almost sundown. Joe lingered outside, watching the sky go purple and the sun turn gold in the crisp winter air. The ranch was in the foothills of the Bradshaw Mountains, and the summits of Towers Mountain and Wasson Peak rose to the north.

"What was that you were saying before lunch, Daddy?"

Joe turned. It was Amy.

"Nothing, honey."

"I'm not ten years old, Daddy."

"It's nothing. Things always cost more than you think, that's all. You say five billion over five years, and it ends up being ten."

Amy looked at him skeptically.

Joe smiled. "When are you going back to Stanford, honey?"

"When you stop changing the subject."

"You coming back to Washington for New Year's?"

"You're worried about something, aren't you? Is it Mr. Montera?"

"A little."

"You think he did something wrong?"

Joe shook his head.

"They're going to roast you over it. We don't need that right now, do we?"

"No," murmured Joe. "We certainly don't."

He put his arm around Amy's shoulder. He had always felt a deep, instinctive connection with Amy. Not that he didn't love Greg. But with Amy it was easy, natural. Sometimes, with Greg, it seemed to him that whatever he did only served to drive his son further away.

"Hugo's a good man," said Joe. "He'll make a good secretary. I need good people. The country needs good people in Washington."

"But they're going to roast you, Daddy. All the way to the confirmation hearings. It doesn't look good, what he's accused of. Even if he didn't do anything wrong, it doesn't look good."

Joe gazed at the last golden sliver of the sun, almost gone now.

"You know, your mom told me, if I wanted her to, she'd give up her job. She said it's not worth all the vitriol that's flying around out there in press-hate land."

"And what did you say?"

"Yes it damn well is!"

Amy laughed.

Joe Benton chuckled as well. He looked at his daughter. "So are you coming back to Washington for New Year's?"

Amy shrugged.

"Is there someone there, at Stanford?"

"Daddy!"

"What?"

"Nothing." She gave him a kiss. "Merry Christmas, Daddy."

"Merry Christmas, Amy."

Tuesday, January 4

Benton Transition Headquarters,
Lafayette Towers, Washington, D.C.

There were two new faces in the room. Joe Benton wanted to keep knowledge of the ESU data to as small a group as possible, including only those who had an essential contribution to make either to the analysis or the strategy. He still hadn't involved Angela Chavez. And after discussion with John Eales, he had decided against involving Andrea Powers, his nominee for secretary of environment, on the grounds that her contribution would come later, in enforcement. But Ben Hoffman was present. Benton had decided they couldn't go much further without his chief of staff knowing what was going on, and he also knew that Ben's conciliatory style would be valuable. Particularly with Larry Olsen present, the other new joiner in the group. This would be the first time he had brought Olsen and Alan Ball together for a substantive policy discussion, and Benton wasn't sure what to expect.

"Everyone have a good New Year's?" he asked. "Jackie, Alan, I've invited Larry to join us for obvious reasons. Sorry, Jackie, do you know Larry?"

"We introduced ourselves while we were waiting."

"Okay. Larry, I apologize in advance for what you're about to hear. I couldn't tell you before, and you'll understand why when you hear it. I mean, I could have told you, but then I would have had to shoot you. Ben . . ." The senator smiled ruefully. "What can I say? Here's another complication to add to the list."

Hoffman shrugged uncomplainingly.

"Okay. Let's get going. John, can I ask you to bring Larry and Ben up to speed?"

Eales cleared his throat. "November tenth," he began, "Senator Benton got a call from President Gartner."

Ben Hoffman looked at Benton in surprise. Benton glanced at him, then turned back to Eales.

For the next fifteen minutes, Eales gave a summary of the senator's conversation with President Gartner and his own subsequent briefings with Art Riedl and Dr. Richards. The senator glanced at Larry Olsen a few times as John spoke. There wasn't a flicker of surprise or emotion on Olsen's face. Just concentration.

Eales finished.

"All right," said the senator. "Jackie and Alan and I have had a couple of discussions about this but we haven't got too far. I'm looking at the people in this room as my core team on this unless anyone thinks we need to bring someone else in."

He waited for suggestions.

"So no one else knows?" asked Hoffman.

"No one but the people in the administration, which we believe are restricted to the president, Art Riedl and Ed Steinhouser, and I guess there must some of their aides who know at least part of it."

"And the top couple of people in Dr. Richards's unit," added Eales.

"So what we need now is a plan." Benton paused. "Larry, you need some time to think about this or do you think you can discuss it now?"

"I think I've pretty much got a grasp of it."

Benton nodded. He pretty much thought Olsen would have.

"All right. January twentieth, what do I do?"

"Senator," said Olsen, "can I ask who were Gartner's people actually talking to on the Chinese side?"

"Chen somebody or other," said Eales.

"Here in Washington? Chen Liangming?"

"That sounds right."

"And who was talking with him from our side?"

"Art Riedl."

Olsen raised an eyebrow. He glanced at Alan Ball and smiled in disbelief. Alan Ball watched him stonily.

"Okay," said Benton. "Let's talk about a plan. Do we talk to the Chinese government, do we not talk to them? If we talk to them, how do we talk to them? What do we start with? What's our road map?"

"I've written a paper with some thoughts on how we use this to regain our leadership role in the Kyoto process," said Ball. "I'll get a copy to Larry and Ben."

"Okay, but do we really believe that's what we should do?" said Benton.

"What?" said Ball.

"What I've seen in your paper, Alan. That we go to the international community and say we have a problem—here's the data—and now let's make sure Kyoto solves it."

Alan Ball narrowed his eyes. "Do I believe it? Which part, Senator?"

"Any part. Every part. I want to test that. John, what about you? Do you believe it?"

"I think there are alternatives," said Eales.

"That we don't go to the international community?" said Ball. "That we don't say Kyoto's the place to solve it? Is that what you're saying?"

"Those are alternatives," said Eales. "Maybe we should test them."

"Didn't Gartner already do that?"

"Good point," said Benton. "Still, I don't know that I'd accept Mike Gartner as the best test of anything, particularly in the circumstances in which he was trying to do a deal with the Chinese."

Ball didn't reply. His glance moved from the senator to Eales, trying to work out whether something had been agreed between them.

"Larry?" said Benton. "What are your thoughts. Do we take this into Kyoto?"

"That's one option," said Larry Olsen.

"What's the other?" inquired Ball.

"Do it outside Kyoto."

Alan Ball pretty much expected that. He knew he'd have to fight Olsen over this. It was the insinuation in Benton's questions that really worried him.

"Nleki's still pushing for a declaration of support," said Hoffman. "Half the EuroCore's demanding it now as well."

Benton nodded. Ever since he announced Olsen's nomination, the demands for him to confirm his support for the Kyoto process had grown stronger. "Larry," he said, "can you explain what you mean?"

"I mean, we talk to the Chinese directly."

"In Kyoto," said Ball.

"Outside it," said Olsen.

"You mean in parallel?" said Ball.

"Or as a substitute."

"What else?" said Benton. "What other alternatives do we have?"

"We don't talk to them."

"How does that get us anywhere?" demanded Alan Ball.

"They know the facts just like we do. According to what John just said, they suffer along their southern coast like us. So we hold out. We wait for them to come to us."

"You got a couple of decades up your sleeve?" said Ball.

"Another option: we develop a coalition with a range of other partners that leaves the Chinese out in the cold."

"Why will it be different from every other coalition we've tried?"

"Because we'll actually do what we say we're going to do."

"And China gets left doing exactly what it wants to do. You reward them for their misbehavior. You think you're going to shame them into compliance?"

"No."

"Then why do you want to take that route?"

"I don't," said Olsen. He smiled. "I was asked for alternatives, Alan. Like I said at the start, I say we talk to them."

Alan Ball gazed silently at Olsen.

"Great," said Ben Hoffman. "Looks like we're in violent agreement."

Joe Benton waited a moment to see if anyone had anything to add. "So it's talk to them within Kyoto, or talk to them bilaterally. Is that right? Whatever way we go, we agree we should be talking to them."

Olsen nodded. Ball nodded grudgingly as well.

"Senator," said Rubin, "last time we talked about whether you were going to cover this in your inaugural or continue to deal with this covertly for at least a time. Can I ask what you've decided?"

Benton wanted to hear Olsen's thoughts on that question.

"Ideally," said Olsen, "I'd like the flexibility we'll get from dealing with this covertly in the first instance. That leaves going public with it as an instrument in our hands, and we can use it when we feel it will provide the kind of pressure we need. But they'll be watching what you say. Whether or not you cover it in the inaugural will send an important message."

"What will it say if I do?"

"You're upping the ante."

"And if I don't?"

"You're frightened of something."

"Or he just doesn't know yet," said Ball. "They might interpret it like that."

"True," conceded Olsen.

"What will make them feel more comfortable?" said Eales.

"If we keep it quiet," replied Olsen. "But do we want them to feel comfortable? I'm not sure. At this stage, probably we do."

"Of course we do," said Ball.

"But not for too long. Senator, you're the new boy on the block. You don't want them to think you're a pushover. That means if you keep quiet on this, you've got to take action somewhere else. You take early action somewhere else so you're sending them a second message that you're not frightened in principle to take action, you're just waiting for the right moment."

"Where do you suggest?"

"I'm not sure. Something limited, not particularly important strategically. Off the top of my head, I'm thinking maybe Haiti. We've been threatening the Corot regime for years to clean up their act or we'll intervene. They've got an election coming up January twenty-fifth. It'll be rigged. We could act."

"Senator," said Ball, "I'm not sure that action so early in you presidency would set the tone you're trying to achieve, either at home or abroad."

"I'll lay out some options," said Olsen. "It doesn't have to be Haiti."

"It doesn't have to be anything."

Benton thought for a moment. "Give me the options, Larry. Now, let's think about talking with China. If it's in Kyoto, it's part of Kyoto. But if it's bilateral, what do we say to them?"

"Depends on what you've done at the inaugural," replied Olsen. "If you've announced it, we have to be hard. We need a proposal. We also have to have a bottom line. You have to get success. Once it's public, you're hostage to it."

"We have to get success anyway," said Eales.

"That's true," said Benton. "Making it public might be a good forcing mechanism."

"Once you make it public, you can never take it back," said Olsen. "I want to hold on to that as a weapon."

"It's a weapon against us as well," remarked Ball.

"Granted. We have to bear that in mind."

"So what if I don't mention it in the inaugural?" asked Benton.

Olsen shrugged. "You can be softer. As I said, you then use the threat of going public as a way of building pressure."

"Alan?"

"I agree. But I'm still not comfortable with this whole line of going outside Kyoto. I've never heard us say that before. Where's this coming from?"

"When we start talking to them, we can't reward them for stringing Gartner along," said Olsen, ignoring Ball's question. "We start right back from square one, we don't concede anything Gartner might have offered. And whatever we do, we move them quickly. We can't let them get comfortable."

"Hold up!" Ball wasn't going to let Larry Olsen talk them into action they'd regret. "Let's just hold up here for a second. China's a serious military power. Let's think about what we're saying. There's absolutely no need for us to go backing them into a corner. We've got four years to solve this, it doesn't have to be done in a day."

"Four years in which the situation gets worse," said Hoffman.

"I'm with Ben," said the Senator. "If we allow ourselves to think we've got four years, we never get it done. Time's critical."

"I didn't say it wasn't."

"Actually, I'm not talking about time," said Olsen. "I'm talking about comfort. Senator, in my opinion, if you let them get comfortable, we've lost it. They have to believe you're going to act. Otherwise they will lie, and when you discover they've lied, they'll take you down the same process again and they'll lie again. I've seen it."

"They've seen it as well," retorted Ball. "From us. We've done plenty of lying of our own when it comes to emissions control. We need to build trust. And whatever you say, that's going to take time."

"No," said Olsen. "It's not going to take time. We don't have the time. So they're just going to have to see that we don't lie. That we take action. We're going to show them, very clearly, and very early. But we cannot let them get comfortable. We cannot let them think they've got our number. Senator, that's the most important thing."

Alan Ball took some papers out of his briefcase. "Here's a copy of a speech President Wen made on New Year's Day."

Olsen rolled his eyes.

"Senator, just look at the speech. I've circled the part of interest." Ball handed him a copy. He handed others out around the table. "He's saying they're committed to the Kyoto process."

"He's not saying that, Alan. You're not the only one who saw that speech. He's saying they'll work with their international partners of good-will. You know that phrase?" Olsen said it in Mandarin. "We've heard it from Wen ever since he became president."

"Senator, he's sending you a very clear message. Why else would he say that at this time?"

"He's sentimental. Wen gets sentimental on New Year's."

"Larry, come on!"

"It's true, it's his daughter's birthday. January first he gets sentimental, and January second he orders the troops into Hong Kong. Anyone who knows Wen knows that."

"Senator, read the rest of the passage," implored Ball. "He says he wants all world leaders to know China's good intentions, those who are new leaders and those who are old. That's you, Senator, the leaders who are new."

Benton read. It was feel-good, internationalist stuff. "Doesn't look very specific."

"It's not so much about the content," said Ball. "It's the timing."

"Alan," said Olsen, "it's New Year's. Wen always makes a speech for international consumption on New Year's and he always says the same thing. The Chinese media hardly even report it. You want to hear what he's saying to his Chinese audience, you listen to the speech he makes on Chinese New Year. More importantly, see how the domestic media cover it. That'll get you a lot closer to his thinking than this will."

"He didn't have to include the reference to the new leaders. That's significant."

"Right. If it's significant it just means he's trying to snow us. All the more reason to go hard."

"If that's all you want to do, Larry, just say so!"

"All right," said Benton sharply. "Let's cool it." He looked at both men impatiently. Half an hour at the same table and they were acting like two kids in the school yard. He put the copy of the speech to one side. "Alan, this is helpful. I'll study it later." He paused, and looked meaningfully at each of the two men again. "All right, here's the thing I don't understand. Why didn't they want a deal? Gartner was desperate and they must have know it. Logic says, do the deal a week before the election. And on the other hand, if they want to do it in a multilateral context, why were they even talking to us? Why didn't they leak what Gartner was telling them and drag it out into the open? Either way, China's going to be hurt by all this as much as we are. They should have done a deal."

"Senator, with respect," said Olsen, "who's *they*?"

"The Chinese government." Benton paused. From the way Olsen was looking at him, he felt there was something wrong with the answer.

"Don't assume everyone in the Chinese government who you think should know about this, does know about it. And don't assume people who shouldn't know, don't."

"But President Wen must know."

"If it's Chen Liangming they were talking to, you can assume so. Chen's Wen's man."

"So why doesn't President Wen want a deal?" said Benton.

"Who said he doesn't?"

"Why didn't he do one?"

Olsen nodded. He was looking at Benton in the same way as before. "We need to educate you, sir."

Joe Benton let that go. "All right," he said. "Here's what I want. I need to know the range of proposals for emissions reduction that we can realistically be looking at. Gartner proposed eighteen percent. Is that too high? Too low? Just right? Jackie, will you lead on that? For the moment a ballpark estimate is fine. John will get you the data and the scenarios from the

ESU. Jackie, tell the guys on your team . . . I don't know, give them a bunch of other stuff to do and say we're looking at a whole range of scenarios."

Rubin nodded. "I know what to do."

"We can still go Kyoto, I'm not ruling that out. Alan, we already have your paper on that."

"I want to expand it."

"Good. Go ahead. But I also want a bilateral negotiation road map. Larry? I want to know our strategies for dealing with various responses. And yes, give me the options for some kind of action in case we need to make the Chinese take us a little more seriously. But limited action, Larry. I'm not talking about putting an army in the Congo."

"In the *what?*" said Alan Ball.

"All right?" said Benton. "Everyone okay with that?"

There was silence. Olsen glanced at Ball. Ball's gaze was cold.

"Let's meet in a week. Ben, can you take the minutes here from now on?"

Hoffman nodded. He had been taking notes anyway.

"One more thing, Senator."

Benton looked at Olsen.

"I need to get you together with some guys on the China desk."

After they had gone, the senator came into Ben Hoffman's office and closed the door.

"I'm glad you stopped by," said Hoffman. "You'll be pleased to know that as of today you're scheduled to make an appearance at eight balls on Inauguration Night."

"Excellent," said the senator. "Good to know you're keeping your eye on the things that really matter."

Hoffman laughed.

"Well?" said the senator. "What did you think just now?"

Hoffman nodded. "I've got to say, it was quite a bombshell."

"I'm sorry I couldn't tell you. I probably should have got you involved earlier."

"And you haven't told Angela?"

"Not yet. I need her out there selling New Foundation."

"What's going to happen with that?"

"That's what I want to talk to you about."

The senator sat at the meeting table in Hoffman's office.

"What I'm thinking is that I'm going to use the momentum of my first year to drive as far as we can on the legislation for the critical elements we need to put in place. Universal health. Education. Job creation. That's the framework for Relocation. If we can put the framework in place, if we can establish the elements of fairness, then we can expand on that, but if we don't have the framework in place and this thing blows up, I don't think we ever get it. I've talked it through with John. I just can't see that we're going to be able to sell a whole bigger package from the start."

Hoffman considered it.

"I want you to think about it, Ben. Set up a time with John and me and we can have a discussion."

Hoffman nodded. "Whose side are you on, by the way? Alan or Larry's?"

"I didn't know there were sides."

"No?"

Benton shrugged. "You know, I was as surprised as anyone that I appointed Larry. But he was cogent. And he made me see something in a way I hadn't seen it before. When that happens, I value it." He paused. "Ben, I'm not saying I like his style. But we can't afford groupthink. That'll kill us. We need a few subversives. If Al Graham had been in that room today instead of Larry, we just wouldn't have had the same debate. We have to be prepared to test our thinking. That's true generally, but if there's any one specific issue we really need to do it on, it's this."

"Well, having Alan and Larry in the same room will certainly make for better entertainment, that's one thing."

"Creative friction," said Benton. "Who was it who had the theory it's the source of all great achievement?"

"I have no idea, but we should invite him to our next meeting."

The senator laughed.

"How did Al take it, by the way, getting the UN?"

"You haven't spoken to him?"

Hoffman shook his head. "He probably thinks I schemed against him."

"Well, he took it," said Benton. "It wasn't pretty. He acted like he was offended. In fact, at first he told me he wouldn't do it. Turned me down flat."

"And then?"

Benton shrugged. "I told him he'd always have a line to me."

"And that did it?"

"Who knows? Al wants to be back in the game, right? The UN's a pretty good stage."

"Sure." Hoffman thought for a moment. Then he smiled.

"What?" said the Senator.

"I just wonder whether you like being told you need to be educated."

Thursday, January 6

Logan Circle, Washington, D.C.

"What the hell is this place?"

Larry Olsen grinned. "It's an apartment I'm using until I get set up in D.C. again. Belongs to my brother-in-law. Come in."

The senator took a couple of steps inside. He looked around. The place was a shambles.

"Come through," said Olsen.

Three people were waiting in the living room. They stood as Benton came in.

"Dr. Elisabeth Dean," said Olsen. "The undersecretary of state for China. Dr. Oliver Wu, one of the China experts at State. And this is Sandy Chan, the Beijing station controller over at the Agency. Technically, I shouldn't have invited her to this meeting."

"Technically, I shouldn't have accepted," said Chan, putting her hand out. "An honor to meet you, sir."

He shook hands with them. They all seemed so young.

"Sit down, Senator," said Olsen. "Scotch? Don't have much else, I'm afraid. You take it neat, as I remember."

"Thanks."

Olsen poured him a scotch.

"We haven't talked about any one specific thing leading up to this meeting, Senator," said Olsen meaningfully. "I've just told the guys you want a general briefing about the state of play in China."

"Thank you," said Benton. "That would be very helpful."

"We're going to have freewheeling discussion." Olsen sat down. "Elisabeth, would you lead?"

"Certainly." Dr. Dean paused for a moment, then began. "Senator Benton, we think China today is pretty much in the same kind of situation it was back in 2013. If you remember, the economy had been growing steadily for about thirty years straight at that point. Politically, the party had achieved a kind of precarious balance. From an external perspective, the nature of the regime and its domestic actions were rarely critiqued to any serious extent by other governments. There was a kind of unspoken agreement by which foreign governments turned a blind eye to the way the party maintained power—paying lip service to concerns over human rights but never doing anything about it—in return for access to China's markets and its low-cost manufactures. Domestically, the legitimacy of the regime depended on another trade-off—as long as the regime delivered growth and political stability, the middle classes focused on doing business and accepted its rule. But it was a precarious balance. The economy was overheated, with inflation continuously threatening to get out of control. There were numerous social tensions that the regime struggled to contain, in particular an extreme disparity in wealth between the cities and the countryside. And within the urban middle classes, which were growing exponentially, increasing demands for democracy clashed with the objective of the party to stay in power and of individuals in the party and the army to keep feeding on the endemic corruption in the state. These tensions had been strong for at least a decade. The global slowdown created by the credit crisis of 2008 and 2009 greatly exacerbated them, despite the Beijing Olympics of 2008, which the party used to stoke nationalist support for the regime and clamp down on dissent. After that, the problems were at breaking point, just waiting for a trigger."

"And then came the fundamentalist coup in Pakistan in 2013," said Benton.

"Yes. Nuclear war between India and Pakistan over Kashmir was a real possibility and the global financial system went back into meltdown. Turned out that for China, 2008 and 9 was only a foretaste. 2013 precipitated the crisis in the Chinese banking system, the collapse of their stock market, urban unrest, then the Hong Kong massacre and the political crackdown that followed. The regime's growth promise—the basis of that precarious balance domestically—had been broken, and the only way the party could stay in power was through brute force. But I would submit it didn't have to be a Pakistani coup. There were numerous potential shocks at that stage, any number of things that could have disrupted the global economy and thrown Chinese growth into reverse. It could have been the crisis over the Iranian nuclear program. It could have been the Russian expulsion of foreign oil companies. It could have been lots of things, it could have happened a few years sooner as a few years later, but when it was the Pakistani coup that acted as the trigger, political upheaval in China was inevitable, because the guarantee of growth, the source of the regime's legitimacy, was broken."

"So what are you saying, Dr. Dean? We're about to see another financial meltdown?"

"I don't know about that, Senator. The reason I've gone through all this is I'm trying to point out the parallels—and some of the differences—in the China situation today. Their first year of significant economic growth after the 2013 crackdown was 2017. That means by now they've had roughly another fifteen years of growth. Today, again, the regime's legitimacy is based on exactly the same trade-off as before—growth for control. We're seeing the same disparities in wealth, the same demands for democratization. The difference, this time, is everything's on an even bigger scale. Their GDP, as you know, is now bigger than ours. Back in 2013 it was under a third of ours. Their middle class numbers some four hundred million, still only a relatively small percentage of the country, but more than our entire population. Consequently, the democracy movement is stronger. The disparity in wealth between the city and the country is even greater than it was—this is a problem the regime just doesn't seem to be able to solve. And this time round there's a new element, an environmental opposition. Back in 2013 this was just developing, and the crackdown effectively stifled it for ten years. The Yangtze landslides got it going again and gave it a momentum that has proven pretty much unstoppable. With the degree of environmental devastation the regime has allowed, it's growing strongly in both the city and the country. In fact, it's about the only issue that unites the two sectors. The party's fear of what will happen if growth ceases, therefore, is extreme. Yet for various reasons, the Chinese economy is as vulnerable to external shocks as it was back in 2013. Arguably it's more vulnerable. The party knows this. In China, vulnerability is not only economic, it's existential. In the U.S., a financial crisis threatens the party in government, not our form of government. In China, it threatens the regime. Maybe even the cohesion of the state."

"So what's the party going to do?" asked Benton.

Elisabeth Dean smiled. "Senator, there are five people in this room. That means we're likely to get five opinions on that question."

"Six," said Larry Olsen. "I'm always good for two."

Oliver Wu smiled.

"Elisabeth, go on," said Olsen, and he took a sip of his scotch.

"The party is divided. There are elements that realize in the long term its model of control isn't compatible with a growing, capitalist society. On the other hand, there are regressive elements that can't conceive of any future but through the traditional form of party control and whose interests are tightly aligned to a continuation of the status quo. What I say about the party goes for the army, you can take that as read."

"Except, if anything, the balance in the army is even more regressive," said Sandy Chan.

Dean nodded. "We face numerous uncertainties, Senator. What are the relative strengths of the factions within the party? What's the strength of the army relative to the party? If it comes to an open struggle, what's the process by which the factions seek to win? Are we going to see a struggle within the party itself? Is the party going to split? Would the army seize control? If it's a crisis that precipitates the struggle, will there be a functional response to the crisis itself, or will it be piecemeal, different things happening in different parts of the country?"

"What happened in 2013?"

"Good question," remarked Olsen, as if he was a professor at a seminar. "Can I top you up, Senator?"

Benton handed him his glass.

"In 2013, Senator, the regressive faction within the party was clearly the stronger and was able to deal quickly with dissent both within the party and the army, and then to deal with unrest within the country in a more or less coordinated fashion. As a result, the response was functional. I mean that in a political sense—it was brutal, but it had clear objectives and it achieved them. The country held together and the party stayed on top. I don't think we can say that would necessarily happen this time round. If the response isn't functional, anything's possible. The country could split apart, effectively if not in name. In many respects, provincial and even municipal government already wield more power than the central government in Beijing."

Benton took his glass back from Olsen. He turned to Sandy Chan. "What's your opinion?"

"I wouldn't dispute anything Elisabeth has said. The opinions vary when you start to look at the relative strength of the different factions, the different individuals, and the ways they might behave. Our view at the Agency is that a considerable amount of positioning is already going on. Our sense is there's a showdown coming, and it's a question of how it's precipitated. External events might do it, but it's just as likely one of the factions will seize on a pretext to precipitate it."

"What does that mean for us?"

"It means we're a pawn in their game, sir."

"Every country is a pawn in every other country's game," said Benton. "I'm wary of making statements in front of four foreign affairs experts, but isn't that a fundamental fact of international relations?"

"Senator, you've got to look at China somewhat differently," said Oliver Wu.

"I'm always a little mistrustful when I hear something like that, Dr. Wu. In my experience, in any walk of life, cases are rarely as special as they seem."

"I understand, sir. But in China . . ." Wu paused. "As we all know, the party isn't a communist party, whatever it calls itself, but it retains an aggressively statist philosophy, that everything can be sacrificed for the good of the state—which in reality, in the terms of their thinking, means the good of the party. And that includes not only domestic issues, but international as well. There is a difference, Senator, between China and most of the other countries you're going to deal with in that respect."

"Which other countries have you studied, Dr. Wu?"

"I'm a China expert, Senator."

"So how can you make that comparative statement?"

"I have some familiarity with other Asian countries. I also have some familiarity with Russia."

"But you're not an expert in those countries?"

"No, sir."

"And you still maintain China is a special case?"

Dr. Wu nodded. "From my understanding, sir, I do."

Benton gazed at him. It was almost arrogant, the way Wu refused to back down. And yet his manner was anything but arrogant. It was almost apologetic, as if he was sorry that he had to keep insisting that he was right—but he was right.

"All right," said Benton, "which faction is on top at the moment?"

Olsen interrupted. "I think maybe we need to give the Senator a brief introduction to the dramatis personae," he said, and he looked in the direction of Elisabeth Dean.

"There's President Wen," said Dean, "whom you know, of course."

"What did you think of his speech last week?" asked Benton.

"His New Year's speech?" Dean shrugged. "Same every year."

"So it didn't mean anything?"

"No."

Benton looked at Wu and Chan. They appeared equally unimpressed. Olsen smiled.

"So where does Wen stand?" asked Benton.

"His instincts have always been progressive," replied Dean. "But he won't sacrifice the party. He's strongly influenced by the history of Gorbachev and the collapse of the Soviet Union. He's studied it carefully. He won't go down that route. When you're dealing with Wen, that's the thing to remember. He wants to be seen to be progressing—and he genuinely does want progress—but not at the risk of the party's role. If he has to choose between the two, he'll choose the party. He'll choose stability."

"So if we can give him a way to look progressive without threatening the party's role, he might be interested."

"That's right, Senator," said Olsen. "That's Wen."

"Right now, he's trying to avoid a showdown," said Chan. "Recently he's tried to do that by building up a group of traditionalists after a period in which the progressives made headway. It's a kind of balancing of forces he's trying to achieve. The premier, Zhai, is a progressive who has seen his influence wane. Xuan Qing, the mayor of Shanghai, is still a force to be reckoned with, and probably the most outright progressive among the senior Chinese leaders."

"What about the vice president?" asked Benton.

"Wen sidelined him years ago," said Olsen.

Dean nodded. "Hui's a nonentity. The most important of the group Wen's promoted recently is Ding Jiahui, who now holds the public security ministry. This gives him control of elements of the security apparatus as well as influence across the provincial governments. There's also Zhou Zhanwei and Wu Kejie. They're all hardline protégés of Ex-president Zheng. Wen sidelined them at the start but now they're back in favor and they've been elevated to full Standing Committee membership. In the meantime, they've all been busy creating independent power bases. Ding's is by far the strongest."

"The patronage system magnifies the effect through the tiers of the hierarchy," explained Chan.

"Also, there are some senior party figures who try to adopt an unaligned stance," added Oliver Wu. "The foreign minister, Chou, and the finance minister, Hu, particularly. Hu tries to maintain a kind of neutral, technocratic stance. But if things get hot, that won't be possible. We think he may come down on the progressive side."

"We're not sure about that," said Sandy.

"In the army, the key figure is General Shen Bihua," said Dean. "He's the ranking military officer on the Central Military Commission. Wen tries to keep him close, but it's hard to say how much patience Shen would show in a crisis. Ever since 2013, the military hasn't had a lot of respect for the political side. The party avoided a coup by a whisker."

Benton frowned. "The message I'm getting is that we're looking at an unstable country with a bunch of unresolved tensions, and the regime is splitting into camps around those tensions, the way you always see regimes doing in these circumstances. You've got those who are intent on retaining the status quo by suppressing the tensions —as they see them—and those who believe the status quo can't be retained, because the tensions can't be suppressed, so *they* have to change. Now, I'm no historian, but history bets on the side of the second group, doesn't it? Eventually, the tensions demand resolution, and in the long run that can't be managed by trying to suppress them."

"In the long run," said Larry Olsen. "But it can be a damn long run, and history tells you that before that bet is won, an awful lot of side bets can be lost."

"Agreed. So what are they going to do?"

"Crisis favors the regressives," said Elisabeth Dean. "Continuity favors the reformers."

"How so?"

"The reformers fear loss of control. They're reformers, not revolutionaries. The regressives also fear loss of control, but feel they can impose it as long as they get started quickly enough. The reformers don't want to have to impose control because that would undo their reforms. It would turn them into regressives."

"So what happens?"

"As Sandy said, there may be an external shock that precipitates events. In that case, they scramble."

"We think the regressive faction is better positioned," said Chan.

"In which case, the reformers themselves may try to precipitate a crisis before that happens. One which they feel they can manage and will leave them in a superior position."

"What if they lose control?" said Benton.

"They may. It's a risky strategy. If they actually do lose control—even in one city, or one province—then they're the emperor with no clothes. That's the end of the ball game."

"What would be the pretext if they had to manufacture one?"

"Taiwan's a perenial possibility, but hard to control, and essentially it speaks to a traditionalist agenda. We don't think the reformers would try that."

"But if they lead in that," said Chan, "they gain the credibility to deal with other issues from a reformist stance. We wouldn't put it past them."

"We think it's very unlikely."

"Senator," said Oliver Wu, "the point here is, the only function of the United States in all of this is the extent to which it helps or hinders each faction's plans."

"I understand," said Benton, and he turned back to Dean. "Let me ask you this. Say I'm involved in a negotiation with the Chinese government, or say I may be considering it, how do I handle it? Generally. What are the guidelines?"

"At the top level—understand who you're dealing with. There is no Chinese government, there's only the party. There is no party, there are only factions. Sometimes there aren't even factions, but only individuals. Understand that person. How much power does he really have? What are his motives?"

"What else?"

"It would depend what the negotiation's about."

"Let's put that aside. What else?"

"I know I've already said it," said Oliver Wu, "but be aware that your only value to them is as a factor in their own domestic political considerations."

"I said I understood that."

"Senator, with respect . . ." Wu hesitated.

"What is it, Dr. Wu?"

"You said that very quickly. But if you think about what it really means . . ." Wu frowned, as if searching for a way to bring it home to the senator. "Sir, think about the way you might approach a major international issue, arms control in space or environmental migration or emissions reduction, for example. If you think about the way you'd approach it, what would go through your mind? I'm guessing here, but you might think of something that's outside your own narrow partisan agenda. One or two things that aren't just about how you'll stay in power."

"Of course there would be."

"Well now imagine that you don't." Wu paused. "Imagine that's the *only* test you use. For everything. How it helps you stay in power. Really imagine what the world looks like from that perspective." Wu paused once more. "Now put yourself back on the other side of the table again, and you're looking at a half dozen people who are exactly like that. And the biggest threat to them staying in power isn't you, or anything you're talking about, but the person sitting right next to them. Or maybe not. You don't know. They might not even know. They might not even know that they don't even know. These are the people with whom you're trying to do a deal."

Larry Olsen sighed demonstratively. "Ah, diplomacy! There's nothing quite like it. The art of maneuver in the darkness. The triumph of perspicacity over uncertainty."

Joe Benton glanced at Olsen impatiently. It was less than two weeks to his inauguration. The time for philosophy was over.

"Senator," said Oliver Wu, "I'm not exaggerating. That's what you're dealing with here."

Tuesday, January 18

Blair House, Washington, D.C.

They were on draft twenty-six.

The inaugural week had begun on Sunday, at Independence Hall in Philadelphia. In conscious reference to the Founding Fathers of the republic, Joe Benton and Angela Chavez and their families met with a descendant of each of the signers of the Declaration of Independence. Then, after a ceremony in the Liberty Bell Center, a train emblazoned with the starspangled banner took them from Philadephia to Washington in time to appear at a concert at the Lincoln Memorial, before going to Blair House, the official guest residence, where they would spend the next four nights before moving across the street to the White House.

Monday was Martin Luther King Jr. Day, and the schedule of events included the traditional governors' luncheon in honor of King at which Benton spoke. The following evening, after a day of engagements, the president-elect held a reception for the Washington diplomatic corps. He gave a short speech outlining his commitment to a secure and prosperous America in a secure and prosperous world. He and Heather appeared briefly at another couple of dinners and didn't get back to Blair House until after ten. Sam Levy, Jodie Ames and John Eales were waiting, along with Barry Murphy, a boisterous, redheaded Arkansan who was on Jodie's staff and had become deeply involved in the process of drafting Joe Benton's inaugural speech.

Benton had his pen out and half-moon reading glasses on his nose as he looked over the draft. Old-fashioned, he still liked to use paper. So did John Eales. Sam, Jodie and Barry worked directly on screens.

The speech started with a reference to the foundation of the republic more than two hundred fifty years before, to the house the Founding Fathers constructed, and which had been built on, generation by generartion, over the quarter millennium that had passed. "Building a house" was the idea they had settled on as the major theme for the speech, which allowed Joe Benton to continue to talk about a new foundation but to extend the rhetoric in a way he hadn't done during the campaign. In parallel, the language of "it's time" would occur on a number of occasions, and at the end the two themes would come together to build the exhortation that would be the speech's finale.

The work was painstaking, line by line. Benton was prepared to spend as long as it took. When midnight came they were still deep in the text.

"I'm not sure about this," said Benton. "Today," he read, "I tell you that we have the opportunity to put behind us once and for all the invidious forces that bring poverty and misery into our communities." Benton paused. "Put behind us once and for all? Are you saying they're going to go away forever?"

"You want to be aspirational," said Levy.

"Aspirational, not naive. Joe Kowalski knows we're not going to change everything."

"I hate Joe Kowalski," said Levy.

"Well, he's my friend." Benton smiled. "Sam, you can do better."

"Yes, sir," muttered Levy.

Benton frowned, still considering the sentence. They talked about it and came up with a better formulation. Benton still wasn't entirely happy.

"Senator, leave this part to us now," said Murphy. "We'll get it right." He glanced at Levy. They weren't exactly a natural pair. Levy liked to work alone, producing draft after draft and polishing up the product. Murphy loved to work with others, yelling ideas across the room and burning bright on shared energy.

The senator read the next sentence. "The fact that I stand today in this high place before you, the bearer of your sacred trust, shows that you know we have this rare opportunity, and that, through me, you want this moment to be seized."

The senator paused, pondering the page. The others waited.

"That's just . . . That's awful."

"That's exactly what I've been saying," muttered Levy, throwing a glance at Jodie Ames.

"How the hell do we still have something like this in there at this stage? Imagine me standing up and saying that. Physically. Try and say it to yourselves." Benton drew a line through the page. "Strike the 'know we have this rare opportunity.'"

Levy nodded. "So you want it to read: 'shows that you, through me' . . . no, 'shows that through me, you want this moment to be seized.'"

"Make that the rare opportunity," said the senator. "Actually, you know that part later with the line about it being a once-in-a-generation moment? We should move that back to here."

"That's good," said Levy. "Explains why it's such a rare opportunity."

"It belongs here," said Murphy.

Levy deftly made some changes on his handheld. "I can streamline a couple of other things on that. That's really good."

Benton was still gazing doubtfully at the line. "You think it's triumphalist? You know, look at me, here I am, in this high place."

"But you've got the humility with the 'bearer of your sacred trust,'" said Levy. "That's why it's there. It's a high place, but you're their servant."

"Then why don't we say I'm their servant?"

"That's a little too much humility. You're their servant, but you're also their president."

"Jodie?"

Ames read the line thoughtfully on her handheld. "I think Sam's got the balance."

"John?"

"I like it," said Eales. "Depends how you read it, Senator."

Benton read it aloud. "What do you think?"

Eales shrugged. "I still like it."

Ames nodded. Levy and Murphy watched the senator.

"'Through me.' I don't like 'through me.' What am I, their savior? That's too much. Change that to 'through my administration.'"

Levy nodded. "That's better."

The senator continued to gaze at the paper. "No, I still don't like it. How about: From this high place, as the bearer of your sacred trust, I pledge that my administration will seize this rare opportunity."

"Say that again, sir," said Levy, tapping it in.

The senator repeated it.

Levy shook his head. "It's got no rhythm. Not when you look at the sentence before."

"You're already changing the sentence before."

"You're right. Leave it with me, Senator."

Benton kept reading. Slowly, they worked through the rest of the speech.

It was past one o'clock when they got to the last sentences. Joe Benton read them aloud.

"My fellow Americans, it's time. Our time. Not a time to take, but a time to give. Not a time to rest, but a time to work. A time to renew the foundations. A time to rebuild the house. To build it strong, to build it sturdy. Come build it with me. And in times to come they will look back and say, in these years, these people built a house to last."

There was silence.

"How do I say it?" asked Benton.

"That was good," said Jodie Ames.

"That was better than good, sir," said Barry Murphy.

"Come on, be hard on me. It's not good enough. Let me hear you say it."

"Who?"

"You, all of you."

They looked at each other.

Murphy shrugged. He cleared his throat. "My fellow Americans . . ." The senator listened.

"I could really get into this," said Murphy when he had finished.

"Sam?"

Levy read it. With emotion. They were his words. Then Jodie Ames read it. Then Eales.

There was silence.

"All right," said the senator. "I'll work on the delivery. Very good. Thank you. Sam, can I have the redraft by seven?"

Levy looked at his watch. That gave him a little over five hours. "Sure. Senator, can I ask you something? Are there going to be any surprises?"

"Sam, you know I always reserve the right to have a couple of surprises."

"I don't suppose you could tell me where they might fit?"

Benton knew that John Eales was watching him, waiting to hear what he would say.

Joe Benton's face cracked in a smile. "Sam, what would be the point of that? If I did have anything up my sleeve, it would just spoil the surprise."

Thursday, January 20

The Capitol, Washington, D.C.

It was the strangest ride. Joe Benton wondered whether anyone who had taken it had ever thought otherwise. He and Mike Gartner sat side by side in the limousine, one the loser, the other the winner who had taken his crown. And yet perhaps there was something wonderful about it as well, he thought, humbling. It made a kind of sense, like the ancient Roman practice of having a slave standing in the emperor's chariot whispering that all the glory before him would soon pass.

Benton glanced at Gartner. The other man's head was turned, looking out the window at the bleachers that had been erected along Pennsylvania Avenue. They were full of people who had opposed him, who wanted to see him gone. People who had come to cheer as he was deposed. Thoughts of tumbrils and guillotines came to mind.

The day was dazzling bright. Cold.

"It rained on my Inauguration Day," murmured Gartner. "It was a crappy day."

Joe Benton remembered. A fine, misty rain. Unseasonably warm for Washington at that time of year. He had watched Gartner's inauguration as a member of the Senate. Back then, a mere four years earlier, it had seemed unlikely the time would ever be right for him to run.

Gartner turned back and sniffed. He had a cold. His big nose was red.

Benton didn't say anything. He respected Gartner's right to his thoughts at this moment.

They had met once more since their secret meeting in November. That was the meeting everyone expected. Gartner had had his secretaries of state and defense with him, and Benton had brought Larry Olsen and his nominee for secretary of defense, Jay MacMahon. The press were there to take pictures. There had been no discussion of the Chinese negotiations, nor any mention of Dr. Richards and the ESU.

Benton had always thought of Mike Gartner as a mediocrity, a timeserver from the right family and the right state who had spent his eight requisite years as vice president and then had proceeded to squander his four years as chief executive in a stuttering series of firefighting actions. If any common thread ran through his policies, it was the naked brazenness with which they maintained the status quo for the Republican party's donors. The presidential pardons Gartner had just handed out on the last full day of his term were egregious even by the standards of that questionable tradition. Yet it wasn't what he had done during his time in power, but what he hadn't done, that was the greater crime. Opportunities lost, one after the other. Joe Benton had promised himself and the American people that his presidency would be everything that Gartner's had not been, fresh, vigorous, purposeful, effective. A complete break. And yet, after swearing the oath, if he made the speech that Sam Levy had finally drafted for him, if he revealed nothing of what he had learned that day back in November, there would be something at the heart of his presidency that wasn't a break with Gartner, but a continuity. He felt, in a way, that he would be complicit with Mike Gartner in a deceit against the American people that the man beside him in the limousine had perpetrated in the final months of his presidency. It was the last thing Joe Benton wanted, to feel bound to this man for whom he had so little respect, to feel that the shadow cast by his action loomed over his own presidency from the very beginning.

But that was the nature of power, he knew, to be confronted by exigencies that didn't fit with your plans. To find yourself with bedfellows you despised. And the successful exercise of power was to steer your way through those exigencies, to walk past those bedfellows, holding fast and trusting to the vision of where you were going, and to get there in the end, if not sooner, then later, if not all the way there, then a good part of it, peacefully and with integrity. That was what he had to do. If he didn't believe he could do it, he shouldn't be in that car.

Maybe that was the speech he should make. Just that. One minute. Wasn't that all that needed to be said?

"You know, you never can tell what's going to hit you next," murmured Gartner gloomily, as if reading Benton's thoughts. "I bet you think you know what I mean, but just wait until you're president."

Gartner gazed at him for a moment, then turned away again.

The car pulled up. A marine in dress uniform pulled open the door.

Benton got out. Above him, in the clear blue sky, rose the dome of the Capitol.

On that icy, dazzling January day, in those last minutes before he was sworn in as the forty-eighth president of the United States, Joe Benton still believed he could manage to do what he had promised, to break with the past, to use his presidency to turn the enormous challenge that awaited the American people into a triumph. Over the last weeks, the structure of his four years had crystallized. It no longer seemed a long time, with scope for trial and error, as it had seemed during the campaign. It was painfully short. The first year would determine his success. He had to go hard, gamble everything. The year was mapped out in his mind. A parallel strategy of two parts. First, the programs, the bills, of which there were eleven major ones. The elements of fairness that would create the new foundation for the country. They would have to be in place by the time he made his first State of the Union address in a year's time. It was a daunting prospect, but with a majority in both houses, it was possible, provided he could keep the swing supporters with him. If he had to, he'd pork-barrel like the best of them. Then at the State of the Union, he would reveal the other side to his strategy. Over the last weeks, almost against his own instincts, he had found himself moving to a decision to deal bilaterally and secretly with the Chinese government over emissions. If all went well, in a year's time, with the elements of fairness in place, he would have a deal with China and be ready to reveal the terms of that deal and take it to the global community.

That was the only way it could be done. Fast, furious. If he got bogged down, he would never extricate himself, and in four years he would be in Mike Gartner's seat. Worse, the once-in-a-generation opportunity with which the American people had entrusted him would be out of reach, and it would be another twenty, thirty years before it would swing back into reach again.

That was the thing that scared him. Not his own fortunes in four years time, but missing the opportunity for the people who had voted overwhelmingly for him to act on their behalf. Being the one to let it slip.

He went up the steps. Gartner climbed them by his side.

"Nervous?" murmured Gartner. "I was nervous as a schoolboy when I walked up here four years ago. Funny. I'd been up there twice with Shawcross, but it didn't matter. It gets you, what you're doing."

They got to the top. The other dignitaries were waiting.

"Good luck, Joe," said Mike Gartner. "I mean that."

Angela Chavez was sworn in first. There was a reading that Chavez had chosen. Then the moment had come. Justice Paula Eagleton, chief justice of the Supreme Court, administered the oath. It would have been a cliché to say it was the most solemn moment in Joe Benton's life as he stood with hand raised, but it was. In the weeks since the election, he had spoken often about the great honor that the American people had bestowed upon him, the awesome burden, his doubt that he was worthy of it, his endeavour to prove that he was. At the security briefing that morning at Blair House, when he had been instructed on the steps his military aide would take if he was to order the launch of nuclear weapons, he had even thought he finally felt what that really meant. But he realized that even then he hadn't, it was only a foretaste of the real thing. It was only now, as he raised his hand, uttered the words, conscious of the people watching and listening to him below, conscious of the cameras streaming the image around the world, that he felt the full force of it. It was as if the weight physically descended on him as he spoke, not a heaviness, but a gravity, and he could feel it settling upon him. He felt himself standing in a line with the forty-six men and one woman who had gone before him. He felt himself unworthy. Deeply, deeply unworthy.

When he had said the words, he shook Justice Eagleton's hand. He shook Mike Gartner's hand, then Angela Chavez's. He kissed Heather and hugged Amy and Greg.

Then Senator Randall Turner, chairman of the Congresional Committee on Inaugural Ceremonies, called upon him to speak for the first time as the president of the United States.

Joe Benton stepped forward. He was conscious of the coldness of the air, the brightness of the sunlight. For a moment the cold seemed to grip his throat. He looked out at the crowd. He thought of Joe Kowalksi, Joanna Kowalski, sitting in a bar in Detroit. In Philadelphia. In Baton Rouge. In Santa Fe. He thought of all the Joe Kowalskis and Joanna Kowalskis he had met, the real ones, the one who had brought him into politics in the first place, the ones who had kept him in it.

"My fellow Americans . . ." he began. "A little over two hundred fifty years ago, a group of men laid the foundations for a house."

In Detroit, in Philadelphia, in Baton Rouge, in Santa Fe, in cities and towns and villages, people watched.

In a crowded office in Lafayette Towers, Sam Levy gazed at a screen, mouthing every word an instant before the president spoke it, his hand gripping a champagne glass so hard it threatened to splinter between his fingers.

He spoke for thirteen minutes. Then he drew to the end.

"My fellow Americans, it's time. Our time. Not a time to take, but a time to give. Not a time to rest, but a time to work. A time to renew the foundations. A time to rebuild the house. To build it strong, to build it sturdy. Come build it with me. And in times to come they will look back and say, in these years, these people built a house to last."

Saturday, January 22

The President's villa, Pingfang, outside Beijing, China

Each of them had a translation of the speech in Mandarin together with the original version in English. There was also a summary of editorial from the American media which had been prepared by the foreign ministry, and an opinion from the U.S. desk head of the Guoanbu, the state foreign intelligence service.

President Wen was looking relaxed in polo shirt and slacks. He was a tall, narrow-shouldered man who had gone a little to fat in recent years. The others were more formally dressed, Ding most formal of all. Sharp Armani suits were his trademark, even in the most relaxed surroundings.

They sat on sofas around a low table. The others present were the prime minister, Zhai Ming, Li Wenyuan, one of the rising stars of the next generation and a protégé of Wen, and General Shen Bihua. Zhai had been disconcerted to arrive and find that Foreign Minister Chou wasn't present. Immediately he felt outflanked.

"It's a domestic agenda," said Li, concluding the overview that Wen had asked him to present. "Nothing appears to have changed from what he was saying during the campaign."

"I'm struck by this sentence," said Wen. He read it in English. "We are a nation of mighty power. But to those who are listening to me today outside these United States, I say, we will not use this power just because we can, nor without care, but only if we must. Let us sit down, let us solve our problems together. Do not leave the table, that is all I ask." Wen looked around. "What do we conclude from this?"

"There are numerous ways to interpret this," said Li. "I think we must look at it in the context of the speech. Only 182 words devoted to foreign affairs, out of a total of 1,644. This is a historically low figure, President Wen. To me this is an important statistic. It couldn't be a coincidence."

"I agree with Minister Li," said Zhai. "I do not take this one sentence to mean so much. His concerns are domestic."

"Are his domestic problems really so great?" demanded Ding.

"Great," said Wen. "The domestic problems of America are always great, and yet the consciousness of the people is so low." He laughed. "How do they do it, Shen? I wish we had the answer."

General Shen laughed, and there were smiles from the others in the room, except for Ding. He interpreted that as a rebuke from the president. Ding Jiahui had little sense of humor, unlike Wen, who projected an easy, avuncular charm.

"If their domestic troubles are so great," muttered Ding, "perhaps they will let us get on with solving our own."

"I believe he is committed to dealing with the domestic issues, and his foreign policy will be minimalist," said Li. "He will act only when forced."

"Why do you say that?"

"I watched him very carefully in the campaign, President Wen. I believe he is driven by a kind of historical mission. He believes this moment is the one when he can put right the great problems in America. He has a sense of historical destiny. Many of his speeches refer to the place of this generation in history."

"Is this some kind of religious faith?"

"No. I conclude that this is a sense of historical mission. In my opinion, the inauguration speech confirms this." Li glanced over the speech, lifting the pages. "Everything he says here fits with that."

"A man with a sense of historical destiny is dangerous," said Zhai.

"Are you saying we have no sense of historical destiny?" Wen paused. "Or are you saying we are dangerous?" Wen roared with laughter. "Ding," he said. "Ding, can't you laugh at anything?"

Ding forced a smile.

Wen became serious again. "So this is his vulnerability? His sense of his place in history?"

"I think so," said Li.

"But Olsen is a pragmatist. Zhai, you know him?"

Zhai nodded. "Olsen is not subtle. His strength is to define his objective, not necessarily in the way he tries to get there."

"Americans are never subtle," said Shen.

"But he is forceful? He will play a role?"

"Yes. Why else has Benton appointed him?"

"Benton will focus on his domestic agenda," insisted Li. "This is what we learn from the speech. And he has a majority in both houses of the Congress, so he has the ability to actually do the things he speaks about."

"If he can get them to do what he wants," said Wen. "That's not always so easy for an American president."

"Every president says the same thing when he takes office," muttered Ding. "Always it's the domestic issues that are on top. Then they get more and more involved outside. Once they have the power, they can't help it."

"I think on this occasion Minister Ding is right," said Zhai. "Every American president comes to power saying he will focus on domestic affairs, and each of them soon becomes embroiled outside."

Ding was silent, and Zhai, although he had referred to him, didn't glance in his direction. There was very little on which the two men did agree, and as Ding's popularity had grown, encouraged and abetted by Wen, Zhai had felt his own authority eroding.

"A new American president always represents an opportunity," said Shen.

"Or a danger," said Zhai.

Wen nodded. "The question for us is whether he knows yet."

"I have thought about that," said Li

"Tell us what you think."

"There is nothing here that deviates from what he said during the campaign. Nothing to suggest he has learned anything new."

"If he wishes to keep it secret," interjected Ding, "why would he say it?"

"That may be so, Minister Ding. But I think something would creep in. A hint, at least."

"What about the sentence President Wen read to us?" Ding searched for it in his copy of the speech and read it in English. "*Let us sit down, let us solve our problems together. Do not leave the table, that is all I ask.* Is he talking to us? Is he not saying that he knows?"

"Who begs in public?" said Zhai coldly.

"Is it begging?"

"I agree with Premier Zhai," said Li. "The fact that he says this, in my opinion, shows that he doesn't know. If he knew, he wouldn't say this."

"What would he say?" demanded Ding. "Since you seem to know the mind of the American president so well."

"He wouldn't say this. What does President Wen think?"

All faces turned to Wen.

Wen shrugged. "Does it matter? If he didn't know, soon he will. What would be the process? When would they tell him?"

There were blank looks around the table.

"Whenever it is, it'll get him shitting," muttered Ding.

Wen smiled. "Let us assume he doesn't know. Now he has made this big speech about solving America's problems, and the next day he wakes up and finds out his biggest problem is with us!"

General Shen laughed. "We should give them a tickle. He'd be too scared to respond."

Wen smiled.

"What is it, Premier Zhai?" said Ding. "Don't you think that's funny?"

Zhai was grim-faced. "Make my enemy comfortable. My enemy's pain is a danger to me."

"And a danger to me makes me strong again."

Zhai shook his head. He looked at Wen. "President Wen, you should call him to congratulate him."

"Ambassador Liu has passed on the congratulations of the government," said Ding. "And President Wen spoke to him after the election."

"Now he is president."

"No need to speak again so soon," said Wen. "When did I speak with Gartner? Hardly ever."

"The relationship can be better."

"Let him come to the president," said General Shen.

Wen nodded. "Let him find out first. Then watch him flounder. Why should we make the path for him? For six months, he won't know what to do."

"President Wen, we should take advantage of his confusion to push him to where we want him to go," said Ding.

Zhai looked at him sharply. "And where is that?"

Tuesday, January 25

West Wing, The White House

The surprise on Chen Liangming's face showed for only an instant, but Larry Olsen saw it. That was exactly the effect he wanted. The invitation had led Chen to expect to be meeting the new president's chief of staff. The extra presence in the room caught him unprepared.

Ben Hoffman shook hands with Chen. "This is Mr. Olsen, the secretary of state," he said.

Olsen smiled. He spoke in Mandarin. "We know each other, don't we Mr. Chen?"

Chen nodded. "Good afternoon, Mr. Secretary. He spoke in English, shaking Olsen's hand. "This is Miss Hu," he said, gesturing to the young woman who had accompanied him. He smiled at the obvious redundancy of her presence. "She is my interpreter."

Ben Hoffman indicated chairs. They sat.

"It's still chaos," he said, waving his hand around his office. "I apologize."

Chen nodded. "New job, Mr. Hoffman."

"Everyone here's got a new job, Mr. Chen. A whole building full of people with a new job."

"I add my personal congratulations to President Benton to those of my government."

"Thank you, Mr. Chen. I'll pass it on."

There was silence.

"You happy to do this in English, Mr. Chen?" said Larry Olsen. He chuckled. "My Mandarin's a little rusty."

"Certainly, Mr. Secretary."

"We can call in an interpreter on our side if we need to," said Hoffman.

"There's no need, Mr. Hoffman, I assure you."

"You might want to . . ." Larry Olsen glanced at Miss Hu, and then looked meaningfully again at Chen.

"My assistant will take care of Miss Hu," said Hoffman.

Chen hesitated for a moment. Then he nodded. "Thank you."

Hoffman ushered the interpreter out.

"I was surprised to receive this invitation," said Chen, when Hoffman came back. "I would think you have many urgent calls on your time during this period, Mr. Hoffman. And of course you, Mr. Secretary."

"Well, we're busy," said Olsen. "I don't think we'd deny that, huh, Ben?"

Hoffman nodded.

"There's something we want to talk to you about," said Olsen. "We're aware that over the six months prior to the last election the previous administration was engaged in a process of negotiation with your government. More particularly, with yourself, Mr. Chen, as your government's representative."

Chen's expression was deadpan. "Our governments negotiate over many things, Mr. Secretary."

Olsen smiled briefly. "Of course they do, Mr. Chen. I think we both know what negotiations we're talking about. Carbon emissions, if you want to be explicit. Now, you should know that we're aware of the scientific evidence that caused these negotiations to start. We're aware of the implications for our country and for yours."

Olsen paused. Chen didn't speak.

"These implications are very grave, Mr. Chen."

Still Chen didn't speak.

"Mr. Chen?"

"Are you aware of the proposal your government put to us, Mr. Secretary?"

"At this stage, that's not a relevant point, Mr. Chen."

"Your government proposed a joint cut in—"

"I don't care what the previous administration proposed, Mr. Chen. My understanding is that your government rejected all the proposals made by that administration."

"The last proposal, Mr. Secretary, is still under discussion in Beijing."

"Three months after it was made? That's a lot of discussion."

"I can only repeat, the last proposal is still under discussion in Beijing."

Olsen shrugged. "Well, it's not under discussion in Washington."

"But the last proposal—"

"The last proposal was not accepted by your government. Mr. Chen, this is a new administration. It will honor any agreement signed by any of its predecessors and duly ratified by the United States Senate. It is not bound by a proposal made by a previous administration to which a response was never even received."

Chen watched him stonily.

"I'm afraid that proposal's no longer on the table."

"Then perhaps you will tell me what is on the table, Mr. Secretary?"

"Nothing. It's your turn, Mr. Chen. We're waiting for your government to put something there."

Chen didn't reply. He glanced at Ben Hoffman.

"You need to give your government a message, Mr. Chen," said Olsen. "Last year, you were negotiating with a president in the last year of his term. I'm sure you understand the way politics works in this country, and I'm sure President Wen understands as well. You're now dealing with a president in his first year of office. A Democratic president with a majority in both houses, which is something that hasn't happened since the 2012 Congress. I'm sure you understand the implications of that, Mr Chen. I'd like to be sure that President Wen understands as well."

"President Wen is fully aware of the political processes in your country, Mr. Secretary."

"Good. Then he'll know he's not dealing with a Mike Gartner now."

Chen allowed himself a slight smile.

Olsen adopted a more familiar tone. "Chen, I don't know why we're arguing here. We know as well as you what's going to happen to your country if nothing's done about this. The Guangxi coast, Hainan island, large parts of the Guangdong coast all the way to Hong Kong are going to be severely compromised if not uninhabitable. Those are some pretty important areas. Chen, you're from Guangdong yourself. What's going to happen to your home village? The relocation plans your government's got in place are woefully inadequate to the scale of what's going to happen if we don't sort this out."

"Mr. Secretary, this is because the United States has been a constant and consistent carbon emitter far in excess of its proportional rights."

"Mr. Chen, isn't it time we stopped playing the poor cousin? Your country surpassed us in carbon emissions back in 2007. That's a full quarter century ago. You're now more than double our size in emissions."

"But with a population four and a half times as large as yours."

"And with an average economic growth rate three times greater than ours."

"And with an average per capita income four times smaller, even now. With respect, Mr. Secretary, don't talk to me about playing the poor cousin."

"All right, I'm not here to negotiate with you."

"These are the facts, Mr. Secretary. I'm sorry if they're inconvenient. These are the facts successive governments of your country have refused to accept."

"I said I'm not here to negotiate."

Chen nodded. "Very well. See? When the facts are inconvenient, it's easier to ignore them."

Olsen raised his hand. "There's something President Wen should understand. A lot of people misunderstand Joe Benton. They assume that just because he talks about domestic issues, he has no interest in foreign affairs. Wrong. President Benton has a keen interest in foreign affairs and an acute understanding of them. If President Wen thinks he's going to sit around and watch while President Benton finds his feet in foreign affairs, I've got a message for President Wen. President Benton has already found his feet. You're looking at them." Olsen paused. "President Benton will act, Mr. Chen. He's not afraid. When it's in this country's interests, he will act. You are going to see this very shortly. Note what I say. In the next few days, sir."

Chen's eyes narrowed.

"President Wen should judge President Benton on his actions. I want that message to be very clear. I'm going to give it to Ambassador Liu when I meet him, but I've got a feeling President Wen's going to get it a lot quicker from you." Olsen sat forward. "Chen, here's the thing. The government of the United States cannot tolerate inactivity on the issue of emissions. It may be the case, that in the past, we haven't acted with as much urgency as we should. Between you and me and Ben here, I'm prepared to admit that in many cases we haven't lived up to everything we've promised, and we're no better than anyone else in that respect. So I'm not getting on any high horse. But what I am telling you is, that's changed. That time is gone. The issue is urgent, and under this administration, when we say we're going to do something, we're going to do it. So this is now the number one priority of this administration. The government of the United States cannot tolerate, and will not tolerate, inactivity." Olsen paused. "But we're only looking for a fair solution, and a just solution, to this problem. This has to be win-win for both our countries, inasmuch as you can even talk about a win in this situation. This isn't a question of an unequal treaty." Olsen stopped again. He wanted to be sure Chen noted the terminology he had used. The agreements imposed on the Chinese empire by foreign goverments in the nineteenth century were referred to as unequal treaties, and their memory still provoked anger and resentment in Beijing. "We understand and accept that. The time for such treaties is long gone, and they should never have happened. But we do need to come to an agreement, one that's fair. As I said, this is our number one priority and that's not going to change. Now, your government has rejected a number of proposals already that were made by the previous administration. So when you come back to talk to me, I would like to hear what your government *would* like. Take your time. Take a week or even two. Ben here is the man to contact when you're ready. In the meantime, I repeat, judge President Benton by his actions."

Olsen sat back.

Chen gazed at him. The muscles in his jaw clenched a couple of times. "The Chinese government is only looking for a just solution as well," he said eventually.

"Good," said Olsen. "Then we shouldn't have any trouble, should we?"

"I'll minute it," said Hoffman after he had shown Chen out.

"Thanks," said Olsen. "What did you think?"

"You were harsh on him."

"You think that was harsh?"

"Isn't there something about not making Chinese lose face?"

Olsen laughed. "Chen and I go way back, Ben."

"Okay. Well, to be honest, Larry, I'm not sure the president expected you to go that far. Do you think it was wise to take Gartner's proposal off the table?"

"Gartner's proposal wasn't on the table. What was on the table—or what would have been on the table—were bits of Gartner's proposal. The bits our friends happened to like. That's not going to work. We're in an endgame, Ben. They have to understand that."

Hoffman frowned. "I'm not sure everyone on our side sees it as an endgame."

"What about you, Ben?"

Hoffman didn't reply.

Olsen nodded. "Watch a little. Just watch what they do."

"Do you think it was smart to tell them how urgent we regard it? Doesn't that encourage them to prevaricate?"

"That's a fair question. To be honest, it could do that. On the other hand, it doesn't look like they've needed much encouragement to prevaricate so far, so what have we got to lose? Ben, this is more about setting a tone. Straight talking. It's like: I know you're going to try to play games with me, but I'm going to talk straight. Because I know you need a deal too. So you can play your games with me, but it won't get you anywhere because I'm not going to play them with you. Nothing's going to change so let's cut the crap and get started."

Hoffman looked at him doubtfully.

"And if you're in doubt," added Olsen, "watch us. We're going to show you we really are prepared to act."

Hoffman thought about it. "What do you think they'll come back with?"

"This time round? Nothing." Olsen smiled. "That's the game, Ben."

Wednesday, January 26

Oval Office, The White House

He gripped the edges of the lectern with both hands. Adam Gehrig was a slim, handsome man, with curly black hair and a dimpled chin. In the Oval Office, the president, Ben Hoffman, John Eales and Jodie Ames were watching him via the feed from the press briefing room.

Gehrig had already announced that Hugh Ogilvie, the British prime minister, would be visiting Washington in mid-February. Next he announced that the president had signed a set of executive orders releasing additional funds for people who had already been moved under President Gartner's Relocation program. Then he got onto the final announcement of the press conference.

"As you are aware, this morning President Benton announced the immediate suspension of aid to both Syria and Iraq until they come to an agreement over sharing the waters of the Euphrates River. The president, of course, is aware of the special U.S. responsibility in these two countries, for reasons that we all understand. He has today spoken to both President Al-Difaari and President Lahoush to assure them of the continuing U.S. commitment to reconstruction in their countries and his hope for the earliest possible resumption of aid. However, this dispute must be brought to an amicable end. Over the last eight years it has resulted in four major border incursions and numerous smaller incidents with considerable loss of life. The president believes a resolution of this dispute is not only possible, but attainable within a short time and strongly urges the parties to resume the negotiations that were broken off in September. To this end, he will be sending as his special envoy General Alger Weiss, who, as you may know, has considerable experience in the region dating back to his service as a marine in the Second Gulf War. A biography of General Weiss is available in the press area of the White House website. The president will meet with General Weiss later today in the Blue Room. There will be an opportunity for photographs but the president will not be taking questions. A statement will be released after the meeting." Gehrig paused. "Now I'll take questions."

They started. But the questions weren't about the Iraq-Syria initiative, nor about the British prime minister's visit, nor about the release of funds for the victims of the Gartner relocation. They were about Hugo Montera.

Gehrig fielded a half dozen of them.

In the Oval Office, Joe Benton watched.

"It's amazing how many ways they can find to ask the same question," murmured Ben Hoffman.

"No, it's not," said Jodie Ames.

They kept watching. Gehrig fielded a final assault. Ben Hoffman switched off the stream.

A couple of minutes later, Gehrig came in.

"The man himself," said Eales.

Benton smiled. "That didn't look like much fun."

"I've had better briefings, Mr. President," said Gehrig.

"Do you think they even heard the announcement on the Iraq-Syria initiative?"

"Well, sir, I told them."

"Jodie," said Eales, "make sure they cover it."

"Is it that important?" said Ames.

"Yes," replied Benton. "Get Hugo Montera off the front page and my initiative onto it."

"With respect, Mr. President, there's only one way to do that."

"Jodie, that's not going to happen. I won't have this administration getting a reputation for being soft in defense of its people."

"Well, that makes it hard, sir. What was happening out there, they figure if they get to a certain point, if they bring the story to a certain level, they've done their job. They deserve the scalp."

"They *deserve* it?" demanded Benton. He avoided looking in John Eales's direction. Eales had already told him it was time to cut Montera loose. "If the time comes, I'll do what I have to do. But I'll be damned if I'm going to let *them* tell me when that is."

There was silence. Ames glanced at Gehrig, who gave a slight shrug.

"Jodie," said John Eales. "Just make sure they cover the action the president's taken over Syria and Iraq. It's important."

Monday, January 31

West Wing, The White House

Chen was alone this time. They got down to business quickly. Larry Olsen didn't have much to say. This time, he was there to listen.

"President Wen wishes me to pass on his commendation of the president's action on the Iraq-Syria Euphrates dispute," said the Chinese diplomat. "Hopefully, this will help bring it to an end. For a number of years it has been the belief of President Wen that this is a destabilizing dispute which is capable of resolution, and the United States is the natural mediator to help bring this about. President Wen said this to President Gartner a number of times."

"Thank you, Mr. Chen," said Ben Hoffman. "I'll be sure to pass on to the president your remarks."

Chen nodded.

Larry Olsen had noted the way Chen referred to President Wen, not the government of the People's Republic. This wasn't accidental, he knew.

"I'm glad President Wen took note of this action, Mr. Chen," he said. "And particularly the swift and decisive nature of it. As you may know, General Weiss is already in Baghdad. I think this illustrates what I was telling you about President Benton last time we met."

"I repeat, Mr. Secretary, President Wen commends the initiative of President Benton, and the People's Republic will be supporting the resolution of the United States in the upcoming vote in the Security Council."

There was silence. Olsen gazed at Chen. Chen stared back at him. Ben Hoffman watched the two men. The silence went on. It was almost unbearable. Hoffman had to hold himself back from saying something, anything, to break it.

Chen spoke.

"President Wen has asked me to state that he has the intention of issuing an invitation to President Benton to visit Beijing if he can be assured that President Benton would be favorably disposed to such an invitation."

Larry Olsen didn't reply.

"As you aware, President Gartner met President Wen on a number of occasions, first as vice president and later when he became president himself. Each of these meetings was fruitful. President Wen regards President Gartner as a personal friend, and he hopes he will have the opportunity to regard President Benton as a friend as well."

Olsen nodded. "I sincerely hope so."

Chen waited for Olsen to say something else. Eventually he continued. "As a mark of respect for President Benton, President Wen would like this meeting to take place as soon as possible. An early meeting would show the world the respect in which each of our leaders holds the other. Provided President Benton is favorable, President Wen believes that it would be possible to welcome the president to Beijing as early as September."

"As early as September?" said Olsen.

"This would be after the G9 meeting in India. Of course, the two presidents may meet then as well, but this is not the same, I think, as a visit to Beijing."

"No," said Olsen. "It isn't."

Chen glanced questioningly at Ben Hoffman.

"There are a number of schedulings I would have to check."

"Of course," said Chen. He looked back at Olsen. "President Wen's view is that negotiations on any matter will proceed more smoothly once he and President Benton have had the opportunity to speak face-to-face. Familiarity makes understanding, Mr. Secretary."

Olsen cleared his throat. "Mr. Chen, I am certain that President Benton would greatly appreciate the opportunity to visit Beijing, and that provided this visit comes at the right time and in the right circumstances it will be, as you say, a fruitful one."

Chen waited for Olsen to continue, but Olsen said nothing more. Chen glanced at Ben Hoffman. Hoffman sat rigidly, trying not to move a muscle.

"Mr. Secretary," said Chen, "do you have a message you would like me to give back to President Wen? The early date that President Wen is suggesting for the meeting with President Benton is a great mark of respect."

"That was the message, Mr. Chen. I just gave it to you."

"I'm not sure I understand exactly . . ."

Olsen repeated the words in Mandarin.

Chen was silent.

"Last time we met, I explained that we were waiting to see the proposal of your government on the issue of carbon emissions. We're still waiting for that, Mr. Chen." Olsen paused, watching the other man. Then he stood up. "Good to see you, Mr. Chen." He held out his hand.

Chen stood up and shook it.

"Mr. Chen," said Ben Hoffman, holding out his hand.

"Thank you, Mr. Hoffman," said Chen.

Olsen watched Hoffman walk him out.

Ben came back and closed the door. He sat down with a troubled look on his face.

Olsen smiled. "Ben, I told you last time not to expect anything back."

"You think they haven't got a proposal?"

"They might have. But our friend Chen sure as hell wasn't going to turn up with it today."

"Meaning he might later?"

"If Wen thinks the door's closing."

"Is the door closing?"

Olsen shrugged. "The door never closes. It just squeaks a little sometimes."

Ben Hoffman frowned. "Maybe the president should go meet Wen, like they say."

"Yeah, right." Olsen smiled, shaking his head. "Like I'd let him do that."

Tuesday, February 1

Cabinet Room, The White House

Joe Benton was late as he walked the short distance from the Oval Office to the Cabinet Room. He had been in an emergency phone conference with Erin O'Donnell, the attorney general, and Sol Katzenberger, director of the FBI. Prior to that he had spoken to Tom Walters, governor of Montana. Overnight an attempted arrest for nonpayment of federal taxes had developed into a siege of a compound near the town of Whitefish. The FBI estimated that ninety people, including up to fifty women and children, were holed up under the leadership of a known extremist called Bill Dare. They were now surrounded by four hundred FBI agents and Montana state troopers. Katzenberger wanted to give the go-ahead for his men to go in and get everyone out in a sharp, overwhelming attack. As long as they went in fast, Katzenberger was confident of minimum casualties. That level of optimism rang alarm bells in Joe Benton's mind. Katzenberger couldn't provide a plan for the assault. The alternative, said the FBI director, was the risk that the situation would develop into a drawn-out siege, ending in a catastrophe like Waco back in the early 1990s, when over eighty people died. In Dare's twisted view of the world, that might have been exactly what he wanted, some crazy kind of martyrdom.

Tom Walters, a republican who had been elected on a hard-line law-and-order ticket, was for immediate action. Erin O'Donnell wanted to wait.

This was the first time Benton had been asked to approve a specific action which might result in a loss of life. He felt the responsibility of executive power more strongly at that moment than at any other time since his inauguration. He weighed the options. Rightly or wrongly, he wasn't prepared to give the go-ahead, not on the basis of what Katzenberger had told him. He asked the FBI director to come back to him within twenty-four hours with a detailed plan for an attack. In the interim, his agents were to act only in self-defense.

He was still thinking about the decision when he walked into the Cabinet Room for his meeting with the legislators. He opened the door and was immediately among a bunch of familiar faces. Kay Wilson, the Senate majority leader, was standing beside the House Speaker, Don Bales. The majority whips of both houses were there, Senator Val Birley and Congressman Paul Rudd. A dozen of the other most influential Democrats on the Hill had also been invited, including Celia Amadi, the veteran senior senator from New York, and Rose Miller, a Florida congresswoman. From the White House, Angela Chavez, John Eales, Steve Kivopoulos, one of Eales's aides, Jodie Ames, Adam Gehrig, Josh Singer, the counsel to the president, and Barb Mukerjee, the president's chief legislative aide, were present. Ben Hoffman was delayed by something and would be along as soon as he could get away.

Benton greeted the legislators and they settled down. As Barb began to distribute sets of stapled pages, he consciously forced the situation that was developing at Whitefish to the back of his mind.

"This is how we're seeing the program," he said as the papers passed along the table. "I'll give you time to look over it."

One or two of the legislators nodded absently. They were studying the paper. None of it was news to them. They had been closely consulted all along as to the scope of the bills and were helping arrange sponsors for each piece of legislation. But this was their first chance to see the entire program laid out in front of them.

Joe Benton glanced at Angela. She smiled back at him. She didn't know that the task of relocation outlined in the introduction to the paper, daunting as it was, was only the beginning, and that the challenge that would face the nation over the next ten years would be threefold or fourfold greater— if he managed to do a deal with the Chinese government. That was a big if. Since taking office, Joe Benton had had zero time to focus on that. The pace over the last two weeks had been unremitting, and keeping the momentum on his domestic program was something he couldn't let up on. He knew that Olsen had been meeting Chen. Ben Hoffman had been keeping him informed. Some time in the next couple of days, he knew, Ben had arranged for the group to convene in order to review progress.

Eventually he had waited long enough for the legislators to look over the paper. He glanced at Jodie.

She outlined the approach they were going to use to announce the program. The president was scheduled to address a joint session of Congress on Monday. Prior to that, he would trail the program in a Friday press conference and in his weekly podcast to the nation that went out on Sunday. He was going to present it as a package. Every bill had to pass, every element was necessary, or New Foundation would fail.

"This is all in a year," said Don Bales, flipping through the pages and shaking his head. "I thought you were aiming to get it done in two."

"We've reconsidered that," said Eales. "If we pitch two, we won't get it done in four."

"I agree," said Kay Wilson.

Benton thought highly of Wilson. She was a self-made business-woman from Kentucky who had been Senate minority leader for four years. He had worked closely with her through six Congresses. He didn't rate Don Bales. Pat Greenberg, the previous minority leader in the House of Representatives, had retired at the last election and Bales, a four-time Democratic representative from California and dark horse for the Speaker's role, had put together a coalition that gave him the vote of the House Democrats. But the way he had been talking since the election, it had been Don Bales, and Don Bales alone, who had delivered the majority in the House at the general election. Benton suspected that the only thing Don Bales really cared about was retaining the majority at the midterm elections to become the first House Democrat to lead a majority in successive congresses since 2014.

Celia Amadi laid the paper aside. "I'm with Kay. It's a demanding list, Mr. President. Enough for the entire Congress. But if we can do it in a year, I say, let's do it."

Benton smiled. He had fought plenty of battles alongside Cee Amadi over the years and had always been thankful they were on the same side. If there was a tougher streetfighter in Congress, he'd like to know who it was. "I would have thought that was right up your alley, Senator," he said.

Cee laughed.

The president looked at Rose Miller. "Rose?"

"You're going to get everything or nothing, Mr. President."

"Every president says he's presenting a package," said Val Birley, "but this really is. If we fight it piecemeal, we'll get picked off. Everyone will object to something."

"Mr. President," said Don Bales, "with respect, I think we're biting off way too much. Even just your health care bill would be a landmark achievement."

"Don, kiss my *tuches*," said Cee Amadi. "Let's be bold. It's all or nothing. Joe won the election saying it was time to do stuff. He has a mandate for change."

"Not this much change."

"You can't have too much change. Not once you start. Bold's best."

The door opened. Ben Hoffman came in. He exchanged a quick glance with the president.

"Sorry," he said. "Did I miss anything?"

"Only Cee inviting Don to kiss her tuches," said Angela Chavez.

Bales ignored that. "Mr. President," he announced, "I don't know if you have the support any longer to get this program through."

The president looked at him incredulously.

"There's a WhichGov poll out today, and it's going to show you at forty-eight."

"No way!" said Ames.

"Jodie, it's showing him at forty-eight. With this Iraq-Syria thing, people are damn scared this president is going to put us right back in Iraq, which it took us ten years to get out of."

"Don," said the president, "it's two weeks since my inauguration. I don't care what a WhichGov poll says. The next election's in four years."

"Less than two, Mr. President, if you'll excuse me. And some of the congresspeople whose support you need do care about this poll."

"This is ridiculous!" John Eales thought Bales was a lightweight and was more than happy to let him know it. "People aren't that stupid. We're not going to war over the Euphrates. Those numbers will be back up next week."

"Mr. President," said Bales. "With respect, I think you just shot a whole chunk of your credit with that announcement."

"Just remember whose credit it was, Don." Benton gazed at him and let it sink in. "I'm not going to get anywhere if I react to every damn poll.

I've done politics a long time and I've never done it like that. Now, what I want to know is whether you can deliver the House for this program."

"And if you can't," said Angela Chavez, "what do we have to do to make sure you can."

Bales glanced at Paul Rudd, the House majority whip. "I'd say two hundred to two ten in the House are rock solid," said Rudd. "You've got another ten to twenty who'll come with you in general. And then you've got . . . it's ten or fifteen . . . they call themselves Democrats, but they're the ones. They're always the ones."

"We'll sit down," said Angela, glancing at Barb.

"Sure," said Rudd. "I'm not saying we can't do it. It's going to take some solid work."

"That's what you'll get," said Benton. He looked around the table. "Whatever you need, you'll get it. From me, from Angela, from whoever can make it happen."

They talked through the tactics. The American people had put Joe Benton into the White House on a platform for change, and not a single member of Congress was going to be allowed to forget it. And if they did, the voters in their district were going to know about it.

"Mr. President?" said Cee Amadi.

"Cee."

"I think you've got us all on your side." She paused and looked around at her fellow legislators, as if to give them opportunity to dissent. "But— and I'm going to be frank—there is something."

Benton smiled. "Cee, I'd never expect you to be anything less than frank."

"I'm talking about Hugo Montera."

Benton nodded. That's what he thought she was talking about.

"Mr. President, we've got people saying they don't like what he did, or what it looks like he did, even if he didn't do it. They're not going to go to bat for him."

Benton looked at Kay Wilson. "He's not going to get through?"

Wilson shook her head.

There was silence.

"The longer you leave it," said Cee, "the worse it is. The Republicans are squeezing this thing for every drop they can. Our people see Montera hurting them. They want you to take that hurt away." She raised the paper with the legislative program. "We want to do this. We really want to do this. But for some of them, this is going to hurt as well. Bad. They can only take so much."

"It's twenty or thirty," said Paul Rudd.

"Andy Burstin holds the South Carolina fourth by twenty-eight votes," said Rose Miller. "He'll back your program, but every time he takes that walk to vote for one of these bills, the Republicans are going to be counting him down like a pack of wolves. 'Twenty-eight, Andy, twenty-seven, twenty-six . . .'"

"You're asking that from him," said Bales, "it's not right to have people calling him up from South Carolina asking why the president insists on appointing an unfair employer as his secretary of labor."

There was silence around the table.

"Joe, you should get it done." The tone in Cee Amadi's voice was one Joe Benton knew from a thousand conversations over the past twelve years. Firm, pragmatic. Brutal, when she had to be. And almost invariably right. "Today. That way, Friday, when you get up in front of the press, you may have a chance of getting them focused on what you really want to talk about."

Benton frowned. "Okay, say I do it," he said quietly. "Doesn't it look weak? Doesn't it look like I'm backing down? Who's going to come out and support me over this package if I'm not strong enough to support my own nominees?"

Cee shook her head. "Once you do it, you get us back. No one wants to see you lose one of your nominees. No one believes Montera really did something wrong. And even if he did, you couldn't have known. We all feel this has been blown way out of proportion and you've been unfairly attacked by the Republicans and the press in what's supposed to be your honeymoon. Once he's gone, that feeling can come out. Our instinct is to rally around you. That'll happen. Mr. President, it's going to make you stronger."

Joe Benton knew it might work like that. He had seen it, been a part of it himself. On the other hand, it could work the other way as well, his perceived weakness making even more of his support ebb away. There was no rule about it. It depended on the feeling on the Hill at the time.

"Everyone agrees?" he said. He looked around the table.

There were nods from the legislators.

Joe Benton had seen enough of other presidents to know that exercising executive power was about keeping your hands as free as you could to do the things that really mattered. That meant making sure they weren't shackled by the myriad things that didn't matter, or didn't matter as much. Joe Benton counted Hugo Montera as a friend, but his nomination was turning into one of those things. Whatever was happening in Whitefish, Benton knew, could easily turn into another. If he had just made the wrong decision about handling the siege, even though it involved only a hundred people somewhere in the hills of Montana, it could shackle his hands by robbing him of the credibility needed to implement bold decisions affecting millions of people all across the country. And he would need that credibility. He would need more of it than he could ever have, without giving any of it away.

He glanced at Cee Amadi.

She met his eyes, and nodded.

Wednesday, February 2

Family Residence, The White House

Amy's face was on the screen opposite the sofa where Heather and Joe Benton were sitting.

"Daddy, I still can't see you," said Amy.

Joe Benton shifted closer to Heather. "How's this?"

Amy smiled. "You're too tall!"

Joe scrunched down in the sofa.

"You're still cut off. Go down a little further."

Heather laughed. "Ladies and gentlemen, the president of the United States." She got up. "Why don't we just deal with the camera?" she said, and she proceeded to adjust the webcam.

It was ten p.m. in Washington, seven p.m. in Palo Alto, on Amy's twenty-third birthday. Joe Benton hadn't spoken to her since she flew back to Stanford after inauguration week, ten days earlier. He made a mental note to make sure he regularly got time to talk with Amy. And with Greg too, if only Greg would make the time himself. No, that would be too much to ask. But if he didn't get someone to block out time for him with Amy, he knew it wouldn't happen. Time would slip away, and before he knew it, weeks would pass.

Time. He looked at Amy's face on the screen and wondered what any father would have wondered. Where had the years gone? His little girl was a smart, beautiful, vibrant woman of twenty-three in her second year of law school. How was it possible? The years slipped away, and before you knew it they were gone.

"I wish you were here so I could give you a hug, Amy."

"I wish I was too, Daddy. That'd be the best present I could ask for. And you too, Mom."

"Did you get the dress, honey?" asked Heather.

"It's beautiful, Mom."

"Does it fit?"

Amy nodded.

"What about the color? They had it in a blue, as well."

"The color's great, Mom."

"You can exchange it. If you don't like the color or the size or the cut . . ."

"No, it's perfect, Mom."

"I hope you're not just saying that. If you want to change it, you go right ahead."

"Honey," said Joe, "you heard what she said. She loves it. Not that I had anything to do with it, Amy. It was all your mom's doing."

"Joe! Don't say that. It's from both of us."

"We should have got you to fly over," said Joe. "I wish I'd got someone to organize that. Huh, Heather?"

Amy laughed. "That wouldn't be very responsible, Daddy. Just when we're meant to be the environmentally trustworthy ones. Imagine what Senator Hoberman would do if he heard you say that."

"Probably demand an inquiry. One flight doesn't matter."

"Daddy, *everything* makes a difference. I seem to remember a certain presidential candidate saying that a few times."

Joe Benton's face cracked in a smile. "Guilty as charged."

"Anyway, I love the dress."

"I think your mother wants to know why you're not wearing it," said Joe in a stage whisper.

"Joe! She doesn't have to wear it. That's not what I'm saying."

"Don't tell me you don't want to see her in it."

"Joe, Amy will wear it if she wants to wear it."

"Guys," said Amy. "I'm still here. I'm going to wear it later when I go out, okay? I'll send you a picture if you don't believe me."

Joe and Heather glanced at each other. They would have preferred a picture of the person Amy was going out with.

"He's just a friend!" said Amy. She laughed. "You're terrible."

"We're just interested," said Heather.

"Well, I'm sure you could find out from the Secret Service report if you want to."

Joe Benton frowned. He hadn't thought of that.

"Don't you dare start spying on me, Daddy!"

"Of course we won't spy on you, honey," said Heather, and she glanced at Joe again, as if she hadn't thought of it either.

"It'd be abuse of presidential power," said Amy. "I'm warning you, Daddy. I'd have you impeached."

Joe laughed. She probably would too.

"Are the agents getting in your way?" asked Heather.

"Not really," said Amy. "They've got a job to do, I know that. And I think everyone on campus is pretty much used to them by now."

"So quickly?"

"You forget, Mom. They've been around since Daddy won the nomination."

"Well, you let us know if they're treading on your toes."

"Daddy, I heard about Mr. Montera."

Joe nodded. Adam Gehrig had announced the withdrawal of Hugo Montera's nomination at that morning's White House press briefing.

"I'm sorry about it. I guess I knew it was coming, but he's a good guy, right?"

"In the end there was nothing we could do. Hugo wanted to withdraw. In fact, confidentially, he wanted to withdraw a week ago but I told him we could fight it through. But you have to know when you've lost."

"Will it hurt you?"

"Honey," said Heather. "It's your birthday."

"Daddy, I want to write him something to say I'm sorry it turned out like that."

"That's sweet of you, Amy. I'm sure he'd appreciate it. I'll get someone to send you his details."

"So will it hurt you? Have you got another nominee?"

"We're working on it."

"So what else is news, honey?" said Heather.

"Nothing, Mom. Dad, are you planning to nominate another Latino in the role?"

"I'll go for the best person I can get."

"I think that's right. You've got Angela, and the Latino community couldn't ask for more high-profile representation than vice president. Particularly because you've pledged she's going to play a real part. And the Latino vote is a natural constituency for you, so you don't need to give them too much. They're not going Republican next time round."

"I can't take that for granted, Amy. I still need to recognize their contribution."

"Honey," said Heather, "we can talk about this another time. It's your birthday."

"Mom's right," said Joe. "We shouldn't talk about this."

"Why not? What should we talk about?"

"Tell us about you," said Heather.

Amy laughed. "What do you want me to talk about? My classes? I'm not in junior high, Mom. Daddy, what are they saying on the Hill? I guess they wanted him to withdraw."

Joe glanced sheepishly at Heather. Heather shook her head, then shrugged in resignation.

He turned back to Amy. "There's strong Democratic support for the withdrawal. Confidentially, there was a general feeling in the caucus that we had to do it."

"Well, everyone loses a nomination, don't they? It won't make a difference in the long run."

"It makes a difference to Hugo."

"I didn't mean that. But in terms of your administration, in four years, this isn't going to make any difference."

"Agreed. But it might make a difference to what I can achieve this year."

"But this wasn't a critical role. It wasn't like he was your secretary of state."

"What should I have done if it had been?"

"That depends," said Amy.

"On what?" said Joe.

Beside him, Heather sighed. So much for the idea of having a conversation in this family—just one—that wasn't consumed by politics. It was one of the things that kept Greg away, she knew. But Amy and Joe both reveled in it. Talking politics with Amy wasn't work for Joe, it was sheer enjoyment, like a game they had played together for years. It was a game that Greg had never been able or willing to play, and Heather felt helpless to do anything about it. Amy was the one who had always been on Joe's wavelength, and as she matured, the more on that wavelength she seemed to be. There was a kind of informal agreement with the press to stay away from her while she was still in education, and Heather did what she could to stamp down on any talk in Democratic circles of a political career for her daughter. At twenty-three, Amy didn't need that kind of pressure. But that was where she was likely headed, Heather knew, and it made her worry. Joe wouldn't have understood why. In his mind, there was no higher calling than public service, and no mode of life more satisfying. Yet the thought of what that kind of life would mean for Amy brought out every maternal, protective instinct that Heather possessed.

And yet despite herself, as she watched Joe and Amy dissecting and analyzing the implications of Hugo Montera's withdrawal—Joe on the sofa beside her, Amy on the screen across the room—Heather couldn't help feeling a satisfaction, a deep sense of warmth, at the naturalness of the bond that they shared.

Friday, February 4

Oval Office, The White House

Joe Benton had just been on the receiving end of a harsh lesson in the art of keeping the press in line with presidential priorities. The Montera issue was over, but at his press conference, which had been scheduled to unveil the New Foundation package, the press was chasing Whitefish, sensing the Montana siege would pose an early test for the new president. As he had feared, the fate of a hundred-odd gun-toting fanatics was getting more interest than plans that would affect tens of millions of people. Benton almost wished he'd told Sol Katzenberger to send in the troops a couple of days earlier and to hell with the consequences. Just get the thing over and out of the headlines. Except that it would still be in the headlines if the attack had turned into some kind of Waco-style catastrophe. Well, he wasn't going to let that happen over the next few days and take the agenda away from him entirely at such a crucial moment. On Monday he would be presenting the New Foundation package to a joint session of Congress. He was going to let the siege run until those idiots in Montana came in starving out of the snow.

He came back from the press conference less than happy. He had a short conversation with Jodie Ames, Adam Gehrig and Barry Murphy, and they went away to work up a strategy to try to get the New Foundation message out again. Then he was scheduled for a meeting of the China group, which was now called the Marion group. Ben Hoffman had said they needed a name for it and there wasn't much point calling it the China group, or the Emissions group, because that kind of defeated the need for secrecy. Somehow he came up with Marion. Joe Benton had no idea why.

Larry Olsen reported on his meetings with Chen Liangming. The Chinese suggestion of an invitation to visit Beijing in September got an enthusiastic response from Alan Ball.

"It's a delaying tactic," said Olsen.

"So we let them delay a little at the start," said Ball. "Let them save some face."

"They haven't lost face yet."

"This way they don't."

Olsen turned back to the president. "Mr. President, there is simply no way you can leave this until September. If you start like that, you'll go on like that. They'll know you'll go with their timetable. We have to impose our timetable, and we have to do it from the start."

"I don't think we're going to get anywhere trying to impose anything on the Chinese," said Ball.

"I accept that, Al. Bad choice of words. But we become the junior partner in this negotiation if we accept their timetable. We become the supplicant at their table. At the very least, we've got to share the table. Mr. President, a meeting with President Wen has to be a reward. We make progress—he gets a meeting. He does nothing—he doesn't get a meeting."

"Maybe I should call him," said Benton.

"That should be a reward as well. Our job is to get you to the point where you talk to him. You're not there yet."

"I'm sorry, I think a meeting is something to consider," said Ball. "Admittedly, September's a long time to wait. We could try to make it earlier."

Benton wanted to know whether his Iraq-Syria intervention had had any effect. Olsen thought the Chinese side had got the message. Hoffman, who had sat in on the meetings with Chen, agreed that they had.

"Now they're testing us," said Olsen. "They're saying, sure, you've shown us you can pick a fight with the hundred-pound weakling, now are you going to come after the two-hundred-pound bully?"

"I suspect they think we're the bully," murmured Alan Ball.

"Whatever," said Olsen impatiently.

Benton thought about it. His immediate instinct was that a visit to Beijing must be a good idea, although, as Ball had said, September was a long time to wait. But Olsen was presenting him with an entirely different perspective. First, that a visit should be an outcome, not merely a step in the process. And second, that accepting a delay until September wasn't only undesirable but would send a message to President Wen that he was prepared to go at whatever pace Wen set.

"Mr. President," said Ben Hoffman, "I think we should get something on the table here. Larry, correct me if I'm wrong, but I think you believe we're in an endgame, and I think that's where your perspective is coming from. And my feeling is that Alan doesn't really have that view. Alan, would that be fair?"

Alan Ball nodded. "I'd like to know how Larry defines an endgame if he thinks we're in one."

"Let's not worry about definitions," said Olsen. "The point is, we have got to do something, and this time it has to be a good, final answer. We don't have the luxury to come back and revisit this in another five or ten years. Whether you call that an endgame or not, I couldn't care less. We have to get a solution. Now, God knows we've been remiss in living up to our obligations, I think all of us will admit that, and I don't think we should try to hide it. But China has never lived up to anything it's agreed to, and we shouldn't try to hide that either. They've been the biggest emitters for twenty-five years, and they've been the biggest economy on the planet for going on five years. That position carries some responsibility. They simply have never accepted the discipline of global responsibility, and they simply have not lived up to the leadership position they claim for themselves."

"A lot of people would say the same about us."

"And they'd be exaggerating. In the Chinese case, I'm not exaggerating. Sometimes they claim to be global leaders, sometimes they claim to be global paupers who are still the victims of colonial policies. Showing global leadership means sometimes you have to think beyond the purely parochial interest of your domestic agenda. Show me one example where the Chinese government has ever done that."

"Africa," said Ball. "We failed on aid for Africa for decades on end. Many people would say any prosperity that does exist in Africa is because of Chinese investment."

"Out of which they've done very well."

"Unlike us in our investments."

"Al, that's not the point! I'm saying that with that level of global leadership comes responsibility, and it's about time we asked them to accept what that means. We have to be prepared to demand more."

Alan Ball shook his head. "We're never going to get anywhere if we're thinking like this."

Benton intervened. "We have to live up to everything we've signed up to. That's the policy of this administration, period. I don't care what anyone else is doing. We live up to our commitments."

"Then, Mr. President, we should show that," said Ball. "Let's show that before we start laying down the law to the Chinese."

"Agreed. We're way behind on Kyoto 3. I'll announce an immediate program to bring the worst offenders in our industries into line in the course of this year."

"Mr. President, with respect," said Olsen, "I understand your desire to comply with what we've promised, and on principle we should always do that, but at this time, it sends the wrong message to Beijing. It's unilateral. It says, you guys, you're in breach, that's fine, stay in breach. We'll do the right thing. That rewards them for misbehavior."

"I'm not rewarding them. This is for us, not them. We need to be clean. We need to be completely clean in the global court of public opinion."

Olsen shook his head. "You're giving them something for nothing."

Benton didn't reply to that. Larry Olsen seemed to see every action either as a reward or punishment toward the Chinese government. Joe Benton didn't share that view, and Alan Ball obviously didn't either. That was one of the differences between Olsen and Ball. Another was becoming clearer as the meeting went on.

"You know," said Benton, "I think one of the things I'm hearing here is there's a difference between you, Larry, and you, Alan, on the question of timing. Alan, I don't think you believe we don't need to do something, but you think we've got time, right? And you think we might be more effective if we use that time. And Larry, you think we don't have time, and that if we take time, we become ineffective. Now, my instinct is to say, like Alan, I've got four years here. One thing that counts against that is the fact that with every day we delay, the physical reality of what's happening out there gets worse, and therefore the scale of the task gets bigger. Let's set that aside. By the yardstick of diplomacy alone, Larry, why don't I have four years to deal with this?"

"Mr. President, it's what I said to you before. You let them start like this, this is how it will go on. No matter what you do, they will never *believe* you're serious. You'll never be able to convince them of that again. We've started by saying, give us an answer quickly, and by the way, take a look at what we're doing with Syria and Iraq to see how quickly we're prepared to act. And what do they do? They say, okay, let's get together in seven months. You agree to that, game over. They'll think you carry a big stick only when you're up against a weakling. You let that go on, eventually you'll have to start a war to make them sit up and take notice."

Joe Benton smiled. "I don't think I'll be starting a war."

"Larry here might," muttered Ball.

"No, what I'm telling you, Alan, is how you *don't* start a war."

Ball's eyes narrowed. He gazed coldly at Olsen.

Olsen turned back to the president. "Another thing, sir, every day that goes by, you become vulnerable to this being made public. They could do that, and you'd look like you're deceiving the American people. That's an enormous weapon to leave in their hands."

"They've already got that," said John Eales.

"Sure, John, but only up to a point. If it does come out, it's one thing to say, all right, we're doing stuff, we're on the case, and the reason we've kept it quiet is so we can make progress. That's an argument. You can sell that. It's another thing to say, well, actually, we're doing nothing. We're just waiting until Beijing decides to roll out the red carpet in September. Just think what that looks like. That's the weapon you give them."

"Unless we put it into Kyoto," said Ball.

Olsen rolled his eyes. He wasn't even going to respond to that.

The president exchanged a glance with Eales. Then he turned to Rubin and Hoffman to see if they had any further thoughts. Rubin said she lacked the diplomatic experience and knowledge of the Chinese government to comment. Hoffman didn't have much to add either. He just thought that after two weeks in office, it might be a little hasty to conclude that they couldn't proceed cautiously for a while longer.

Joe Benton was inclined to agree.

"Let's try to get to a conclusion on this," he said. "Alan, you first. What do you suggest?"

"I think we should accept President Wen's invitation on principle," said Ball. "I think we try to bring it forward, but we accept it. And in the meantime, we continue talking with Chen, or whoever they're using, to see if we can make progress."

"And what do I take when I meet Wen?" asked the president.

"We'll take him some kind of proposal. It depends on what will have happened before that."

"Nothing will have happened before that," muttered Olsen. "Once you accept the invitation, everything freezes."

"So? That wouldn't be a disaster. Mr. President, it'll be a first meeting. A first meeting doesn't have to produce anything. People understand that. Besides, there'll be the usual cooperation agreements and business deals set up for you to sign. You won't come out of it empty-handed."

Benton turned to Olsen. "Larry?"

"It's what I said. We ignore this invitation. We set out a timetable to Chen by which we expect to reach an agreement."

"How long?"

Olsen shrugged. "Six months? We can work out the details. But this can't be indefinite. Both sides know the facts of the case, it's only a question of how we accommodate each other."

"Larry," said Eales, "if you give them a timetable, what's to stop them procrastinating around it like they're already doing now?"

"It includes an escalating set of penalties."

"Wait a second." Benton looked at Olsen. "Penalties? Larry, what do you mean by that?"

"Sanctions. In three months, say, if we haven't achieved progress—a certain set of sanctions. Three months after that—another set of sanctions."

This was new. Benton looked around at the others.

"Larry, what kind of sanctions are you thinking about?" asked Jackie Rubin.

Olsen shrugged. "Trade. Education. We can work something out."

"We have agreements," said Alan Ball.

"So do they. All kinds of agreements they've never kept. Al, you ever bought a Rolex on the street in downtown Beijing? If you paid more than five bucks you got ripped off. How hard do they act to crack down on that stuff? We've got to stop holding them to a different standard. It's what I said before, we have to be prepared to demand that they should be delivering. Why can't we say, you don't keep your agreements, we don't keep ours?"

"What do they do in retaliation?" demanded Rubin, still shaking her head incredulously. "Crash the dollar? They hold three trillion in reserves. What do they do? Sell down our bonds?"

"Who to? They sell that kind of volume, who's buying? Hurts them as much as us."

"Exactly. You shut down their trade, you shut down ours."

"True."

"You keep their students out, you hurt our universities."

"True again."

"Hold on," said Ben Hoffman. "Is there any sanction that would hurt them more than us?"

Jackie shook her head. "You know what, Ben? I don't think there is."

Olsen looked around the room. "Let's be clear about this. This whole thing is about pain. When we finally do get to an agreement with the Chinese government, it's going to hurt. So let's be absolutely clear here. This is about the historic moment of accepting that everything can't keep going like it's been going, that this is the moment when we have to stop and pay the cost." Olsen looked at Benton. "Or have I got the wrong end of the stick here?"

All eyes turned on the president. He thought about it. It was about pain. In one way or another, that was what he had said to the American people throughout his campaign, that the time had come to pay the cost of what had not been done over the past thirty years. And yet something in the way Olsen was talking about it seemed to be showing it in a different perspective. Joe Benton had the feeling that after all this discussion—some of it not particularly good-natured—they were finally getting to something important.

"What do you mean, Larry?" he said. "Go ahead."

"Mr. President, we are going to have to demonstrate to the Chinese government that we—the United States—will absorb pain. There is going to be no deal with them, nothing even close to a deal, unless they believe that. Now, you know what? Right now, I don't think they do believe it. And if I was in their shoes, I wouldn't either. As a country, the United States has never done anything to convince anyone otherwise. But if we're going to get this done, other people have to believe it. Not only the Chinese, but the rest of the world. We are going to have to be prepared to demonstrate that we will take our medicine, no matter how bitter it is."

"Mr. President," said Jackie Rubin, "you put sanctions in place, and you're going to come under *so* much pressure. Every special interest group in the country will start screaming. I'm thinking about your legislative program."

"Larry," said Benton, "I hadn't considered sanctions."

"We can't do without them. At least not the threat of them. And if we make the threat, we have to expect they're going to call our bluff."

Benton didn't say anything to that. It was the language of threat and ultimatum. That was Larry Olsen's style, but it had never been Joe Benton's. He didn't think it was about to become his style now, whatever his secretary of state said.

"Mr. President," said Alan Ball, "nothing Larry has said makes me think differently. Maybe we will end up talking about sanctions, but we're a long way from there. It's like you said before, Mr. President, it's about timing. We're going down this track way too fast. You should meet President Wen. Let's start with that."

"Talk to Wen without the threat of sanctions and you may as well be talking to yourself," said Olsen.

John Eales held up his hands. "Let's step back for a second. How did we get to sanctions? To demonstrate the willingness to inflict and absorb pain. Okay. But the Chinese government knows that if it doesn't act, China's going to hurt just as bad as we are. They're not dumb. They've seen the numbers, they've seen what happens to their southern coastline. There's your pain, Larry."

Olsen shook his head. "That's their pain, not ours."

"Exactly, and they're going to feel it!"

"In about ten years. John, you're talking about a corrupt and brittle system under enormous tension. Right now, the party obsesses about whether it's still going to be in control in ten months, not ten years."

"Larry," said Hoffman, "you said it yourself to Chen. They're going to have to relocate millions of people, uproot whole areas of their manufacturing base. Factories, warehouses. Hong Kong itself may not even be viable."

"Sure I said it," said Olsen. He smiled.

"What's funny?" asked Hoffman.

"It's beside the point. That's why it didn't make any impression on Chen. I didn't expect it to."

"What is the point, Larry?" said the president.

"Mr. President, these things aren't a problem for the Chinese government. Not the same kind of problem they are for us, anyway."

"You're saying relocating millions of people isn't a problem?" demanded Jackie Rubin.

"Yes, I am, Jackie. Alan knows what I'm talking about. Al, how many did they relocate when they built the Three Gorges Dam? Two million, right? And then another *four* million when they figured out what the true environmental implications were. Am I wrong, Alan? Tell me if I'm wrong."

Ball silently shook his head.

"And after the Yangtze landslides? No one knows for sure, but it was probably close on another ten million. And all of this without a whimper, Mr. President, without a fight. Look at us. Gartner tries to move a hundred people out of some bayou in Louisiana in his first act of relocation, and the whole country goes crazy. Those factories in Guangdong, Jackie, who do you think owns them? Let's look at the figures. Seventy-five percent of factories in Guangdong are foreign co-owned or sponsored. That's an important fact. It means it's not them who's going to pay to move them. You know who it is? Us! One way or another, directly or indirectly. And while we're at it, the factory workers are internal migrants. The average time they spend in these areas is less than three years. The government isn't going to relocate them, they're going to relocate themselves. And Hong Kong? It's been a thorn in their flesh ever since the Brits handed it back. A lot of people in the party would be very happy if Hong Kong just quietly sank beneath the waves." Olsen stopped. There was a hush. "Alan? Have I said anything you disagree with? Correct me if I'm wrong."

Ball maintained a stony silence.

"So what are you saying, Larry?" said John Eales. "You're saying they want this stuff to happen?"

"I wouldn't go that far. What I'm saying is, it's not going to hurt them like it's going to hurt us. Even if the numbers are big on their side—and they are, really big, way bigger than ours—big numbers aren't as scary for them. So let's not kid ourselves. They can outstay us on this. We have to find something that will hurt them."

"Even if it hurts us?"

"*Especially* if it hurts us. That's the point I'm making. It has to hurt us and they have to see that. We have to be prepared to bleed. They don't believe we ever will. That means we have to think about what's going to make them think otherwise."

There was silence.

"Alan?" said the president.

"Like I said before," said Ball quietly, "I'm not saying we won't get there. I'm just saying we need to test it a little more. We need to give it more time."

"Al, forget the timing!" said Eales impatiently. "In principle, do you or do you not think at some point we are going to have to demonstrate that we will take pain in order to get China to the table?"

Ball hesitated for a moment. Then he nodded, avoiding Larry Olsen's glance.

"Well, if that's the case," said Eales in exasperation, "we may as well do it now!"

"Except for the legislative program," objected Jackie Rubin quickly. "Except for what it does to that."

Ben Hoffman put his head in his hands and groaned.

"All right," said Benton. "I want to reflect on this. We obviously can't get to a decision today." He paused. "Jackie, we need a review of possible sanctions, as broad as you can take it. Costs, legal position, economic implications. Alan, we need an analysis of the likely Chinese retaliatory responses."

"How many do you want? I can give you a hundred right now."

Benton ignored that. "The other question in my mind is, if this is where we're headed, should we be starting to work with anyone else on this? Should we be trying to build a coalition to support us or is it too early?

If so, with who? India? Russia? The EuroCore? If we're saying sanctions really are a possibility, even a remote one, we're going to need support. Larry, that's yours. I'm meeting Prime Minister Ogilvie . . . When is that, Ben?"

"In a week's time."

"I'll sound him out privately. Let me see if I can get some idea about where the EuroCore will come down if we really need to go to them." Benton paused. "Now, I have one more question. Is there anyone else we need in this room?"

"The way Larry's talking," said Ball, "it won't be long before we need the secretary of defense."

"Alan, is that a serious suggestion?"

Ball didn't reply.

"All right," said the president. "Larry, I'll tell you who I want. You remember that guy I met when you got those China people together? That young man."

"Oliver Wu."

"I'd like a China expert in the room. No offense, Larry, but someone who's completely up to date and studying their leadership team a hundred percent of the time with this in mind."

"I agree," said Olsen.

"Unless you can think of someone better, let's bring him in."

Olsen nodded.

"All right. I think we're done. Ben, can you schedule another discussion for the group? Larry, can you stay for another minute?"

The others got up. Alan Ball made a point of catching Benton's eye before he went out. Benton watched him leave.

When the door was closed again, the president turned back to Olsen.

"Ben tells me you've been pushing Chen damn hard."

Olsen shrugged.

"I didn't tell you to push him hard."

"You told me to negotiate with him, sir. I know Chen. That's how you do it."

"Maybe we better agree next time what kind of tack you take."

"You have to trust your negotiator, Mr. President. You can't script him. If you feel you have to script him, you'd better get rid of him."

Benton gazed at Olsen.

"Mr. President, we'll agree on it next time." Olsen said it in as close to a conciliatory tone as he was capable of. "I'll explain to you in advance."

Benton nodded. "Thank you. And as far as today goes, I want to be clear. When I asked you to come on board, I said I'd let you be heard."

Larry Olsen nodded.

"I think I did let you be heard."

"Yes, sir. I think you did."

"But I haven't decided. And on something of this magnitude, it'll be my decision."

"That goes without saying, sir."

Benton watched him for a moment, trying to sense if there was anything behind that. "Okay." Benton stood up.

"Mr. President?"

"Yes."

"About Oliver Wu."

"What about him?"

"He's a good choice."

"Good."

"And when you meet Prime Minister Ogilvie, sir, in your private talks, don't take this the wrong way, but . . . be careful what you say."

Benton looked at Olsen. He hardly thought he needed to be told something like that.

"He's an affable guy, Mr. President. He's good at what he does. It's easy to say too much."

Saturday, February 12

Camp David, Maryland

Joe Benton had met Hugh Ogilvie a number of times before. His conversations with the leader of Britain's Labour-Liberal Democrat government had been brief, usually with a group of other senators. He wondered how the relationship would work with a man who had gotten on famously well with Mike Gartner.

The first day of the visit was spent at the White House in discussions attended by cabinet secretaries, ambassadors and aides. Benton had a half hour alone with Ogilvie prior to the state dinner he hosted in the prime minister's honor. Joe Benton also had a chance to meet Ogilvie's wife, Anthea, whom he had never met, and the Ogilvies met Heather. On the morning of the second day the presidential and prime ministerial parties flew to Camp David. The idea was for the two couples to spend time getting to know each other, with only the minimum complement of aides to accompany them, before returning to Washington Sunday afternoon, when the Ogilvies would head back to London.

After a day with Ogilvie, Benton was warming to his guest. He was starting to appreciate the other man's moderate approach and understated sense of humor. He also realized that Ogilvie's previous relationship with Gartner didn't necessarily signify much. Getting on with U.S. presidents of whatever stripe was probably pretty high on the list in any British prime minister's job description.

The couples had lunch together in Laurel, the main gathering cabin at Camp David. Later, Joe Benton asked Connor Gale, the young aide who accompanied him pretty much everywhere and whose job was to see to it that he arrived where he was meant to be, to find out if Ogilvie wanted to take a walk with him. Gale spoke to Ogilvie's chief political aide, Jonathan Coomb. He also spoke to Ben Hoffman, who turned up five minutes later at the president's cabin.

"It's just a *walk*, Ben," said the president. He knew nothing made a political advisor more nervous than the sight of two leaders heading off by themselves. "I'm not going to revoke the Declaration of Independence."

He picked Ogilvie up at Sequoia, the newly refurbished main visitors' cabin. The president could see, from the look on Jonathan Coomb's face as they left, that Coomb was just as unhappy as Ben Hoffman at seeing his man go out alone.

Joe Benton chuckled as they set off. "They don't trust us, Hugh."

"Can you blame them?" said Ogilvie. "We might actually decide something."

They walked, crunching over brittle filaments of ice. Off the path, there was a dusting of snow. Ogilvie was rugged up in an overcoat and scarf. Benton wore a skiing jacket. The cold pinched at his face.

"Not too cold for you?" he said.

"Bracing," replied Ogilvie, and he clapped his gloved hands demonstratively.

The path crossed another. Benton stopped, looking from side to side.

"It's rather a nice walk down there," said Ogilvie.

Benton laughed. "How many times you been here, Hugh?"

"Five, I believe," replied Ogilvie.

"That's five more than me," said Benton.

"I thought as much."

"So? Down there?"

"Why not?" said Ogilvie. "It's very nice, as I recall."

They walked. The crunch of their footsteps filled the air.

"So what do you think of the state of the world, Hugh?" said Benton eventually. "Just between you and me?"

"Oh, it's chugging along, I suppose."

"Chugging along. I like that. How long have you been in office now?"

"Seven years."

Benton shook his head admiringly. "Two elections and a third coming up, right?"

"Luck rather than good management, I'm afraid."

"At least we never have to go past two elections over here."

"Yes, there's a point," mused Ogilvie.

"They give you a hard time when you started?" said Benton.

"My own party, do you mean?"

Benton laughed. "I'm taking a hell of a beating from the media. You wouldn't believe this stuff about Heather. Like there's nothing else for them to worry about. The woman's got a job. Get over it!"

"It does sound like it's been awful for her."

"But they'll use that, right? Anything they can. They'll use that to divert attention from the issues."

Ogilvie nodded.

Joe Benton shook his head in frustration, and kicked at a fallen pine cone that lay at the side of the path. It skidded away across the snow.

"I watched your address to the joint session," said Ogilvie.

Benton looked at him in surprise.

"Your legislative program is extremely impressive."

"Is that British for downright crazy?"

Ogilvie smiled. "I think it's fantastic. It's not my place, but I wanted to tell you that."

Benton laughed. "Go ahead. You can tell me stuff like that any time."

"It's bold. It's visionary."

"And it's got every special interest group in the country out to wring my neck. You'd think I'd shoved a red-hot poker up their ass."

"Well, in my experience, for what it's worth, it's only when they act as if they're skewered with a red-hot poker that you know you're doing the right thing. When you feel their claws sunk into your flesh, as one of my predecesors said, that's when you know you're on the right track."

"I can feel them, Hugh."

"Well, there you go. But I'm serious, Joe. What you're doing truly is a new foundation. If you pull it off, in my humble opinion, you'll do something extraordinary for this country."

Benton stopped. "Thank you, Hugh. I value your opinion. You know, I really believe, the Relocation, we have to see it as an opportunity. Otherwise, it'll be a burden that will crush us."

"That's what I try to make people understand. The scale of our relocation is much smaller than yours, of course, even proportionately. But even so, it's desperately hard to make people see how we can use it as a chance to build. That's the British for you, I suppose. Never see the silver lining if there's a chance of seeing the cloud."

"No, Hugh, it's hard. It really is."

Ogilvie nodded. "Anyway, it's not my place to draw comparisons, but there isn't one. With your predecessor, I mean."

Benton smiled. Then he started walking again.

Ogilvie asked about the Iraq-Syria initiative, and Benton talked about progress in the talks, which wasn't substantial.

"Well, it certainly sent a message to anyone who was watching," said Ogilvie.

Benton looked at him. "What message?"

The prime minister's lips twitched in a slight smile. "That you will deal with things. I presume that was the intent."

Suddenly Benton felt as if he had got a glimpse of the acuity behind Hugh Ogilvie's agreeable exterior. "I think that's a good message."

"I think probably it is. Provided, of course, you can keep your domestic support onside while you do these things. I'd imagine you need every bit of support you can find to get your program through Congress."

"That's the truth."

"And of course the question we're all asking outside the U.S. is, what's the next thing you're going to deal with?"

"Maybe there isn't a next thing."

"Mr. President," said Ogilvie with a hint of mischief, "there's always a next thing."

Benton didn't say anything to that. After they had walked a little longer, he stopped. "You want to head back? It's damn cold." He looked around. "I hope you can remember how we got here, because I sure as hell can't."

They turned and walked in silence for a while.

"What do you think about Kyoto 4?" asked Benton eventually.

There was a change in Ogilvie, almost imperceptible, but something about him became a little more cautious, more guarded, as if he sensed they had got to the thing the walk was really about.

"I don't have particularly high hopes of it," he replied.

"No?"

"With respect, Joe . . . the United States hasn't been a great adherent of the Kyoto process."

"You think that's the problem?"

"I think it has been. A big part of the problem."

"I appreciate your frankness, Hugh. But I don't think anyone has been a particularly assiduous adherent of the process. I don't think even Great Britain's record is perfectly clean."

"True. But you see, Joe, when the United States is the delinquent, everyone else feels they have a license to offend."

Benton nodded. "That's well put."

"Hardly original, I'm afraid. I said exactly the same thing to President Gartner. And to President Shawcross, if it comes to that."

"That's even better put," said Benton.

Ogilvie smiled.

"It's ridiculous, though. Hugh, the Chinese have been bigger emitters than us for twenty-five years. Their emissions are more than double ours today. Even if we wanted to solve all the world's emissions problems ourselves—even if we just shut the United States down and stopped our emissions cold, right now, this minute—it still wouldn't be enough without China. And yet it's us everyone points at."

"An historical irony. Um, Joe. I think we might want to go up there."

Benton, stopped, looking around at the crossroad where he had just turned right. "You sure?"

"Trust me. Cook, Shackleton, Ross. Nation of great explorers, the English."

"All right, if you're sure."

They turned.

"What were you saying, Joe?"

"I was going to ask you about the EuroCore."

"What about the EuroCore?"

"What do you think they really think about Kyoto 4?"

Ogilvie considered the question. Benton waited to hear what he would say. As Britain had continued to stand outside the European currency zone, while remaining a member of the European Union, it had become increasingly detached from the Franco-Italian-German-Polish dominated

EuroCore. Its main claim to a place on the international stage was now as a bridge between the EuroCore and the United States, a middleman able to understand and interpret each party to the other. Although it was Washington that tended to place a value on this role. More often than not, the Europeans saw London as an unnecessary nuisance.

"The EuroCore," said Ogilvie eventually, "doesn't see itself as a major player in this area. Not in the sense of having to lead the way."

"I know, and I don't understand that. Nine percent of the world's emissions come out of the EuroCore. Surely that puts them in a critical role whether they like it or not."

"The EuroCore's a funny thing. It's got quite a schizoid personality. Sometimes it speaks utterly with one voice. Other times, it conveniently fragments into its constituent parts. And when that happens, given the voting arrangements, there's no way for those who want to speak as a bloc to be able to do so. This is one of those issues. The EuroCore—or certain countries within the EuroCore—think they can slip in under the radar. All they have to do is stand back and let the United States fight it out with China and India. They know that's where the process is going to fail again. So they don't need to be the bad guys. In fact, they can be the good guys. You're going to see them proposing quite extraordinary reductions and of course they don't have the slightest intention that any of this will happen."

"No change there, then."

"Well, I'm afraid not, Joe. I'm sorry, but I'm going to be frank. I take on board what you said about the level of Chinese emissions. But as long as the United States continues to provide this convenient umbrella of noncompliance you just have to expect everyone else to come in and shelter underneath it."

"Including the United Kingdom?"

Hugh Ogilvie didn't reply to that.

They crunched over the ice. They were almost back at Sequoia.

"You want to take this discussion inside?" said Benton.

"Sure."

Benton took him back to Aspen, the presidential cabin. Connor Gale was inside, playing a computer game.

Benton smiled. "None but the brightest and the best," he said, as they went past him to the study. "Yes, Connor, you can tell Ben we're back."

"I think he knows already, sir," said Gale, nodding at the window. Hoffman was coming toward the cabin through the snow.

"Well, we're not done," said Benton, and he closed the door of the study.

There was coffee on the sideboard.

"Coffee all right for you?" asked Benton. "Or should I call for tea? Something stronger?"

"Coffee's fine," said Ogilvie.

"You want something to eat?"

Ogilvie shook his head.

Benton poured. He sat down, took a sip, felt the coffee warming him.

"I don't think Kyoto 4 is going to be enough," said Benton. "Even if we get agreement." He looked to see Ogilvie's reaction. "What would the world say if it knew that?"

"Hallelujah, I suspect. The emperor's been wandering around without any clothes for too long now, don't you think?"

"Thirty years."

"That's right."

"So what do we do, Hugh?"

Ogilvie frowned. Benton could see him considering carefully what he should say next. "The United Kingdom is committed to the Kyoto process, Joe. We don't think there's a better alternative."

"But it's a busted process, Hugh. You said so yourself."

"Maybe now's the time to fix it."

"I don't think so."

"Then what are you proposing?"

"I'm not proposing anything." Benton paused. "I'm just saying, confidentially, that we ought to look at what we've got here. We've got negotiations for a treaty in a process where three previous treaties have failed to deliver, and if you ask me, that doesn't sound like there's much hope for the fourth. And the way it's shaping up, even if the fourth one gets delivered down to the last subclause of a subclause, it still won't be enough."

"Won't it?"

Benton hesitated, wondering how much to reveal to Ogilvie. It would be easy to tell him everything. He remembered what Olsen had warned him about the British prime minister.

"Let's just say our analysis suggests that it won't."

"Using what data?"

"Hugh," said Benton, and he held up his hands.

Ogilvie smiled, like a kid caught with his hand in the cookie jar.

"The point I'm making," said Benton, "is we're kidding ourselves on Kyoto."

"Well, a little is better than nothing, even if it's not as good as a lot."

"Yeah, I've heard that before, just once or twice. I don't think that's good enough anymore. Hell's bells, Hugh! The world can't wait for Kyoto 4 to fail. It doesn't have the time."

Ogilvie put his fingertips together thoughtfully, almost in a manner of prayer. "There are two things here, Joe. There's the process and there's the content."

"Agreed."

"Let's distinguish. I suspect you're right on the content. Will it be enough? Probably not. You may know more than I do about that." He paused meaningfully. "On the process, I suspect that's where we differ. The United Kingdom does believe that a multilateral, UN-mediated approach is the only way to ensure an equitable and truly global solution."

"Which this same approach has failed to deliver for thirty years," pointed out Benton.

"Which *we* have failed to deliver for thirty years, Joe."

"All right, I accept that. What's going to change it now?"

"You?" Ogilvie looked at him questioningly. "Take away the umbrella, Joe. Stop being the delinquent."

"Let's say I was prepared to do that. What's to stop everyone else still offending?"

"I can't guarantee that."

"That's the point. It's not good enough. I can't take that to the American people, they'll never buy it. I can just about take them something saying the whole world is going to do its part, and yes, it's going to cause some pain. I believe the American people will accept that. But if they're going to take pain, I've got to be able to tell them they're not the only ones."

"Well, what I can guarantee," said Ogilvie, "is that if the United States *doesn't* stop offending, no one else will."

"Agreed. I have no argument with that. That's the bind we're in." Benton tapped his finger on the arm of his chair. "I want to know why the others *will* stop. Tell me that and I'll have something to work with."

Ogilvie opened his mouth to speak, then thought better of it.

"They'll have signed up, right? That's what you were about to say, isn't it? They'll have treaty obligations."

Ogilvie didn't reply.

"What about sanctions?" said Benton.

"They've never been a part of the Kyoto process." Ogilvie shrugged. "Maybe they should be."

"You think anyone's really going to sign up to that? You said yourself, Hugh, no one expects they're really going to implement the full cuts they've signed up to."

"Joe, I think I can say, if you show you're going to keep every single word of your commitment, and if you show real initiative in the level of cuts you propose, then the United Kingdom will be able to support you if you push to have serious, genuine sanctions written into the treaty."

Benton gazed at him.

"I can see you're less than overwhelmed," said Ogilvie.

"What are we going to do, Hugh? Set up a court to monitor compliance? And then have two-, three-, four-year legal processes to figure out whether sanctions should be applied? Look at the WTO. Look how it works there."

"Perhaps we could streamline it," said Ogilvie. "I'm thinking off the top of my head now. Maybe we could work out a regime where the sanctions are applied and the scrutiny comes later."

"Same problem," replied Benton impatiently. "Anything that really looks like it's going to bite, I don't think it'll happen."

"That's rather a pessimistic outlook."

"Exactly. And this is me talking. I'm the biggest optimist in my administration!"

Ogilvie smiled slightly.

"Hugh, let me be hypothetical. Will you permit me?"

Ogilvie waited.

Joe Benton sat forward in his chair. "Let's say, I went outside the process. Not against it, but in parallel with it."

"Joe, Britain is committed to a multilateral process. I don't know what you're asking, but I can't see us realistically supporting a competing approach."

"In parallel, I said. Just hear me out." Benton paused. "Let's say the United States decided to impose sanctions on a particular country. It doesn't matter which. And not being the delinquent anymore, as you describe it, but making serious cuts, deep cuts in our own emissions, and expecting the other country to do the same. Now, I won't ask you what the position of the United Kingdom would be, because I don't think that's fair. And anyway, since I wouldn't take any action that wasn't in our mutual interest, I would assume the United Kingdom would support us." Benton waited just long enough to make sure Ogilvie got the point. "What I would like your view on, is what do you think would be the attitude of the EuroCore? Would they support it? Could I rely on them to impose similar sanctions themselves to really make it work?"

Ogilvie frowned uncomfortably. "I take it this is a significant country you're talking about? A major emitter?"

"It ain't Albania."

Ogilvie's frown got deeper. "I think it's very hard to answer those questions without knowing the details of the situation."

"I understand. It's hypothetical. Fill in any details you need to fill in."

Ogilvie was silent. Benton waited.

"I doubt it," said the British prime minister at last.

"That they'd support it?"

"Yes, that they'd support it. Rumain, definitely not. Sometimes I think his whole raison d'être is to throw spanners in the works of your foreign policy. DiMarco? Not at this point. Ingelbock, maybe. Koslowski, he's a hard one to judge. The Poles have a number of issues with Russia at the moment, and if you gave them something on that . . . I'm not sure what it would be, but if you could give them something in that area, maybe they'd get behind you. But I'm guessing, Joe. And it's just as likely they'd all give you no support at all. More likely than not, actually. If this was a significant country, as you say, your sanctions would open up opportunities for them."

Benton nodded. It wasn't too much different from what he'd expected to hear. "What about Russia?"

"Russia." Ogilvie nodded. "You'd certainly want Russia to support you if this country you were talking about happened to be China. Choke off their Russian energy supplies, that's the one sure way of getting them. But what would Russia want in return? That's the question, isn't it? Ask them to cut their energy supplies to China, and how much do you knock off their GDP? And what does it do to their economy in the long term if we all cut our fossil fuel consumption?"

"You're way ahead of me," said Benton.

Ogilvie looked at him knowingly. "Of course I am. This is all hypothetical."

There was silence.

"You'll be invited as a guest at the EuroCore summit in June," said Ogilvie. "You'll get to hear everyone's views for themselves. I'm sure there'll be a spirited debate about Kyoto at the summit." He smiled slightly. "There always is."

"I'll look forward to it," said Benton.

Hugh Ogilvie looked at him seriously. "It isn't my place to give you advice, Joe, but you've got a hell of a legislative program on your plate. People elected you knowing you were committed to Kyoto. Presumably that's one of the reasons they supported you. It seems odd that you'd put that support in danger. Wouldn't it be easier to go along with Kyoto like you said you would, at least until you've got your legislation in place?"

"It would be easier."

"Then why don't you do it?"

"I haven't said I won't."

"Of course not, and I realize this is a confidential discussion. But I just think . . . from where I sit, it looks as if you'll need every bit of support you can get to drive your program home. I just can't see that you can afford to alienate any of your natural constituency." Ogilvie shrugged. "Or maybe I'm wrong."

"No," said Benton. "You're absolutely right."

Friday, February 18

Oval Office, The White House

Dr. Richards was on her feet. The latest data, she had explained, were tending to confirm the mid to upper level of the trends she had presented to the president at his first meeting with President Gartner. On the screen behind her she projected a series of maps to demonstrate her scenarios, each showing various parts of the coastal fringes of the continental United States in red. As each scenario grew more extreme, the areas in red expanded.

It was Oliver Wu's first meeting as a member of the Marion group. He sat silently, staring at the screen, listening to Dr. Richards's presentation and the questions that came from the others. Larry Olsen, who was on a visit to Pakistan, had filled him in a couple of days earlier, but it hadn't seemed quite so real, quite so bleak, until he found himself actually sitting in the Oval Office with the president of the United States and his chief political advisor and the White House chief of staff and the national security advisor and the budget director and he began to see these maps coming up on the screen in front of them all.

"So it's a question of degree, not whether this is happening?" said the president after Dr. Richards had finished.

"That was the case last time we met, sir. What we're seeing now are trends confirming the upper range of the predictions."

"When will you have a definitive answer?"

"After this summer I believe we'll be in a strong position to give a narrow range of likely rates. By October, sir, after we analyze the data."

The president nodded. He looked around the room to see whether anyone had other questions.

"Larry," he said, "anything from you?"

"No," said Olsen's voice out of a speaker. "I'm fine." He was calling on a secure connection from the Karachi embassy, where it was one thirty in the morning.

"All right," said Benton. "Dr. Richards, can you show us the impact on China?"

Richards called up a series of maps. Same format as the ones for the U.S.—red showing areas that would be uninhabitable, blue for areas of partial viability, yellow for the rest.

Wu stared at the screen, scanning the maps, utterly absorbed in what he was seeing. Benton glanced at him. With a pointed chin and short black hair that stood up like bristles on a brush, Wu looked too young to know anything about anything, thought Benton. But he was thirty-four, with a doctorate from Harvard and three years of postgraduate work in Beijing before joining the State Department.

"Larry," said Eales, "we'll make sure you get to see these later. Suffice to say there's going to be a whole lot of water down there in the south of China."

"That's fine," replied Olsen. "I don't need the detail now."

Dr. Richards went on to the next series, showing the impact on India. "We've got the whole subcontinental area here," she said as the first map came up. "As you can see, there's not much left of Bangladesh."

"Is that inundation or storms?" asked Alan Ball.

"At a certain point in that part of the world it becomes the same thing," said Dr. Richards. "We have more detailed charts showing the distribution, but effectively the flow-off capacity will be so limited that the areas in red will become permanently flooded. At that point the question's moot."

There was silence. The northern end of the Bay of Bengal was a red flare on the map. India was almost entirely red-fringed, and there appeared to be a loss of about a quarter of the Sri Lankan land surface.

"Go on to the reduction scenarios, please, Dr. Richards," said Eales.

Richards had been asked to have her team model the effect of a number of different levels of global emissions, ranging from ten percent reduction over ten years to a thirty percent cut over five years. She talked through the results. Even with the most extreme reduction schedule, the U.S. population requiring relocation would range from twenty to twenty-five million. And even in that scenario, Miami went under.

"Can you give us an estimate of the population at risk in other countries?" asked Eales.

"I believe we can do a country-by-country estimate if that would help. A significant amount of modeling will be required so it may take a little time. A week perhaps. Would that be quick enough?"

"That would be very helpful."

Richards nodded.

"Can you summarize the qualifications to your presentation, Dr. Richards?" said Benton.

"I believe the only major qualification, Mr. President, is our uncertainty over the level of increase that our data are showing. But if you take the upper case and the lower case for each scenario, the real outcome will almost certainly lie within that range. Other qualifications are the normal ones around mapping, demographic projections, etcetera. I would estimate these amount to no more than a five percent variance, which is not material to the directionality of the projections."

The president looked around the room. Then at the console. "Larry?"

"I'm fine."

Benton nodded. "Thank you, Dr. Richards."

"Is that all, Mr. President?"

"Thank you. You'll make sure Mr. Eales has this presentation? He'll be in touch if we need any further analysis at this time."

"Mr. Eales, I have to get to you the relocation impact of the scenarios on a country-by-country basis."

Eales nodded.

"Thank you, then." Richards pulled her drive out of the desk console. Ben Hoffman got up and showed her out.

The sound of the door closing behind her left a hush.

"Jackie?" said the president.

Jackie Rubin got up. She went to the desk console and inserted a drive. She had asked her team to model the economic effects of the same reduction scenarios Dr. Richards had been given.

"These are scary numbers, Mr. President," she said before she showed any of the slides. "Whatever happens, this throws us into reverse. In the worst case, we have an average nine percent contraction of the economy year-on-year for four years. That's almost unimaginable, sir."

"Just take us through the numbers, Jackie," said Benton quietly.

She projected a series of tables showing growth rates in key economic parameters. All in the early years were negative. The bald columns of numbers belied the misery they foretold for millions of people.

"Is it really that bad?" asked the president. If we're relocating people, doesn't that create jobs? People have to build new places, the reception areas need more teachers, more doctors."

"But you've got the loss of the productive capacity of people during the transition, Mr. President. More importantly, you've got the loss of the productive capacity of the assets that are being abandoned. Both of those factors drive down overall productivity. Plus, who pays for the new infrastructure? We accept that a lot of it's got to be taxpayer funded, but where's the tax coming from if you have a lower productivity base? And if we borrow to fund it—which is inevitable, at least for a sizable chunk of it—you're sucking money away that would otherwise be used for consumption or business investment, and you're driving up interest rates, both of which hit jobs in other ways."

"But we had a plan to turn our original relocation package into a net economic benefit over the course of the program," said Ben Hoffman. "That was a central plank of the campaign."

"Ben, this is a whole different scenario. It's about timing and scale. The idea with Relocation in the New Foundation package is that we do it systematically, prime the receiving communities with infrastructure ahead of time and as much as possible allow old infrastructure to downgrade naturally so what we're really doing, effectively, is redirecting resource from renewing infrastructure in affected areas to building new infrastructure where it's needed. Add to that universal health care, adequate education and job stimulation, and put the whole thing in a reasonable time frame, so you can phase relocation, and that actually gives you growth. This is a whole nother thing. Many more millions of people will be moving over a much shorter period. That means you have much less freedom to phase it, and you're going to abandon infrastructure you'd still be using. That's an enormous net loss to our asset base, like what happens in a war. And the relocation is going to be like accepting millions of refugees at the same time. Except it's a double impact. Those refugees, if you will, aren't just a burden on our resources, until the day before they were actually producing some of those resources."

"I won't have the American people spoken of as a burden on resources," said the president quietly.

Rubin nodded. "I was speaking as an economist, sir."

"I'm not sure if I'm missing something here." It was Larry Olsen's voice. "I'm just listening to you all and it sounds like you're making us out to be the bad guys. Every one of our scenarios factors in our relocation plan, right? Even the one with no emissions reduction?"

"I haven't done one with no emissions reduction," said Jackie.

"Well, that's the problem. You need one with no emissions reduction and no relocation plan, and you need to show us how bad that looks when everything finally falls apart. That's the true comparison. Show people that and *then* ask them what they want us to do."

Rubin wasn't sure that would be persuasive. "The pain will be greater, but it's going to be a lot further away. We're talking twenty, thirty years. Maybe more."

"That's always been the problem," said the president. "Thirty years ago that's exactly what people thought, and you know what? That's why we're sitting here today. If Kyoto 1 or 2 had been bold enough, we wouldn't be talking about relocation at all."

"It's a political question," said John Eales. "Not an economic or a social one. Economically, ever since the Stern Review, it's been a no-brainer. We have no excuse, none of us."

The president nodded. "Do that scenario, Jackie."

"Doesn't matter if it's going to happen to their grandkids," said Eales, "let's show them what it's really going to mean."

Rubin nodded.

Benton felt they needed more policy thinking around this. How could they maximize the outcome of the action they would have to take? Hoffman suggested a subgroup of the Council of Economic Advisors. Eales liked the idea.

"Pitch it as a blue sky group, Ben," said Eales. "Radical thinking on carbon emissions control, something like that. They don't need to know the context."

Hoffman nodded. "I'll set up time with Sandy Winter."

"Set it up for me. We can make it look like some kind of thing I'm doing so it doesn't look like it's directly coming from the president."

Benton looked around the table. "All right, we just have to persuade the American people to take a huge hit for their grandchildren's sake. Easy. That's part one. Let's move on to the second part. Can someone tell me how we get the Chinese to play ball?"

No one volunteered an answer.

"Dr. Wu," said the president, "you're up. We've had some discussion about how we might handle the Chinese government. I'm not sure if Secretary Olsen has filled you in. On the one hand, we could move hard with a threat of sanctions. On the other hand, we could go slow."

"Yes, sir," said Wu. "I understand."

"Have you seen the papers?"

Wu nodded.

"Do you have a view?"

"On that specific question, Mr. President? On sanctions?"

"On anything," muttered Ball.

"Do you think President Wen is sitting with a bunch of guys someplace in Beijing having a discussion like this?" asked Benton.

"Perhaps he doesn't know these facts, sir."

"Assume he does."

"When you mean this kind of discussion, Mr. President, you mean what measures he can use to get the United States to drastically cut its emissions?"

"I guess so," said the president.

"Then no, sir. He is not having this discussion."

"Is he having any kind of a discussion?"

"Yes."

"What's it about?"

Wu was conscious of every eye in the room watching him, conscious that no one in this gathering was going to pull their punches if they thought he was wrong. In particular, Alan Ball.

"It's about China," he said.

"How China deals with this?"

"Not exactly. How China benefits from it. The mindset is—China continues. Whatever happens to it, China continues. War, natural disasters, human disasters—China continues. So how does China benefit from this? It's a zero sum mentality. Which means, for example, if you propose emissions reduction, how does China benefit from this? One simple answer is if it forces you to take more reductions than it does."

"That's obvious," said Alan Ball. "Tell me a country that wouldn't."

"Really?" said Wu. Nervousness made the reply come out more sharply than he intended. "I'm sorry, Dr. Ball. What I mean is, we haven't. Unless I've missed something today, we haven't been talking about how can we force China to take bigger cuts than we will."

Benton smiled. "Maybe we haven't got round to it. What else?"

"There's the party angle," said Wu. "How does the party use this?"

"Will they try to use it?"

"Absolutely, if they can. Mr. President, as I understand it, President Gartner tried to do something very similar in the context of our own political system. Multiply that tenfold in the Chinese context."

"What would be their attitude if Hong Kong had to be abandoned?" asked Ben Hoffman.

Wu smiled. "Unfortunate. Very unfortunate."

"I'm sensing irony, Dr. Wu," said the president.

"Yes, sir. To be serious, it would be difficult for China economically, of course, very difficult, but politically it would have its attractions."

"What else?"

"President Wen will be talking to different people, and he'll be saying different things. They'll know he's saying different things, although they won't know what those things are. Wen's a classic power broker. He plays cliques. There are at least three potential successors, Zhai, Xuan and Ding. No one knows which one will succeed."

"Does Wen know?"

"That's an interesting question, sir. There's quite a lot of debate about that. Even if he does know, anything can happen between now and the party congress next year when he's due to announce his successor. Each of the three heirs apparent are using this time to shore up support. That's support through Wen, to keep his favor, and independent of Wen, so that if Wen turns against them, they've got their own power base. Ding's the wiliest, but the others are no slouches. You don't get to a high position in the party without knowing what you're doing. What we're talking about here sounds big, Mr. President, possibly the biggest thing since the troubles of 2013. Everyone will use it for their own purposes if they can."

"What about sanctions?" asked the president.

"They'll outlast us. I've read the papers that were circulated. Anything we can do, they'll sustain it for longer."

"Exactly," said Ball.

"Unless it's in someone's interest not to."

"Explain," said the president.

"Say, for example, we impose sanctions, and Wen resists. Say Ding Jiahui thinks—for whatever reason—this is a time he can push against Wen and establish his place in the succession beyond challenge. It doesn't have to be Ding. It could be Zhai, it could be Xuan. Each of them controls media outlets. They'll use that control to work up a case against Wen, tying him to the sanctions and the pain it's causing. Two months later, you might find you're talking to someone who wants the sanctions lifted and is prepared to cut a deal."

"But it wouldn't be Wen?"

"It could be Wen. He could do the exact same thing in reverse. Say he's decided to take Xuan out of the equation. He uses Xuan as his mouthpiece in defying you to impose sanctions, and Xuan does it, thinking he'll build his relationship with Wen and achieve national approval. Then Wen changes course, uses Ding to cut a deal with you, and Xuan is discredited."

"Dr. Wu," said Eales, "I think we need something on the likely ways this might play out."

Wu nodded.

"Can you do that?"

"I can. But I have to say, there are numerous ways this could go. I can try and say which scenario is more likely, but that still leaves considerable uncertainty. I'd be more comfortable if I could take this out to some other people at State."

"Not yet," said the president. "Just give us your thoughts, for a start."

Larry Olsen's voice came through from the speaker. "Maybe we should get Chen in and give him a hint. Mention the S word."

"Sanctions?" said Eales.

"Why not?"

The president was watching Alan Ball. Ball's face was grim.

"Just to see what happens," said Olsen. "It might be interesting."

Benton thought about it. "It might be."

Alan Ball asked for a few minutes of the president's time at the end of the meeting. He stayed behind as the others left the Oval Office.

Benton waited to hear what he wanted to say.

Ball's face was grave. "Joe, I have a real concern. I know you'd want me to be open with you. Olsen's pushing us way too fast. If we're not careful, we're going to find ourselves imposing sanctions on China."

Benton smiled. "I think we're a long way from that, Alan."

"Not in Larry's mind. Is that what you really want?"

Sanctions against China were the last thing Joe Benton wanted to invoke, and he thought Alan Ball ought to know it.

Ball hesitated. His voice dropped. "Joe, I think you should reconsider."

"Reconsider what?"

Ball didn't reply.

Benton stared at him. "You think I should reconsider Larry?"

"I don't mean to talk out of turn."

Benton watched him. He had already spoken out of turn, and must know it. Benton also found something unpleasant in the fact that Ball was doing it when Olsen was out of Washington.

"I wouldn't be saying anything if I didn't think this was really important. I think we have a real problem here."

"Go ahead, Alan," said Benton quietly.

"You appointed Larry because he gave you a perspective you value, one which was different from the perspective that myself and Al Graham and a number of other advisors shared. I understand that. By all means, Joe, use him as an advisor. Get his input. But putting him in as secretary of state . . . He's rash. He's aggressive. He's putting us in a position that's way too hard. Now he wants to start imposing sanctions."

"He said something about a hint. I don't even know what that means yet."

"That's what I'm worried about."

"It's okay. We have an agreement. He's not going to say anything to Chen before I speak with him."

Ball shook his head in exasperation. "He's . . ."

"What, Alan?"

"He's not the right guy!" Ball's hands were clenched in exasperation. "Ask anyone who worked with him at State. I'm just being completely frank with you."

"I appreciate your frankness," said the president evenly.

"Really, he isn't. Joe, if you've made a mistake, it's best to recognize it early and do something about it, not keep going so one mistake gets compounded by another."

Joe Benton was silent for a moment.

"I hear what you're saying, Al, but I'm not sure if I have made a mistake. To be fair to Larry, I'm not sure at what point I'd say he's done the wrong thing. Where he's been too rash, as you call it. And in the end, I take responsibility for the decisions this administration makes. Me, not Larry." Benton paused. "But I will think about what you've said. And I will talk to Larry and see exactly what he means to say to Chen before he meets him."

Ball's face was a picture of misery. "Please, Joe. Please, don't let him talk to Chen."

Chen Liangming looked around the room. "I see our numbers are growing," he remarked.

"Mr. Chen, this is Dr. Wu," said Larry Olsen. "He works at the State Department. You may know him."

Chen shook his head.

Oliver Wu extended his hand.

"We have no intention to ambush you, Mr. Chen," said Ben Hoffman. "If you're uncomfortable being here as a lone hand, we can rearrange this meeting so you have the opportunity to call on additional resource."

Chen smiled. He shook his head again.

"Then would you care to sit?"

Chen sat. The others took their seats as well.

"It's about three weeks since we met?" said Olsen.

"Yes, Mr. Secretary."

"I hope you had a good Chinese New Year."

"Thank you, Mr. Secretary. I was fortunate to be able to go home."

"To Guangdong?"

"Yes. To Guangdong." Chen turned to Wu. "Where is your home village?" he said in Mandarin.

"I met Ambassador Liu the other day," said Olsen. "We had a very good talk."

Chen gazed at Wu for a moment longer, then looked back at Olsen. "So I understand, Mr. Secretary."

"The ambassador expressed his hope that I would soon meet Foreign Minister Chou."

Chen nodded.

"I look forward to that as well."

"Yes, Mr. Secretary."

"Mr. Chen, I believe we're still waiting for a proposal from your government."

"Mr. Secretary, we are waiting for an indication from President Benton whether he will accept an invitation from President Wen."

"As I told you last time, Mr. Chen, such an invitation would be warmly accepted at the right time."

"Am I to deduce that this is not the right time?" inquired Chen.

"Yes, Mr. Chen. I think that's a fair deduction. You can also deduce the time won't be right until President Benton has seen your government's proposal."

Chen didn't reply immediately. He glanced at Wu again. Oliver Wu was accustomed to those kinds of glances from Chinese officials, accusatory, hostile, as if to ask him what kind of a traitor he was to be working with the Americans, betraying his own people. None of them ever seemed to consider that he was a third-generation American, born in Sacramento where his father was a California state official, educated at Berkeley and Harvard, and that the citizens of the United States, not China, were his people.

"Mr. Secretary," said Chen, "as I said last time, the last proposal made by President Gartner is still under consideration. President Wen has serious reservations about this proposal and its manifest unfairness towards the Chinese people, but perhaps there is some way in which we can continue to talk about this. If President Benton chooses to show his willingness to accept President Wen's respectful invitation, I'm sure we will find a way to achieve this."

Olsen was silent. He closed his eyes for a moment, then looked at Chen again. "All right, Mr. Chen, I'm going to explain one more time. You can tell your government to stop wasting its time with the Gartner proposal, because it is no longer on the table with the Benton administration."

"But it's a commitment from the United States government, Mr. Secretary. If the Chinese government cannot rely—"

"No, sir, it was not a commitment from the United States government. Let's get that clear once and for all. If there's any doubt, I have a copy right here. The Gartner proposal was an unofficial, time-limited framework— not even a proposal in the true sense, but a framework—that has lapsed. If the Chinese government wasn't able to respond in a timely fashion, so be it."

"But, Mr. Secretary . . ."

"Mr. Chen, let's not get bogged down over that. It's done. It's finished. Your government had the chance to take it and it didn't. Since it was manifestly unfair to the Chinese people, as you put it, I presume you're glad it didn't." Olsen paused. "So now we're clear, correct? As to President Wen making a proposal dependent on President Benton accepting an invitation to Beijing, at this stage that isn't going to work. Let's be realistic."

"President Wen believes this is a very realistic channel to a resolution of this issue. He is prepared for the government of the People's Republic of China to issue a formal invitation as soon as it has President Benton's assurance of acceptance."

Olsen sat forward. "Chen, that's not going to happen. You and I know each other well. So please stop suggesting that because every time you do I'm just going to have to tell you again it isn't going to happen."

Chen was silent. He looked at Wu. Wu held his gaze, knowing it was important not to be stared down.

"What we're waiting for, Mr. Chen, is a proposal from your government. We're only looking for a fair agreement, not an unequal treaty. I would like to be able to tell President Benton when we're likely to receive that proposal. Mr. Hoffman, the president is eager to know, isn't he?"

Ben Hoffman nodded.

"Mr. Chen?" said Olsen.

"I can of course relay your request to my government."

"I'm assuming you've already done that. After all, I put this request to you at our first meeting a month ago. Didn't you relay it then?"

Chen didn't reply.

"Did you not relay it, Mr. Chen? It's critical that I know that when I speak with you I can be sure President Wen knows what I have said."

"I relayed to my government a full account of our meeting, Mr. Secretary."

"Including my request?"

"I relayed a full account," repeated Chen quietly.

"Very good. And you'll relay a full account of this meeting as well, will you not?"

Chen nodded.

"Well, when you do, make sure you tell President Wen this. The government of the United States, if it must act without the cooperation of the government of the People's Republic of China in a matter that is crucial to the future of our planet, will take actions that reflect this fact. We are friendly to your country and wish to remain so, but any government that does not cooperate with the United States in solving a global problem of this magnitude, a problem of carbon emissions that affects us all, cannot count itself a friend of this country, and cannot expect to be treated as one. Now, in relation to unfriendly governments, the United States exerts reasonable, peaceful sanctions, to encourage a return to friendship. Do you understand that, Mr. Chen? Do you understand what I'm saying?"

"Are you sure you want me to tell this to President Wen?"

"Very sure."

Chen smiled.

"You find that funny?"

"I fear your country will find itself much alone if it goes this way, Mr. Secretary."

"The United States of America has often been alone. That's what leadership demands. Some of this country's greatest moments have been because it was prepared to stand alone for what it believed was right. You forget, this country was born in an act of standing alone against the oppression of empire."

"Very patriotic, Mr. Secretary." Chen nodded. "I applaud you." His tone was heavily sardonic.

Olsen stood up. "Until we have a response to our request, there is very little further for us to discuss. I look forward to your government's answer."

Chen stood as well. He shook hands with Olsen and Hoffman. He threw a glance at Oliver Wu and then walked out of the room.

Olsen sat down once the door was closed.

"What do you think?" he said to Wu.

"He's like I've heard about him."

"And he's Wen's man?" said Olsen. "That's still true, right?"

Wu nodded. "He was close to Zhai for a while, but when he had to choose, he came home to Uncle Wen. At this stage, whatever happens, Chen'll have no career after Wen's gone. He doesn't have to worry about the struggle over the succession. He's Wen's man, heart and soul.

"So when we talk to him, the message gets through?" asked Ben Hoffman.

"To Wen? Sure, unless Chen chooses not to give it. And there'd be no reason for him to do that. His role isn't to filter, it's to let Wen know exactly what he sees and hears. That's his value to Wen."

"And what comes back from him comes from Wen?"

Wu smiled. "What comes from Chen Liangming, Mr. Hoffman, is *one* of the things that comes from Wen."

Tuesday, March 8

Air Force One, east of Seattle

They were ninety minutes from landing. Around Joe Benton, in his office on the plane, sat John Eales, Jodie Ames, Sam Levy, Hilary Battle, the secretary of education, Amanda Pavlich, Battle's spokesperson, Ewen MacMaster, the White House education policy aide, and a couple of additional aides whom Battle had brought along.

The president worked through the speech that he was to deliver that evening at the University of Washington. The next day he was going to a tour a high school, visit an elementary school, and address a town hall style meeting at a state college. The speech at the university was to be a keynote on the administration's education policy, a careful mixture of policy and aspiration tying education into the broader New Foundation program, and it had been crafted largely by Sam Levy and Ewen MacMaster. Hilary Battle and her people were still fighting over the nuances, trying to reduce the references to other elements of New Foundation and focus the speech more exclusively on education. Joe Benton had had no time for the speech, and far too little time for education policy in general since he took office. But Sam, Ewen and Jodie Ames knew the president's mind better than Hilary Battle, they knew the strategy for selling New Foundation as a package, and they had got the balance about right. As he reviewed the speech, Benton was changing very little.

There was a knock on the door. The president looked up from his pages as Connor Gale came in.

"Mr. President, I've just been speaking with Mr. Hoffman. There's something he wants you to see."

"Now?"

Impatient glances were being sent at Connor from all around the room.

"Yes, Mr. President," said Gale. "May I?" He turned on the screen set into the panel opposite the president's sofa. MacMaster and Levy had to move aside so the president could see it.

Connor logged into the FoxBloomberg website. A reporter was on the screen with a skyline of towers behind her. The footer on the screen said Shanghai.

The reporter was in midsentence, saying something incredulous about the sheer volume of business that was included in the memorandums of understanding that had been signed.

The screen cut to the FoxBloomberg anchor in New York. "And all of this out of the blue, Melanie?"

Back to Shanghai. "Not exactly, Pete. These contracts have been under negotiation for some months, but my sources tell me that a major push to get these matters settled has been on for the last couple of weeks, culminating in this marathon session that apparently started before the weekend and lasted all the way into Wednesday. Pete."

"What's the broader implication of this? Forty-nine billion dollars of business wrapped up in one big package. Can you remember anything like it, Melanie?"

"Pete, to be honest, I can't. What the implications are . . ." On screen, Melanie shrugged. "I guess an awful lot of people will be pondering that today. But there's one thing I will say. There's going to be a lot of happy companies out there after this morning, Pete."

"And all of them in Europe, apparently. Thanks, Melanie. That was Melanie Chu in Shanghai reporting on the announcement today of a mammoth package of contracts awarded by the Chinese Ministry of Trade, including power plants, aircraft, heavy engineering and a new high-speed rail link out of Shanghai. At the moment, we don't have exact numbers, but we understand the value of the deals is in the region of forty-nine billion dollars, which we are informed would comfortably make it the largest single trade package ever agreed. A joint press conference is scheduled with the Chinese minister of trade and his counterparts from the UK and the leading EuroCore countries, who flew to Shanghai overnight when it became clear the package was going ahead. We'll be going live to that conference when it takes place a couple of hours from now. But first, what's gone wrong? How could it be that not a single American company succeeded in getting a share of this business? What has our government been doing? To discuss this, I'm joined by Ed Logan from the Brookings Institute and Harry Birnbaum from Goldman Morgan. Gentlemen, who's to blame?"

"Turn it off," said the president.

Gale logged off the stream.

"Tell Mr. Hoffman I'll call him as soon as I get a chance."

"Yes, sir. Anything else?"

"Not right now. Tell him I'm busy."

Gale went out.

There was silence. Jodie Ames exchanged a glance with John Eales.

"Let's go," said the president, waving the speech.

When they were finished, Sam Levy headed out to work up the final draft. The others left the office as well. John Eales stayed behind.

Connor Gale put his head around the door. "We've had calls from Dr. Ball and Secretary Sellers, sir."

"I'll get to them."

"Yes, sir," said Gale, and closed the door again.

The president nodded at the screen, now blank. "What do you make of that?"

"I think Mr. Chen just gave us our answer," said Eales.

"Yeah, I think so too." Benton hit a button on his desk console. "Can you get me Mr. Hoffman?"

A moment later Hoffman was on the line.

"Ben," said the president, "I've got John here. We both think this is a reply from Chen."

"I've spoken to Paul Sellers," said Hoffman. "We were on track for half those contracts as late as last week."

"What time is it in Shanghai, anyway?"

"Right now, it would be about eight in the morning," said Eales.

"So they must have announced it around seven? What kind of time is that for an announcement?"

"Apparently they've been negotiating all night," said Hoffman. "I think someone leaked. They were going to announce formally at this press conference they've got organized."

"Okay, Ben. Let me know if you find out anything else."

Hoffman went offline. Benton sat back on the sofa. "They've called our bluff, right?"

Eales nodded. "We threaten sanctions, they announce fifty billion dollars worth of deals with Europe. They'll all be conditional. None of these deals will go ahead if the Europeans join us in any kind of sanctions."

"They should have known something's going on."

"Who?"

"The Europeans."

Eales laughed.

Joe Benton shook his head. "Hell's bells, John! How did we miss this? We should have known we had this much business at stake. How come we didn't see this coming?"

"We did. It's in Alan's paper as one of the possible measures the Chinese might take. He'll tell you as soon as you talk to him."

"Great." There were a hundred things in that paper. This would give Ball ammunition in the war that was obviously developing between him and Larry Olsen. Benton was seriously beginning to wonder whether it would be possible to keep both men in his administration.

"Joe, in principle this doesn't change anything. You figured the Europeans weren't going to come on board. Now you know for sure."

"Yeah, but now I'll have half American business baying for my blood."

"They were going to start baying sometime."

"I don't need it now." Benton was silent. "I would not have figured . . ." He shook his head disbelievingly. "I wouldn't have figured they'd come back so hard. We only talked about sanctions. It was only supposed to be a general warning."

"Maybe Olsen went further."

"No. Ben was there. Hell's bells! It's a damned aggressive thing to do. It's like a punch in the face."

"Joe, we can use this if we want. Start painting the Chinese in the kind of colors we want to paint them in. Unfair, discriminatory in trade matters. We could use this as a reason to escalate action. If we're going to have to do it, like Larry says, then we're just going to have to do it. May as well start."

Benton frowned. "I'll say one thing. This is a smart move. The ball's back in our court. If we don't do something, they figure they've won, right? And we're finished. That's it, for the rest of my presidency."

"A month or two in I don't think you can say anything's finished for the duration."

"No, I think Larry's right about one thing. We don't do anything now, the more we have to do later to convince them we're serious. That's exactly what they're saying to us. We know you can deal with the hundred-pound weaklings, now can you mix it with the big boys?" Benton shook his head in frustration. "Damn!"

Eales looked at his watch. "I'll tell Jodie to put together a communication strategy. We'll seek clarification, we'll defend U.S. interests, we'll review contracts in process with Chinese companies . . ."

"Make sure she talks to Paul. Make sure he's in the loop.

"I'll talk to him as well. And to Alan."

"I'm going to talk to Ogilvie," said Benton. "See what he knows."

"Yeah, well, sounded like the Brits got a chunk of that business as well."

Joe Benton stood up. He looked out the window. It must be Idaho down there, he thought, or maybe they were already over Washington State. Thirty-five thousand feet below, through breaks in the cloud cover, he could see patches of green. He knew what he was going to have to face now, the right-wing press, business groups, congresspeople with affected districts all screaming and complaining. All of it way out of proportion. It wasn't just a smart move by the Chinese, it was a stroke of genius. Put pressure on him in a way that was exquisitely effective against an American president, without revealing anything publicly of the cause.

It was as if he could feel—literally feel—the heat of a brewing crisis coming all the way up at him from thirty-five thousand feet below.

Behind him, Eales got to his feet. "Joe, I'll deal with this now. Jodie and I will get on it. Today's about education. You need to give some time to Hilary. I'll go get her."

Benton nodded. Eales went out.

A moment later the secretary of education came in.

Joe Benton turned to her. His face cracked in his trademark smile.

Sunday, March 20

Benton Ranch, Wickenberg, Arizona

He could still smell the smoke. Days earlier, spring wildfire had swept from Mexico into southern California, which was in its fourth year of drought. From San Diego up to San Marcos and inland to Julian, a million and a half people had been evacuated, and at the height of the crisis the fleet in port at Naval Base San Diego had put to sea. The fire service had been joined by hundreds of volunteers to battle the blazes. Joe and Heather Benton had toured the area with Mary Okoro, California state governor, and Lou Katz, director of the Federal Emergency Response Authority. They helicoptered over a blackened landscape, where the remains of destroyed homes still smouldered. Fourteen firefighters were dead. Benton talked to their comrades, so exhausted they could barely stand. In the emergency centers, he and Heather visited with families who didn't know if they had a home to go back to. A child who had nothing but the clothes he wore wept over a lost dog, and in front of the cameras Joe Benton knelt to comfort him. At the foot of a hillside of charred stumps he pledged federal funds for emergency relief and reconstruction. But in his heart, he knew that reconstruction would be temporary. The desertification of southern California was irreversible. The full Relocation that was coming would sweep these people away.

And still the furor over the Chinese business contracts went on. Every special interest group in the business sector was squealing. Andrew Tollson, head of the American Business Forum, had described Joe Benton as the worst president for American business since Herbert Hoover. The right-wing press seemed to find a sadistic pleasure in repeating it.

His schedule was upside down. There wasn't time for him to have a day at the ranch on the way back east to Washington. He told Ben Hoffman to make the time.

He needed to think, to get out into the brush on one of his horses, into the ruggedness, the vastness, with the smudges of the Bradshaws rising in the distance. He needed to pull himself out of the detail and think about the big things, remember what they were, remember why he had even wanted the job he was doing. Even if it was only for a few hours. And even if he was never quite alone, and a Secret Service SUV or an agent on horseback was always somewhere in the corner of his vision, like a reminder of the morass of overwhelming detail that wasn't gone, just momentarily forgotten.

So many things seemed to be coming at him, had been from before his inauguration. Some big, some small, the media didn't care as long as they had something to fling at him. The worked-up outrage over Heather's decision to keep her job, the attack over Montera. Now the siege at Whitefish had dragged into its fifth week and was heading for who-knew-what-kind of resolution. Activity against U.S. troops in Colombia had increased as a challenge from the insurgents to test his resolve, and had pushed the casualty rate to more than twice the average of the past couple of years. The Republicans had seized on a statement by a newly appointed Justice Department official about federal prison release policy—the kind of poorly judged, ambiguous statement that inevitably gets made by someone in a new administration and which has to be retracted three hours later—to run a scare campaign and try to pass a House resolution condemning the administration's prisons policy. It was one thing after another. Where was the perspective? Four years of drought in southern California, that was important. People whose houses had burned down and who were camping out in a shelter, that was important. The New Foundation program that he and Angela Chavez and the rest of the administration were trying to put in place, that was important. Compared with that, who cared about a slip of the tongue by a junior official?

And yet he knew he ought to be grateful, because the media didn't know about the biggest thing. Joe Benton felt his presidency was in crisis. Not because of all the little things that kept getting thrown at him. They were par for the course for any president. And not even because of the hate and anger that were being turned on him after the loss of the Chinese contracts. But because of what lay behind the loss of those contracts, the limitation of his ability to exert U.S. influence on the international stage.

People sensed the Chinese government had challenged him when it awarded those contracts to Europeans, but no one outside the Marion group could put their finger on what the challenge was about. Yet the Chinese government knew, of course. If he allowed that challenge to pass, he would be beaten. His ability to exert influence with the Chinese regime would be gone. That would soon become evident to other countries. And once it was evident that he couldn't exert influence with China, the only other country on the planet with a claim to be a superpower, his ability to exert influence with anyone would go the same way.

He had got hold of a copy of James Alderson's study of the Bay of Pigs and read it on the flight into Phoenix. That was the analogy that immediately sprang to his mind. Within three months of taking office, Kennedy had been publicly beaten, humiliated, and discredited—far more publicly and more comprehensively than had happened to him—yet had recovered and gone on to exert considerable international influence. But there was an important difference. In the Cold War World of the 1960s, there was a hunger for American leadership against the Communist bloc. Kennedy stepped into that role and, despite his humbling over the Bay of Pigs, made it his own through his handling of the Cuban missile crisis eighteen months later. Seventy years on, in Joe Benton's world, there was no hunger for American leadership. Anything the United States proposed was going to meet with skepticism. Add a lack of credibility in exerting American influence, and it was going to be met with derision.

He read Alderson's account carefully. Kennedy had gone with a plan the CIA had already prepared. It chimed with his instincts, and he didn't know enough to say no. He, Joe Benton, hadn't gone with a plan from the previous administration. It was his own plan. So the responsibility, in that sense, was more squarely on his shoulders than it had been on Kennedy's.

Two months after his inauguration, his power on the global stage was potentially shot. That had to be his fault. The buck had to stop with him. What he needed to understand now was how it could have happened. And what, if anything, he could do to rescue the situation.

He rode slowly along the horse track above the house. He had taken out a chestnut mare called Martha. It was the first time Joe Benton had been back to the ranch since the inauguration. A crisp spring wind blew in his face. As he rode, he glimpsed spring wildflowers, pink verbenas and yellow poppies, scattered through the brush. He thought of the fire survivors he had seen the previous day. Exhausted, bewildered, scared.

He turned his mind back to his predicament. How had he got to where he was? Two things came to mind. First, he had acted unilaterally. He hadn't tried to build an international consensus. But for what? He hadn't planned on doing anything yet. That led to the second thing. He had made a threat of sanctions—even if only a veiled threat—sanctions that he himself hadn't yet identified or figured out how he was going to implement. Perhaps a smarter man, a wiser man, would have realized you couldn't act so quickly and so much alone. Perhaps if he was in the third year of his administration, and not the first, he would have acted differently.

But there was another point there. He hadn't actually decided to use sanctions. He had simply agreed that Olsen could raise the prospect with Chen. That was a failure of process. If he had forced himself to make an explicit decision to use them, the debate leading up to that decision would surely have been more robust, more searching, the implications more carefully considered. The decision to drop a hint to Chen, if he still had made it, would have been made with a greater awareness of what might happen next and greater care in timing and preparation.

But would he really not have made it? Would the decision have been any different?

Anyway, that was done. The question now was whether he wanted to escalate. Whether he had to escalate. Or could he back down? How much of his credit with the Chinese had he really blown?

He could make the visit to Beijing, as the Chinese were suggesting. See what would come of that. That was what Alan Ball was proposing.

But not Larry Olsen. Olsen had managed to find a way of claiming the contracts debacle as a success. Benton had to admire his chutzpah, if nothing else. According to Olsen, they had flushed the Chinese out, discovered how aggressive they were prepared to be—very—and now they knew the kind of game they would have to play. If losing the jobs that would go with forty-nine billion dollars of business was a success, Benton didn't want to see what Larry Olsen would count as a failure.

Why hadn't Olsen predicted this? Surely, when he suggested making a threat of sanctions, it should have been obvious the Chinese would come back as hard as they could to test him out, a new president, to see if they could make him blink. It certainly was obvious now it had happened. That was the kind of thing he and Wu and the other China experts at State should have understood. Maybe they did. Maybe Olsen actually wanted this to happen as a way of escalating the process even faster.

Was it the case that he was being manipulated by his own secretary of state? Was that possible?

Perhaps he really had made a mistake in appointing Olsen. If he put his pride aside, maybe Alan Ball was right. Yet when he looked back on it, the thing that stood out was that he had chosen to follow Olsen's advice straight down the line. If Olsen was the wrong man, why had he done that? Surely he wasn't so weak in judgment, even in foreign affairs, to be overly influenced by his secretary of state against the reality of the situation? If he was, how could he safely lay claim to the presidency?

He had gone with Olsen. And right now, apart from being more explicit about the decision to make the threat of sanctions, he still couldn't find the point at which he should have decided to go the other way. Which meant that fundamentally he was in line with Olsen. And yet look where that had got him.

He gazed at the peak of Towers Mountain in the distance. The mare, as if sensing his preoccupation, had stopped.

Why had he followed Olsen's line? He had only one answer. Urgency. That was the thing Alan Ball didn't seem to get. Maybe he should have taken Ball with him to San Diego to see what could happen in California after four years of drought. Olsen, whatever else you said about him, got it. And Ball just didn't seem to.

Joe Benton felt it strongly. As president, it was his responsibility not to prevaricate around the issue, but to face it. The need for action was urgent. History would judge him harshly if he failed to respond. In all this mess, that was the one thing he was certain of.

And yet if you act too hastily, he knew, project yourself beyond the limit of your credibility, then you lose the ability to have any effect at all. Anyone who had ever exerted any kind of power successfully knew that.

But there was no option to act slowly here. The way to recover his credibility had to be through action, not by retreating to the edge of where it extended already.

Suddenly he became aware that the horse had stopped walking. He leaned down and ran his hand over the horse's flank. "What do you say, Martha. Huh? What do you say, girl?" He straightened up. "Come on," he said, and at a slight pressure from his knees, the mare walked on.

Joe Benton's way with any serious problem had always been to work through it, once he had gathered views, more by going away and thinking it through than to talk it out. But at times even he reached a point from which the only way to progress was to talk, when he was so deep or so lost in it that he needed someone else to help haul him back above the landscape to get perspective. He had reached that point now. He tried to think of the right person. It couldn't be anyone who was involved in the process, not even John Eales. Marty Montag, the long-serving ex-senator from New Hampshire, had been a mentor to him. But he would have to tell Marty everything, and he didn't feel he could do that. What about Gartner? There was no one else in the world who could appreciate what he was going through like an ex-president. But he didn't respect him, nor Shawcross, who had preceded him. Shawcross had always struck him as complacent and lazy, favored by a global upswing that did more for the economy than any of his policies, smugly governing through an immense appetite for delegation and a stubborn willingness to postpone dealing with any of the major issues the country faced. As for Gartner, he was crafty, altogether darker. Maybe it was hubris, but Joe Benton didn't want to expose himself to either of those men.

He respected Currie, who had preceded Shawcross, and he probably would have called the ex-president if it was possible. But Pat Currie was far gone into the world of Alzheimer's. That left him without any ex-presidential counsel he could call on.

It left him with only one person.

Heather made coffee after he came in from his ride. She sat on the sofa beside him.

Joe sipped the coffee.

"So are you going to tell me what's on your mind?" said Heather eventually. She took his hand and looked at him questioningly. "Is it California? It was awful, wasn't it?"

Joe nodded. "Thanks for coming with me. It made a difference. To people, I mean." He was silent, reflective. "How are you finding it? When we agreed I'd run I knew this was going to be asking a lot of you, but I don't think I realized how much."

"It's fine, Joe. You know, it's not often you get to spend twelve thousand dollars wallpapering a room."

Heather was redecorating the White House, as new first ladies traditionally do, and the usual ridiculous allegations were coming out in the right-wing press.

Joe smiled.

"It's fun."

"I know it's hard work."

"Well it is hard work. That's true. And there are things like California. Even there, you can't really do anything, but just being there makes a difference to people, like you said. And that's worthwhile."

"I appreciate it, honey. I want you to know that."

"You know, it made me think, maybe I will give up my job."

"No!" Joe looked at her, aghast. "There's no way we're going to let those—"

"Joe, hold on a minute. It's not because of them. I'm just not sure there aren't more things I'd like to do as first lady. I'm beginning to think I could achieve more that way."

"I'd hate to see them push you out."

"They're not pushing me out."

"I'd hate for them to think so."

Heather nodded. She didn't say anything to that.

"I'm sorry, honey. I've got no right to say that. It's your choice. I don't want to play politics with your life."

"Well, I haven't decided." She paused. "Maybe I'll leave it a little longer. Maybe next year."

Joe nodded. Heather nestled into the sofa, drew up her feet and pushed her toes under Joe's thigh. She wriggled them.

"What about you, Mr. President?"

"What about me?"

"Like hearing 'Hail to the Chief' every time you walk in a room?"

Joe smiled. "That's something, isn't it?"

"So?"

"So what?"

"So you get them to bring us here and then you go riding for four hours by yourself." Heather raised an eyebrow. "I know you, Joe."

Joe frowned. The frown got deeper. At last he took a deep breath.

"It's confidential, Heather."

Heather rolled her eyes.

"Really, honey. About a half dozen people in the whole country know about this."

Heather's expression turned serious. Joe had told her confidential information before, plenty of times, when he was a senator. But this sounded as if it was on a whole new scale.

"You sure you want to know?"

She wasn't. But she nodded anyway.

He told her. Starting at his first meeting with Gartner, all the way through to the Chinese action in response to his clumsy threat of sanctions. When he stopped, he looked at her sheepishly.

She was deep in thought.

"I'm sorry I didn't mention anything before. You know . . . I couldn't."

Heather shook her head quickly, dismissing the thought.

"I'm boxed into a corner. Two months in, I've thrown out a challenge to the only other major power in the world, and they've met me. If it's a bluff, they've called it."

"Is it a bluff?" asked Heather quietly.

"It wasn't. But doesn't look like I thought it through carefully enough. So maybe it is."

"That's bad then."

"I didn't set out to bluff them."

"But maybe that's what you've done. Don't bluff if you're not prepared to get called, Joe Benton."

Joe didn't reply. He found himself wishing he'd spoken to Heather sooner, as he knew he would. When he talked to her like this, she was always logical, objective. Just as he needed her to be. Comforting came later.

"Joe, you knew the Europeans wouldn't support you. You said that's what Ogilvie told you. Well, all that's happened is the Chinese have shown you that."

"No, they've shown me they know it as well."

"Same difference."

"They're saying they knew it all along, so my threat was empty."

"Why? Are you saying it's only a real threat if the Europeans join us. We won't go it alone? Are you saying the United States won't go it alone?"

"I'm not saying that."

"But that's the question, isn't it? If we won't go it alone, it's a bluff. If we will, it isn't."

Joe nodded. That was exactly how it was.

"What are our options?"

"Well, we go ahead, I guess, or we back away. If we back away, we do it with some kind of secondary action." Joe paused, thinking over all the discussions he'd had with Eales and Ball and Olsen over the past days. "We show some kind of aggression to send the message that we're backing off on this but that doesn't mean we're going to be weak on anything else."

"What kind of aggression?"

"Something peripheral."

"Another Iraqi-Syrian thing?"

"Maybe something closer to home. We could make some kind of show of support toward Taiwan, but that might be a little too inflammatory. They might interpret that the wrong way. There's aid to Korea for the ex-North. They can always use more of that, and the Chinese hate it when we do anything to build Korea up. Or those contracts the Chinese government awarded . . . Apparently there were some quite advanced memorandums of understanding with some of our companies and we could challenge what they did on those. That might be kind of smart because the Chinese could give on that as a way of letting us know they've got the message."

"Which is?"

"That we hear them on the big issue, and we respect them on that, but they better respect us as well."

Heather didn't look impressed. "Doesn't sound like you're asking for much respect."

"If we keep going, if we go it alone, Heather, I don't know what that means. I don't think any of us knows what that means."

"What about talking with President Wen?"

"No one seems to think that's a good idea right now. Not even Alan."

"What do you think?"

"You know, I actually don't see how it's going to help. Wen must have authorized what they did. If he didn't, he could reverse it."

"But surely it helps to talk?"

"That's what you'd think. But they all tell me no, not right now." Benton smiled ruefully. "When Alan and Larry agree, you've got to think there must be something in it."

"Things are bad between them?"

Joe shook his head and laughed. "Honey, I don't know which one I'd fire first. Alan came to me and told me I should sack Larry."

Heather stared at him.

"He said it straight."

Heather frowned. "So if you did take some kind of action—I mean in relation to China—when would they be expecting you to do it?"

"Soon, I guess. Soon enough for it be clear that what we're doing is a response, that we're not prevaricating. It's nearly two weeks already. If we look like we're prevaricating, that just makes us look weak again."

Heather was silent. She drew her knees up under her chin, hunched her shoulders, frowning in thought, holding her coffee mug in both hands.

"If I keep going with this, it'll be what the Benton presidency ends up being about," said Joe quietly. "That's my fear."

Heather nodded.

"Nothing else will matter."

Heather looked up at him. "What else does matter, Joe? You ran against Gartner saying it was finally time for someone to stop telling lies, to admit we faced a problem and it was going to hurt but if we worked together we could get through it and come out the other side a better country. And the American people trusted you to do that, to tell them the truth, to deal with it, to lead them through it. And that hasn't changed. It just turns out the lies have been a little bigger and the truth is a little harder."

"A lot harder."

"So does that mean suddenly *you* stop trying to deal with it? Because suddenly it's too hard? To me, it seems like it's the opposite. The harder the truth, the more important it is to grapple with it. If the situation is as bad as you say, if action is needed as urgently as you say, then . . . I don't know, personally, Joe, I'd rather see you try and fail than not try at all. I don't give a damn about the Benton presidency. I give a damn about Amy and Greg and the kind of world their kids are going to grow up in."

Joe gazed at her for a moment. Then he drew her to him.

"So you don't think I'm an awful president?" he said eventually.

"I think you'll get better."

Joe drew back and looked at Heather in mock dismay. Heather smiled.

"You'll have to make the case, Joe. You're going to have do something, and you're going to have to sell it to the American people."

"I know."

"When?"

Joe shrugged. "I hate even having to think about this. We've got the health summit this week. That's what I want to be doing, Heather. Things that are going to make people's lives better."

"You can still do that, Joe. This isn't stopping you."

"Not yet. That's the one thing we've got on our side, none of this is out in the open. We've still got control of the public agenda."

Wednesday, March 23

East Room, The White House

The president stood in front of the Gilbert Stuart portrait of George Wash
ington in the East Room, the oldest object in the White House. On his right
were five of the key people from the health care sector who had taken part in
the daylong summit on health that he had just chaired. On his other side stood
the secretary of health, Mary Lawson, the surgeon general, Eric Boulier, Jodie
Ames, and the chairs of the House and Senate health committees.

Adam Gehrig opened the press conference by reading a communiqué
from the summit. It stated that the group was committed to reform and
the participants would be putting in detailed responses to a series of measures that Secretary Lawson had proposed. Jacqueline Russel, president of
the American Medical Association, and Bill Overton, representing the
Association of Managed Funds, both of whom were in the group on the
president's right, had fought bitterly over the wording "commitment to
reform." They had wanted something like "willingness to explore reform"
or "interest in continuing improvement in patient care" or something even
more meaningless. So had the Republicans from Congress. Joe Benton had
rammed the wording through. He was committed to reform. If they weren't
committed to reform, they were going to have to get out of his way.

In the past days, the furor over the loss of the Chinese business contracts had abated. Jodie was confident that today the journalists would be
engaged in the issue at hand. As an inducement to get them to stick to the
matter, she had offered the prospect of another presidential press conference within two weeks with a general scope. The first question, from the
Washington Post correspondent, was right on the money, asking if the president could summarize the reforms that had been discussed during the day.
The president certainly could. They were the reforms Joe Benton had been
calling for all through his campaign: universal coverage obligation through
managed funds supported by a levy on sales of tobacco, fast foods, motor

vehicles and other major causes of morbidity and mortality; guaranteed access to pharmaceuticals through centralized purchasing at state level; development of competition through genuine transparency of fees and outcomes of physicians and health funds; and a program of targeted investment by federal government to provide hospitals and other infrastructure in key locations of need, in particular the Relocation states. "And I have to say," concluded the president, "there was a remarkable degree of support around the table for each of these measures."

He didn't look at Jacqueline Russel as he said it. He didn't need to in order to know the kind of look she must be giving him.

"That simple, huh?" said the *Washington Post* man.

The president smiled. He turned to someone else.

"Elly Meyer, *Journal of the American Medical Association.* Mr. President, don't you think the reforms you've mentioned strike at the heart of patient autonomy and choice that has been the basis of our medical system for the past hundred years and more."

"Ms. Meyer, our medical system has failed the American people of the past hundred years and more." As if Jodie Ames hadn't anticipated this question and given him a dozen sound-bite options. "It has failed our poor, it has failed our unemployed, it has failed our old, it has failed our young. Just about the only people it hasn't failed are the people your publication represents. Let me give you some statistics." He did. They were impressive. He knew it. As an American, they made him feel ashamed, and he said so. American physicians should be ashamed, and he said that as well. He didn't see how anyone could argue for the status quo when faced with those numbers.

Elly Meyer didn't have a follow-up.

"Next question. Pete," he said, pointing to Pete Abernethy from Issues.com.

"Mr. President, why do you think this is going to work? Why do you think you're going to succeed where so many of your predecessors have failed?"

"They didn't fail, Pete, they gave up. Over and over, we've had good presidents come to this office with good intentions to reform our health care system and one after the other they've been beaten down by parochial interests. Well, I don't think the American people are prepared to see that happen again. I'm not prepared to see it happen again." Benton smiled. "A previous president once famously said he'll be with you till the last dog dies. And that still wasn't enough. Understand this. I'll be with you not only until the last dog's dead, but until he's good and buried too." There was laughter from the press. "And you know who's going to be burying it? Me!" There was more laughter. Benton glanced at the group on his right, Jacqueline Russel and Bill Overton among them. "I think we all understand that now." He looked around. He nodded toward one of the raised hands. "Matt?"

"Mr. President," said Matt Ruddock, "can you outline the process going forward? You've had this summit today, and I wonder how that translates into something more than hot air."

"This is a step on the path. It's important to talk. It's important to hear each other's views and understand where we're all coming from. That's what we were doing here today. So as you've said yourself, it's an important part of the process, and there'll be more days like this. But the process moves on. Secretary Lawson will shortly release a detailed consultation timetable. This is something we are moving on and will continue to move on so we'll have legislation on the Hill in the fall just as we've planned to."

"Isn't that an ambitious program, given everything that's happened in the last couple of weeks?"

"And what would that be?" replied Benton. There was a moment of silence. Then Benton smiled, and he raised his hands helplessly, and more laughter broke out among the journalists. For some reason, the mood in the press corps was good today, and Joe Benton felt it. "Is it an ambitious program? Hell yes. You want some cautious little incremental piecemeal thing, then the American people elected the wrong guy. They elected me to be ambitious. Because they're ambitious, and so they should be. Is it ambitious? I hope so. You tell me if it isn't."

Ruddock grinned. "I will."

"Okay. I'll be listening." The president looked to the other side of the room. "Phillip?"

"I love this idea of taxing fast food companies for the health costs of their product. But what happens if you're successful, Mr. President? People stop eating fast food, where's the tax money going to come from?"

"People stop eating fast food, Phillip, and they'll be that much healthier that we won't need it."

"Don't you think it's kind of anti-business?"

It took all of about thirty seconds for Benton to deal with that one. A reporter from FoxBloomberg asked him why he thought he had the right to tell Americans how to live—what to eat, what to drink, how fast to drive—and he swatted that away just as easily. He was on a roll. He looked around the room again. He took another couple of questions. "I'll take one more." A dozen hands were in the air. His eyes stopped on a young woman whose hand had been raised since the beginning. He nodded at her.

"Michelle Kornhaus, *Toronto Herald*."

"I'm glad to see our Canadian friends have sent someone along."

"Is it true, Mr. President, that you have recently received a report showing that sea level rise over the next twenty years is likely to occur at least twice as fast as previously estimated and will require the evacuation of eighteen million people in the United States in addition to those already to be relocated, including the Florida Keys and the cities of Miami, Galveston, and the lower San Francisco Bay area?"

For an instant, Joe Benton's mind was blank. He glanced at Jodie Ames. Jodie was staring back at him.

He turned back to the Canadian journalist.

He smiled. "That's like asking a man whether it's true he beat his wife."

"I'm not asking whether you beat your wife, Mr. President. I'm asking whether you've received a report showing—"

"And I'm explaining there are some things, entirely false, you can give credence to just by denying them. Do I let my dog Bertie pee on the White House furniture? No." There was a scattering of laughter. "By the way, I don't have a dog called Bertie." There was more laughter. "See how that works? Now I'll take one more if someone has a serious question they want me to answer."

He took another question on the health program and handled it briskly. "Okay, I want to thank you all, and I particularly thank everyone who participated in the summit today. We're at the start of a long road, but it's not going to be as long as some people think, and we'll get to the end of it successfully."

He turned, shook hands with the people who had been standing beside him as he spoke, and left. Jodie Ames came with him.

"That was excellent, sir."

Benton nodded, not replying.

"And that ridiculous question from the *Toronto Herald,* I promise you, sir, I'll find out just what the hell she thought she was doing. I thought you handled it very well."

Joe Benton wasn't so sure. He wished he hadn't said that thing about the dog peeing. It had just come into his head. It was condescending and sounded as if he was trivializing the issue, and it was the kind of thing that would come back to haunt him. Someone would drag those words up one day. But the thing that really worried him was the look he had given Jodie. He could remember glancing at her. He didn't think that would have looked good, a glance to the side like that. It had probably looked shifty. There had been three cameras in the room, and by now there'd be a thousand sites on the Net with the footage, including their own.

"Let's see it," he said when they got back to the Oval Office. He tossed the control to Connor Gale, who logged in to the White House site. "Skip to the end," said the president impatiently.

There he was, turning to the *Toronto Herald* reporter. Her question. Then he was staring. For an instant. Like he was stunned. Then the sideways glance. Benton's heart sank when he saw it. "Help me out here," it was saying. "I don't know what to say." Worse. "How the hell did she find out about that?"

It's the cover-up that gets you, he thought, not the misdemeanor. That was the great lesson Richard Nixon handed down to posterity.

He looked around. Jodie Ames was staring at him, as if she had just seen that glance for the first time.

"Is it . . ." She stopped before she uttered the word she wouldn't be able to take back. Besides, she didn't need his answer. She could see, from that look. It was true. She didn't want to make the president lie to her.

"Should we take the footage off the site?" she asked quietly.

Benton shook his head. "That'll turn into another story."

News moves fast through the West Wing. John Eales came in. A moment later Ben Hoffman arrived.

"We need to prepare some kind of communication," said Jodie. "My phone's going to be running hot."

"The president gets risk assessments and scenario analyses all the time," began Eales smoothly, as if he was giving dictation. "Some of them are designed to be purposefully extreme. It's possible there was an analysis that used assumptions along these lines, but it's only one of many, and it's not White House policy to comment on every scenario analysis that's provided to it because if we did, that's all we'd ever be commenting on . . ."

Benton stopped listening. His mind was following another line of thought. Someone had leaked. Who?

"Show me what you've got when it's ready," said Eales.

Benton was aware that there was silence in the room. Jodie was looking at him. "Are you happy with that, sir? What John just said?"

Benton nodded.

"Okay." Ames threw a last glance at the screen, now showing the White House website home page. "I'll try it."

She left.

Benton turned to Eales and Hoffman. "What do you think?"

John Eales threw himself down in a sofa. "Joe, you looked guilty as hell."

Thursday, March 24

Oval Office, The White House

His day was meant to have started at eight o'clock with the morning CIA breifing followed by a meeting to review communication strategy after the previous day's events. It started at six a.m. with a phone call from Erin O'Donnell.

Something had happened at Whitefish. It was unclear yet whether some or all of the group had attempted a breakout, or whether they had simply provoked the FBI into a firefight. All O'Donnell knew was that in the pre-dawn darkness, shots had been exchanged.

Katzenberger rang a couple of minutes later. It turned out the firefight was still taking place. The FBI was going in.

From that moment, through everything else that happened that day, Benton was conscious that the final assault at Whitefish was under way. It was as if he could physically feel the shackles on his hands constraining him from what he wanted to do. If the siege ended well, those shackles would be loosened. If it ended in a massacre, they would be screwed tighter than ever.

At 8:15, Ames, Hoffman and Eales were in the Oval Office to go over the communication strategy. Jodie's face was grim.

"Jodie, it couldn't be that bad," Benton chivvied her as he sat down.

Ames shook her head. She wasn't in the mood to smile.

"What's happening?"

"The environmental groups are having a field day. They're saying the figures the *Toronto Herald* journalist gave out are a good scenario. They're saying they've been telling us this since the moment they took office. Apparently, they've sent us these figures."

The president glanced at Hoffman. "Have they?"

"Probably. You wouldn't believe what we get. There's some guy who keeps sending e-mails that the end of the world's coming tomorrow . . ."

Ben stopped in midsentence. "That's a thought. Why don't we get some journalist to stand up at your next conference and ask if it's true you've had a report that the world's ending tomorrow?"

The president stared at him. So did Jodie.

Ben glanced at Eales. "Why not? It might work."

"Mr. President, the problem," said Ames, "is it's becoming a trust thing. You've never been doubted on the trust issue. Whatever else anyone's thrown at you, you've always been rock solid on trust."

The president waited. He knew he wasn't going to like what was coming next.

"NewsPoll ran a sample last night, divided between those who had seen the footage and those who hadn't. The question was simply: Do you trust the president? Those who hadn't seen the footage, seventy-eight percent, right up where you normally are. Those who had seen it, fifty-four."

"That's NewsPoll," snarled Eales. "A bunch of self-selected, self-important respondents who haven't got anything better to do than sit around doing online polls. We'll get our own polling. I'll get Chris Plenty to take a look."

"John, everyone knows the NewsPoll methodology is hardly scientific, but I think they're picking up on something here. More importantly, every other press outlet agrees. They're all quoting the NewsPoll numbers.

"Jodie, what do you suggest?" asked Benton.

"I want to lay out a defense of everything you've done. We can show without question that you've moved to carry out your major campaign promises in your first hundred days faster and more comprehensively than any other president in modern times. If that's not a trust issue, I don't know what is. I've had Barry do some research on Gartner." Jodie glanced at her handheld. "Of the eighteen major pledges during his campaign for his first term, only four of them received any kind of action during his first year in office. And we can show that already a good twelve of your pledges are being actioned. That's a proud standard and we should put it out there."

"Comparing ourselves to Gartner is not a proud standard," said Eales, "no matter what we've done."

"We can check Shawcross."

Eales shook his head.

"Jodie," said the president, "I think what John's saying is we don't want to fight them on this. And I agree. I don't want to make trust an issue by responding. If we do that, we'll be arguing about trust for the next four years. Trust is something you earn by doing, not by talking. If you need to address the issue, just tell them that, and then focus on what we're doing."

"I still think—"

"Sorry, Jodie. Maybe we'll use the comparison some other time. Not now. What else can you suggest?"

"We could bring forward our announcement of the Teacher Support Program. We were planning that for next week, but we could advance it. Personally, I don't favor that. It smacks of trying to divert attention. The press won't buy it, and if it doesn't work, we lose the mileage we could have got out of it."

The president glanced at Eales.

"Sounds to me that idea works both ways," said Eales. "It's a pledge you made back in the campaign, and Jodie, it lets you make your point, we're fulfilling promises."

Ames shook her head. "They won't go for it. We'll just lose it."

There was silence.

"And what am I saying on the other thing?" asked Ames. "The sea levels, the evacuation of Miami?"

"What we agreed yesterday," said Eales. "We get all kinds of scenario analyses, including extremely hypothetical ones, and we don't comment on them. As far as action is concerned, there's an established multilateral procedure going on, the planning for the Kyoto 4 round under the auspices of the United Nations. The United States will play its part, and we'll share what we know with our partners in that process."

"Can I say the president personally is fully committed to that process?"

"Go with the wording John just gave you," said Benton quietly.

Ames shook her head. "The press isn't going to like it. This is just like what we did over the Chinese contracts. It's a generic response. There's no specifics. They want something real."

"You can say I'm going to meet Nleki."

Eales and Hoffman looked at the president in surprise.

"Ben, let Al know. Let's not do the meeting too soon, huh? Spin it out a couple of months."

"You sure you want to meet him?" said Eales.

"There's no reason for me not to."

"You want me to let Larry know?" asked Hoffman.

"No, I'll do that."

Jodie frowned. "So I go with the same line as yesterday, but I say you're going to meet the UN secretary-general?"

"As part of the U.S. commitment to playing its part in the process. That's it. That's as far as you go."

Jodie still didn't look happy. "That's better. It's not much, though."

"Jodie," said Benton, "there's something else happening that you need to know about. At Whitefish. It started a couple of hours ago. We're going to finish the siege."

Now the expression on Ames's face changed. "Can we leak that?" she asked eagerly.

"No, I'm not going to compromise the operation. Once it's finished, it's all yours."

"How soon will they be done?"

"I don't know."

"Well, it'll get Miami off our backs. It'll knock it right off the front pages. That's great."

"Not if it ends up like Waco," said Hoffman. "Already we've got a trust issue. We're not going to look too good if we end up with a hundred dead rednecks on our hands."

Eales smiled. "Come on, Ben. No one cares about dead rednecks except other rednecks."

"I'm hoping it won't come to that," said the president.

"I'll get Barry to prepare our case," said Ames. "We'll lay out the way you've handled it, Mr. President, show that you've been moderate and patient. Whatever happens, everything you've done you've done to protect the lives and property of U.S. citizens. It'll be ready to go." Jodie Ames had brightened up. "Okay. I'll get to work."

Ben and John stayed on after Jodie left.

"The wonders of the modern news cycle," said Eales. "In't it great?"

"You think Katzenberger's guys know what they're doing out there?" asked Hoffman.

"I hope so," said Benton. "They've had seven weeks to figure it out."

There was silence.

Benton looked at Eales. "Are we trying to find out who leaked?"

The president wasn't talking about Whitefish now, and Eales knew it. "Likelihood is we won't find the source. It's probably someone on the Chinese side anyway."

"Or some do-gooder at the ESU," said Hoffman.

Benton didn't reply. He had his own suspicion.

"This is going to hurt us, Joe," said Eales.

Hoffman nodded. "The Budget Reconciliation Bill goes to the Hill next week. Then we're scheduled for the Small Business Bill two weeks after that. They're both crucial."

"And they're all going to take months," said Benton. "Let's not panic. A dip in my ratings now doesn't make any difference as long as we can bring them back. We just need to keep the momentum going until the ratings come up."

"As long as they do."

"They will."

"If Whitefish goes Waco it'll be a fucking disaster," said Eales. "If these bills stall, we're dead."

Hoffman's face was grim. If things started stalling, they would never get the package through.

"I'll talk to anyone in Congress I have to talk to," said Benton. "All day and all night. Talk to Barb. Just set it up."

Hoffman nodded. He had already started doing that. The president's diary for that day had been thrown out and it was now filled with meetings with key congresspeople. The secretary of the environment, Andrea Powers, was on the schedule as well. She had demanded a meeting with the president and from the tone of her voice it sounded as if she was going to resign by e-mail if she didn't get it.

"I have another question," said Eales. "Are we still on course with this strategy? Do we push through the bills for New Foundation first and then migrate public opinion to the true size of the relocation? Because we could use this to change course. Go public with what we know and push for everything at once."

Benton shook his head. "John, look at the craziness we've got here when this stuff just comes out as a rumor. What happens if we come out and say it's true? We don't just stall, we lose control. Unless we can say we've got a solution, we can't do it. We've got to be able to say we've got a solution. Until we get to that point, the strategy is to get the elements of fairness in place first. I'm not changing direction."

"We may have no choice. Events may have overtaken us."

"Well, let's see about that. Jodie's out there saying this is simply one extreme scenario. If they buy that, we're okay. They get hung up on White-fish, in a week's time this is just some other crazy scenario some journalist was talking about."

"The longer we leave it now, the harder it'll get if we have no choice," said Hoffman.

"Maybe. Eventually, if we're forced to, we come out and say, sure, we got this report as you all know, we've done some more work to verify, now we're in a position to say this is what we expect to happen. Makes us look judicious."

Hoffman glanced at Eales doubtfully. "Okay," he said. He stood up. "We'll try to keep everyone on track."

"I'll talk to anyone," said Benton. "Just let me know who I have to talk to."

Hoffman nodded. "To start with, you've got Andrea Powers coming in about ten minutes." He smiled. "Good luck."

Hoffman left, closing the door behind him. Benton was silent for a moment.

He turned to Eales. "I want to ask you a question, John. On the question of who leaked. I'm not sure if this is completely crazy but . . . You don't think it could have been Larry?"

Eales was genuinely surprised. "Olsen? Joe, there's a whole bunch of people with a motive."

"You think Larry has one?"

"What? Ramp up the confrontation?" Eales thought about it. "That risks bringing it out into the open. Larry doesn't want to do that. If anything,

Alan's motive would be greater. He wants it in the open. He wants this in Kyoto."

"No, not Alan." Benton thought about it. "Alan wouldn't do it."

The phone rang. Katzenberger was on the line. They had nine of the Whitefish people in custody. Two were confirmed dead. There had been no sighting yet of Bill Dare, the leader of the group. FBI and state troopers were moving on the main compound. Apparently the shooting so far had happened at a couple of outposts.

The president told Katzenberger to minimize the use of force. And to keep him informed.

He told Eales what was happening. "I just pray they don't go in there and slaughter a slew of them."

"No agents killed so far, right? Well, maybe they'll take it easy. If agents start to go down, the others'll go fucking postal."

There was silence. Half of Benton's mind was on Whitefish, half on Olsen.

"I'm going to talk to Larry," he said. "I've got to be clear on this."

"You're going to accuse him of leaking?"

"You think I made a mistake? Appointing him?"

Eales opened his mouth to reply.

The phone rang again. It was Eleanor Gottlib, the president's assistant, to say that Andrea Powers was there. Eleanor asked if the president required a note taker for the meeting. He told her that he didn't. As he spoke, Benton signaled to Eales to leave the office.

Eales went out through the door to the president's private dining room.

There was a moment of awkward silence after Andrea sat down. Then she spoke. Within about a minute it was clear she had come to resign. She felt she had been kept in the dark about the report over Miami—even if it was only a scenario—that the press had seen she was out of the loop, and her position now was impossible. Benton tried to placate her. Somewhere in Montana at that moment, several hundred trigger-happy FBI agents were storming the hideout of a bunch of overarmed, overaggressive lunatics, including sixty women and children, and he could only imagine what was about to happen. Now one of his cabinet members wanted to resign.

Whatever damage had already been done by yesterday's confrontation over the emissions scenario would be made ten times worse if his environment secretary walked out. More importantly, he didn't want to lose her. Andrea Powers came with a dream résumé for the role. Formerly CEO of Amberton Systems and head of the Business Forum on Social Responsibility, she was one of the few people in the country who could talk credibly to business leaders about the environmental perspective and to environmental leaders about the business perspective. And she could get things done. In the short time she had been in office, her work on driving compliance had been extraordinary.

Powers's anger was palpable. Benton tried to assuage it, but she wouldn't be placated. Eventually he fell back on the ultimate argument at his disposal. If she wanted to achieve what she obviously felt so passionately about, serving in the administration was the only way to do it. Had she really lost the credibility to do her job or was it her pride talking? She could leave the administration, but if she really cared about what she was doing, how would that help? He asked her to consider that.

Powers did. Eventually she said that if she was going to do her job, she had to be kept informed about anything touching her area of responsibility. Benton committed to keep her informed of everything he could. That wasn't quite the same thing, but it was close. Benton told her to think about it, and if necessary they could have another conversation. By the time she left, Joe Benton was pretty sure that Powers was going to stay on. But there was a wound now, he knew, and it would take its time to heal.

After that he faced a day full of meetings and calls. It was amazing how much damage could be done with a look. There seemed to be a general belief the Miami scenario was true. Or at least everyone needed reassurance that it wasn't. Benton didn't say that, he just kept saying it was one of a number of scenarios, saying it nonchalantly, matter-of-factly, to show that he wasn't perturbed by it, so why should anyone else be? He said it when he met with Dan Bass, the recently appointed director of the National Relocation Commission, and he kept saying it in the afternoon-long series of meetings he had with worried congressional leaders. Between the meetings he was getting updates from Whitefish, where the operation was in progress but details were frustratingly few. And somehow in the midst of all that he had to find the time to call Larry Olsen.

He didn't have the time for niceties, and he didn't much feel like them anyway. "Larry, I'm going to ask you straight out," he said. "Did you leak that report yesterday?"

There was silence. Olsen's face on the screen was hard to read.

"With respect, sir," he said eventually. "That's a crazy question. It's also insulting."

"Well, I'm asking it. I'll apologize for the insult once you give me an answer."

"Mr. President, I think if that's where we are, you probably have your own answer and you don't want me in your cabinet. And if that's what Alan's telling you, that's fine."

"Alan's not telling me anything of the kind," said Benton.

"Really?" Olsen's expression was skeptical. "Well, is that what you're saying, that you don't want me on board? Because if you are, Mr. President, just say it and I'll get out of your hair."

Benton shook his head.

Olsen took a deep breath. "Then for the record, Mr. President, I didn't leak it. And for the record, I would never do such a thing."

Benton was silent a moment. "All right, then. I apologize."

"Sir, I have no more idea than you who leaked it. If I had to say, probably someone from the Chinese side."

The idea that he had even suspected Olsen suddenly seemed ludicrous. Joe Benton was embarrassed. How could he have thought that? It was crazy. He had to get his head clear. He had to break out of this circle of guess and secondguess where he was trapped.

"I'm going to talk to President Wen," he said suddenly.

"With respect, sir, I don't think—"

"Why shouldn't I?"

"It makes you look weak. We're still waiting for a response from them. You don't talk to them when you're waiting for a response."

"What response?"

"Their proposal."

"Larry, they're not giving us a proposal. You've said it yourself."

"They haven't told us that. Technically, we're still waiting for it."

"Hell's bells, Larry! I don't care about technically. This is nuts. I'm going to talk to him."

"As your secretary of state, sir, I advise you not to."

"And as president, I thank you for your advice."

Benton cut the line. It was rare for Joe Benton to be genuinely angry, but he could feel his heart pounding. He picked up his phone and got through to Ben Hoffman and told him to set up a call to Wen. Hoffman must have heard something in Benton's voice because he simply asked when the president would like to make the call, as if he had been just waiting for the request.

This was madness, thought Benton. Everything was out of control. Anything could be happening right now in Montana, and if it went wrong the press would be all over him. On Capitol Hill, some kind of craziness seemed to have taken hold and even normally solid congresspeople were panicking over a single rogue report from a journalist at some second-rate Canadian newspaper. And people were telling him he couldn't pick up a phone to talk to another world leader about an issue that was of crucial concern to both of them and to the whole world, as a matter of fact. And he couldn't *talk* to him? He had to get back on top. He had to start following his gut a little more. He had to listen to himself a little more, and to the so-called experts a whole lot less.

Friday, March 25

Oval Office, The White House

On the screen, an FBI agent was standing in a cellar full of weapons. Rounds of ammunition and rocket-propelled grenades were on the floor at his feet.

"They should get that fucking guy out of the shot," muttered Eales. The agent was in a bulletproof vest with FBI written in fluorescent letters. "The conspiracy junkies will think it's staged. They'll never believe they gave up without using that stuff."

The Whitefish siege had ended shortly after five a.m. Only six were reported dead in the compound, including Bill Dare, the group's leader. A slightly larger number had been injured. Two state troopers had died.

Joe Benton had felt an enormous surge of relief when he heard the news, almost had to remind himself that two law enforcement officers had died. He felt the shackles around his hands loosening. When he talked to President Wen, he could talk to him knowing he had earned at least a little extra freedom of action.

Now he was waiting for the call, which was scheduled for eight thirty a.m., eight thirty p.m. in Beijing. Olsen and Ball had arrived an hour earlier to brief him, and Eales came to sit in on the call along with Oliver Wu, who was going to interpret and take notes. They agreed on what the president would say. Then they waited, watching coverage of Whitefish on the screen.

Toward the end of the siege, most of the group had surrendered. Resistance folded after Dare died. Looking at the weapons in that basement, Benton wouldn't like to think what would have happened if Dare hadn't died when he did.

"I heard one of his own guys shot him," said Alan Ball.

"First sensible thing any of them did in two months," muttered Olsen.

"We ought to get some of their guys on camera saying there were no wanton killings. I'll talk to Katzenberger." Eales glanced at the president.

"Jodie's going to set up a press call for you with Katzenberger and Erin. Let's make sure you get some of the glory."

Benton nodded.

They had to wait a little longer. Finally the call came through.

Joe Benton waited for President Wen to come on the line.

"President Wen," he said in an upbeat tone. "I'm glad we are able to talk. I hope you're well."

Wen returned the pleasantry in Mandarin. Wu translated. "President Benton, it's a shame we have not been able to meet."

Wen hoped that they would meet soon. In fact, he hoped they would meet in Beijing soon after the G9 summit in India.

Benton said he hoped they could meet as soon as the conditions were right, which was the line he had agreed with Olsen and Ball. Then, as they had planned, he went on to say directly that he was disappointed U.S. companies hadn't won any of the contracts that had been awarded by the Chinese authorities a couple of weeks back.

"I regret, . . ." translated Wu, "I have no influence over commercial decisions, President Benton . . . These were commercial decisions that were made by the responsible authorities . . . You too do not interfere in commercial decisions. We should cooperate as much as we can within the limits of our power."

Olsen rolled his eyes.

"I would like to send my secretary of commerce to meet with your trade ministers," said Benton.

"Certainly . . . He would be welcome . . . United States ministers are always welcome."

"We need to cooperate as much as we can."

Wen agreed. He asked what else President Benton had in mind.

Benton said he would be open to any proposals President Wen wished to present.

There was a hush in the Oval Office.

Wen didn't speak.

"President Wen," said Benton, "together we can make great progress for both our countries. If we do this carefully, and with good faith, there can also be stability. That is the prize we can have, progress with stability. History will judge us kindly if this is what we achieve. But this requires us to agree, and to act. We must act now. Now is the moment."

There was silence on the line again. Then Benton heard Wen's voice start up in Mandarin.

"To seize a moment in history . . . This requires good faith."

"I agree."

"Before proposals must come . . . trust between the leaders. Then there can be proposals. Then the moment in history can be seized." There was a pause. "Trust comes from knowing the other . . . A telephone is good, but face-to-face is better."

"Face-to-face is good when there is something to agree on," said Benton.

As his translator interpreted the response, Wen laughed.

"Let us agree generally," said Wu, translating Wen's response, "and agree on specifics later."

"President Wen, time is short. We need to be bold in the levels of emissions cuts we propose. If we can find a way of getting twenty to twenty-five percent in cuts, then we can really get somewhere." Benton paused, listening for Wen's response. He avoided looking at the others in the Oval Office. In giving specific numbers, Benton had gone further than agreed or even discussed. "President Wen, this is necessary for both our countries. We need to agree on the kind of magnitude, the ballpark, and then our people can get down to details."

Wen's voice started up in Mandarin. A second later Wu translated. "First we should agree generally."

"Yes. Exactly. If you and I can agree generally right now on the magnitude of the cuts, then that pushes everything ahead. That's what we need. Can we agree that our people should be working on mutual cuts in the range of twenty to twenty-five percent?"

Benton waited tensely for Wen's response.

"I heard that the difficult situation in your . . . in Montana was resolved with little bloodshed today."

Benton frowned at the jump in subject. "Yes."

"I am glad."

"Thank you. I appreciate your saying that. It was a difficult time, but our forces did a fine job and I'm proud of them. But to come back to—"

"We sometimes have difficulties as well. Sometimes we also are called upon to act inside our own country."

Benton didn't reply to that. "President Wen, I want to come back to what I was saying. Can we agree on what we should be doing?"

"Of course. First we must meet face-to-face, then comes trust. I met President Gartner a number of times."

Benton didn't know what to say in response. He glanced at Larry Olsen. Olsen shook his head emphatically. He cut his hand crisply through the air. This wasn't going anywhere. Wen wasn't going to be drawn. Anything else Benton said would just create a hostage for the future.

Benton tried again. Wen wouldn't be drawn.

"We must talk more often," said Benton eventually.

"I agree," said President Wen.

"This is very useful."

"Yes."

There was silence in the Oval Office after Benton put down the phone.

"Have you ever heard such crap?" exploded Olsen. "Comparing our action at Whitefish to some of their dirty internal repression?"

"He didn't necessarily mean that," said Ball.

"He damn well did. You watch, that'll come back at us. Next time we say something about their repression, they'll start yelling about Whitefish."

"You don't give them credit for anything."

"Don't I? Well, we're not getting any proposals from them, that's for sure. Wen's just going to sit."

"We should go meet him," said Ball.

"Yeah, right."

There was silence again.

Joe Benton was frowning, staring at the phone. He felt somewhat troubled now for having said as much as he had. Suddenly, as he spoke to his Chinese counterpart, it had occurred to him that he could cut through everything by throwing out the numbers. Yet it had had no effect. The other leader was obviously willing to sit back and wait. Now Benton wondered whether he had made a mistake. He had revealed something, and the other man hadn't, and that didn't feel right.

Or maybe it wasn't so bad. The numbers weren't a secret. At some point, Wen had to know them.

And yet, it did feel unbalanced.

Benton looked up at the others. "I don't think that did any harm, right? I don't think that set us back."

Oliver Wu thought it was unlikely that President Wen himself sanctioned the leak to the press.

"It makes you lose too much face, Mr. President. The contracts, that's one thing. Only we know what the connection is. It's a strong public act, but it gives you room to back down privately. It's different if you have to back down from something in public, that's when you lose face. At this stage, I don't think Wen would want that to happen. It would make you harder for him to deal with later, if he wants to, because you'll lack credibility. Making your opponent lose face is always a two-edged sword. Wen would be very sensitive to all of this. Losing face is probably a more powerful weapon in his mind than it is in yours."

Benton smiled ruefully. "I don't know about that."

"Also, the Chinese press has barely mentioned it since the leak happened. That's another important indicator. If Wen was really using this to make you lose face, it would be everywhere."

Jackie Rubin wasn't sure they needed to be thinking only about Wen. "Someone else over there could have leaked it, couldn't they?"

"True, but what would they have had to gain?" said Wu. "If it's someone else in the upper echelons of the party, then this isn't about us. It's about them and their position in the party. That's not to say they wouldn't use it, because they would. But I've gone through all the likely instigators—Ding, Zhai, Xuan, Ma, Li, even Chou—and I don't see what it does to build anyone's position. If someone in the Standing Committee had come out and said there's no risk of anything, then, yes, it makes sense to plant that question in a news conference with the president, for example, to discredit him. But no one's said that, at least not publicly. There's no context for this. Without context, without some kind of relationship to the ground on which power is being struggled for, a leak has no value."

"What if it's designed to create context?" said Eales. "It might be a first step. Next thing they might leak that we've been meeting with Chen."

"Then they'd be attacking Wen."

"That's possible, isn't it?"

"Yes, sir. But this is a very roundabout way of doing it. I'd expect to see more context first. I could also be wrong on the first count. Maybe Wen does want the president to lose face. That's possible for reasons we don't understand. I'm not ruling it out. I just don't see it as being high on the list of probabilities, and there was nothing in the conversation with Wen that even hinted at it."

"So what are we saying?" said the president. "The leak didn't come from the Chinese side?"

"I think what Oliver's saying," said Larry Olsen, "is that it's probably not Wen, and if it's not Wen, and yet if it did come from within the party, and yet without any context, it's a reflection of an internal tension that's too subtle for us to see right now. So we should come back to what we need to decide today, which is what we do now."

Benton agreed. What he wanted out of this meeting was a conclusion, even if only a preliminary one, about what should be done next.

"Go ahead, Larry," he said.

Olsen glanced at him. Benton knew what was in that look. Inevitably, there was a residue left from his accusation about the leak.

"Go ahead," said Benton again.

"There's a number of things. First, we haven't done anything since those contracts were given away. That's almost three weeks ago now. Second, this thing comes out about Miami going underwater, and we don't say anything except that we support the Kyoto process and a multilateral approach. Third, Mr. President, you talk to Wen and he won't engage on anything but setting up a meeting. I think he thinks you're backing down."

"Or that we're going to start using a more conventional approach," said Alan Ball pointedly.

"That's not how they'll be looking at it. They think we're beat. That's what they'll be saying to themselves."

"Thank you, Larry," said the president. "You've made yourself clear. Dr. Wu?"

"I agree with the secretary, Mr. President."

"We know they're not sending Chen back with anything," said Olsen. "That much is clear. So where are we? We make a noise, they call our bluff. Now what?"

"Sanctions, right?" said Ball impatiently.

"I'm sorry, Alan, but if not, they really have called our bluff. They win. Fine. Just so long as I know. I'll go put this file at the bottom of the pile and see if I can bring peace to the Congo."

"Mr. President," said Ball. "Wen invited you again to come to Beijing. Why not build trust in the way he says?"

"Sure," muttered Olsen. "Let him give us a banquet in the Great Hall and prevaricate for another year."

"I have a suggestion," said Ben Hoffman. "Why doesn't Larry go?"

"When?" said Eales.

"Now. As soon as he can. It just seems to me there's an awful amount of uncertainty. For one thing, we don't know what Chen's been saying to Wen. Even after your conversation, sir, we don't really know what Wen's trying to say to us. Why don't we go find out? If going to meet President Wen yourself is too big a thing, Mr. President, then let's get Larry to go."

"Wen won't talk to me," said Olsen.

"You can talk to their foreign minister, though, can't you?"

"I don't know if Chou's in the loop. He's got no power."

"He's not the only one you'll meet, right?" said Eales.

Olsen frowned. "What's the message here? They blow us off on the contracts, the president calls Wen. Wen doesn't give him anything, so I come supplicating. What are we trying to say to them?"

The president smiled slightly. He didn't see Larry Olsen supplicating to anyone.

"What's the message?" said Olsen again.

"No message," said Hoffman.

Olsen shook his head.

"You're just going to talk," said Eales. "Larry, they know we care about this. They know we want action. It's no secret."

"They'll see it as weakness."

"You already said they think we're beat. How much more weakness can we show?"

"John's right," said the president. "Larry, I don't see what we've got to lose here. You said yourself, they think we're beat. If we're going to show them otherwise, we're really going to have to do something. So before we take some kind of action, if that's what we're going to have to do, don't you think it makes sense to try to gather a little more information? Wen might meet you. If not Wen, Chou. Chou might be in the loop."

"Mr. President . . ."

Benton smiled. "Dr. Wu, you don't need to put our hand up."

Wu nodded quickly. "Sorry, sir. Well, in my opinion, the secretary's right. Our going there will be seen as weakness. It will be seen as supplication. That's a very bad way to be perceived from the Chinese political perspective."

"Then we just have to be prepared to follow it up with action. I like this approach. Alan?"

Ball shrugged. "It's better than slapping on sanctions and getting into a trade war."

"How long would it take to organize?"

There was silence from Olsen.

"It could be quick," said Wu. "A couple of weeks if Chou's agreeable."

"Larry? What are your thoughts?" The president watched him. Even if Olsen didn't want to do it, maybe he should. In fact, maybe it was important he did it *because* he didn't want to. It was about time, Joe Benton thought, that he saw Larry Olsen carry out an action that wasn't his own idea. If he couldn't do that, perhaps Alan Ball was right. Perhaps there really was no place for him in the administration.

He glanced at Ball. Ball, who had hardly looked at Olsen during the discussion, was watching him expectantly.

"Larry?" said Benton.

Olsen frowned. "Let me think about it."

Tuesday, April 26

Zhongnanhai Government Complex, Beijing

Lights flashed as the photographers snapped their shots. Olsen's visit had commenced the previous evening with a banquet hosted by Foreign Minister Chou. Now, at ten o'clock in the morning, Larry Olsen was sitting opposite Chou at a table in one of the meeting rooms of the massive government complex off Tiananmen Square. Along his side of the table were another dozen people, including Elisabeth Dean, the undersecretary for China at the State Department, and Alvin Finkler, the U.S. ambassador to Beijing. An equal number of Chinese officials were drawn up opposite.

They had an hour planned at the table, then ninety minutes in smaller groups to discuss a number of agreed issues. During this time, Olsen would confer with Chou. In the afternoon, more discussions were scheduled. Olsen would meet Zhai Ming, the premier, and Ma Guangen, the vice premier. A twenty-minute slot was also penciled in for a meeting with President Wen, but the Chinese side had been clear that this was unconfirmed and should not be released to the press as part of the scheduled agenda. That would end the official element of the secretary of state's stay. In the evening there would be drinks with members of the Beijing American chamber of commerce before dinner as guest of honor with the Association of American Universities in China. The following morning Olsen was scheduled to have breakfast with a group of selected CEOs before leaving for Tokyo, where he would spend twenty-four hours before heading back to the States.

The photographers were ushered out of the room. Chou spoke. The Chinese foreign minister was a native Shanghainese speaker and Olsen found his Mandarin hard to follow. He gave up concentrating and focused on the translation of Oliver Wu, who was sitting on his left. Chou was expressing his hopes for a successful meeting. Olsen responded. An interpreter sitting behind Chou translated Olsen's words. "This is our first meeting," concluded Olsen. "I appreciate your hospitality, Minister Chou. Let's make sure we get off to a good start."

There were smiles and nods all round.

They headed into the agenda. Olsen had asked Dr. Dean to lead the discussion. The man sitting beside Chou, the director general for North America in the Chinese foreign ministry, did most of the talking on the other side. The topics were ones that would have been on the agenda of almost any U.S.-China bilateral in the past two decades: trade, Korea, energy security, various regional affairs. Off the agenda were ones that were listed publicly only at times of tension between the two countries: Taiwan, free access to the Internet, human rights, the U.S. military presence in Colombia, which the Chinese side raised whenever the U.S. raised human rights. Those were the things Olsen would get to with Chou in private.

The meeting broke into groups. Chou and Olsen, together with their interpreters and an aide on each side, were ushered into another meeting room. This time they sat in armchairs. Tea and coffee were brought.

"Can we get you something else, Secretary?" asked Chou in English.

"Coffee's fine, thank you," said Olsen. The young woman who had brought it in served them. She served tea to the others and left.

"Mr. Secretary, I am very glad to have this opportunity to get to know you," said Chou.

"Likewise, Minister," said Olsen. He had met Chou briefly at a couple of diplomatic functions but had never spoken with him at length. Chou Yongyue had a reputation as a prickly, long-winded character who was quick to react to anything he perceived as a slight toward China or the party.

"There are some things I would like to discuss with you."

"Please," said Olsen.

Chou switched into Mandarin. He started talking about the case of a Chinese student who was in prison someplace in Kentucky. Olsen hadn't been briefed. All he could say was he'd look into it. Chou took an envelope containing the details from his aide and handed it across. Sounded like the kind of thing you'd normally deal with at embassy level. Chou was probably going on about it to preempt the human rights conversation which he knew was coming.

Olsen turned to his own aide and was passed a sheet with the details of the latest group of detainees, mostly cyberdissidents and environmental campaigners, whose cases the United States wanted to raise. Chou took the list with a fatalistic expression and listened as Olsen detailed the president's concern for action on these cases.

"We would very much like not to have to continually make such representations, Foreign Minister."

"Then don't make them," said Chou in English.

"We are committed to supporting the process of democratization wherever we feel it is possible. This has been the policy of the United States government since as far back as President Truman, and this administration takes that responsibility seriously. We will help in any way that we can."

"The government of the People's Republic does not require the help of the United States in this," replied Chou in Mandarin. The translator, a young woman, spoke in flawless, American-accented English.

"What help does it require from the United States?" asked Olsen.

Chou smiled. "That is a friendly question."

"We are all friends, I hope, Foreign Minister."

"I hope so, Mr. Secretary."

"Do you have an answer? President Benton would only be too pleased to know."

Chou passed the list to the note taker. "I have taken note."

"Can I tell President Benton anything specific?"

"My government is concerned at the continuing occupation of Colombian territory by military forces of the United States. China cannot support the occupation by one country of another sovereign country's territory."

Olsen sighed. They were going to have to go through the charade of talking over the Colombian intervention, as if the Chinese government really cared.

Chou then proceeded to give a rundown of the history of the U.S. involvement in Colombia since President Shawcross's decision to send troops. Olsen responded by pointing out certain discrepancies between Chou's version and reality. He also pointed out that President Benton had met with President Lobinas, the Colombian leader, only a week previously in Washington, and President Lobinas had reaffirmed his support for the Cartagena Points, which outlined the objectives of the American intervention. Chou responded by saying that the Cartagena Points required modification. "Mr. Secretary," he said, "I advise you that we will continue to call for this in international forums, and the progress of relations between our two countries cannot be divorced from this. Nor from the stand of the United States towards the province of Taiwan. Since this is our first meeting, I would like to make clear the position of the government of the People's Republic of China on this matter."

It was one of the clearest positions in the whole world, but that wasn't going to stop Chou laying it out, which he did, over most of the next hour, going all the way back to the surrender of Japanese forces at the end of the Second World War and progressing methodically through every twist and turn in the saga, including the U.S. Congress's Taiwan Relations Act of 1979, the Four Communiqués, and the Manila Understanding of 2017, which set out ceiling levels of PRC troop, naval, and air deployments in the three provinces facing Taiwan and in the Taiwan Strait. He lingered particularly over the Manila Understanding, lambasting it for its manifest unfairness and the sheer impossibility of maintaining its conditions. Part history lesson, part polemic. The Chou treatment, as it was known to foreign ministers around the world. Everyone had to experience it, at least once. At the end of it, their time together was almost up.

"There's one more thing I'd like to raise," said Olsen.

Chou stared back at him blankly.

"Foreign Minister, shall we have a moment in private?"

"If you wish," said Chou. He glanced at his interpreter and note taker and gestured to the door. Oliver Wu and Olsen's aide left as well.

"Foreign Minister, I would like to discuss carbon emissions," said Olsen in English.

Chou looked at him as blankly as before. "What is to discuss, Mr. Secretary?"

Olsen hesitated. "Are you satisfied with the Kyoto process?" he asked cautiously.

"The Kyoto process throughout its history has been extremely unfair to developing economies," replied Chou, giving the standard response.

"In which you include the Chinese economy, I suppose?"

"Of course."

"Even though your GDP is now greater than that of the United States."

"With 1.6 billion people to feed, Mr. Secretary. How many mouths in the United States?"

Olsen nodded. He didn't want to get bogged down on that. He tried again. "And apart from the Kyoto process?"

"Mr. Secretary, what is there apart from the Kyoto process?"

Was that a question, wondered Olsen, or an answer?

There was silence.

Olsen was aware of Chou watching him expectantly.

"What is it specifically that you wish to discuss, Mr. Secretary?"

"I want to be sure our two countries will work together to deal with this. I'd like to be sure that this is as high a priority to the government of the People's Republic as it is to the government of the United States."

Chou shrugged. "The developmental stage of each country must be taken into account. When the United States, the EuroCore and the other developed economies accept their responsibility in this, then the Chinese government will do all in its power to achieve a just agreement for this problem."

Olsen gazed at him. That was the standard line. There didn't seem to be any more, not a hint that anything at all was to be read into that statement beyond the actual words. Chou probably didn't even know about the negotiations that had been taking place in Washington. It was a waste of time having come here, thought Olsen, or at least having talks with Chou. He had no power in the hierarchy.

"Is there something else?" said Chou.

"No," said Olsen.

Chou got up. "Come, Mr. Secretary, let us have lunch."

Afterward Olsen had meetings with Zhai and then Ma, each of which Chou attended. Of the leading figures in the party, Olsen knew Zhai best, having worked with him in the negotiations for the establishment of the UN's permanent peacekeeping force years earlier. They had spent plenty of long, bleary nights on opposite sides of negotiation tables. More rarely, on the same side. They greeted each other like old friends.

The discussions were superficial. Ma said nothing when Olsen raised Kyoto. Zhai came out with Chou's line, although delivered in a more amicable manner. Olsen got Zhai alone for ten minutes as they walked from one room to another, dropping back behind the pack of officials, and still there was nothing. They were giving him a united front. It was Kyoto or nothing. And Kyoto, of course, weak and unenforceable as it was, was tragically unfair to China.

The last item on the schedule was the meeting with Wen. Twenty minutes. Five minutes photo op, fifteen minutes talk. But you could say a lot in fifteen minutes, Olsen knew. Sometimes it was only one or two sentences that mattered.

Chou and Olsen, accompanied by Ambassador Finkler, Elisabeth Dean and the whole entourage from both sides, walked down a red-carpeted corridor toward a meeting room. The first thing Olsen noticed when the door opened was that no press was there. Hui, the vice president of China, was waiting for him. Hui was nothing but a figurehead. Olsen saw someone else beside him. Ding.

Hui started to speak. An interpreter began speaking almost simultaneously.

"Secretary Olsen, please accept President Wen's deepest apologies. He is unable to meet you today and has asked me to humbly express his regrets." Hui came forward to shake Olsen's hand.

"Please tell President Wen that I appreciate his sending you, Vice President Hui, in his place."

"No one can take the place of President Wen, Mr. Secretary," said Ding.

There were smiles at the remark.

Ding came forward to shake Olsen's hand as well. "President Wen also asked me to send his apologies."

"Thank you, Minister Ding."

"Let us sit," said Hui, gesturing to four armchairs, behind which stood two upright chairs for the interpreters.

They sat. Chou occupied the fourth armchair. The others in the entourage stood at the other end of the room.

"President Wen would like to know whether your meetings have been fruitful," said Hui.

"Very fruitful," replied Olsen. "Although it is a great disappointment not to be able to meet President Wen."

"Yes," said Hui.

"Still," said Ding, "many photographers would be with us now if President Wen was here. We could not have this quiet talk."

"The photographers would go," said Olsen.

"Yes," said Ding, "but the press is sometimes troublesome, don't you think?"

"I guess that's the price we pay."

"Such an irritation," said Hui, and he laughed.

There was no sign of humor on Ding's face. "Sometimes the troublesome press is more than just an irritation, wouldn't you agree, Secretary Olsen?"

Olsen gazed at Ding, wondering why he was pushing the point. "A free press is an important part of any democracy, Minister Ding," he said carefully. "The irritation we sometimes feel with it is a price worth paying."

"I think President Benton was irritated some weeks ago with the press, is that not so?"

Olsen didn't reply. He watched Ding intently.

"President Wen sends his regrets that that occurred. He takes no satisfaction in this."

Olsen glanced at Chou. The foreign minister was looking at Ding without any sign of particular interest on his face. Hui's look was similarly unrevealing.

Olsen turned back to Ding. "As I said, the occasional irritation from the press is a price worth paying."

Ding nodded. "As you say, Mr. Secretary."

"President Benton hopes there will soon be greater cooperation between our government and yours," said Olsen.

"Yes," said Hui, smiling. "Our governments must cooperate."

"President Wen would like you to pass on his words to President Benton," said Ding. "He asked me to tell you this. It is important to him."

Ding was watching him closely. Olsen nodded. "Tell President Wen that I certainly will."

Wednesday, April 27

United States Embassy, Tokyo

It was midnight in Tokyo, eleven a.m. in Washington. Larry Olsen was on the secure connection to the president, highest level of encryption, and Alan Ball and John Eales were listening in. The president asked Olsen to tell him once again what Ding had said.

"So it was one of Wen's guys who leaked?" said Eales. "One of his guys leaked and now he's saying sorry."

"Not necessarily," said Olsen. "Wen's saying he's sorry it happened. He's not saying he's sorry he did it. Mr. President, we don't know whether Wen's admitting some kind of responsibility, but what seems clear is he didn't want to see you put on the spot. Even if the leak didn't come from them, he's saying he's sorry if you were embarrassed. He takes no satisfaction from that, to use Ding's words."

"And is that good?" asked Benton.

"I think so. It means he's not treating you as an enemy. Your enemy, you want him to be humiliated. When you have a friend, you don't want him to lose face. If he loses face, it's hard for you to be his friend even if you want to be. So that's good."

John Eales glanced at the president. "It could be a lie."

"What was that, John?" said Olsen from Tokyo. "I didn't catch it."

"I said it could be a lie. Wen could have been happy to see us humiliated, if that's what he thinks happened. He might be telling us he wasn't so he can set us up again."

"I don't have that feeling, John."

"So you take it at face value?"

Olsen laughed. He didn't take anything at face value. "I think what Wen's saying here is, there was obviously a moment of embarrassment for the president—maybe he knows how it happened, maybe he doesn't—but anyway, he's sorry it happened, and he doesn't want us to think that he either engineered it or feels that he benefited from it. As we noted at the time, Mr. President, the Chinese press made very little of it, which is consistent. I think the message must have gone out from the government pretty damn quickly that this thing wasn't meant to be covered."

Benton was silent for a moment. "So where does that leave us?"

"Well, it looks like Wen is managing this himself," said Olsen. "That's number one. Number two, he's saying he's not trying to hurt you in public."

"Who else knows?" asked Benton.

"From what they said to me yesterday, none of them. Not even Zhai broke ranks. I gave him an opening, but he didn't say a thing."

"Larry, that's not possible, is it?" said Eales.

"No, I don't think so. Some of them must know."

"Ding?"

"He might not. Wen could have just told him to say what he said to me. He would have said it."

"How do we know Wen told him?" said Ball. "It might have been his own idea."

"He said it in front of Hui and Chou. If Wen didn't tell him, it'd get back to him."

Benton wondered if the way Wen was handling this made him vulnerable. "If he hasn't shared it with Zhai or Chou, but he has, say, with Ding, where does that leave him? What if one of them finds out?"

In Tokyo, Olsen rolled his eyes. "Mr. President, I do not think you want to go playing Chinese party leaders off against each other. That's a minefield. You don't want to even take a step into that."

"But it's something to keep up our sleeve, right?"

"Up our sleeve, Mr. President. A long way up our sleeve."

"All right." Joe Benton glanced at Eales and smiled. Scaring Larry Olsen wasn't something you could do every day. "Incidentally, where are the Japanese on the Kurils?"

The dispute between Russia and Japan over the lower Kuril Islands dated back to the Second World War, when the U.S.S.R. took control of the territory. It flared periodically between the two countries and had come to the fore again in the past year with a series of incursions by Japanese fishing vessels into the area. Japan was angling to get the islands back, and Olsen knew before he arrived in Tokyo that he was going to be pushed for U.S. support.

"Honosawa gave me a solid half hour today on how it was time for Japan to have them back and it was the historic responsibility of the U.S. to help."

Eales snorted "What did you say?"

"I gave him a solid half hour back along the lines of how he should take a look at what happened in the ten years before they lost the Kurils before they start talking about historic responsibility. We've definitely got some leverage there. But even if we helped them on the Kurils, whether the Japanese would put their relationship with China at risk by coming in with us on sanctions, I think that's another question. Anyway, Russia's the better choice for us. I'd trade the Kurils for Russian energy sanctions any day."

So would Benton. If they did get to the point of launching sanctions against China, Russian support would be crucial, and it didn't take a foreign policy expert to figure it out. The Russian republic supplied a third of China's oil needs and close to eighty percent of its gas.

Benton glanced at Alan Ball. His face was grim.

"All right," said the president, "we're getting way ahead of ourselves. This isn't about getting Russia to apply sanctions. Let's get back to Wen. Where are we, Larry? Summary. What have we learned, where do we stand?"

"The key thing, Mr. President, is like I said, it's personal with Wen. He's taking charge of the issue."

"And his view is?"

"That's harder to judge. When I hinted to Ding that we needed to work together better, there was nothing back."

"So what are you saying, Larry?" asked Eales.

"My sense is it's one of two things. One, Wen's happy. He's sitting pretty. He thinks he's got us beat, and he's just waiting to get the call saying the president's coming over in September. Two, alternatively, he's still pretty happy, but he doesn't know what to do with what he's got."

"Which presupposes he wants to do more," said Eales.

"That's right. If he does, he probably feels he's won the first round, but now, having won it, he's not sure how he gets to the second. Or even what the second round looks like. He's probably waiting for us to show him."

"I can let him think he won the first round," said Benton. "I can live with that."

"I disagree, sir. Letting him think he's won anything is a bad idea."

Alan Ball muttered something about the stupidity of people who tried to win every battle when it might cost them the war.

"Sorry, Al," said Olsen. "I didn't catch that."

"Larry, I don't care how we get to the second round," said Benton, "as long as we get there."

"We don't know Wen's even looking for a second."

"So what *do* we know?" Joe Benton's impatience was getting the better of him. "You know, I'm giving an interview this afternoon for my first hundred days. And on this issue, I don't think we know any more about what we're doing than we did the day I was sworn in. We don't have a proposal. We don't have a negotiating partner. We don't even know whether Wen wants to talk. That's a *hundred* days gone. For nothing."

"With respect, sir," said Olsen, "I think we've learned an enormous amount. It's what we do with it now."

"Hell's bells, Larry! If we learn this much again over the next hundred days we won't even know what our own names are."

Benton shook his head in exasperation. He had spent a solid chunk of the previous afternoon rehearsing for the hundredth-day interview, with Cindy Ravic, one of Jodie Ames's aides, playing the role of Emmy Peterson, the NewsLog interviewer who was going to be conducting the interview. Of all the questions Cindy had thrown at him, only one—in all the variants Cindy had tried—kept resonating in his mind after the rehearsal was over. What mistakes had he made? What had he learned? What would he do differently? He could answer it—it was easy enough to give an impression of thoughtfulness and humility without admitting anything specific that could be used against him. Jodie Ames had given him a half-dozen sound bites to throw in for good measure. And yet it had stuck with him, made him think, because that really was the question. If the hundred-day milestone meant anything, it was because it was a time to sit back and reflect. What had he learned? What would he do differently?

He glanced at John Eales. "John," he said, after Ball had left, "there's something I think we should do."

John Eales tapped on his handheld, and a slide came up on the screen.

"Our involvement in this began November fifteenth, when President Gartner invited the president and myself to see him outside D.C."

Eales clicked again. A new slide came up. Over the next ten minutes, he ran through every step in the chronology that had brought them to this point in the process with the Chinese government. At the end he had a numbered summary slide.

"One," he said, "we used Gartner's channel. Two, we confined knowledge of the situation to a small subgroup in the administration. Three, we took off the table the offers Gartner had made in the past, including the final one that the Chinese side claimed, probably falsely, was still under consideration. Four, we demanded a proposal from the Chinese government. Five, we turned down a suggestion for a presidential visit in September. Six, when a proposal wasn't forthcoming from the Chinese side, we threatened sanctions, although we ourselves hadn't decided what sanctions we might impose and in fact we hadn't made an explicit decision that we were going to follow through and actually use them. Seven, when the Chinese responded by awarding business contracts to European competitors, we made no direct response. Eight, later, as an indirect response, we spoke to Wen without having a definite program or demand in mind. Nine, as an extension of that indirect response, we sent the secretary of state to Beijing to see whether we could get a better insight into Wen's perspective, and learned only that Wen claims not to have wanted to see the president embarrassed by the press leak about the emissions data. The thing with the leak, we don't know where it came from, and our feeling is it probably wasn't from the Chinese, or if it was, it was a mistake. So I'm setting that aside. Those are the nine key decisions we took. I'm not saying any of them was right or wrong, but that's how we got to where we are."

Eales sat down. The slide with the nine points remained on the screen.

"I asked John to summarize those steps," said the president, "because I want us to question them. If we accept that where we are today is not the best place, I want us to think through each of those steps and understand where we might have acted differently, whether we should have acted differently, and what that means for what we do from now. If we made mistakes, it's crucial that we identify them and learn from them before we go any further."

"Well, it's clear," said Olsen immediately, "We haven't taken any action. We were okay until seven, but you can't threaten something and then not do anything, especially if the other side comes back and does something first. After seven, we lost it."

The president let that stand. He waited for someone else to speak.

"With respect, John," said Alan Ball, ignoring Olsen's remarks, "I think you've missed a point. We made a decision to go the bilateral route rather than bringing this into the open. That's a crucial decision and it isn't on your summary. You start from where we decide to use Gartner's channel, but prior to that a decision was made to continue bilateral and secret negotiations."

"Alan's right," said Benton. "That was our first decision."

Eales picked up his handheld and typed the point in at the top of the slide. There was a moment of levity as he struggled to get the points to renumber.

"Mr. President," said Ball, "if we're trying to be genuinely open, if we're going to question what we've done, we have to question that as well."

"Go ahead," said Benton.

Alan Ball laid out the case for looking for a solution within the Kyoto framework. It was still possible to bring the scientific data into the public domain—the leak might turn out to be a blessing in disguise, preparing the way for the release of extreme projections. Even if information about the negotiations with Chen then leaked, these could be pitched as preliminary discussions. Why not come out into the open now, releasing the data and affirming commitment to the Kyoto process? It could all be done around the meeting that had been arranged beween the president and Secretary-General Nleki in New York in May.

Larry Olsen snorted. "I wish we were living in the kind of fantasy world Alan thinks is out there."

"Larry, what's your argument?" said the president sharply.

Olsen laid it out. In essence, it hadn't changed from the argument he had presented the first time Benton met him. It was based on the likelihood of achieving a meaningful result in a multilateral forum, compared with the ability to use a bilateral result between the two key global players to unlock the rest of the world.

"Larry's position is as much fantasy as mine," said Ball. "He's assuming you can pressure the Chinese bilaterally. Go do it! Surely you've got more chance pressuring them with the rest of the world lined up behind you."

"Go get the rest of the world lined up first," retorted Olsen. "*That's* the point. Look, Alan, in the end we both want the same thing—an agreement with everyone. We both agree China's key to that, both as the world's largest polluter and its largest economy. All we really differ on here is which step comes first and which comes second. Do you do the deal with China, and believe that will make everyone else follow, or do you do the deal with everyone else, and believe China will follow?"

"No. Don't misrepresent what I'm saying. China wouldn't be following. It would be part of the deal with everyone."

"You can't regard China as just another country." Olsen turned to the president. "On this issue, there are two countries everyone watches, us and them. No one's going to move an inch unless they believe we're both in. Now, given that we're in, I say it's got to be China first, and then everyone else follows. Alan's saying it's everyone else first, and then China follows. I say we've had thirty years trying the route of getting everyone to do a meaningful deal and stick to it. Hasn't worked. What's changed this time round?"

"Our level of commitment," said Eales.

"True. But it's going to take ten years to demonstrate that, ten years before anyone believes it. We don't have ten years."

"Well, we've tried what you're suggesting," said Ball. "Look where that's got us."

"No, we haven't tried what I'm suggesting! That's exactly it, Alan. We haven't carried through." Olsen pointed forcefully at the screen. "Step seven—sorry, it's eight now—after step eight, we back down. The president asked why we find ourselves in the position we're in. That's it right there. Round one, Wen outplays us. He was smarter. He was quicker. He was prepared to act and he knew where we'd hurt. So far, we're all talk. That's why we are where we are, not because the strategy is wrong."

"Excuse me," said Jackie Rubin. "I'd like to say something. We're forgetting the domestic program here. Instinctively, I agree with Alan—although I agree with Larry that we haven't carried through the game plan we started with, so it's difficult to judge whether it could work. But even though I'm inclined to agree with Alan, if we turn around now and come out with these projections and raise the Relocation number from ten million to, say, thirty million, everything stops. Every one of our bills. People just aren't going to know what we're saying anymore. What *are* we saying? Are we saying New Foundation is enough? Is there going to be more? Is it the end or the start?"

"We're going to paralyze the process," said Ben Hoffman.

"Absolutely. Paralyze it. We agreed on that right at the start and in retrospect I think that was the right call. If anything, it's even more true now."

Benton was glad Jackie had raised the point, because it was what he believed as well. He wanted to see if he would hear it from somewhere else.

He glanced questioningly at Alan Ball.

Ball threw up his hands. "I'm here to advise you on national security policy, Mr. President. Your domestic program is outside my remit."

Larry Olsen smiled.

The president looked back at the screen. It seemed to him there was agreement in the room on the conclusion to be drawn , or at least as much agreement as he would ever get with Alan Ball and Larry Olsen sitting at the same table. "If we look at this road map, and if we accept that decision one was right—and I accept, Alan, that was a distinct decision and it's open to question, and I know you would still question it—then the problem is we didn't take action after step eight. Is that right? Does anyone disagree? Alan, is that correct in your view?"

Ball nodded grudgingly. "If you believe in the bilateral approach," he muttered. "That's a big if."

"Agreed. Let's set that aside." Benton paused. "So what's it going to take? If Wen genuinely opposes this, what kind of action will bring him into line? Here's what I don't understand. How can he be against this? How can he honestly not want to do a deal on this? Maybe we went out too belligerent, and he figured he had to do something to show we're not in charge, but now he's done that. How can he not want to do a deal now?"

"Maybe he does," said Jackie Rubin.

"He hasn't shown it. He's just sitting back. This isn't a zero sum game. It's not we win, they lose. If we don't do something, this is a disaster for everyone. How can the leader of any country who understands that not want to do a deal?" The president glanced in the direction of Oliver Wu. "I know what you're going to say, Dr. Wu. It's China, China continues, and the pain they can take outlasts anything we can take, so they'll let the pain begin and then we'll be the ones who fold. But is that still true? I may not be a China expert, but I question that. They have a middle class, they have an economy, this isn't the China of Deng Xiaoping coming off the back of the Cultural Revolution. You told me yourself they have a serious problem with a democracy movement and an environmental movement, both of which pose threats to the party hegemony, and don't tell me the kind of pain we're talking about isn't going to make that worse. Now, I can't see how any kind of leader isn't going to say, let's deal with this in an orderly fashion. Let's get to grips with it. That's the best way we have of securing ourselves."

"Not if the solution causes instability," said Olsen.

"Well, maybe it does cause a little instability."

"And if it does," said Olsen, "it does it now. Whereas the issues we're talking about don't do it for maybe twenty years. And in the meantime, if we resist—I'm talking as the Chinese side here, on the extreme side, Ding for example—if we resist and the big bad Americans try to force a solution, we're seen as the victim and we're standing up for our rights and we use the nationalist argument to strengthen our hold, as the party, and to create a context in which we can clamp down on those elements that are destabilizing us. Mr. President, we've been through this."

"But we don't *know*."

"No, we don't know. There's always stuff you don't know. That's the nature of the game."

The president closed his eyes. "I cannot believe a leader would do that. I can't believe he'd be prepared to do so much damage to his own people."

He looked up. Olsen was watching him skeptically. The others were watching him as well. "Am I being naive?"

Olsen threw back his hands, as if it wasn't for him to answer.

"Alan?"

Ball shrugged.

He looked at Wu.

"That's not a word I'd really use . . ."

"To my face you mean." Benton smiled ruefully. "Huh?"

"I don't know. I'm . . . sorry, sir."

There was silence. Benton understood that no one else around the table, at least not the foreign policy experts, shared his incredulity.

"It seems to me there are two possibilities here," said John Eales. "One is that Wen doesn't understand what we're dealing with, or what he was being offered by Gartner, or he doesn't believe it. Possibly he hasn't even had it presented to him properly, since we've got no idea what Chen actually said to him. And the other possibility is, he does understand it and, yes, he's doing what Larry says he's doing, and might even end up using it as an instrument to deal with domestic political problems."

"Or he does know, and he does want to do a deal, but he's constrained," said Wu. "With respect, Mr. Eales, that's a third possibility. He may not have the power on this we think he has."

"Then if we take some kind of action, that just makes it worse for him, doesn't it?"

"Not necessarily," said Wu. "It might empower him by discrediting the people who are constraining him."

"This is just great!" Benton shook his head in frustration. He thought American politics was complex, and it was. He was constrained on all sides, and nothing significant got through Congress without its share of pork barreling. With all the legislation he was sending to the Hill, he was up to *here* in that stuff. But at least he understood it. It even had a kind of transparency. But this . . . this was surreal. This was straight out of Kafka. "There must be an alternative to confrontation," he said.

Olsen shrugged. "There is if we back down."

"I'm not backing down. The United States can't do the cuts in emissions for the whole world, and no one else will join us if China doesn't. So

China has to do it, that's a given. But I'm not prepared at this stage to do something that creates an irreversible step that puts us in confrontation. Now, we agree it's possible that President Wen doesn't know all the facts, or that he doesn't understand the implications. I'm not saying that's definite. I'm not saying he isn't using this for domestic purposes or that he's not constrained. But I'm saying we don't *know* that. It's possible that he doesn't know everything we think he knows. We just don't know enough."

Olsen watched the president skeptically.

"We don't know, objectively, what Chen told him," said Eales. "That's a fact, Larry."

"Chen's Wen's man."

"But we don't know what he told him."

"Before I take another step," said Benton, "I need to be sure, exactly, what Wen's been told. I'm not going to escalate on the basis of a false premise." Benton looked directly at Olsen. "This isn't prevarication, Larry. I'm just not going to be irresponsible."

Olsen shrugged, as if the thought that Benton was prevaricating had never entered his mind.

Benton glanced at Eales. Eales nodded slightly. The president turned back to Olsen and Ball.

"You two get together. Find me someone who can get to Wen. Someone you can agree on."

Monday, May 9

Oval Office, The White House

F. William Knight was sixty-eight, a silver-haired banker who had first gone to China as a young Morgan Stanley associate in the gold rush days of the nineties and had been there, more or less, ever since. During the financial crisis of 2013, he was one of the few respected Western voices in the country when party officials were blaming foreign banks for everything from the collapse of the stock market to the condition of the roads in downtown Beijing. At that time Wen Guojie, a young party leader and nephew of a former premier of China with a power base of his own in Shanghai, was given the post of finance minister and told to clean up the mess. Knight had known him for years. Wen gave Knight a desk in his office and for the next eighteen months they worked literally side by side. The fact that the Chinese banking system didn't disappear into the almost bottomless pit that had been dug for it by the failure to introduce adequate reforms over the previous decade was attributed to Wen and fuelled his subsequent rise to the top of the hierarchy. In reality, to the extent that any one man was responsible, it was F. William Knight.

Larry Olsen was with the president when Alan Ball brought Knight into the Oval Office. Ball, who knew the banker better than Olsen, did the introductions.

Knight was a tall man. Thin. Almost gaunt. The skin hung loose at his throat. Joe Benton wondered whether he was ill.

"I think Dr. Ball has explained something to you of what this is about," said the president when they were sitting.

"Some, Mr. President."

"Enough to get you to take the trouble of coming back from Shanghai. I thank you for that, Mr. Knight. I'm sure your time is scarce."

Knight nodded slightly.

"I want to ask you, Mr. Knight, about your relationship with President Wen. Perhaps you can give me a quick summary of the history."

Knight cleared his throat. "President Wen, as you know, had a background in . . ." He cleared his throat again, frowning as he did, as if there was something he couldn't quite get out of there. "Wen was always in the banking and the financial side, so I had quite a lot to do with him, probably from about 2003 or four. I first met him . . . this was before he was a minister, he was a vice president of the Bank of China at the time. I was senior vice president for Morgan Stanley, as it was then, for China. This was around the time when the first wave of foreign ownership was coming into the big four banks in China, you may remember, and of course Morgan Stanley was a player. And I would say, after that time, there would rarely have been more than a few weeks when I didn't meet Wen in one context or another."

"Tell me about 2013."

"Well, 2013 was something else." Knight gave the story of how he had worked with Wen.

"What about the Hong Kong massacre? Did Wen have anything to do with that?"

Knight closed his eyes briefly, as if being asked to look at something distasteful. "There was enormous repression across China in 2013 and fourteen, more than most people in the West knew about. To my knowledge, Wen wasn't directly involved. He was utterly focused on the financial issues at that point and, in fact, as far as Hong Kong goes, I remember him being totally incredulous because of what it would mean for the recovery."

"Slowing it, you mean?"

Knight nodded.

"And that was the only reason?"

"Wen Guojie is no more an advocate of massacre than you or I, Mr. President. But I concede there was a serious wave of repression at the time— I remember people saying it was the biggest crackdown since Tiananmen, and actually it extended quite a lot further, and certainly went on for longer—and I guess any senior party leader must have had some knowledge of that and at the minimum must have acquiesced. So I'm not trying to exonerate Wen Guojie. I'm just saying he had little direct responsibility, and in fact, given his role, repression, at least in Hong Kong, Shanghai, and the other financial centers, worked against what he was trying to achieve."

"I'm just trying to understand what his mindset might be," said the president.

Knight didn't reply.

"What about since then? After the crisis? What's your relationship?"

"I would say that Wen has always treated me as a private advisor on economic affairs. He'll receive his advice from his ministries and then he might call me in and we'll have a discussion. He rarely invites me to be present when there are officials around. The discussions we have, you understand, Mr. President, are quite informal. It's usually over a drink."

The president smiled. "What beverage does President Wen favor, as a matter of interest?"

"Single malts," said Knight.

"When you have these talks, does he do what you say?"

"Sometimes," said Knight. "The quality of his advisors has vastly improved over the years. His need for my input is far less than it was."

"Do you ever disagree with him?"

"Often," said Knight.

"Do you tell him that?"

"Of course. I doubt he would have asked my advice all these years if I didn't."

"Then he's a wise man," said the president.

Knight nodded.

"Tell me about him. What's he like?"

Knight frowned. He cleared his throat. "I regard him as a friend, sir. That's . . . pretty much all I would say."

Benton nodded. Nothing the banker had said until now couldn't have been discovered from other sources. Benton hadn't heard anything he hadn't already seen in the briefing on Knight that he had been given. Except the part about Wen favoring single malts, and that was probably well known, anyway.

"You don't want to say anymore?" said Benton.

"Not gratuitously, Mr. President. Friendship involves trust. Trust isn't a thing I take lightly."

Benton watched him.

"How can I put this, Mr. President?" Knight cleared his throat. "Any American businessman living in China for any length of time is almost certain to be approached by various agencies of our government. This complicates things enormously, as you can understand. I've always avoided entanglements. I'm sure the briefing you must have seen about me mentions this."

"President Wen knows this, I presume? That you avoid entanglements."

"I presume he does. I also presume he knows I'm here now, or will very soon."

"But you didn't tell him?"

"No, sir. I don't feel obliged to tell him about my activities, nor does he expect me to. As I said, we count each other as friends."

"And you don't think this is an entanglement, as you put it?"

"Not yet." Knight cleared his throat. "I didn't feel it was my place to refuse, sir. I'm an American citizen. It would be an act of unconscionable pride to refuse a request to speak to one's president."

The president gazed at F. William Knight. The other man was detached, controlled. He was a proud man, with a strong sense of honor. An act of unconscionable pride to refuse to speak to one's president, he had said. But possibly not to refuse to carry out one's president's request.

"Tell me something," said Joe Benton. "I'm curious. You've lived in China for . . ."

"Forty years, give or take."

"You care about China?"

"Of course. I've seen the country progress on every front. In my opinion it still has an enormous way to go, but if you compare the China of today to the China I found when I first went there in 1991, it's just not the same place."

"And you're proud of that. Proud of the contribution you've made."

"I think I have made a contribution. If I have, yes, I'm proud of it."

"So if it came to choosing between the United States and China, what would you do?"

Knight looked at the president, eyes slightly narrowed.

"Say it was a choice, Mr. Knight. I'm curious. How do you deal with something like that?"

The president waited. The security assessment on F. William Knight had been in the briefing Benton had been given, as Knight himself realized. The president knew that Knight had repelled so many advances from the CIA that the Agency had stopped trying. He also knew there was no evidence that Knight had ever worked in any covert way for the other side. It really must be very easy, thought Benton, to find oneself entangled, living the life F. William Knight had lived, with contacts reaching to the very top of the Chinese regime. To have avoided even the suggestion of such an entanglement over a period stretching forty years must have required exceptional, scrupulous care.

"That's a hypothetical question, Mr. President, and a very difficult one," said the banker at last. "Everything I've done to help China . . ." Knight cleared his throat. "I've always felt that a vibrant, prosperous China is a good thing for the United States. I've never felt there's been a conflict."

"I don't think anyone in this room would say there has been," replied the president. He paused, as if to give a chance for Olsen or Ball to dissent. "But what if there was, Mr. Knight? Sometimes circumstances can lead to that. You wouldn't be the first citizen with divided loyalties."

"Well . . ." Knight cleared his throat. "As I said, I haven't felt circumstances have lead to that until now."

"I'm not saying they have now either, by the way. On the contrary. I was just interested, that's all."

Knight nodded.

"Let's hope we never get to that point, huh?"

"Let's hope so, Mr. President."

The president smiled. He wasn't warming to F. William Knight. He found him cold, passionless. But if everything Ball and Olsen had said about the banker was correct, Knight had access to Wen. The only person outside Wen's closest circle in the party, perhaps, who could get thirty minutes with him alone. That far outweighed the question of whether he was likable or not. And he was trustworthy, the president could see that. Knight would certainly deliver a message, if he first agreed to do it.

"Mr. Knight, let me ask you straight out," said Benton. "If I asked you to deliver a message directly to President Wen on my behalf, would you be prepared to do it?"

"Why me, sir?"

The president smiled. "That's a fair question. We have, as you know, a vast hierarchy of people all dedicated to making contact with their Chinese counterparts. Yet, the funny thing is, it's very difficult to be sure that one is getting to President Wen himself. Almost impossible." The president paused. "As it is to me, I guess."

"Surely you'll be meeting President Wen," said Knight. "You'll be able to give him your message then."

"I would like to do it much sooner than that, Mr. Knight. Tomorrow, if I could. And much less publicly."

Knight cleared his throat. But he didn't reply.

"You're not comfortable with what I'm asking, Mr Knight?"

Knight didn't reply to that. "May I ask, Mr. President, have any attempts already been made to deliver this message to President Wen?"

"Yes."

"And you're sure the message didn't get through?"

"No, Mr. Knight, we're not sure of that. In fact we think the message did get through. What we don't know is what form it got through in."

"Have you reason to believe it was distorted in some way?"

"Mr. Knight, the issue we're talking about is of such gravity that I can't afford to take even the slightest chance that some kind of miscommunication has taken place. I need to be one hundred percent sure the message I am giving reaches President Wen in precisely the form I'm sending it. The whole message and nothing but the message. I'm sure you can understand the importance of that."

F. William Knight nodded.

"Let me assure you, Mr. Knight, in case that's what's worrying you, this is not something that pits the United States against China. On the contrary, this is very much a matter that is to our mutual benefit, one that's in the interest of the entire world."

Knight was silent.

"This is something that will hopefully mean that people like yourself, Mr. Knight, don't have to make that terrible choice we were talking about. Between one country and the other." Benton paused. Knight was gazing at the rug, a frown on his face. "You still don't look comfortable, Mr. Knight."

Knight shook his head. "I . . ." He cleared his throat. "I've always tried to avoid being caught in the middle. That happens to people in China all the time. That's how you lose your credibility."

It occurred to Joe Benton that the gaunt, silver-haired banker might really be about to turn him down. He glanced at Ball.

"Bill," said Alan Ball. "You've got forty years of credibility behind you. We both know that's not going to disappear overnight."

Knight shook his head, still staring at the rug. "I realize this must be important," he murmured. He cleared his throat.

Joe Benton wondered once again whether the other man was ill. He was agonizing over the decision, Benton could see that. He was really torn.

"Bill," said Alan Ball, "what's the point of all that credibility if you never get to use it? It's like money in the bank. At some point you've got to take it out and spend a little."

Knight looked at Alan Ball.

"Now's the time, Bill. If there ever was a time, trust me, this is it."

F. William Knight was silent for a moment. Then he turned to Benton and nodded. "All right, Mr. President. I'll do it."

Joe Benton leaned forward. "Now, you know, before we go any further, you have to be a hundred percent clear you're prepared to do it. You can still say no, Mr. Knight. I want you to be clear. You're making a commitment."

"I realize that, sir."

"Your commitment is to take my message quickly and secretly to President Wen—and only to President Wen—and to deliver it exactly as you're given it, and to bring back to me exactly his answer, whether written or verbal. Nothing more and nothing less. I need you to make that commitment before we go any further. If you need to think about it a little more, tell me."

"I don't need to think about it any more."

"Are you sure?"

"I'm sure."

Benton stood up. He put out his hand. "I thank you, sir. Your country is in your debt."

Knight stood up and shook the president's hand.

"How soon do you think you can talk to President Wen?" asked Benton.

"Within a few days, I would imagine. Is that soon enough?"

"It is. Secretary Olsen and Dr. Ball will brief you. You'll be given a packet to deliver."

Saturday, May 14

Family Residence, The White House

"You looked distracted tonight," said Heather.

"Did I?" The president, taking off a sock, looked up at her.

He had been guest of honor at a dinner for the Young Democratic Achiever award. There had been some truly extraordinary stories of courage and determination, and he hoped he hadn't given any sense that he didn't value them.

"You didn't like my speech?"

"Your speech was fine. It was the way you wandered off during the conversation."

"Maybe it was the conversation."

It was the stories of the young achievers that were inspiring. Unfortunately, the young achievers were seated with families and friends, all brought in for the event, and the presidential couple were seated with Mal Jackson, chair of the Democratic Party, his wife and a bunch of party apparatchiks.

Heather laughed. "I've seen you survive worse than that, Joe Benton."

"Well, maybe that's true. Being president requires a fine ability to tolerate banal conversation. They ought to put that in a warning somewhere."

Heather folded her arms. "So what is it?"

Joe sighed. "Well, let's see. Could be the fact that Senator Edwards has said he's going to withhold support for the Teacher Support Bill unless we award one of our new integrated viral research grants to the University of Arkansas, which has rather a dubious claim to it, given that the University of Arkansas hasn't exactly undertaken the world's greatest viral research in the past. Or it could be that the military is already attacking us over our alleged plans to reduce funding for the self-propelled battle tank, which, by the way, haven't even officially been presented to me yet, let alone reduced. Or it could be the fact that the Polish president, who was meant to be in Boston next week—and no, don't ask, I have no idea why he's going there on some kind of semiprivate visit—but the Polish president has now taken exception to some remark made by Congressman Batty and has decided he might cancel unless Congressman Batty retracts the comment, which normally I wouldn't worry too much about, if not for the fact that Senator Wojciek, who's also a little shaky on the Teacher Support Bill, has decided that she absolutely has to host President Koslowski at some dinner she's organized, and she doesn't think she's going to look too good if we can't lean on Congressman Batty, who, by the way, is exactly as his name suggests, and has built his entire career on his legendary ability—self-proclaimed, I should add—*not* to be leaned on." The president paused, looking at Heather expectantly. "Should I go on?"

"I don't believe you gave Senator Wojciek a moment's thought tonight."

"True," said the president, pulling off his other sock. "But I should have. And that's even more of a problem."

Benton tossed his socks on the floor.

"You're not happy with him? The guy you sent to China. You don't think he was the right choice?"

"No. He was the right choice. I didn't much like him, but he was the right man for the job."

"So?"

"He's meeting Wen tomorrow."

"Sunday?"

"Alan told me today."

"So that was on your mind?"

"It's kind of important."

Heather nodded. "When will you hear?"

"Depends how long Wen takes to get back to him. Could be a couple of days. Could be a week." Joe lay back on the bed and stared at the ceiling. "I don't even want to think about what we're going to do if he comes back and says Wen's not interested."

"But he won't, will he? Joe?"

"I don't know. I really don't. They all tell me that's what they're like. China goes on. China can absorb more pain than we can. Therefore China will out-wait us."

"I don't believe that," said Heather quietly.

"That's what they keep telling me." Joe got up on one elbow. "I don't know. But I tell you one thing. I can feel time slipping away. There's a historic moment here, and if that's the attitude the Chinese government takes, it's going to go. And that means we'll be condemning another generation or another two generations or I don't know how many generations to suffering that we could help them avoid."

"Did you put that in your letter to Wen?"

"Sure, along with a lot of stuff about stability, which is apparently all he cares about."

"So the letter's some kind of ultimatum?"

Joe smiled, shaking his head. "No. It was just . . . let's deal with this. Now. Together. Let's do what leaders are supposed to do." Joe was silent, thinking about it. Then he sighed. "Whatever it is, the answer's not going to be simple. It's not going to be a straight yes or no, that's one thing I can be sure of. And in the meantime I'm meeting Nleki, and what am I meant to say about Kyoto? They all want to hear me say Kyoto's the be-all and end-all. I can go ahead and say it, but it isn't true."

Heather frowned. "Maybe he'll get back to you before you meet Nleki."

Joe shrugged.

There was silence.

"I miss having the kids around," Joe said suddenly. "Do you miss them, honey?"

Heather smiled.

"Seems like they used to be around more before."

"Joe, they haven't been around for years. Have you just noticed?"

"Amy used to come back more for weekends, didn't she?"

"Not since she went to Stanford, Joe. That's almost two years ago."

"Really?"

"You'll see more of her in the summer."

"She's definitely interning with that firm?"

Heather nodded.

"But that's in New York, right?"

"We'll see her."

"Yeah, I guess so." Joe frowned. His resolution to make time to speak regularly with Amy had proven a lot easier to make than to keep. "What about Greg?"

"Greg's okay, honey. He's just in a phase."

"He's been in a phase for about ten years."

"He'll come back. You just need to give him time. All of this . . . it complicates things for him."

Joe frowned. "I don't think I was ever in a phase."

Heather laughed. "You wouldn't know what a phase is, Joe Benton. You were always way too focused."

"Is that a good thing?"

"I don't know."

Joe nodded. His thoughts drifted. His face grew serious again. "If Wen says he isn't interested . . . We're going to have to do something, and it's not going to be pretty." He frowned, gazing blankly at the rug. Heather watched him. Suddenly he looked at her. "You want to go to church tomorrow?"

"If you like."

"Let's go to church. We haven't been since . . . when was the last time?"

"Easter."

"That's right. What do you think? Do you want to go? Do you want to go or not?"

"If you want to."

"Calvary?"

Heather nodded. Neither she nor Joe were regular churchgoers, and if it wasn't for political reasons, they probably wouldn't have gone but once a year. To the extent that they did attend, Calvary Baptist on Eighth was the one they had used since Joe came to D.C. as a senator all those years ago. They counted Seb Miles, the minister, as a personal friend.

Joe picked up the phone. The White House duty administrator answered and the president asked to be put through to the duty officer in charge of the Secret Service detail. It was a Lieutenant Koposi. The lieutenant said he would find out what time the service started at Calvary and arrange for the president and first lady to be there.

"Joe," said Heather, when he had put the phone down, "you realize now that poor boy has to work out a whole security plan, and he probably has to wake someone up to get authorization, and you're probably going to have a dozen guys working all night just to get this organized."

"You think I should call him back and tell him to forget it?"

"I think you should give them a bit more warning next time."

"But I didn't think of it till now." Joe frowned. "You think I should call him back?"

"No, Joe." Heather took his hand. "I think we should go to church."

Wednesday, May 18

United Nations Headquarters, New York City

Hands were going up. Al Graham and Jodie Ames watched as the president and the UN secretary-general, Joseph Nleki, stood side by side behind a pair of lecterns at the press conference following their meeting. Nleki was a small, meticulously groomed man, formerly a South African foreign minister, and Joe Benton towered over him.

"Michel Temple, *Le Monde,* France, for President Benton. Mr. President, your predecessor famously described the Kyoto process as something that would be a dead duck if it was even a duck. What kind of a duck is it to you?"

Joe Benton smiled at the journalist's question. "President Gartner had quite a turn of phrase. It's not any kind of duck, let me say that right away." There were smiles among the journalists. "And it's not a goose, either," he added to laughter. Then he was serious again. "I said throughout my campaign, and I've repeated it since I came to office, that my administration will engage with any and all parties on all major issues, including environmental ones. The Kyoto process is a major element of that engagement, and the United States will play its full role in the upcoming round over the next eighteen months, starting with the time-tabling talks that are under way. In fact I think Secretary Powers has already shown a clear intent in this regard. Andrea Powers is a fine secretary, and she's doing a fine job and my administration is lucky to have her."

"If I may follow up, Mr. President? The EuroCore, as you know, has stated that the Kyoto process is the only process that it recognizes in order to prevent a fragmentation of effort and a true transparency. In particular, it has condemned bilateral and regional approaches. I suppose my readers, and I suppose all of Europe, would like to know whether your support of Kyoto extends to that degree, whether you accept it as the sole process, or whether you leave the door open to competing approaches, in particular bilaterals and regionals?"

"I have today explained to Secretary Nleki that the United States government does support the Kyoto process, and we will be playing our role in it, and I think that statement stands for itself."

"But if I may, would you explain to us, Mr. President? Does your statement exclude other approaches?"

"Nothing about my position has changed since what I said during my campaign, and I think that was very clear. The United States is fully behind the Kyoto process and will engage strongly in it, in a way you certainly wouldn't have seen under the previous administration. What I'm saying is that I see the Kyoto process as a very important part and, yes, a primary part, you can say the most important part in dealing with the world's environmental issue. And when there's a primary part in a process I think you can say that's a pretty important part, and I think that ought to be enough for anyone, so I think that answers your question."

He glanced at Nleki. The secretary-general nodded thoughtfully. Anyone who knew the secretary-general knew that didn't mean anything. As head of the UN, Joseph Nleki spent a good part of his time nodding thoughtfully as leaders spoke beside him, whether or not he agreed with what they were saying.

In the car to La Guardia, Al Graham was on a high. He thought the meeting with Nleki had gone well. It was clear the secretary-general felt a lot more comfortable with Benton than he had ever felt with Mike Gartner. There was just one thing that worried him.

"Your answer on Kyoto, Joe. I didn't get that. What is it? Are we looking at other things?"

Benton knew he hadn't fielded that question well. He had felt his own ambivalence coming through, even as he tried to conceal it.

"Al," he said, "Gartner said he didn't believe in Kyoto for four long years, and he didn't do a single thing about creating an alternative. I said that we see Kyoto as the primary part of the process. That's a big step. They ought to be happy with that."

"But you'd tell me, right? You'd tell me if we were cooking up something else."

Benton nodded.

Graham watched him.

"Al, of course I'd tell you."

"Joe . . ."

"Look, I'm not going to rule it out in public, am I? Where does that leave us if I do? The EuroCore, you know the game Brussels plays. I don't have to play that game."

"But you'd tell me, right?" Graham turned sideways in his seat, looking full on at the president. "Joe, I'm going to look an awful fool if you turn around here and announce something else."

"Al, I'm not announcing anything else."

"But you'd tell me, wouldn't you?"

"Al, stop it. That's the line, okay? What I said today is exactly what I planned with Jodie."

"Not Larry?"

"If you want clarification on the line," said Benton impatiently, "talk to Jodie."

The convoy swept onto the tarmac and came to a halt. The door swung open.

Benton hesitated. He felt bad. "Al, look, come on. It was a good meeting. You said so yourself. Don't spoil it."

Graham didn't reply.

Benton got out. The door closed behind him. As he took the steps up to Air Force One, the limo with Al Graham inside it pulled away.

On the plane, Alan Ball and Larry Olsen were waiting with F. William Knight.

The president held out his hand. "Sorry to do this to you, Mr. Knight. Looks like it was the only slot we could find. I appreciate your flexibility."

The four men sat down and buckled themselves in. The tone of the plane's engines changed and the aircraft began to move.

"All right, Mr. Knight, tell me what happened."

Knight cleared his throat. "I told President Wen what I had been asked to say, and then I gave him the dossier that I was given." The banker paused. The plane was gathering speed.

"Go on."

"He . . . um, he looked through the dossier while I was there and said he would need time to consider it. Then he asked me to come back the next day, and then there was another delay of a day so it was only yesterday I met him again."

"And did he make any other remarks at your first meeting?"

"We exchanged news," said Knight. "Personal things."

The president nodded. The plane took off and pitched up.

"We also exchanged thoughts on the economy. After President Wen had looked at the dossier and said I would have to come back, we had a brief discussion, just as we would normally do."

"What happened when you went back?"

"President Wen said the issues you raised are grave."

"Was that his exact word?"

"I'm translating, sir."

"What language do you use with him?"

"Mandarin, mostly. Technical economic stuff, we sometimes go into English. He has excellent English."

The president nodded. "I interrupted you."

Knight cleared his throat. "He said the issues are grave. They require much thought. They will affect the lives of our children and our children's children. He gave me a letter, sir. He asked me to be sure to deliver it to you personally."

Knight pulled a plain envelope out of his jacket pocket. He unbuckled his seat belt and handed it to the the president.

On the envelope was written, "For the President of the United States." For a moment it struck Benton as funny, like something a kid would write if they had to send a letter to the president.

Benton slid a finger under the flap of the envelope and tore it open. He pulled out the single page that was inside.

To His Excellency Joseph Benton, President of the United States of America.

I thank you for your letter and the information you have sent me. You have chosen a good man to carry your word. Our world faces a grave danger. As you have written, this is truly a historic moment, and it is our duty, as the leaders of the two greatest economies in the world, to lead the world out of this danger. The People's Republic of China is prepared to fulfill its historic role at this time. Together, our two great countries can lead the world to a brighter future. Let us try to find the way. Let us not have people who come between us. When we speak, let our words be carried direct to the other.

Sincerely yours,
Wen Goujie
President of the People's Republic of China.

The president looked up. Ball, Olsen and Knight were watching him.

He handed the letter to Ball, who was sitting closest to him. Ball scanned it and gave it to Olsen.

Knight cleared his throat. "President Wen asked me to say, after you had read the letter, that he would consider a channel to take this matter further."

"Bill," said Alan Ball, "is he expecting you to come back with an answer?"

Knight nodded.

"Mr. Knight," said the president. "You've done a fine job for your country. I want to ask if you'll wait outside."

"Yes, sir." Knight unbuckled his harness and stood.

Ball got up as well and took him out.

The president looked at Olsen. "This is good, huh?"

Larry Olsen nodded cautiously. "He didn't say any of the information we gave him was new."

"So what?"

"Why's he changed his mind?"

Ball came back. "We're in business!"

Benton smiled. "Larry's got doubts."

"You don't say."

"All I'm saying is that he didn't say the information was new. So why does he want to do anything different than he did before? And by the way, he had a channel. Chen."

"Maybe he doesn't trust Chen."

"Then why not send someone he does trust? Why act so aggressively and then change course just because we send him the same information we sent before."

"Because he finally realizes he's talking to someone who's serious," said Ball.

"Or because he thinks he can still keep control as long as he's talking to us. That's how he can keep stringing us out."

"Hell's bells, Larry! What else could you have wanted?" Benton glanced at Alan Ball in exasperation.

"A rationale," said Olsen. "I want him to say, 'Gee, I didn't realize things were that bad. Now I see why I have to act.'"

"Look at what he does say. He recognizes the historical imperative to do something."

"And he didn't recognize that before? You mean someone had to point it out to him? Are we going to believe that?"

"Larry, I'm sorry." Benton found himself straining to control his frustration. "It may be that he's not going to give you everything you want in exactly the way you want it. Live with it."

"I'm not saying we don't talk to him. I'm just saying—"

"Mr. President," said Ball, "we're not laying on sanctions after a letter like that."

"Of course not."

"That's exactly the point," said Olsen.

"Larry, I don't know what the hell *more* you could have wanted!" Benton struggled to restrain himself. "We're going to talk to him. All right? The man says he wants to talk, we're going to talk. We're going to tell Bill Knight to go back and say we'll talk, we're serious about negotiating, we're nominating someone who'll have a direct line to me. That's what we're going to do, period."

Olsen nodded.

Benton sat back in his chair and shook his head. "All right. Let's focus on what we do next."

"We need a negotiatior," said Ball. "Someone really good. I've got a couple of—"

"This is a State responsibility," said Larry Olsen. "State will find a negotiator."

"Two minutes ago you didn't even want—"

"This is a *State* responsibility." Olsen gazed at the president. "State will find a negotiator."

Benton glanced at Ball. "Larry's right."

Ball clenched his jaw.

"Just keep Alan in the loop."

"Sure," said Olsen. He looked at Ball.

"How quick can we make this happen?"

"As quick as Wen wants," said Olsen.

"Then to your point, Larry, that'll show how serious Wen is. All right, where are we going to do it? It can't be Washington. Can't be Beijing."

"Oslo," said Olsen. "We tell them there's some incredibly sensitive negotiation between us and China. They'll think it's about Taiwan. We'll tell them it has to take place in utter secrecy and would they mind hosting it?" Olsen smiled sardonically. "Norwegians love stuff like that. They'll wet themselves."

Thursday, May 26

Eidsvoll, outside Oslo, Norway

The road led through a forest of fir and spruce. In the back of the car, along-side Oliver Wu, sat Pete Lisle, a tall, reddish-haired man in his fifties with a big blade of a nose and a chiseled chin. A State veteran, he had brokered the Turkish-Kurdish autonomy deal that put an end to decades of bloodshed in eastern Turkey. That had taken four long years of his life, half of it on horse-back in the mountains of Kurdistan. He had succeeded through incredible patience on detail combined with unsentimental, ruthless decisiveness in forcing the crucial compromises at the crucial times, together with an un-canny ability to gain the trust of the people he negotiated with. No one at State knew more about getting a deal on the table and making it stick.

It was a warm spring morning. It reminded Lisle somewhat of spring mornings in the forest valleys east of Diyarbakir.

"I bet this place is cold as hell in the winter," he murmured, staring out the window.

Oliver Wu nodded.

"I hate the cold. Comes from growing up in Chicago. When I retire I'm going to southern California."

Wu began to laugh at that, then stopped, thinking of the data they had in their briefcases. Southern California wasn't necessarily going to be much of a place to live.

Lisle turned to look at him. "Believe an agreement can be reached, Dr. Wu." Pete Lisle held up a finger. "Lisle's first law of negotiation. You have to believe it can be done. And then it can. It's never rocket science. The answer's never something no one's thought of before—it's just some-thing one side or the other hasn't been prepared to accept."

Wu nodded, wondering whether the Chinese side was really prepared to accept the full cost of what had to be done. Or whether the United States was either, when it came to it.

Eventually the car turned onto a drive and pulled up at a house. It was a classical Scandinavian country lodge, two-story, white, formerly a hunting lodge for the Norwegian royal family. A pair of small pointed turrets poked up out of the roof.

A man from the Norwegian Foreign Ministry was waiting to welcome them. The driver, another Foreign Ministry employee, pulled their cases out of the trunk.

"We the first ones here?" asked Lisle.

"The other parties are scheduled to arrive this afternoon, Mr. Lisle," said the man from the Foreign Ministry, and he led them inside.

They knew who to expect. The Chinese side had forwarded two names, and the CIA had provided background on each one. Lin Shisheng was a talented Bank of China executive who had worked closely with Wen back in his Finance Ministry days and was often called upon, according to the CIA, when Wen needed someone for a particularly sensitive mission. Gao Jichuan was a more shadowy figure who had been around Wen for years as a kind of general aide or factotum. The creativity in the negotiation, if there was any, would come from Lin. Gao's role was probably to hold him within the limits of whatever bounds Wen had set.

The objective of the initial phase of the discussion was limited. At this point, the aim was to share information with the Chinese side. In the planning sessions with Larry Olsen, there had been much discussion about the amount of information they should provide. Pete Lisle had been insistent that they supply everything they were going to provide up front. Olsen wanted to keep some of the data up his sleeve, but Lisle wouldn't budge. The day he had to admit he had something more, he said, was the day he would lose his credibility with the other side. Eventually Olsen agreed, with the exception of data that would reveal the specialized sources operated by Dr. Richards's unit. Lisle still wasn't sure he had everything, but he knew he had as much as he was going to get.

The Norwegians had arranged for the negotiators to have a light meal together in the evening before a first, brief discussion session. Lin was of middle height, with receding hair and a round, lively face, and it was soon obvious that he was talkative and sociable. Gao was taller, heavy-featured. As they ate, Lin launched into a long story about his first visit to the United

States as a student, culminating in a ludicrous incident when he was mistaken for the brother of a notorious gangster in San Francisco's Chinatown. It was hilarious the way he told it, but almost lethal at the time. Lisle reciprocated with a story about being caught in the crossfire between two warlords in Kurdistan. Or what he and his guides thought was crossfire, but turned out to be two wedding parties on either side of a valley that had become a little too competitive with the celebrations. Lin laughed appreciatively. Gao gave a slight smile. It wasn't clear how good Gao's English was. Wu said something in Mandarin about his closest brush with death being the time he tried to teach his sister to drive. Lin laughed at that as well. Gao smiled the same stiff smile.

After the meal, a Norwegian official took them into a room where there was a table and a sideboard with refreshments, and then withdrew, closing the door behind him. Lisle glanced at Wu, who excused himself and went up to his room to get the dossiers that had been prepared for them. When he came back, Pete Lisle was in the middle of a story, and Lin was listening with a smile of expectation on his face. Gao was stony-faced. Lisle got to the punch line and Lin rocked with laughter.

Wu put the dossiers on the table.

"Okay," said Lisle, and he pushed the two dossiers across the table. "Here's what we've got. Everything's there. All the key data."

Lin opened the file and began to leaf through the pages. Gao didn't touch his copy.

"We're putting everything on the table," said Lisle. "No point beating around the bush. This is stuff that affects us, it's stuff that affects you, so you may as well know it. I don't know how much of this your people have seen already, but I want you to understand that we don't have anything else. You read that, you know as much as we do. As much as President Benton does. I want to be very clear on that point."

Lin looked up and nodded seriously. Oliver Wu could see that this move had an immediate effect on him. He had probably expected to receive nothing but a general description of the problem at the first session, and then to have to drag out the data piecemeal over the next few days.

Wu looked around and found Gao gazing at him.

Lin closed the folder. "We will have to look at this," he said.

"Naturally," replied Lisle.

"We should meet again tomorrow. Let's say tomorrow evening. Then we can at least have made an initial study of the document."

And have talked to Beijing, thought Wu.

"Of course," said Lisle. He stood up. "After you."

He waited for Lin and Gao to gather up their dossiers and leave the table. Then he waited for Wu to get up. As they left the room, Lisle surreptitiously pulled a map of the Taiwan Strait out of his pocket and left it on the sideboard for their Norwegian hosts to find.

Saturday, May 28

Eidsvoll, outside Oslo, Norway

Lisle and Wu were on a secure connection. Larry Olsen took the call at home.

"They say they need to go back to Beijing to consult," said Lisle. "They pushed hard yesterday for more. I told them that was it, that's all we had. I think they've finally accepted that."

"Let's park that for a minute," said Olsen. "Tell me what your general feeling is. How do you think it went, giving them everything up front?"

"Definitely not what they expected. I think we short-circuited a month of demand-and-answer just by putting it all out there."

"I agree," said Wu. "They weren't expecting it."

That was good. Olsen was determined to force the pace. "The president thinks he's won some kind of victory just by getting these guys to sit down and talk with us. He thinks Wen's serious because it only took a week to get going. I think that doesn't mean squat. It's once you start talking you discover whether there's going to be any progress. And look what we've got. Two days in, they're already stalling."

"Mr. Secretary," said Lisle, "I wouldn't go so far as to say they're stalling. If they believe they've now got the full set of numbers they genuinely are going to have to go back and consult."

"Granted. But if this whole thing is a ploy by Wen to drag everything out—which I suspect it is—we need to expose that quickly and show the president so we can go in a different direction."

"Mr. Secretary, it's too early to say from what we've seen here what Wen's intention is."

"Okay, but my sense from what you're saying is that we're pushing a little more than they're comfortable with. That's what we need to do. Now, tell me, what do you make of them?"

Pete Lisle glanced at Wu before he answered. "Pretty much like we expected. Lin's sharp, but he likes to be friends. That may be something we can use. But he's smart, so it may be something he's consciously doing. We'll have to see."

"And Gao?"

Lisle laughed. "You remember those *Addams Family* films when you were a kid? They had a servant, right? A tall, silent guy like Frankenstein."

"Lurch," said Olsen.

"That's him! I couldn't remember the name. Gao's like Lurch. Big guy, kind of spooky."

Olsen laughed. "I loved those films."

"He doesn't say a damn thing."

"He's there to keep an eye on Lin?"

"Looks like it."

"Oliver, what do you think?"

"I never saw those movies. What did you say they were called?"

"Doesn't matter. What do you think?"

"I agree with Pete. Looks like he's just watching."

"I wouldn't underestimate him," said Lisle. "When it comes down to it, he may be the one Wen's going to listen to more."

"What would he be saying about you?" asked Olsen.

"What would he be saying about us, Oliver?"

"He doesn't like me. Overseas Chinese. I'm betraying the motherland."

"You think we shouldn't have you there?"

"If it creates an obstacle. If it gets personal, I guess we shouldn't."

"You think they're irritated because you're there?"

"It's possible."

"Pete? What's your take?"

"I think there is a certain . . . hostility's too strong a word. But there is some resentment. Especially from Lurch. But maybe that's okay. Shows them this is a genuinely shared issue. Cuts across nationality, religion, whatever."

"Forget that," said Olsen. "I kind of like it if they're irritated. We're not kowtowing, right? That's what this shows. We pull Oliver, next thing they'll ask to nominate the people we send. Oliver, ramp it up a little more. Talk up. Make them engage with you."

Wu glanced at Lisle questioningly. Lisle shook his head. He wasn't going to let someone who had never even sat down with these guys dictate the way they should be handled. "We'll play that by ear, Mr. Secretary. Let's see how that goes."

"Well, don't let them intimidate you. Oliver, you hear what I said?"

"Yes, sir."

"Okay. So what's the next step? They take our numbers and go home and discuss it? Is that what you said?"

"That's right," said Lisle. "I can't see how we can object."

"Okay, but the truth is, there's nothing there they don't know already, unless Chen didn't tell them. So we haven't actually got anywhere."

Lisle disagreed with that. "Mr. Secretary, we had to get this done. This gives us a firm base of shared data. Wen knows he has everything we have, and he knows we know it. Whether they've seen that stuff before or not, that doesn't matter. What matters is now there's no more room for excuses."

"Okay," said Olsen. "Fair enough. We had to do this. What next?"

"Next round of meetings, we talk solutions," said Lisle.

"Have they agreed to that?"

"No. We haven't discussed that yet. That's what I want to check with you, sir. My instinct is to say at this point, after they look at the numbers, we both come back with proposals."

Olsen thought about it.

"I don't think there's anything else now, Mr. Secretary. They have the numbers, same numbers that we have. Now it's time to talk about what we do."

"Go on," said Olsen.

"If they don't actually put something down, and we do, then we end up giving them stuff and negotiating against nothing. That's always a mistake. They'll pocket what we offer and come back for more. So what I want to say to them is, next time, each of us comes back with a proposal. Neither proposal is binding on the party that makes it. They can put in whatever they want, and so can we, and there's no commitment. Then we work through the differences. Only when we both agree on something, does that thing become a commitment on either side."

"You think that's the way to do it?"

"In my experience, Mr. Secretary, given what I've been told about what's already happened, that's the only way we're going to get something out of them. They have to come back with something. It also protects our position. It means we can present something and they can't pocket it. That's critical. The same rules have to apply to both sides."

Olsen liked the approach. That was the level of pressure he wanted to apply. "Sounds good."

"Before I do that, Mr. Secretary, I need to make sure it's okay. I want to be able to say to them that if they don't have a proposal next time we meet, we don't sit down."

"That's okay. Say it."

"Mr. Secretary, they might come back with nothing." Lisle paused. "Before I do this, I need to know the president would agree to me laying it out as an ultimatum in this way. Would he be comfortable with that?"

"The president's not running this negotiation," said Larry Olsen.

Lisle glanced at Wu. "Mr. Secretary, they *really* might come back with nothing. Mr. Secretary? If I say this, and they do come back with nothing, I need to know the president is going to back me a hundred percent when I walk away. Because if he doesn't, if he makes me sit down with them, you'll have to find yourself a new negotiator. My credibility will be shot."

Lisle and Wu stared at the phone, listening for Olsen's response.

There was silence.

"Mr. Secretary, if you need to talk to the president, I can wait. I can wait until tomorrow. I don't need to tell them tonight. But I need to know he's going to back me."

Still there was silence.

"Mr. Secretary?"

"Tell them tonight."

"Are you sure?"

"I'm sure." There was another moment's silence on the line. "How long do you think you should give them to come back? If we can get there, the president's talking about announcing the deal on the Fourth of July."

"The Fourth of July?"

"You don't think it can be done?"

Pete Lisle frowned, calculating. "I guess it's not impossible, but I wouldn't bet on it. If we're shooting for that, we can't give them more than two weeks to come back. I'll give them a week, and if they push, I'll give a little and make it two. I guess we'll see how they respond."

"Let's get it started," said Olsen. "Tell them tonight. They can take the data, but when they come back they come with a proposal, or they don't come back at all."

Friday, June 10

Oval Office, The White House

The discussion was getting heated. Jackie Rubin had just summarized a set of scenario outputs for the Marion group. While the negotiations in Oslo had been getting under way, she had pulled a group together to work intensively modeling the economic impact of different emissions reduction options, among which were the ones Pete Lisle and Oliver Wu might be taking back to Oslo. Joe Benton listened to the discussion in the group and made notes on a pad. When about twenty minutes had gone by, he called the discussion to a halt.

"Let's get back to what we're trying to do here," he said. "We have four objectives." He read from the notes he had made. "One, to determine the level of global cut we need to get. Two, to figure out how we apportion shares between us and China, in the first instance, on the understanding that other major emitters will follow suit. Three, to put that into a formula we can sell to the Chinese. Four, to figure out the negotiating strategy so we end up with that formula." He looked around. "Have I missed anything? Okay, let's start at the top. What level of cut are we looking for? From what I understand, Jackie, at a minimum we need twelve percent over the next five years, and another twelve percent in the five years after that. Do we agree that's right? Is it enough? Is it more than we need?"

"Mr. President, as I've said before, this is a judgment," said Rubin. "If you're prepared to accept economic ruin, you can stop environmental degradation in its tracks. But if we're looking at something that's reasonable as a way of balancing action on emissions with the economic implications—and that's the balance we've got to get right—our initial analysis showed that the optimal Relocation ceiling is in the region of thirty-five million people here in the U.S., so that's what we worked from. To keep the Relocation to that level, those are the kind of emissions cuts we're looking at. As I said, the exact numbers, as close as we can say, are 12.3 percent in the first five years and 11.4 in the following five."

"Let's stay with twelve and twelve," said Benton. "It's easy, it's clean. Can we agree on that?"

Rubin nodded. The others were silent.

"Jackie, what if you change the Relocation ceiling?" asked John Eales.

"To get Relocation down significantly below thirty-five million will take emissions cuts that inflict extraordinary economic damage. And if you go the other way, because of the geography of the sea levels and the demographics, until you're prepared to accept a sixty or seventy million Relocation, the level of cuts doesn't come down much. Twelve and twelve is the optimal level." Rubin turned back to Benton. "Mr. President, there's an important assumption here that the cut will be shared globally in proportion to current emissions. If the United States has to take a bigger hit, the numbers are different. You also talked about exempting the poorest twenty percent of the world's population from any cuts. You should be aware that adds another half percent to the rest of us. It's not much, but it's something."

"So what if we have to end up taking proportionately bigger cuts because of our starting position as the highest emitter on a per capita basis?" asked Benton.

"We modeled a whole bunch of these scenarios. For example, say we agree to take a fifty percent greater cut proportionately, we couldn't realistically do it in the timescale. So if the rest of the world made their cuts in two equal five-year lots, we'd have to go roughly sixy percent of our allocation in the ten years and the other forty percent over another eight."

"So we trade that," said Eales. "Timing for volume."

"We could. I don't think that's something we can decide now." Rubin glanced at Pete Lisle and Oliver Wu, who were back in Washington and sitting in on the meeting. "That's something for the negotiators to bear in mind."

"All right," said Benton. "We're saying twelve and twelve globally. The half percent issue isn't material, so let's leave it off the table for now." The president looked back at his pad. Working out the total level of required cuts was the easy part. It was figuring out how to divide it up and sell it to the Chinese that worried him. "Let's say we take this to the other side as it is. What do the Chinese say to it?"

"No," said Alan Ball.

"Reason?"

"It's absolute numbers. Like Jackie said, these cuts are based on the absolute volume of each country's emissions. First thing they're going to say, look at our populations. We'll cut emissions, but we'll do it on a per capita basis."

"What about on a GDP basis?"

"Their GDP's higher than ours so that makes it just as bad for them."

"It's not quite as bad for them," said Rubin, "because proportionately their share of global GDP is lower than their share of emissions. But yes, if they have to use absolute GDP numbers, it's still higher than ours, so they still won't like it. If I was them, I'd go per capita, like Alan says."

"And that argument lets India and Brazil and Russia off the hook right there," said Larry Olsen. "It catches us, Japan, and the EuroCore. We can't admit that argument."

"So what are you going to do?" demanded Ball. "Put your hands over your ears?"

"It's no-win for us."

"Why do they care?"

"Hold on," said the president. Hoffman was trying to break into the exchange between Olsen and Ball. "Ben, what did you want to say?"

"What's the principle here?" asked Hoffman. "If we have to agree on something, there has to be a principle of equity."

"Sure," replied Ball. "Their principle's going to be everyone should have the same standard of living. Every person. There it is right there, GDP per capita. That's the measure. That's a tough argument for a democracy like us to rebut. Every person's life is worth as much as everyone else's, right? Are you going to say our citizens have a right to a higher standing of living than they do?"

"We *have* a higher standard of living than they do," said Olsen. "They have to take that into account."

"Exactly. Here's an opportunity to address that imbalance."

The president glanced at Alan Ball. He was taking almost too much pleasure, Joe Benton thought, in playing devil's advocate.

"What about an equality of pain?" said John Eales. "We take away from each country equally."

"Per capita?"

"Maybe."

"In percentage or absolute terms?"

"We could run that," said Rubin.

Alan Ball shrugged. "Same situation. You start with less per capita, you should have less taken away. Look, we've got a fundamental problem here. It's a long time since the United States was either the world's biggest emitter or its biggest economy in absolute terms, but we're still the biggest per capita on both criteria. So you can look at what we've got left or what you take away, but either way, on a per capita basis, we're going to hurt the most."

"Which is why you don't admit the argument in the first place," said Olsen.

"Which is why the other side says thank you very much and walks away."

"Jackie," said the president, "what does it look like for us if we do it on GDP per capita? Have you looked at that?"

"We're in the stone age." Rubin consulted the handheld in which the models were stored. "We modeled a scenario where we take total global emissions down twelve and twelve percent, roughly, over the next ten years—which is what we've been talking about—but distributed in proportion to the GDP per capita for each country."

"Which means we take the biggest hit?"

"Correct. Followed by the EuroCore."

"And?"

Jackie tapped a couple of times on the handheld. "We contract eight to nine percent year on year for at least four years. We won't be growing again for six."

The president made notes on his pad. "And what if we weight it based on absolute GDP?"

"China takes the biggest hit—because they've got the biggest GDP—followed by us, followed by the EuroCore, followed by Japan, then India."

"And the numbers in that case?"

"This is pretty close to the unweighted scenario I outlined at the beginning. We shrink thirteen percent total over three years, then we're static for two, then we start growing again."

"China?"

"For various reasons, its dip is slightly shallower than ours, but longer."

"How long?"

"Eight years before they grow."

Joe Benton made a note, then looked at Oliver Wu. "You think the party would survive that?"

"The question, sir, is whether the party thinks it would survive it. The party's source of political legitimacy is prosperity. What happens if the Chinese economy not only doesn't grow, but contracts? The party might be able to weather a year or two, but I don't think they believe they'd be able to survive the kind of contraction we're talking about, not one that goes on for eight years."

"So they won't risk it?"

"If I was Wen—unless I was incredibly motivated to deal with this issue and I was prepared to gamble everything in the attempt, including the party's actual existence—I wouldn't. And frankly, Mr. President, nothing in Wen's record suggests he'd be thinking like that."

"Except the note he sent me," said Benton.

"Whatever happens," said Eales, "they have to face up to this."

"But they don't have to agree to the cuts we demand," said Wu.

"What happens to *them* if it goes on a GDP per capita basis?" asked the President.

Jackie Rubin worked at her handheld. "They shrink only four percent over two years, then they're growing again in three."

"Well, there you go," said Alan Ball. "That's it right there. Dr. Wu just told us they can live with that, and they have a principle of equity that gives it to them. That's what they'll go for. I bet they're doing the same calculations right now."

Jackie Rubin shook her head. "In that scenario, six years out, we're not much more than two thirds of the economy we are today. That's not possible, Mr. President."

"Agreed," said Benton. "Our society would tear itself apart. That's not a principle of equity we can live with."

There was silence. The faces around the president were grim.

"Mr. President? May I?"

It was Pete Lisle. Benton nodded.

"I'd like to put this in a slightly different way. With all due respect to Mr. Hoffman, this isn't about equity. Not in an objective sense, anyway. In a negotiation, equity is subjective. It's really about what each side, for their own reasons, is prepared to take. When I'm approaching a negotiation over an extremely painful issue—when the outcome for each side is inevitably going to involve pain—there are two things I'm looking for." Pete Lisle paused. "I don't mean to be lecturing, so I'll stop if I'm out of order."

"No, go ahead Mr. Lisle. I'd like to hear what you have to say."

"Two things. One, both parties have to believe they have to do a deal. Because no matter what the deal is, both of them are going to hurt. So if even one of them believes they don't absolutely have to do a deal—that they might do better later if they hold on now—they won't. The second thing, they have to be able to sell it to their base, by which I mean their support base that's going to let them ratify the deal or make sure they don't get voted out of office or not get overthrown in a coup or whatever's relevant in the political context. They have to be able to sell it so it looks like a success to their base. When it's a matter of pain on both sides, that success often means making it look like the other side is taking more pain than it was prepared to. In other words, making yourself look tough, so even though you're taking pain, it looks like you got away with less pain to yourself than anyone else would have managed."

"What do you think the Chinese need to be able to sell the deal to their base?" asked John Eales.

"Mr. Eales, I'm not a China expert so I'm not best qualified to say. That's why we've got Oliver here, to tell me stuff like that. But one thing I will say. At this stage, from what I'm hearing, I'm not even sure about the first thing, that the other side is convinced—really, truly believes—that they have to do a deal."

Oliver Wu nodded.

"I guess we find out when we see the response to the data," said Eales.

"I agree," said Lisle. "That'll be the best indication. Our argument, what we're saying, is that the data says we all have to do something. If they don't buy that—or if they think that, even if they agree they have to do something, they can't sell it to their base—we're not going to get anywhere."

"And if they do accept it?" said the president.

"We may have to give them enough so they can take the deal to their base and make it look like they beat us up. We may have to be prepared to hear them say that."

"We can't give them parity of reduction on a per capita basis," said the president. "We can't live with that."

"That's clear. That's something they're going to need to understand. There's another principle that's relevant in a negotiation—at some point, each side needs to understand what's genuinely impossible for the other. They need to know what's negotiable and what isn't, otherwise they'll keep pushing on everything. The only question is *when* you let them know. In this case, I'd be inclined to let them know early."

"We could give them a little," said Eales. "We start with a case for cuts on an absolute basis, they're going to come back with a case for cuts on a per capita basis, so we give a little, we find some formula that gives them a percentage point or two. They can represent that as a victory over us, they forced us to concede."

"True," said Lisle. "On the other hand, their opponents can represent it as defeat. Always remember what it looks like from the other side. Let's say we go twenty-five percent of the way towards their position—their opponents can say their own side came seventy-five percent of the way to our position."

"So you're saying we have to go more than fifty percent towards them?" said the president.

"I don't think that's possible on the numbers," murmured Jackie Rubin.

"I'll need to know what is possible," said Lisle. "If they need to understand what isn't possible for us, it goes without saying that I do. But the other thing is, we need to think broadly about what they need to satisfy their base. It could be that it's something outside the narrow confines of this particular issue. What else do we have that they want? In this case, it would have to be something really significant. If we can give them that, then that might be the thing they represent as a victory, and the fact that they don't get much on actual emissions might not even figure."

The president glanced at Wu. "What else do we have that's important enough to them?"

"Only one thing, sir."

There was silence. Everyone knew what it was.

Joe Benton took a deep breath, let it out slowly. "I can't sell them Taiwan," he said quietly.

"If that's the case, and that's all we have . . ." Pete Lisle shrugged. "Well, we've given them the data. Now they have to produce a proposal. When we see it I guess we'll know if they really believe they have to do a deal."

Friday, June 17

Hotel Kirchhoff, outside Cologne, Germany

Joe Benton was taking a hammering. He had been expecting it, but that didn't mean he was enjoying it now that it was happening. He had been invited to attend the final day of the European Union summer summit. The morning had started amiably enough with a breakfast at which he sat next to Ruud Blok, the Dutch prime minister. Blok impressed him. The Dutch had taken an early decision to retreat from virtually all the land reclaimed since World War Two and were the first country in the world to implement an explicit relocation program. After breakfast, the initial working session on trade issues passed off without much dispute. Then it started. Kyoto. The German prime minister, Ingelbock, introduced the topic and set the scene with a vigorous attack on unnamed leaders whose commitment to the Kyoto process never seemed to get beyond generalities. Suddenly they were lining up, Rumain of France, DiMarco of Italy, Blanco of Spain, Pavel of the Czech Republic, Vidic of Serbia and a dozen others. Hugh Ogilvie exchanged a knowing glance with Benton. The European leaders wanted a clear statement on the U.S. president's commitment to Kyoto as the one and only channel through which to deal with the world's major environmental concerns. Benton stuck to his "primary role" line and refused to be drawn further. One leader after another lauded Kyoto and attributed its shortcomings to America's failure to engage fully on previous occasions. China, India and Russia didn't get a mention. The style varied from leader to leader but the content was pretty much the same.

Larry Olsen, who was sitting with a number of aides behind the president, leaned forward.

"Mr. President," he whispered, "I've got to step out for a minute."

Joe Benton turned to him and smiled ruefully. He wouldn't mind stepping out as well, and not just for a minute. Olsen got up and one of his aides moved forward into his seat.

Outside, Olsen walked across the grounds and sat on a bench under a tree. The hotel was surrounded by parkland. In the distance, a squad of soldiers stood beside an armored vehicle at a point on the perimeter of the zone that had been closed for the meeting.

Olsen tapped on his handheld and raised it to his ear.

"Mr. Secretary?" It was Pete Lisle, calling on an encrypted line from Oslo, where he and Oliver Wu were meeting the Chinese delegation for the first time since their initial meeting three weeks previously.

"Go ahead, Pete. What's happening?"

"Mr. Secretary, we don't have the result we want."

"What's in their proposal?"

"They don't have one."

Olsen wasn't sure he had heard right.

"They say they want more information."

"We don't have any more information."

"They say they want to see the raw data."

"They can't see it. The raw data doesn't tell them anything different."

"I told them that."

"Did you tell them you expected them to come back with a proposal? That was the agreement, right?"

"They know that. They say they need to see the raw data."

"You haven't given them our proposal, right?"

"No, sir," said Lisle. "I haven't given them our proposal."

Olsen frowned. He watched the soldiers across the park. A couple of them had got into the armored vehicle, and it was moving away, leaving four of them behind.

"What's really going on, Pete?"

"They may not believe we don't have any more," said Lisle. "But if they do believe us, it's one of two things. Either they're stalling, or they're trying to figure out where the data's coming from."

"What's the atmosphere like?"

"Same as last time. Lin and Lurch. Lurch isn't saying much. Lin's friendly. It's like, we need more, help us out here. It's not our fault, Beijing's making us ask. Please just give us what we want."

"You think maybe they don't believe we've interpreted our data correctly?" said Olsen.

"I guess that's possible as well. They might figure we've gone too far in our interpretation."

Olsen thought about it. It was possible they really did want to check the raw data for themselves, but it was more likely they were stalling. Anyway, they couldn't see the raw data. Doing that would be as good as revealing the existence of the ESU.

"What do you think?" he asked eventually.

"We say yes to this, Mr. Secretary, and we're opening Pandora's box. We'll end up in endless arguments over detail. They'll ask for verification, they'll ask for trends, they'll ask to see the next set of data. They'll probably ask to be involved in collecting it."

Olsen agreed.

"I think we should indicate we have sources they're not aware of. I think we should offer them to come on board and collaborate once we have a binding deal. We can even make the deal dependent on them seeing the raw data. But I don't want to go down this path of questioning the data and verifying the data and anything like that before we get agreement. We've given them what we've got. They can go correlate that with anything they've collected, and if they see some kind of discrepancy with their data, fine, let's get the experts together and work through what it is exactly. But if what we've shown them is in keeping with what they have themselves, then they're just going to have to accept the rest of it."

"Did you tell them that?" said Olsen.

"In a way. I'll go harder when I speak to them again. One of the reasons I wanted to speak with you was to agree how hard I should go. Last time I told them if they didn't come back with a proposal, that would be it. We'd have nothing to talk about."

"They didn't have any specific discrepancy they wanted to clarify?"

"No. Just a general request for more data, then the raw data."

Olsen gazed across the lawns at the soldiers on guard in the distance. "They're stalling," he said.

"I think so."

"Go back and give it to them as hard as you want. They agreed we'd each come back with a proposal. Tell them they don't have a proposal, that's it. We walk away."

"Mr. Secretary, its not that simple. We need to find a way for them to give us a proposal. Once I go hard with them, if they don't have a way back, this channel's going to shut down."

"Pete, the president thinks Wen really wants to cut a deal. I think this is all bullshit. All they've done so far is deign to meet us and take away our data and then ask for more. We've got to push them till they bust. I want to find when that point is, and I want to find it quickly. If they don't bust, fine, then we've got a deal and no one will be happier than me. But I won't believe that until the ink's dry on the paper."

"I have no argument with that, sir. But now they've tried it, and we're showing them we're not going to stand for it, they can't just turn around and say, okay, actually, we had a proposal all along. They're going to lose too much face. At the very least, they'll have to go back to Beijing so they can pretend to convince Wen to make a proposal, and then come back with it. That's at a minimum."

"Well they can do that," said Olsen. "One more chance. But no misunderstandings now. There's no more data. Tell them next time we sit down, that's it. That's it! If they don't have a proposal there's nothing and we walk away. If that's not okay, they may as well tell us now and we can all save ourselves a lot of time and trouble."

"Okay. That's fine. That's what I wanted to check." Lisle paused. "Mr. Secretary, I also had another thought. You said when we first spoke you've got someone with a direct line to Wen."

"Yes," said Olsen.

"I'm just thinking. We could go two, three rounds here with them coming back and still asking for more data or finding some—"

"We'll walk away," said Olsen. "I thought we just agreed that."

It wouldn't necessarily work like that and Pete Lisle knew it. "Let's say they come back and say they've looked at our data and there's a discrepancy with something they've got. We'll have to look at that. And then there might be something else, and realistically, even with the line I'm giving them, they could find ways of stalling for three, four, six months, and each time we'd find it hard to actually be sure there isn't something in it. Believe me, sir. I could do it. And if I could do it, they'll be able to do it."

"Even if you tell them what we just agreed?"

"Abolutely. Even if I tell them. So what I'm thinking is, if you've got someone with a direct line to Wen, maybe this would be a good time to send him back over there. He could say to Wen, our guys can work with your guys, but they've got to be serious. Now, even if there are small discrepancies in the data, it's not material to the overall size of the problem. So if your guys come back one more time with these questions, with these tactics, we'll know you're not serious and it's over." Lisle paused, listening for a response from the secretary. "To your point of pushing the pace, I think we'll get a better effect if we do it like that. And if they keep coming back with this stuff, after that, then we can be sure Wen's not serious."

Olsen thought about it. The Oslo channel wasn't going to work unless both leaders were fully committed to getting a deal. At the last Marion group meeting they had agreed that the Chinese proposal would indicate how committed Wen was. And the Chinese side had turned up with nothing.

He could get F. William Knight to go back to Wen. That wasn't a problem. But if Knight was going to go back, Olsen would have to get the president involved. Apart from unavoidable forays such as this one to the summit in Cologne, Benton was focused on driving his domestic agenda, which was requiring an enormous amount of congressional lobbying, and was leaving Olsen to manage the China track negotiation. That was exactly the way Olsen wanted it. It was driving Alan Ball crazy.

"This won't change what I'll tell the guys on the ground here," said Lisle. "I'm still going to tell them, if they don't come back with a proposal next time, that's it. This is just to make sure Wen knows we're really serious, that this is his last chance."

Olsen was silent.

"So what do you think about sending your guy to Beijing?"

"Do you really think now's the time?" said Olsen.

"Mr. Secretary, I can just see we're going to have this sequence of stuff and it's going to be very difficult to be sure we have enough evidence that they actually aren't committed to enable us to talk away. I've seen it happen. A leader-to-leader contact, even through a trusted intermediary, is what we need to short-circuit that."

"You don't think it might confuse things?"

"No. You said you wanted to find the point where they bust. You said that was critical. Mr. Secretary, believe me, that's going to take forever unless we do this."

There was silence again.

"Mr. Secretary?"

"Let me think about it."

Thursday, June 23
President's Study, The White House

It was the heat coming from the Taiwan lobby that Benton found perplexing. For a couple of weeks they had been talking up, with a number of congresspeople who were in their pocket making statements calling on the president to affirm his support for the continuing autonomy of the island. Joe Benton had made no specific statements about Taiwan during the campaign, and it had never featured as a major element on his agenda. Why were they starting now?

Otherwise, the news was better. F. William Knight was back from Beijing. He reported that it had taken him only a day to see Wen and their conversation had had a notably positive tone. Wen said he understood President Benton's interest to advance to substantive proposals. He said he wasn't aware his people had gone back to ask for more data and he promised to look into it and see whether any more data were really needed before progress could be made. If not, he would send his negotiators back with a proposal and the talks could proceed.

"That sounds about as good as we could expect," said the president.

Olsen didn't reply. He could have scripted Wen's response himself.

"What do you think we'll get back?" said John Eales.

Olsen shrugged. "Any proposal that does come back will likely have caveats about verification of the raw data. They have to do that to save face. They can't demand access to the raw data one day and then turn around and say they don't need it the next, not without paying some kind of lip service to that point."

"They can have their caveats," said Benton. "We can live with that as long as they come back with a serious offer and we can see they want to do a deal."

Olsen nodded. The skepticism was in his eyes.

"I realize we haven't passed that test yet, Larry."

"They're going to start with cuts on a per capita basis. The day we see them moving from that, that's the day we know we're in business."

Benton shook his head, smiling. He felt a lot more hopeful than his secretary of state.

"How long until we expect to see their proposal?" Eales asked.

Wen had told Knight he didn't want to delay. "If he wants to show us he's serious," said Olsen, "probably two to three weeks."

"They must have had some kind of a proposal ready when they were talking to Gartner."

"Not necessarily. If they never treated it seriously, it's possible they never formulated a position. Just kept saying no and watched Art Riedl turn up with something new every time. My guess," said Olsen, turning to the president, "is that they do have something and have had for a while. But they can't come back with it tomorrow. They have to make like they're only doing it now because they only just accepted our data."

"Well, if they have to do it like that, they have to do it. Whatever. You think two or three weeks?"

"I'd say that's optimistic."

The president thought about the implications of the timing. The opportunity for a Fourth of July announcement had closed, but that had always been a remote possibility, and an arbitrary deadline. There were more important considerations. The budget bill, which was the linchpin of the New Foundation package, was still caught up on the Hill, and he and Angela Chavez were having to spend all the time they could find lobbying the waverers in both houses. The G9 meeting in India was coming up in a little over a month. Time-tabling meetings for the fourth Kyoto round were about to start, and the first UN-sponsored agenda discussions were due to begin in Bangkok in November. Benton was under extreme pressure to go further publicly in his commitment to Kyoto. His secretary of environment, Andrea Powers, was becoming increasingly frustrated at his unwillingness to do that. And now there was this sudden awakening of the Taiwan lobby. That disturbed him. It made him feel how vulnerable he was to a leak about the Oslo channel—not necessarily the content of the talks, but even a rumor that talks were taking place—and how painful the ramifications would be for everything he was trying to achieve.

"What do we know about this Taiwan thing?" he asked.

"I'm meeting Alderman and Tang tomorrow," said Eales, naming two of the congresspeople who were most vocal on the issue. Eales had had people trying to find out why the lobby was talking up. He had put off meeting with the congressmen in case his interest fuelled their activity, but he hadn't been able to get to the source of the matter any other way.

"You think someone's picked up a hint about talks between us and the Chinese and jumped to the conclusion it's about Taiwan?"

"That would be logical," said Olsen. "Any substantive talks between us would be assumed to include Taiwan."

"You think the Norwegians have leaked?"

"They're usually pretty good."

"Anything could have happened," said Eales. "Some journalist in Oslo spots us coming or going . . ."

"John, we don't exactly line up at immigration." Olsen turned to the president. "Let's remember, Mr. President, we're in a negotiation. Everything's a weapon for your adversary."

"Larry, seriously, you think Wen's behind this?" Benton smiled. "You're starting to worry me."

"It's like a pressure valve. Mr. President, don't fool yourself. Wen can turn the pressure up on you just by getting his people to put out a hint to the Taiwan lobby that we're talking. We don't have that kind of weapon to use against him in China. But he has it here, and he'll use it."

"I don't buy it," said Eales. "Larry, it works against him. Pressure from the Taiwan lobby makes it harder for us to do a deal with him."

"Does it?" Olsen looked at Eales knowingly. "Or does it makes us want to do it quicker? Wen's smart. If the pressure's getting too much for us to bear, maybe we'll give him more in Oslo just to get it done."

It happened quicker than Pete Lisle expected. Less than four weeks after the last, aborted meeting in Oslo, they were back again. That was encouraging. What happened next wasn't.

Pete Lisle opened his briefcase and reached inside.

"We are pleased to say we are authorized to receive your proposal," said Lin, "even before you provide the data we requested last time."

Lisle stopped, hand on the file with the U.S. proposal. Neither of the Chinese delegates seemed to be getting anything out of their briefcases.

He let go of the file and closed his case. "We're exchanging proposals, right?"

The Chinese pair looked at him blankly.

Lisle glanced at Oliver Wu, then turned back to the Chinese negotiators on the other side of the table. "We're swapping proposals. That was the deal we agreed." Lisle made a giving movement with one hand, and a taking movement with the other. "We give you ours, you give us yours."

"We are authorized to receive you proposal," repeated Lin. "As you remember, last time we asked for further information and the raw data so that we could perform an independent analysis, but out of consideration for the seriousness of the matter and his regard for President Benton, President Wen is prepared to consider your proposal even without receiving this, although we must later receive this as well."

Pete Lisle stared at Lin. "Let me get this straight. You haven't brought a proposal?"

"Please show us your proposal," said Gao Jichuan. His English was more heavily accented than Lin's. "The reason we are here is we understand you have a proposal."

Pete Lisle took the briefcase right off the table. "We swap proposals. That's the reason we're here."

"Are you saying you don't have a proposal?" said Gao.

"I'm not saying that. I'm asking you for yours."

"President Wen has made a very generous concession to consider your proposal even though the data has not yet been given to us," said Gao. "To ignore the gesture of President Wen is a great insult."

Pete Lisle glanced at Lin. The other man didn't meet his eyes.

Lisle turned back to Gao. "We have no intention to insult President Wen."

Gao smiled. "Then please show us your proposal."

"I'm unable to show you anything unless you provide your proposal as well."

"Do you want me to insult President Wen with that answer?" said Gao.

"I'm not insulting President Wen."

"Then hand it over," said Gao peremptorily. "Give us the proposal and we can move on."

"I'm not handing anything over. You provide your proposal as well, like we agreed, and we can talk."

"Are you stopping the talk? Is that what you want to do? You came to us! You came to us and said you want to talk and now you want to stop it? The fault will be on your hands." Gao lapsed into Mandarin, talking rapidly to Lin. Wu listened. It was meant for him, he knew.

"They know the risk they're running," Wu whispered, translating Gao's words for Lisle as the Chinese negotiator gesticulated. "They know the risk they're running and they still want to do it. President Wen won't send us back again. This is their last chance and they refuse to go on."

There was silence.

Lin Shisheng smiled at Lisle. "Pete, you should give us the proposal. Then we can see what happens. Don't let us finish like this. President Wen has made a big concession."

Asking for something he was never going to get, thought Lisle, and then trying to gain an advantage by conceding that he wouldn't demand it after all. Like that was a trick he hadn't seen before—about a thousand times.

"I'm sorry, I'm not in a position to do that," said Lisle.

"Then please consult your president."

"No. I can't consult the president on this. I have clear instructions. Lin, we have an agreement."

"President Benton would not want to insult President Wen," said Gao. "I can only imagine President Benton is not aware of the concession President Wen has made."

"President Wen would not want to go back on a deal he has done," said Lisle. "I can only imagine, therefore, that President Wen's instructions have been misunderstood."

"You should consult."

"*You* should consult."

Gao smiled derisively.

There was silence.

Suddenly Lisle stood up. "This is impossible. We're leaving."

Oliver Wu scrambled to his feet.

"All right," said Lin hurriedly. "Nothing's impossible."

Lisle waited, still standing.

"Let us consult. Give us an hour."

"One hour?"

Lin nodded. Gao stared on, stony-faced.

"Okay. One hour."

Lisle and Wu left the room. They stood in the corridor. "Let's get out of here," said Lisle. "I've gotta cool down."

They strode out into the July sunshine.

"First law," said Lisle. "Never get angry." He was silent for a moment. "*Damn* these guys!" he muttered through clenched teeth, slamming a fist into the other hand.

"Were we going to walk?" said Wu.

"Absolutely! We *were* walking. I'm not bluffing these guys. I'm not going to bluff them even once, and pretty soon they're going to understand that. We're going back in there in exactly sixty minutes and if they're not there then we're leaving."

Oliver Wu was impressed by Lisle's decisiveness. And somewhat scared by it.

"If we walk out, could we come back?"

"You can always come back," said Lisle darkly. "Once someone wants to do a deal, you can always come back. Until that time, there's no point being here."

They sat down at a bench across the lawn from the front of the house.

"They don't want it," said Wu suddenly.

Lisle looked at him. "How do you know?"

Wu shrugged. "They don't. I can tell."

"I don't think you can. Not yet." Lisle's anger had passed. "That little performance in there, that could have been one last ruse. Wen might not even know. Our friend Lurch might just have thought he'd try one last time and see if he could be a hero."

"Well, they don't want it enough, anyway," said Wu. "They have to want it as much as us, and they don't. And they can see that. Everything President Benton does shows he's desperate to do a deal."

"Not everything's visible to them, Oliver."

"I'm talking about what *is* visible to them." Now it was Wu who was angry. He felt they weren't working with a strong hand because of the president's approach. "We shouldn't have sent Knight. What was the point of sending Knight? They come back once with nothing, we're not happy, we send Knight. It's like begging. Way too fast."

"That was my idea," said Lisle.

Wu looked at him in surprise.

"I don't think we'd have even got what we've got if we hadn't sent Knight."

"What have we got?"

Lisle smiled. "Listen, Dr. Wu, at this stage, we're not trying to do a deal. We're trying to see if they're serious enough to want to do one."

"And you think we'll be able to tell that?"

Pete Lisle looked at his watch. "I think, in about fifty minutes, we'll have a pretty good idea."

They went back in when the hour was up. There was no sign of Lin or Gao in the room. Wu looked at Lisle questioningly. The other man smiled. "I'm going to be firm with these guys, but I'm not crazy." They waited. Half an hour later, Lin and Gao turned up.

Lisle watched them expectantly. Gao reached into his briefcase, pulled out a file, and handed it to Lin. Lin put it down on the table.

"That's the proposal of the Chinese government?" asked Lisle.

Lin nodded.

Lisle pulled the U.S. proposal out of his briefcase and placed it on the table as well. He left his hand flat on the folder.

"Now, just so we're all clear. This is not a commitment by the government of the United States. Nothing in this paper represents a commitment by the government of the United States until a final agreement is reached between our two governments, at which time, only the conditions in the final agreement will be those to which the government of the United States is committed. If there is no such final agreement, nothing in this paper represents a commitment by the government of the United States as the basis for any future discussions." Lisle paused. The conditions were set out explicitly at the head of the paper. It was the oldest trick of the negotiating book for one party to pocket a suggestion made by the other as part of a proposal, despite refusing to agree to anything else, and to try to use that as the starting point for negotiations in a future round. "Do you understand these conditions, gentlemen? Do you accept them?"

Lin nodded. Gao didn't respond.

"The same conditions are true for our paper," said Lin.

"That's fair," said Lisle. "We will read your paper on that basis. Now, what we've agreed—again, just to be clear—is that we will look at the two papers and we will then work together to produce an integrated version with the differences between us in brackets. Once we've done that, we will negotiate only on the parts in brackets. Are you still comfortable with that as the process?"

Lin nodded.

"Good. Then we'll proceed on that basis."

Lisle pushed his file across the table toward Lin. Lin pushed the Chinese proposal in the opposite direction.

The proposal that Pete Lisle had provided proposed a cut of thirteen percent in emissions in the first five years, followed by an eleven percent cut in the second five years, apportioned between the two countries on the basis of average national emissions over the three years previous to the agreement. Other clauses dealt with details of timing, verification, penalties and subsidiary issues. It came to sixteen pages. The document inside the file that Lisle now opened was only two pages long.

The total global cut suggested by the Chinese side was fourteen percent over eight years. The apportionment between the two countries was according to GDP per capita. But the sting in the tail came when Pete Lisle turned to the second page. An additional weighting was to be applied in the apportionment, reflecting total emissions per capita over the previous fifty years, on the grounds that emitted carbon dioxide remained in the atmosphere for at least this period.

Pete Lisle didn't know—he would have to provide the numbers to Jackie Rubin in Washington so the figures could be analyzed—but he was guessing that if that weighting was applied, China probably wouldn't have to cut anything at all.

Saturday, July 30

Lake Palace Resort, Udaipur, India

Joe Benton glanced across the table at President Wen. It was a huge round table, and another seven world leaders sat around it, each backed by entourages of a dozen or more people.

It was the first G9 to be hosted by India, which had been admitted to the club four years earlier. Consciously adopting the role of spokesperson for the still-developing world, the Indian government had stated that the focus of the meeting would be threefold: the final liberalization of trade in agricultural products, which would require termination of the remaining subsidies in developed countries; transition to a new patent regime for genetically modified crops; and support for environmental refugees by reception countries in the developing world, most of which lacked the resources even to manage the internal migrations being forced upon them by climate change. In the days before the meeting, as if to make the point, an early monsoon had put almost a fifth of the Bangladesh land surface under water and sent another four million refugees streaming toward the Indian border to join the estimated twenty million who were already living on the other side. Terrible scenes had taken place along the border until world opinion had forced the Indian government to let the refugees through. No one was prepared to admit it yet, but everyone knew that few of them would ever go back. Joe Benton had come armed with a generous aid package for the Bangladesh refugees and he planned to use his announcement of the funding as a spur to the other governments of the G9 to address the problem on a systematic scale. But the most important part of the meeting, for him, wouldn't take place in the main meeting hall in the presence of eight other leaders and two hundred staff. It would take place in a private discussion, scheduled for later that day, between him and President Wen.

In Oslo, Pete Lisle and Oliver Wu had been negotiating intensively with Lin and Gao for nearly three weeks.

The initial proposals were a million miles apart. For the first few days the two pairs of negotiators ignored this as they worked on creating an integrated document with an agreed scope and set of clauses, leaving all the differences in brackets. This itself had proved a demanding task. The Chinese proposal, for example, had said nothing about verification, while the U.S. paper offered suggestions about the method, frequency and depth. Should verification go into the paper at all, and if so, what level of detail was appropriate? Eventually the two sides agreed that the paper should include verification as an item, but every specific clause on the subject in the U.S. paper ended up in brackets, like so much else, to be negotiated later. The integrated paper that emerged out of those first days was little more than a framework on which these sets of brackets could be hung. Yet those early days brought other benefits. By working together without having to settle the important differences, the two pairs of negotiators got to know each other. Solving a problem together—even a trivial problem over wording or location in a text—builds trust and a sense of shared purpose. Lisle tried to find ways of engaging Gao. He had forced him to back down when Gao claimed the Chinese government wouldn't provide a proposal, and Gao had lost face. Lisle wanted to repair that damage, but it wasn't easy. He made a point of giving in to Gao on a number of small issues. Gao remained aloof. Lin, on the other hand, needed no encouragement. He had obviously been embarrassed by the charade over the proposals and was relieved to be working collaboratively, and he found every means of letting Lisle and Wu know short of actually saying it.

By day six, there was a single paper, approved by Olsen in Washington and, Lisle assumed, by whoever Lin and Gao were talking with in Beijing. Then the hard part began.

They sat down to start talking about the contested details in brackets. As a rule, there are two ways of doing this: start with the hardest part in the hope that everything else will fall into place if the greatest obstacle can be overcome, or start with the easy bits in the hope that early success will make it easier to resolve the biggest problem. Either way, everything has to be settled. Lisle chose to go straight to the most difficult part, the formula for the emissions cuts. A week later, they were still talking about it. As Lisle had guessed, the Chinese suggestion, combining a relatively low level of cut

with a per capita apportionment, and an additional weighting for historical emissions levels, meant that China ended up with a two percent cut in
emissions over the next ten years, compared with around forty percent for
the U.S. That simply couldn't work, and Lisle said that to Lin and Gao at
the beginning. They asked for a counterproposal. Lisle wouldn't give them
one—they would take the new proposal and pocket it, so that he would
have given something away while getting nothing in return. If he was going
to provide a counterproposal to their position, he asked them to provide a
counterproposal of their own to the U.S. position. They refused, saying the
U.S. position was so historically unfair there wasn't any way even to begin
to address it. Lisle tried to explore ideas without putting anything in writ-
ing. What if he agreed to consider taking some account of GDP per capita—
would they agree to remove the weighting for historical emissions? Would
they increase the total size of the cuts? Lin spoke about the historical injus-
tice of a developed country asking for equivalence from a developing country. Wu asked if they would agree to equivalence if China was considered a
developed country. A futile debate ensued, taking the best part of a day,
over the definition of a developed versus developing country and whether
China should be considered one or the other. Lisle asked for an exchange
of counterproposals once more. Lin said no counterproposal was possible
until the American position became more realistic. After a couple more days
of this, in consultation with Olsen in Washington, Lisle decided to give the
Chinese side a new proposal incorporating a number of concessions as a
means of seeing whether they could unlock the process. They realized the
Chinese would pocket the proposal but the concessions were ones which
Lisle knew he would have to make anyway. Predictably, Lin and Gao welcomed the concessions and then said the proposal was still so far from ac-
ceptable that they couldn't come back with anything new from their side.
They asked for another proposal. That triggered one of Lisle's rules of negotiations. You can let the other side pocket something once, but never
more than that. You can't give them another proposal until you get a proposal back. Six more days of talks went nowhere.

They were stalled. Lisle suggested an adjournment. He and Wu went
back to Washington, Lin and Gao went to Beijing.

Joe Benton and President Wen went to India.

* * *

They met in a room with a magnificent balcony overlooking the water and the yellow hills beyond. The luxury resort the Indian government had chosen for the summit was built in the middle of a lake and was accessible only by helicopter or boat. It also had only fifty-eight suites, which meant that a fleet of boats continuously crisscrossed the lake, taking hundreds of aides and jounalists who accompanied the G9 leaders to and from hotels around the lake where they were being accommodated.

Close to fifteen of the scheduled forty-five minutes allocated to the meeting were gone by the time the photojournalists were cleared out of the room. The two presidents remained sitting in armchairs, with interpreters behind them, and a small entourage on a sofa on either side. The two parties had agreed to bring three officials each. On the sofa beside Benton were Larry Olsen, Bob Colvin, the treasury secretary, and Ellen Wainwright, the U.S. trade representative. Flanking President Wen were Foreign Minister Chou, Finance Minister Hu, and Minister Li Wenyuan.

The two presidents made general remarks. Wen talked about this being their first face-to-face meeting and hoping there would be many more. Benton responded appropriately. The two leaders discussed a recent bombing that had taken place in the Philippines and the need to cooperate against terrorism. Then Wen started talking about whaling and his hope that the industry could be outlawed forever. Benton wondered why Wen was devoting time to that, and responded by talking about his hopes that business links between the two countries would soon be as strong as ever—an oblique reference to the contract debacle back in March—and said that in token of American seriousness in this area he had brought Ellen Wainwright, the U.S. trade representative, to the meeting, along with Bob Colvin. Ellen nodded in acknowledgment. Wen said he was aware that Minister Hu knew Wainwright well and Hu nodded in turn. They would meet together afterward. More superficial remarks were exchanged. Joe Benton was aware of time passing. He had told Olsen that with about ten minutes to go he was going to suggest that Wen and he have a few minutes in private. Olsen had tried to discourage him, but Benton had overruled his objection. His gut told him this was what was needed. Direct, him and Wen, face-to-face, without the pressure of anyone else looking on, so they could be completely open with each other. That was the only way to break the deadlock in Oslo. Eventually he made the suggestion. Wen held up his hand as the interpreter began translating and said in English that he would be pleased to speak in private with the president.

The entourages stood. Wen glanced at his interpreter and she stood as well. Everyone but the two presidents left the room.

There was silence for a moment. Both men savored the rare treat of being left unattended.

Joe Benton smiled. "I'm afraid it's going to take a little while until we get to know each other and how we each do things."

Wen smiled as well. "That is the problem with world leaders, is it not? As soon as one gets to know another, the first one is gone." Wen laughed. "We should all be leaders for life!"

Benton chuckled along. "I don't know about you, President Wen, but I'm not sure I'd want to inflict something that awful on the American people."

"What? Me or you?" said Wen. The two presidents laughed again.

"Call me Joe," said Benton.

"Frankie," said Wen. He had picked up the moniker when doing postgrad work at Harvard thirty years earlier, and there were at least four different stories in the diplomatic world supposedly explaining how he had got it.

"Okay," said Benton. He sat forward. "Here's the thing, Frankie. My guys tell me we're stalled in Oslo."

Wen looked at him with interest.

"They're stuck."

Still Wen didn't reply.

"Okay, I'm going to be completely open. Your proposal is way below our bottom line. We're not bluffing, it's just way below it. We can't do it. We've given on some things, but nothing's coming back. I'm being completely open. Neither of us is going to get anywhere from here if we don't see any movement on your side."

Wen nodded.

"This is difficult for all of us," said Benton. "I know that. But President Wen—"

"Frankie."

Benton nodded. "Frankie, if we can pull this off, the world is going to thank us for generations to come."

"It would truly be a historic step," said Wen.

"I know you have to be sure there's stability at home. I understand that. And whatever way you want to sell it at home, that's okay. I know, I just know, that if we both want to make this happen, we can do it. There's got to be a way we can find to get this done. What choice do we have?"

The Chinese president gazed at Benton.

Then he spoke, and his voice shook with emotion. "This is a time for leaders, Joe. This is a time to do the hard things."

"It is." Benton felt it strongly, and his voice almost shook as well. He felt that the Chinese leader understood. For the first time, he felt that he really had a partner in this process. "It is, Frankie. A time for leaders."

"Tell your men to go back to Oslo."

"I want to do that, but I can't send them back if there's not going to be anything new."

"Joe, trust me. Send them back."

When they came out, it was twenty minutes after the scheduled end of their meeting. The entourages waited outside in two small groups. The presidents were chatting as they emerged. Wen said something, and Benton laughed.

Olsen sought his eye.

Benton winked, head still half-turned to listen to something else that Wen was saying.

Three days later, Lisle and Wu sat down in Norway across the table from Lin and Gao. Lin pulled a file out of his briefcase. He presented a redraft of the integrated paper.

The demand for an adjustment to reflect historical levels of emissions had disappeared.

Thursday, August 18
Benton Ranch, Wickenberg, Arizona

Joe Benton listened to what Lisle was telling him from Oslo. The rest of the Marion group were patched in on the call from wherever they were on vacation. After two weeks of intense bargaining, the difference between the sides was a matter of timing. One year.

The team in Olso had expanded. Lisle and Wu had been joined by an analyst from Jackie Rubin's team, who was able to model the economic and demographic impact of each option as the negotiation continued, and by an experienced drafter from the State Department. The Chinese team had expanded as well, with four support officials flying in from Beijing.

They had moved to an agreed emissions reduction of twelve and ten percent in the two five-year periods, less than the U.S. had wanted but a lot more than the Chinese had started with. That meant relocating approximately another two million American citizens than would have been the case with the larger reduction. On the apportionment of the cuts, the negotiation had been difficult and demanding. At various points, at the end of late nights, each side had threatened to walk out. According to Pete Lisle's laws of negotiations, that was good. If a side didn't threaten to walk out, they weren't feeling any pain. Ideally someone actually should walk out, at least once, but for everybody's sake Pete was prepared to forgo that step. Yet they hit a wall after agreeing to base the apportionment on the absolute level of national emissions—which was in the United States' favor—adjusted to take account of per capita GDP—which was in China's favor. The U.S. position was to adjust twenty percent of the cut by the per capita formula, the Chinese position to adjust fifty percent. On the basis of the modeling, and after extensive phone consultation with Olsen, Rubin and the president, Lisle knew the U.S. couldn't go above thirty percent. He offered twenty-five, the Chinese came back with forty-five. Halving the difference wasn't going to get there. Lisle offered thirty. The Chinese didn't budge. Either that was the Chinese bottom line, or they were seeing if they could get more. They now had thirty in their pocket, which was the actual U.S. bottom line. They may or may not have realized this. Lisle was prepared to let them know that, and he did. Did they believe it? Another two days of fruitless negotiation ensued. They had been negotiating for ten days solid. They were exhausted. Lisle suggested they all take a day off.

At this point, Pete Lisle didn't know where to go next. He didn't want to reopen the principle of absolute emissions with a partial adjustment. It had taken ten excruciating days to get there and if he reopened that, he knew, they were back to square one, or worse. Yet there seemed to be an unbridgeable gulf of fifteen percent in the weighting proportion, and since the effect of the per capita weighting was so great, that was simply too big.

Lisle decided on a break in the talks and took the American team into Oslo for a day of sightseeing, trying to get everyone's head clear. Todd Anderson, the modeling guy, was a naval history buff and was desperate to see the Viking Ship Museum in Oslo. Soon they were all staring at the long, curving, scroll-prowed hull of a ninth-century Viking ship—apparently the best preserved ninth-century Viking ship in the world —all except Todd, who wasn't staring but walking excitedly around the thing like a kid in a candy store. As he looked at the vessel, Pete Lisle thought how fitting it was that they were here. Their negotiation, and the deal they would do if it succeeded, was just about as fragile a vessel as this canoe-like thing in which men had set out to cross oceans. Were they insanely brave or simply idiotic? Was there a difference? And it was while he was pondering this that Andy Rawlins, the drafter, who was gazing at the tapering hull of the vessel as well, had an idea. What if they tapered the adjustment, working up from twenty percent across the ten-year period?

Two minutes later, they were out of the museum, dragging a protesting Todd Anderson with them.

The modeling went on all night. The next morning, they presented their proposal to Lin and Gao. Apply the per capita adjustment to twenty percent of the reduction at the start, and in year three begin tapering it so that it would reach forty percent in year ten. Privately, Lisle was prepared to go to forty-five percent in the last year.

Lin and Gao came back with something different. Start the tapering in year two.

Todd Anderson had already tried that and it didn't look good. They went away and ran the numbers again. The trade-off between the extra five percent at the end, which Lisle was prepared to give, and the earlier start up front, was disadvantageous to the U.S. Approximately an extra half point of economic contraction.

When they reconvened, Lisle offered the extra five percent at the end if they would agree to start the tapering in year three. Lin and Gao stuck. Start in year two or don't start at all. It was a matter of timing. One year.

"Give me those numbers again, Pete," said Joe Benton in his study at the ranch.

"An additional half percent decline in GDP. That's as close as Todd can estimate it."

"When does the additional decline hit?" asked Jackie Rubin, who was patched in from Maine.

"Year four," said Lisle. "You should be able to access the spreadsheet on the secure server."

"I've got some kind of glitch up here. I can't open it."

"A half percent," said Benton. "Jackie, is that a deal breaker?"

At her kitchen table in Maine, Rubin rolled her eyes. What was another half percent when you were already fourteen down?

"No," she said. "I don't think so at this stage."

"And this makes a real difference to them?" said Benton.

"Not that we can tell," said Lisle. All through the negotiation, Anderson had been using the models to analyze the impacts on China as well, together with the effects of the various options on other major economies. But their level of knowledge of the Chinese position was limited, and they had no real understanding of how the Chinese government planned to handle relocation and the impact of economic contraction. Differences that looked trivial to them might have significant implications to the Chinese government in ways they didn't understand.

"Pete," said Benton. "Give me your sense. What do you think?"

"I think this is it," said Lisle. "I think this is as good as it gets. But whether that's good enough, that's something I don't know. Mr. President, I'm here. I'm in it. You've got to take that into account." Pete Lisle knew that after a time, in any intense negotiation, the negotiators become invested in the process. They have a stake in reaching a result. They develop a relationship with their counterparts on the other side. They get weary and just want to get it finished. All of that can lead them to recommend agreements they ought to walk away from, or give too much to the other side in order to get a deal done. As an experienced mediator in other people's disputes, he had seen it happen. It was always a mistake to persist with a deal under those circumstances. If you wouldn't be able to sell the deal to your base, or if it wasn't sufficient to deliver the minimum it had to deliver, you were better off to walk away no matter how much blood, sweat and tears had gone into the negotiation. Any agreement you did make would soon be repudiated by your own supporters, and the betrayal felt by the other side would make it that much harder to start again.

"Oliver?" said the president.

"I don't think we're going to get anything more."

Joe Benton considered the numbers he had written on the pad. They were worse than he had hoped for. But according to the models, the numbers on the Chinese side didn't look too pretty either. Everyone was going to take pain. There was no way around it.

He looked out the window at the field behind the house. The sky was blue, piercing blue. Outside, it was over a hundred degrees.

"Let's assume this is the best we can get," he said. "Do we take it? What does everyone else think? Alan?"

"It's not as if I've had any time to think about it," muttered Ball resentfully. The first he knew of the details of the deal were on this call.

"What's your feeling?" asked Benton, ignoring Ball's insinuation.

"If we do this, and we bring it into Kyoto, will the others follow?"

"We have no choice but to make sure they do." The figures were based on the assumption that cuts would be achieved globally. "Personally, by going out in front like this along with China, I think this is the best way to make that happen. Alan, do you have any other objection?"

There was silence for a moment.

"No," said Ball.

"Larry?"

Larry Olsen was on Cape Cod. He was amazed that there seemed to be a genuine deal on the table, one in which China took real pain. He had never believed it would get to this point. "I'm still not happy with where we are on verification."

"It's not optimal," said Lisle. "At this stage it's a statement of principles. We agreed we'll have a working party that will come up with an agreed procedure within six months."

"You think they'll stick to that? They won't use that later to renegotiate?"

"I think they're committed to the numbers we've agreed on. Whatever happens on verification, we're not going to reopen those. And we start implementation even if we don't have verification finalized. That's critical."

"Yeah, well, there goes verification," said Olsen.

"I don't think so, Mr. Secretary. We've agreed penalties. Until we have verification, if one side shows the other is noncompliant in *anything*, that's sufficient for the full penalties to kick in. After that, it's up to the guilty party to prove it's compliant again. That argues that both sides should want verification."

"Is it definite they won't reopen the numbers?" asked John Eales.

"We agreed that anything we agreed on is a firm commitment. We've agreed on the numbers."

"Maybe you can still try to harden the verification principles," said Olsen.

Lisle was extremely reluctant to do that. "Mr. Secretary, what we have now is a package. I don't think we can unpick one part of it without them unpicking something else."

"Larry," said the president, "I'm happy to have verification principles at this stage and go with the working party on procedure. Is there anything else?"

Olsen was silent for a moment. "No."

"Then I'm going to put you down as a yes. Ben, what about you?"

"I'm in," said Hoffman.

"Jackie? I take it you're okay?"

"I haven't seen the spreadsheet, but as I said, a half point isn't a deal breaker."

"John? What's your position?"

"I'm go."

"Are there any other thoughts?"

Benton listened. There was silence on the line. Nothing. It was his decision now. He looked at the numbers he had written on the page as Lisle had been talking. To him, they weren't just numbers. He couldn't see them, probably didn't know any of them and never would, but as a result of this final tweaking he would probably be putting an extra few hundred thousand people out of their jobs, their families into hardship. More suffering to add to the suffering of the he-didn't-know-how-many people who were going to be hurt by the economic contraction and the Relocation that were coming. They were people to him, not numbers.

But if he didn't do the deal, how many more would he be condemning, and to what greater misery? And if he said no, how did he know that he would ever get a better agreement? Or any agreement at all?

Diplomacy was about getting the best result in conditions of mutual uncertainty. Larry Olsen had said that to him, or something like it. At that moment Joe Benton was reminded of it.

And he had a deal. He actually had a deal. In his study in Wickenberg, Joe Benton smiled. Suddenly it was real. He glanced at the date on his screen. August 18. His mind was working. August 28. If Lisle could get it finalized and Olsen could get out to Oslo to initial it, he could announce it on the anniversary of Martin Luther King Jr.'s "I have a dream" speech. That was rich with resonance. What greater dream could a president have than to make the planet healthy and fit for future generations? Already, phrases and sentences were forming in Joe Benton's mind.

"Mr. Lisle, Dr. Wu," he said. "I thank you for your work. Let's do it."

Larry Olsen was expecting Premier Zhai or Foreign Minister Chou. But when the door opened, it was Ding Jiahui who walked in.

The arrangement was that a senior government official from each side would sign the preliminary agreement in Oslo. The two presidents would then simultaneously announce the deal in public at an agreed time, and later meet at a summit to sign the final agreement.

Olsen shook Ding's hand.

"I'm glad to see you again, Minister," he said.

Ding responded in Mandarin, even though his English was flawless. He had brought his own interpreter with him. He was immaculately dressed, as always. Larry Olsen, as always, was wearing a much-used and crumpled suit.

Lin introduced himself and Gao. Olsen introduced Pete Lisle and Oliver Wu to Ding. Ding said something to Wu in Mandarin. Wu said yes, he had been in Beijing with Olsen back in April.

"Much has happened in the four months since then," said Ding.

"Much," said Wu.

They sat. Lisle produced two copies of the memorandum, each with an English and Mandarin version that had previously been agreed and initialed by the four negotiators. Lisle handed one copy to Ding and the other to Olsen.

"I take it you have President Wen's authority to sign on behalf of the government of the People's Republic," said Olsen

The interpreter murmured needlessly in Ding's ear. Ding nodded.

"I have President Benton's authority." Olsen smiled. "You'd better look this over to make sure we haven't tried to pull a fast one."

Ding began to scan the pages. First the Mandarin version, then he turned to the English.

"Once we do this, we just need to figure out when President Benton and President Wen announce it," said Olsen. "President Benton's keen to announce it in a speech he's making Sunday. I think you guys already know that."

Ding nodded absently, still scanning. It was taking a while, as if he was actually following the text.

Olsen glanced at Pete Lisle. Lisle shrugged.

At length Ding was finished. He looked up.

"We okay?" asked Olsen.

Ding smiled pleasantly and said something. The interpreter spoke. "There is no rec ognition here of the historical responsibility of the United States."

"The United States isn't admitting any," said Olsen.

"There must be recognition of the historical responsibility." Ding gazed at Olsen as the interpreter translated.

Olsen glanced at Lisle. Lisle shook his head slightly but emphatically.

"Minister Ding," said Olsen, "this is the agreement. Mr. Lisle, this is the text that was agreed, correct?"

"It is, Mr. Secretary."

"Mr. Lin?"

Lin glanced at Ding.

"Well, I think you'll find that Mr. Lin and Mr. Gao's intials are on this draft."

Ding pushed the paper back across the table toward Olsen. "There must be recognition of the historical responsibility." Ding paused. "Five percent of the world's population, twenty-five percent of its emissions. For so many years. There must be a recognition of this."

"Why didn't your people say this before?"

There was no answer from the other side of the table. Ding continued to gaze at Olsen. Gao watched stony-faced, as if it had nothing to do with him. Lin avoided Pete Lisle's eyes. Lisle wondered whether he had known this was going to happen.

"Minister Ding, can you give us a moment?" said Olsen.

"Certainly," replied Ding.

Olsen got up, taking his copy of the memorandum. Lisle and Wu went with him into the corridor outside the room. A man from the Norwegian foreign ministry was waiting there in case they needed anything. Olsen smiled at him briefly, and they went further along the corridor.

"What the fuck is he doing?" hissed Olsen.

Lisle shook his head. "I have no idea."

"What does he want?"

"I don't know," whispered Lisle. "Historical responsibility. I don't know what he wants."

"He knows we're not negotiating here, right? He knows this is a done deal?"

"They know."

Olsen looked at Wu.

"No question," said Wu.

Olsen shook his head in disgust. "What the fuck do they want?"

"Sounds like some kind of admission that it's our fault."

"The United States isn't admitting that! Can you imagine what that might mean? Who knows where that might lead?"

"It's crazy."

"I'm going to tell him to go! We're not here to negotiate. He wants to negotiate, we're finished!" Olsen paused, fuming. He glanced along the corridor at the Norwegian official for an instant, and then looked back at Lisle. "What do you think? Could we do some kind of preamble? Not admitting anything."

Lisle shrugged. "We can probably find a form of words—"

"This is outrageous! I'm not going home and coming back. If we can't work it out today, that's it. Jesus Christ! I'm ready to turn around right now."

"Maybe we can find a form of words," said Lisle.

Olsen shook his head. He shot a glance at Wu. Then he shook his head again. "All right, let's go back. Pete, I'll let you do the talking. We're not admitting historical responsibility, whatever he thinks he means by that. But if we can craft something today, and if the president agrees . . ." Olsen's expression showed how repugnant he found the situation. "This is out-fucking-rageous!"

They trooped back past the Norwegian official into the room. Ding was still sitting on the other side of the table, flanked by his interpreter, Lin and Gao.

"Minister Ding," said Lisle, "this agreement was drafted and agreed as it appears, so we are extremely surprised that you have raised the question of historical responsibility today."

Lisle paused. Ding watched him impassively.

"The United States believes this should be a forward-looking agreement between our two countries. Dwelling on the past is unhelpful." Lisle paused again. "However, it may be possible that we can find a way to put this agreement into its historical context. We could expand the preamble slightly, perhaps, and find a form of words that would satisfy your desire without compromising the strong spirit of friendship in which this agreement was written. Would that be a way forward for us?"

Ding nodded and said something in Mandarin. "Words are not sufficient," said the interpreter beside him.

"Excuse me?" said Lisle.

"One does not feed the people on words, Mr. Lisle. One does not replace the house a man has lost in the flood. With words, one does not remove from the sky the gases your country has pumped into the air for the past fifty years."

"Although your country has been the biggest emitter for the last twenty-five of those years," said Olsen, unable to contain himself.

"Five percent of the population, twenty-five percent of the emission," repeated Ding. "For so many years."

"If you want to quote numbers," retorted Olsen impulsively, "things have changed a little. You guys are sitting on forty percent of the world's emissions for a quarter of the population. So right now when you're saying that, Minister Ding, you're sitting in a big, fat house of glass."

Ding smiled. "You want our cheap manufactures, the emissions are the result. These are still your emissions, Secretary, they just happen to be taking place in China."

"*Jesus Christ!*" hissed Olsen, almost unable to contain himself. "Now I've heard it all."

"Words are not enough," said Ding. "Too many times your country has ignored its historical responsibility for great injustices. No more." Ding tapped his finger on the agreement, even as his interpreter was translating his last sentence. "No more unequal treaties."

"This is no unequal treaty!"

"Never again. You must adjust this formula to recognize the historical responsibility."

"We're not adjusting any formula!"

"You must adjust the formula because the gases in the air today are your gases and if there is no room for more it is because of you. When you adjust the formula, we will have an agreement."

Olsen, Lisle and Wu all stared at him. An adjustment for historical emissions was off the table. It was the first thing that had gone after the two presidents met in India.

"That isn't possible, Minister," said Olsen quietly, trying to get control of his anger. "I think you know that."

Ding shrugged. "The United States must accept responsibility."

"We can say something."

"That is not enough."

"We went through this with your people. We've got an agreement."

"It is not signed."

"It's agreed!"

"An unequal agreement is worse than no agreement."

Olsen shook his head, literally clamping his teeth together to contain his anger.

"Mr. Secretary," said Lin, "I'm sure there's something we can—"

Ding yelled at him in Mandarin.

"He had no right to make such an agreement," Wu whispered to Lisle and Olsen. "He exceeded his responsibility . . . he should shut up . . . he should go. Now! Go! Now!"

Lin got up. He didn't dare look anyone in the eye. Hurriedly, he left the room. The door closed behind him.

Ding gave a brisk shrug of his shoulders and straightened his tie. Olsen watched him carefully. That could have been a show, he knew. A piece of theater designed to convince him they had no deal unless they caved.

"I apologize for Emissary Lin," said Ding through the interpreter. "He has exceeded his authority, and I myself was unaware of this until today. Now, if the United States is prepared to acknowledge its responsibility, and to match that acknowledgment with a just and fair formula, perhaps it will be possible to commence discussions again. If you would like to consult with Mr. Lisle and Dr. Wu, please . . ." Ding held his hand toward the door.

"We're not adjusting the formula," said Olsen. "That's off the table."

"Then you must find another way."

Olsen stared at him.

"This is only one part. Historical injustices and divisions must be repaired."

There was silence. Ding gazed meaningfully at Olsen. Now Olsen knew what this was about. At last, they had got to it. "Historical injustices and divisions." In Chinese government-speak, that was code for only one thing. Ding was holding the emissions agreement hostage to it.

Olsen shook his head. "The discussions are over. That's why you and I are here, Minister Ding. Because the discussions are finished, and we have an agreement. There is no other way."

"Then we do not have an agreement."

"Let me make this very clear. Maybe—maybe—we'd be prepared to change the preamble to better reflect the historical context of what we're doing. But nothing else is going to change, and nothing else is going to be included in this deal. There is no other part to this." Olsen paused, staring fixedly at Ding. "We're here to sign this agreement, and if you want an agreement that's what you'd better do. This is the only one on offer."

Ding smiled briefly. He pushed the memorandum back across the table, and looked into Olsen's eyes.

"I hope you know what you're doing," said Olsen quietly. "We are ready to sign, Minister Ding. Do you understand that? We came here to sign." He pulled his handheld out of his pocket and held it up. "President Benton is waiting for my call to tell him its done."

Ding didn't bat an eye.

"Call President Wen. Call him and tell him what you're doing. We're going to walk away from this. If President Wen thinks he can get something else with this agreement, he's wrong. This is the best deal you're ever going to get from us. President Wen's making a very big gamble and he's about to lose." Olsen held out the phone to him. "Call him and let him know exactly what's going on."

Ding made no move. Olsen slapped the handheld down on the table in front of him.

"I think, Secretary Olsen," said Ding, "the one who is losing the gamble is you." He stood up.

"You're letting a historic opportunity slip away." Olsen was shouting. "You're walking away from the best deal you're ever going to get. Don't come back asking for it again. You walk away, it's off the table!"

But Ding was walking away. Literally. Followed by Gao and his interpreter, he went out the door.

Friday, August 26

Benton Ranch, Wickenberg, Arizona

It seemed that for three days he had thought about nothing but Oslo. Everything else Benton had to deal with, the steady stream of phone calls and papers that needed attention while he was on vacation at the ranch, were interludes between trying to understand what had gone wrong. Trying to make some kind of sense of it. He talked it through with Heather, but still couldn't find a way to resolve it in his mind. Amy was at the ranch. They went for long early-morning rides together, as they had always done, before the heat of the Arizona summer days got going. He tried to enjoy the time with her, so fleeting, so precious. But he fell into silence, brooding. Amy rode in silence alongside him. After the first time she asked what was going on, she knew better than to ask again.

It was the time it had taken. That was the thing he found most discouraging. Three months since the negotiators had gone to Oslo. Three months just to get to a breakdown. It wasn't long, he knew, by the standards of these things—in fact, incredibly fast—but an eternity in the face of the urgency he felt. The hurricane season was well under way, and in the past two weeks alone he had toured scenes of devastation on both the Florida and Lousiana coasts. There would be more of that, he knew, this year, and next year, and every year after that until those coasts were abandoned. And now three months of hard, painful work had gone up in smoke. If they had to start again, how many more months would it take? Joe Benton felt sick at the thought of it.

He had tried to call the Chinese president, but Wen wouldn't make himself available. He had also refused to see F. William Knight.

Now the entire Marion group was squeezed into the president's study at the ranch to figure out what to do next.

"I want to be clear one last time," said the president. "There's no way this could have been a mistake? There's no way Ding could have genuinely thought he was coming to negotiate?"

Lisle shook his head.

"And we have absolutely no reason to imagine Ding would have gone freelance on something like this?"

"We have no indication of anything going on in the Politburo," said Oliver Wu. "I've spoken with people at State and at the Agency and they have no indication of anything significant under way. The Chinese hierarchy is incredibly sensitive to even minor shifts in power. Wen's not taking any kind of action against Ding, so even if Ding did go freelance, Wen's approved it."

Olsen nodded. "Before or after the fact, it doesn't really matter."

There was silence.

"I should meet him," said the president.

"Who? Wen?" Olsen's face was incredulous. "With respect, sir, he won't even take your call."

"I'm sure I can talk to him."

"Mr. President!" Larry Olsen stopped himself, took a breath. "Mr. President," he began again, "with respect, sir, you seem to be trying to find a way to exonerate President Wen. Don't do that. Wen wanted this to happen. If you feel like someone's kicked you in the gut, that's exactly what he wants you to feel. Wen knows what he's doing. This way, when he comes back for more, he figures he'll get a better deal."

"Larry," said the president quietly, "you've told me that already."

"Sir, with all respect, you're making the mistake of thinking Wen's like you. That he thinks like you, that he has the same values as you. He doesn't. Ask Alan. I know we don't agree on a lot of things, but I bet we'll agree on this."

Ball didn't respond. Silence was about as close as he could bring himself to saying he agreed with Larry Olsen.

"Democratic leaders . . ." Olsen shook his head, as if he was almost too exasperated to speak. "Sir, democratic leaders always make this mistake when faced with authoritarians. It's classic, all the way back to Hitler and appeasement. Democrats think authoritarians think like them, so they'll back down. Authoritarians think democrats don't have the cojones to do anything, so they don't back down. Before you know it, it takes a war for each side to find out the other was wrong."

"Larry," said the president. "Don't say things like that."

There was a troubled silence in the room.

"All right," said Eales. "Let's look at this more objectively. There are two possibilities here. One is that Wen never intended to do this deal. He's pushed us as hard as he could to see where he can get us to, and now he's found out. If that's the case, he'll probably come back at some point and try to use that to get what he really wants, like Larry says. Second possibility is that he thought he could do a deal and then he found out he couldn't sell it to his base."

"And the third possibility," said Oliver Wu, "is that we're not even dealing with President Wen, or at least not only with him. He may no longer be in control of this process."

"Is there any way of knowing that?" asked Benton.

"Not that I can see, sir. Not at present."

"So let's work with what we do know," said Eales. "Either Wen never intended to cut a deal, or he decided in the end he couldn't sell it. If he decided he couldn't sell it, don't we have to ask ourselves what we can do to help him sell it?"

"I believe he told us," said Olsen.

"Then we may have to think about giving it to him," said Pete Lisle.

"No." Olsen was adamant. "You cannot do business like this, and Wen's smart enough to know it. This whole deal is about trust, trusting the other party that over five, ten years they're going to do what they say. Trusting them, by the way, to put in a verification mechanism they couldn't even agree to already. You cannot agree to a deal like this and then send someone and say at the last minute, oh, by the way, how about giving us Taiwan as well. Even if we did want to give them the go-ahead on Taiwan—and that's absolutely impossible—you don't do it like that, you don't hold everything hostage to it at the very end. It destroys trust. And you know what? It's destroyed my trust!"

It wasn't doing much for Joe Benton's trust either. He had genuinely liked Wen when he met him at the G9. The Chinese leader was humorous, personable, intelligent. He had seemed to understand the historic importance of what they were doing. Now he seemed crafty. Joe Benton was beginning to feel that Wen had made a fool of him. More than that. He felt a sense of almost personal betrayal.

"Maybe Wen had no choice," said Hoffman. "Ding could have threatened—"

"Please!" said Olsen. "I'm sorry, Ben, but I'm getting sick of this let's-find-excuses-for-President-Wen society we've got going here. Yes, it's possible he wanted to do a deal and then found he couldn't unless he got Taiwan as well, but chances are he didn't. And if we said yes to Taiwan, what he's going to come back with next? Maybe we'd still have to readjust the formula. And then what? Maybe he'd like us to shut down a bunch of Internet sites like he does it at home. Why don't we just go ahead and do that for him right now? Look, he's pushed us as far as we'd go, and that was always his intention. He's going to come back at some point and start from this position and ask for more, and he thinks he'll get it because we don't have the stomach to go through the same thing again. *That's* what he's done. When are we going to hold this man to account?"

"We can't give any more," said the President.

"He won't believe that. He'll play for time, wear you down. He's taken four months by doing this, moved us to a position, and still been the one to walk away. He'll see that as a victory."

The frustration of the last three incomprehensible days welled up in Joe Benton. "Where's the victory? Another four months gone with no action! Four months when we could have *done* something."

Olsen leaned forward in his seat. "Mr. President, please, you must stop thinking he thinks like you."

"He's not a monster."

"I'm not saying he's a monster. I'm not saying he's good or bad. It's not a value judgment. It's a fact, he has different priorities. That's what's motivating him. From his perspective, everything he does is making sense. We've got to see this from inside his head. No matter how likable he is when he talks to you, Wen is not going to risk the party. Nor would any other Chinese leader, by the way. You might be prepared to risk your chances at the next election to get a deal like this done, Mr. President, but whatever he's really thinking, I can tell you one thing—Frankie Wen ain't risking a revolution."

Joe Benton shook his head. He gazed out the window. Over the course of his years in public life, he thought he had developed a pretty good knack of understanding the way other people saw the world. The deals he had cut in the Senate wouldn't have happened if hadn't been able to see things from the other person's point of view. But those years had been devoted to domestic political issues, with domestic politicians. Maybe he really was falling into the trap Olsen was talking about.

And was Wen even in charge on this? That was a whole different question, and Benton found it intensely troubling. If Wen wasn't in charge, who was calling the shots?

"All right," he said eventually. "What do I do?"

"By not taking your call, and by refusing to see Knight," said Ball, "President Wen has sent a very clear message that he wants to leave this for a while."

"How long?"

"I don't know. We need to respect what he's saying."

"To hell with that!" said Olsen.

"We can't leave it," said Benton.

"*He* can." Olsen prodded the air forcefully. "Mr. President, you've hit the nail on the head. He can, you can't, and he knows it. That's what he's just shown you. And when he's sure the message has sunk in, *then* he's going to come back for more."

"Your view is so simplistic," muttered Ball. "So black and white."

"In the meantime," added Olsen, ignoring him, "maybe he turns up the heat on you as well. Get the Taiwan lobby going again. Maybe get the China lobby going."

"Mr. President," said Ben Hoffman. "I agree with Alan. I think we're going to have to leave him for a while. We're pursuing him too hard. We're just going to drive him away."

Ball turned his eyes to the ceiling. "Thank you! Finally! A word of sense. The more we say we want to progress this now, the more he'll hold back."

"No no no no *no!*" cried Olsen. "For once, let's do what *we* want. Let's be the ones who set the agenda."

"Isn't that what we were doing in Olso?" snapped Ball.

"Does Tuesday seem like it was what we were doing in Oslo? Wen wants to let it rest. Fine, let's not let him rest."

"And how exactly do we do that? You want the president to go crawling to Beijing?"

"Sure I do," said Olsen sarcastically. He gave Ball a scathing look, then turned to the president. "We've spent eight months now, one way and another, talking to the Chinese, trying to get them to play ball. Our timetable has been determined by them, by their willingness to engage. All the way, the only weapon we've had is the implicit threat that if they don't play ball, we're going to do something. Well, you know what? They don't want to play ball. That's what this whole process in Oslo was about, and now we've got to the bottom of it. They do not want to play ball. So it's time to make good on our threat."

"Which is what exactly?" said Eales.

"We have to *do* something. Something that says, we're not sticking to your timetable, we've got our own. And not behind closed doors. When they gave those contracts to the Europeans, it wasn't just some speech they gave behind closed doors. It was real. The rationale might have been secret, but the action was public. They're in breach of a hundred trade agreements and intellectual property agreements. We don't even need to make a new case. Let's just do it!"

"Mr. President, this is not the right thing," said Ball. "President Wen has sent a clear message that he wants to let this settle for a while and we're not going help things by trying to push him. It'll just entrench him."

"Then we've got to dig him out."

"Mr. President, this kind of thinking isn't going to get us anywhere."

"You call where we are somewhere?" demanded Olsen. "Look where we are, Alan. We act now or we can forget it."

"Mr. President, this is a mistake. If we wait on this, in three months, six months, you may well find President Wen is coming back to you with some idea of his own and then you'll be in a much stronger position to drive the process and you'll avoid this confrontationalism."

"Six months?" said Olsen. "Twelve months? Eighteen months? Jesus Christ! How long do we wait for Wen Guojie to decide to put on his party dress again?"

"Why?" shot back Ball. "Can't you wait to go to the prom?"

"All right, that's enough!" The president looked at Olsen and Ball. "Hell's bells, you guys! You have *got* to learn to work together."

There was silence. Ben Hoffman and Jackie Rubin exchanged a glance.

Joe Benton was aware of the anger within himself over the sense that Wen had made a fool of him. It would be easy to strike back impulsively with some kind of retaliation, as Olsen was suggesting. Maybe striking back was the right thing to do, but if he was going to do it, it had to be for cool, strategic reasons, not out of anger. And it was hard for Benton to believe that really was the right direction to take, that between two world leaders, between two grown men of any type, demand and counterdemand, strike and counterstrike, could ever be the answer.

He turned to Ball. "Alan," he said. "Convince me. If I wait, what's the best that happens?"

"Wen comes back and says he's ready to do the deal."

"The same deal?"

"Possibly. Maybe by then we can figure out if there's some way we can help him sell it."

Olsen rolled his eyes.

Ball saw him. "I'm not saying Taiwan! I'm just saying, when he comes back, and *he's* had time to think about it, maybe there's something more reasonable we can work out."

"How long does it take for him to come back?" asked Benton.

Ball shrugged. "I don't think it'll be that long."

"How long is that?"

"There's no way of knowing, sir."

Benton nodded. In his mind, an image came back of the wreckage he had seen along the Louisiana coast the previous week, a sodden, stinking street lined with houses that the hurricane had reduced to splinters. Further down the street, out of range of the cameras that were filming him, he had caught sight of a drowned dog bloating in the sun. He thought of the people he had met who were being housed communally in municipal halls upstate, people who told him they had been driven out of their homes two, three, four times in the past fifteen years, people who couldn't bear the thought of rebuilding only to be driven out again, who said they wouldn't go back even if it was only to wait for the relocation program to resettle them.

He shook his head. "You know, Alan, I just don't think that's good enough."

Sam Levy stood in the wings. From here, he could see the president as Joe Benton stepped forward to the lectern. Jodie Ames was in the wings as well, along with Connor Gale and a half dozen other aides and assistants. Sam could feel Jodie glancing at him. Of all the people looking on, only he knew what the president was about to say.

He hadn't found out until a couple of hours previously, on the plane. The president hadn't asked him to prepare a draft or even write a line. In fact, until three days before, Benton hadn't even been scheduled to appear at this conference, which was a meeting of leading environmental experts as one of the preliminaries to the opening of the Kyoto 4 agenda talks in Bangkok in November. Until the president had himself included in the schedule, Andrea Powers was slated to speak for the administration. And then Benton had asked Levy to come on the trip, and it was only when they were airborne that he had called Sam into his office and shared with him the draft of his speech and asked Sam to work on it with him, and Levy had discovered what was going on.

Jodie Ames was still in the dark about it. Now, as they waited for the president to begin, she gave Levy one last, intense, questioning glance.

Then Benton began, and they both turned to watch him.

The president opened by saying that he wanted to confirm the United States' commitment to the Kyoto process. Then he paused. If he was going to do that, it would have to be a Kyoto process that was different to that which had come before. Not an ever-extending round of piecemeal cuts, but a single, final, decisive round, which would face up to the full magnitude of the problems the world faced and deal with them responsibly, not defer them for the next round of piecemeal cuts, and the next round, and the round that came after that.

Sam nodded as the president said it. It was a recurrent theme that Benton had worked into the speech, piecemeal cuts, and Sam had given him an obvious phrase toward the end that would help it stick.

Then Benton said the United States—and a number of other developed countries—had to acknowledge responsibility for disproportionate use of resources and emissions of pollutants, including greenhouse gases, over the past fifty years. He accepted that the world felt a sense of grievance at this, and the United States had to recognize that. He and his administration did recognize it.

It was the moment of self-deprecation, confessional, humility, that comes before an attack. In the original draft, it had been somewhat understated, and Sam had built it up. The platform needed to be strong for the assault that was coming next.

The president launched it. His tone was serious, decisive, mind made up, the trust-me-I'm-sure-about-this tone that people loved about Straight Joe Benton.

Other nations could no longer hide behind that historical argument. While the United States would acknowledge its past actions, other nations could not use this as a reason to act just as irresponsibly in the future. In fact, more irresponsibly. The time had come for the major emitters in the world to accept the fact that, whatever had happened in the past, they were the major emitters of the present. And that the past wouldn't, couldn't make the future better. Only the present could do that. And no country in the present had to do more to change its attitude, its behavior, its willingness to take responsibility, than the world's leading emitter, which had surpassed the United States in that position fully a quarter century before.

Here the president paused, long, meaningfully, so there could be no doubt about the message. Everyone knew who the world's leading emitters were.

He named them. China. Then he hammered at them, jab after jab. China must join in the Kyoto process as leaders, not spectators. They must agree to take their fair share of the pain that everyone would be called on to experience. Whatever had happened in the past, they could not expect others to take an amount of pain that was impossible to bear while they took none. They must join in the quest for a better world for all, not only for themselves. They must accept the responsibility that came with their economic size and place in the world. The time for special pleading, special consideration, special exemptions was over. The United States would expect them to act as full partners in solving a problem that affected every single human being on earth, and of which they, now, were the leading cause. When they were prepared to do that, the United States would take its fair share, fully its fair share, of the burden.

He returned to Kyoto, to the piecemeal cuts. If the Kyoto process continued as it had over the past three decades—agreements to inadequate targets, ratifications, failure to achieve even the inadequate targets that had been agreed, more agreements, more ratifications, more failure—millions of people, hundreds of millions of people, would find their lives disrupted, blighted, even destroyed. It was too easy to sign agreements that were never going to be fulfilled. The United States could not be a party to this any longer. For one last time, it was committed to the Kyoto process, to one last round, as long as it was fast, as long as it was decisive, as long as it dealt once and for all with the problem. In his administration, the world would find an American government prepared to think the unthinkable—not one that would be party to a process that allowed the world to die a death of a thousand cuts.

He paused. Then he ended on a threat, and Sam Levy, knowing Joe Benton, knew that he must have thought long and hard about doing it, tried every which way to find another way out of the problem.

If this round failed, said Joe Benton, the United States couldn't stop. The problems weren't going away. If Kyoto, as a multilateral process, couldn't deal with them on the world's behalf, someone would have to take the responsibility to do it. The United States would use every peaceful means at its disposal. It would hold countries to account, it would impose penalties until cooperation was achieved. The problem had to be solved. Kyoto had one last chance to solve it.

Benton stopped. There was silence in the hall. From his place in the wings, Sam couldn't see the faces of the audience. It felt like the half-stunned, half-stupefied silence of an audience wondering whether it had truly heard something as momentous as it thinks it has heard. The kind of silence that can turn into repudiation or acclaim.

Then he heard applause. It started uncertainly. It swelled. It rose higher, kept going. There must be people on their feet out there, Sam knew. He glanced at Jodie Ames, who was looking at him.

"I hardly made a change to it," he said.

"Death of a thousand cuts?"

Sam smiled. "Jodie, you know me too well."

The president strode off the stage.

"Awesome speech, sir," said Jodie.

But there was nothing triumphalist in the president's demeanor. Suddenly he looked tired. "Let's get out of here," he said.

The Death of a Thousand Cuts speech, as it came to be known, got blanket coverage, positive and negative. Some commentators focused on the sense of resolve in the speech and detected an unprecedented commitment by the United States to engage as a Kyoto partner with the rest of the world. Others focused on the strident tone and predicted a resurgence of American imperialism. Some claimed to be amazed by the hypocrisy of a president who acknowledged past excesses by the United States yet apparently asked for equal sacrifices now. But everyone realized that the president had thrown down a gauntlet to the Chinese government, one which had never been thrown down before. The threat of sanctions was unmistakable.

It was as close as anyone could remember President Benton coming to an unequivocal ultimatum. Some said it was rash, others said it wasn't unequivocal enough. Some said China would ignore it, others said China couldn't afford to and the crucial question, now, was how the Chinese government would respond.

The interview with Andrew Laycock had been recorded that afternoon. Laycock, a Democratic member of the House Environment Committee, was strongly positive on President Benton's stand, which had dominated commentary and analysis since the speech in San Diego two days previously. Now Eleanor Engers and Fran O'Lachlan were in the edit suite with Dave Odgers, one of the technical guys, who was helping them cut the Laycock piece down to a four-minute segment for the late-evening political review.

Ben Lacey knocked on the door and put his head in.

"I'm busy," said O'Lachlan, not even looking up.

"Fran, there's something out here you'll want to see."

"I'm busy."

"President Wen's giving a speech. ChinaCom's put out an alert to foreign news agencies. They've flagged he's about to start talking about the U.S."

In the newsroom, a screen on the wall showed Wen speaking in front of a uniformed audience seated at long, curving desks in a huge hall. An English translation followed a few seconds behind his words.

The journalists in the room stood around the screen in silence. One of them made way for O'Lachlan to come through.

"Who's he talking to?" asked O'Lachlan.

"Some kind of army congress," said someone.

"And they're streaming this live? With a translation?"

"Apparently."

"We are good friends to the United States," said the voice of the translation, a female Chinese voice in lightly accented English.

"What time is it there?" said O'Lachlan.

"About nine o'clock tomorrow morning. He obviously wants to hit the late night shows over here."

Wen was talking again in Mandarin. The translation went on. "When the United States comes to us and says, help us with . . . help us with a problem, of course we say, how can we help? When it is a problem we all share, we say, what can we do? When they came to us, we said, look at us, we have 1.6 billion people, look at you, you have three hundred fifty million. Now, who should emit more? That is what we said, and how can anyone say that was wrong? Was that not helpful? But if a man is dying of a thousand cuts, I ask myself who gave him the first nine hundred and ninety-nine? Not who gave him the last cut, who gave him all the others? That is the person I say who bears the responsibility. I ask our friends to ask themselves that. And what if the one who gave all those cuts is that person himself. Who is the one who should save him then? Shouldn't he be the one to start? The United States . . . The United States should understand that when friends are talking to each other . . . there is no place for threats. If we disagree . . . I should warn the United States that if we disagree, then we disagree. No one will ever again dictate to China what it can and cannot do. Foreign powers that are wise will understand that and those that are not wise will discover . . . they will discover that the time is long past when foreigners can dictate to China what it will do. And if they want to test this, let them test it. If they give us one cut, we will give them a thousand back. I myself promise this."

Wen stopped. There was prolonged applause in the hall.

On another screen logged into a business news site, headlines of the speech were already scrolling under the panels of data. Other headlines started coming up. In Shanghai, shares were down three percent since Wen had started speaking.

"That's the most belligerent thing I've heard from Wen in years," murmured Fran O'Lachlan.

He was talking again.

"So, let us hope that our friends in the United States . . . and other parts of the world . . . will have sensible proposals and not make demands . . . demands that are the attempted imposition of a foreign will that the Chinese people will reject. Let everyone not forget that the Chinese people must have all restitution of . . . historical injustices and divisions. And they will have it."

Wen stopped. He bowed his head. The audience in the hall stood behind the desks and applauded.

"That's Taiwan," said Ben Lacey. "That thing about divisions, it always means Taiwan."

The image on the screen cut from Wen in the hall to a commentator in a studio who began talking in Mandarin.

The journalists began to disperse to their desks.

"He said when they came to us," said Eleanor Engers.

O'Lachlan looked at her.

"He said, when they came to us. In the speech. When they came to us."

"Who came to us?"

"Us, I guess. He was talking about the United States." Eleanor looked at Dave Odgers, the tech guy. "Dave, can we replay it?"

"If it's on the site."

In the edit suite, Odgers logged into the ChinaCom newstream that had carried the speech and downloaded it.

Engers waited. Odgers fast-forwarded through a portion of the speech. They got to the relevant part.

"*When they came to us, we said, look—*"

"Dave, stop it . . . Start it again. From there."

"*When they came to us, we said, look at us, we have 1.6 billion people, look at you, you have three hundred fifty million. Now, who should emit more? That is what we said, and how can anyone say that was wrong? Was that not helpful? But if a man is . . .*"

Engers turned to O'Lachlan and Lacey. "He says, when they came to us. It's the past tense. He didn't use that anywhere else."

Lacey shrugged. "It's a translation. Could be wrong. You know Chinese tenses."

"They streamed this live with a translation," said Engers. "This was meant to be heard outside China. Dave, can you go back and play it again?"

Odgers played it again.

"Can you take the translator's voice off?" asked O'Lachlan.

"I can try," said Odgers. "Give me a few minutes."

Odgers set to work. O'Lachlan picked up a phone. "Sally? Can you come into the edit suite?"

Sally Lu came in. A few minutes later, Odgers had taken most of the translator's voice off the file. He played it. He turned up the volume to make Wen's voice louder.

"It's past tense," said Sally.

"They came?"

"They came, we said. That's what the grammar's saying. Its distinctly past."

"It's probably a mistake," said Lacey.

"Wen's mistake?" Engers shook her head. "Wen wouldn't make a mistake like that."

"So what are you saying?"

"I think what Eleanor's saying," said O'Lachlan, "is that despite everything President Benton said in San Diego about being committed to Kyoto, President Wen would like us to know that we've been talking to them."

Saturday, September 10

Oval Office, The White House

If there was any doubt about what President Wen had intended to say, the official translation of the speech removed it. Benton knew that Wen was trying to put him under pressure, but he didn't know if Wen realized just how much pressure he had created. The Chinese president probably had no idea what it was to be on the receiving end of a free press in full cry or what impact it could have on the political process in a democratic country.

It was in full cry now. The memory of the Miami scenario in March was dragged up, and suddenly everyone was making the connection between it and the discussions that had apparently been taking place with China. Benton's legislative program was clearly going to stop cold, and if the major budget bills hadn't passed before the August recess the country would have been facing a government shutdown at the end of September. The markets were in turmoil, falling on rumors of a rift between the world's two great economic powers, rising on speculation that an agreement between them was in prospect. The right-wing press was going wild with conspiracy theories about a Democratic plot to sell out the United States to China. Every Republican pressure group from the NRA to the Sisters of the Stars and Stripes was going wild. A bunch of right-wing lawyers were talking about launching a suit against anyone in the administration who could be shown to have engaged in covert negotiations with the Chinese government. The mood was so crazy that some mainstream journalists were actually taking that seriously. John Eales had the results of snap polling. Mistrust of the president was back on the agenda.

Kay Wilson, Don Bales, Cee Amadi, and a dozen other key legislators had been in the Oval Office or on the phone to tell Joe Benton about the confusion and sheer bewilderment in Democratic ranks. Within the next week there would almost certainly be a Republican move to launch a Senate inquiry. Kay Wilson wasn't sure enough Democrats would stand firm to block it.

Bob Colvin and Henry Schulz, chair of the Federal Reserve, were communicating heavily to try to calm the markets. Their message was that, as far as they were aware, nothing had changed in the U.S. or global economies as a result of President Wen's speech. At the White House, Jodie Ames's line was that the administration didn't provide commentary on remarks made by other leaders. If people wanted to ask President Wen what he meant, they should go talk to President Wen. But they didn't want to ask President Wen what he meant. They wanted to ask President Benton what he had been doing. Had there been negotiations with the Chinese over cuts in carbon emissions or had there not? When? Where? How deep were the cuts? How far had the talks got? What did this mean for Kyoto? In the press briefing room, Adam Gehrig took a battering that made his first outings back in January look like a walk in the park. His stonewalling only convinced his interrogators that there was more to be told.

Congressional leaders and other respected Democratic figures, privately and publicly, were calling for the president to respond. Benton's staff was divided. Some wanted an immediate statement, others thought a statement would just whip up the storm. Benton himself knew that he had to speak. With every day that passed, he felt that his silence became less comprehensible to the country. Yet still he held back, despite the temptation to come out quickly and say something. He had to do better than that. He had to do more than merely provide an explanation of what had happened. That would hand the initiative back to his critics. He had to say what was going to happen next, outline a plan and put momentum behind it. That was what he was trying to figure out. Eales, Rubin and Hoffman were working round the clock with their teams and other officials to put options together for the actions he might need to take.

In the midst of all this, other key members of the administration had to be brought up to speed with what had been happening. Benton felt a certain degree of discomfort at confessing a covert operation of this importance from which he had chosen to exclude them. In the case of Angela Chavez, the feeling went beyond discomort. As he outlined the full extent of the negotiations, he saw at firsthand her personal sense of betrayal. His assurance that her role in driving New Foundation had been invaluable didn't assuage her hurt. He had promised Angela Chavez that she would be an active part of the administration. Joe Benton knew what she must be thinking now. Week after week, while all of this had been happening, he had sat at their private Wednesday lunches, face to face with her, and hadn't said a word. He didn't know whether their relationship could ever recover. He met with other officials who now needed to know. Bob Colvin and Henry Schulz. Jay MacMahon, his defense secretary. Alan Ball briefed Lou Berkowitz, the director of National Intelligence, Stuart Cohen, CIA director, and Paul Enderlich, chairman of the Joint Chiefs of Staff. The president also made time to see Andrea Powers. Andrea had been supportive of his Thousand Cuts speech, she only wished he had told her about it beforehand. She too felt Kyoto 4 had to be different from the three treaties that had preceded it. After the speech she had told him that she felt it positioned her to go in and make that happen.

Now she sat down in the Oval Office and told him she couldn't see how it was possible for her to stay in his cabinent.

This was the second time, thought Benton, she had sat in the Oval Office and said that. But this time, she didn't seem mad. She seemed calm, cool, detached. Like someone who had already, mentally, left her job.

"I guess you'd like my interpretation of what President Wen said in his speech," he said.

Powers nodded fatalistically. "Mr. President, I'd just like to know what's been going on. I just want some honesty. It's clear there's been a dialogue between you and President Wen on environmental issues, and I'm assuming some other people have known about it, but you've kept me out of that loop. That's your right, of course, but I don't think I can serve in those circumstances."

"I understand," said the president.

There was silence.

"You don't have to tell me," said Powers. "I'll just quit now, if you'll accept my resignation."

"Andrea, let's take it a step at a time."

Powers waited.

"There has been something going on. I wouldn't exactly call it a dialogue between myself and President Wen."

"For how long?"

"Actually, it goes back to the last six months of President Gartner."

Powers stared at him.

The President shrugged. "It was a very small group of people who knew, on both sides. It's nothing personal, Andrea, there were good reasons for it. It's possible that I should have involved you, and I certainly did consider it. It was a tough call. But to be honest, I don't believe there would have been an additional contribution you could have made that wasn't already represented in the group, and it would have distracted you from the excellent work you've been doing in driving compliance with our existing obligations. That's been incredibly important."

"Doesn't feel like it."

"Well, it has been. And it's going to be even more important as we go forward. We need to be scrupulous in compliance if we're going to bring anyone with us on this. As far as keeping you out of the group who were involved, I've explained why I did it, but I do apologize, on a personal level, for any hurt that's caused." Joe Benton paused for a moment. "You've got to understand, the conversation we're having today could easily have been different. I could have been sitting here telling you that you're going into the Kyoto process backed by an agreement between us and the Chinese government for extraordinary, radical action, and sanctions to be applied to any other state that didn't comply. I *should* have been telling you that. We were *that* close."

Powers was silent.

"I'm going to tell you exactly what's been happening." The president told her going through it in a fair depth of detail. "Now, you can say I was wrong to have done it like that, but it was my judgment, and I guess we're going to see now whether a more public process will work, although you may well say the chances are low because the Chinese are angry and that's my fault. And if that's the case, the buck stops with me and I accept it."

Powers frowned, trying to absorb everything she had been told.

"You're sure the predictions are right?" she asked.

"The range is right. Dr. Richards is going to be presenting the latest data, taking account of the summer findings, in about a month. But the range is right."

Powers was silent.

"All right, Andrea, tell me this. You think if I put all this stuff on the table now—in the Kyoto process—you think if I put all this stuff on the table we've got a chance of getting the deal we need?"

"Can I ask you a question first? Why do you think the Chinese government didn't cut a deal in Oslo?"

"That's an excellent question. I really don't know. I'm waiting for someone to tell me."

"You think they might think there's more credit for them in cutting it as part of the Kyoto process?"

The president shrugged.

Powers thought about it. "If they don't want to do it, they won't do it under any conditions."

"That's what I think." Benton looked at her. "You still want to quit?"

Powers shook her head regretfully. "Mr. President, I don't see how I can continue after I've been undermined like this."

"By who? Me? You've got my full support, you know you have."

"I haven't got any credibility left."

"Nor will anyone else who comes in to replace you. It's the credibility of your office that's been undermined. You can rebuild it."

Powers gazed at the president skeptically. "With respect, sir, it's me who's been undermined, not the office."

"All right, it's both of you. Come on, are you in or not? There's work to be done here, Andrea. Serious work. That's what you joined the administration for, isn't it? You won't have a chance to do it outside."

Powers smiled sadly. "Mr. President, I have a powerful sense of déjà vu right now."

"Well, I guess there's only so many arguments a president has at his disposal."

Powers threw back her head and closed her eyes for a moment. She took a deep breath. "Mr. President, if I'm going to stay, I'm going to have to ask you for a promise. You may think it's out of line, and if so, I apologize and I'll leave. On this issue, I have to be in the loop. I need to know everything."

"Done," said the president.

Powers stared at him doubtfully.

"Welcome," said the President, spreading his arms. He smiled. "To the loop, I mean."

Powers shook her head.

The president was serious again. "I'm going to tell you what I think. I'm going to be completely honest with you, Andrea, because I value your opinion on this." Joe Benton paused. "I don't think we can do this through Kyoto."

"What about what you said in the speech?"

"That speech was a question for President Wen. If he'd come back and said, 'We endorse the American position on Kyoto, and we'll be in the front ranks of trying to find an imaginative solution'—something like that—then, sure, I'd have a lot more confidence. Some confidence, anyway."

"But you threatened him."

"Maybe that was a mistake, but what I've learned is that Wen doesn't seem to respond to anything else. You know that's not the way I do things. That's Larry Olsen's style. But I've learned over these last months that's the only way with President Wen. Otherwise, he just snows you."

"Now he's given you a threat right back."

"Agreed. But at least we have that much. Don't get me wrong, Andrea. I'm prepared to try a Kyoto round if there's a realistic chance of success. I just want someone to show me why I should believe there is. It took four months of painful, painful negotiation to get to the point where Wen walked away. And that was just between two parties. Put in another half dozen—and I'm only talking about the major emitters, that's before the other hundred fifty countries have their say—and how do you get agreement on something so hard? I was hoping to send you into Kyoto with a rock solid deal between us and China, but if there's conflict between us, everyone else is going to slip into that crack. The EuroCore, India, Brazil, Russia, they'll all find a place to hide. And it's going to drag on like it always has, and we're going to come out with some godawful thing, and in another ten years someone else is going to be sitting in this office facing exactly what I face today, only it's going to be that much worse, that much harder to deal with. And maybe then the Chinese government will realize they have to do a deal, but that'll be ten more years lost, and I don't think we can afford that. Andrea, I know we can't afford it, so I can't let that happen. Not on my watch. Not without a fight."

"What are you proposing?" asked Powers quietly.

"I want to hear what you think. Maybe I'm wrong. Maybe Kyoto's the way to do it. I sure wish it could be. So tell me, if we sit down at this Kyoto round in March—now that you know all the facts—do we or do we not get the deal we need?"

Powers was silent for a good minute, appearing to study the rug. "I'd like to say so," she said eventually.

"What does that mean?"

She looked back at the president. "We could use the same moral argument. We're taking a lead. Here's the deal, the same deal you agreed in Oslo, the same cuts. This is it, follow us."

"Without China?"

Powers shrugged.

"Andrea, I can't sell that to the American people. Not if we actually have to start implementing those cuts and there's no watertight, copper-bottomed, sanctions-backed guarantee that anyone else will fulfill their side of the bargain. Do you think we can sell that to the American people?"

Powers didn't reply.

Benton nodded. That was as good as an answer.

"So are we pulling out of the Kyoto process?" asked Powers.

"That's a possibility I'm considering. Or maybe we should threaten to. See who really wants to make it work and what they'll do about it."

There was silence.

"Andrea, you can quit if you want to. You were strongly committed to Kyoto, and I led you to believe that I was—which I was, back then, before I knew what we were actually dealing with. So you can, if you really feel you want to, you can quit."

"I'm not quitting. Not unless you want me to."

"Hell's bells, you know I don't want you to."

"Then I'm not."

Benton could see Powers sit up straighter, regrouping. It was about the only cheering thing he had seen in the past forty-eight hours.

"What's the next step?" she said.

"There's a bunch of options being developed. Jackie Rubin's bringing them together. Talk to Jackie and she'll let you see where we're at. I'll let her know you can see whatever she's got. If you have any thoughts, feed them in to her."

"When are you planning to finalize this?"

"Soon as I can. None of the options is what I want to do, but I'm going to have to do something. The better we think it out, the more chance it'll have of working."

Powers nodded.

"I'm going to call the cabinet together Monday and then I'll give an address to the nation. I'd do it tomorrow if I could."

"Tomorrow's not the day for it."

"Good God, no. Not tomorrow."

Sunday, September 11

Family Residence, The White House

It was like a moment of calm between two storms. The one day in the year when partisan politics in the United States were truly put aside. Even this year, in the midst of everything that was happening, that was true. For Joe Benton, it was an all too brief moment of quiet after the raging seas of the days before, an interlude of tranquillity before the new waves that would surely crash against him after he did what he had decided to do the following day.

When he stood up to give his 9/11 address at Memorial Park in New York City, flanked by Heather, Amy and Greg, he said this wasn't a day for politics, this wasn't a day to point a finger of blame or ask questions of division, it was a day to bow the head, to remember those who had been taken, in the first 9/11 of 2001, in the second 9/11 of 2015, and in every other violent outrage that had been perpetrated by one human being against another. It was a day, beyond remembrance, to pledge oneself to build a better future for every fellow human being, without thought of party, creed, color, or nationality. The words, as he spoke them, had a truth that moved him. They seemed especially appropriate now.

By late afternoon he was back at the White House. He walked into a meeting with his key people. Jackie Rubin, Bob Colvin, Angela Chavez, Jay MacMahon, Larry Olsen, Alan Ball, Andrea Powers, Erin O'Donnell, John Eales, Ben Hoffman and Jodie Ames were there. He made decisions on the last, critical questions. The outlines of the plan that he would launch—how far it would go, how aggressively, how quickly—were now set. The details needed to be completed. Over the next twenty-four hours, before he announced it, very few of the people in that room would get more than a couple of hours sleep.

In the evening he, Heather and Amy hosted a 9/11 dinner for fifty survivors of terrorist atrocities who had become leaders in their communities. Greg had stayed in New York. The president had individual conversations with a good number of the survivors. Most pledged their support in what they knew were difficult days for him. A number of them said they knew he'd do the right thing for the country. Joe Benton was heartened by that. The natural faith and optimism of people gave him strength. It was the thing that had brought him into politics and it was the thing that had kept him going through many a dark day in the past.

After the dinner, he spent an hour in his study with Sam Levy and John Eales, working on the address he would give to the nation the following evening. Sam went off to work on the speech. Benton took Eales down to the kitchen for a late coffee. Heather joined them.

"I guess you'll have Sam working all night," said Heather.

Joe smiled. "First draft on my desk six a.m. tomorrow."

"Poor boy."

"He loves it. Does his best work at night."

"Thanks to you he does his only work at night," said Heather.

John Eales, who was pouring the coffee, grinned.

"And you," said Heather, "you're no better. You should go home to Annie."

"She'll be asleep by now," said Eales, handing a coffee to the president.

"Does she ever get to see you?"

"I believe she has a photo on the wall somewhere."

Heather shook her head.

"Heather? Coffee?"

"John, you know I won't sleep."

"You want decaf?"

"No."

"Hot chocolate? There must be a beverage I can get you."

Heather laughed.

John came over, bringing his own coffee. He sat down at the table with them.

Joe Benton sipped his coffee reflectively.

"You know what those people said to me tonight? They said they knew I'd do what was right." He put his cup down and smiled ruefully. "I wish I had that faith myself."

"Of course you'll do what's right." Heather put a hand on his arm. "We all know that. The whole country knows that."

Joe frowned. "The thing is, I know it's slipping away and I can't do anything about it. Jodie said it straight. Her first reaction was, this is going to kill everything else. Everything we're trying to do. Health, education . . . Everything I came into office to do, it's all going to stop. This is going to be so divisive, it's going to kill it all."

"Well, that's Jodie for you," said John.

"She's right."

"It's not going to make it easier, I'll agree with her on that. But we're not done. What was that thing you said that time, about burying the dead dog? It's not dead yet, Joe. Just a little sick."

Joe smiled.

"Just yelping a little."

Joe shook his head. The smile on his face faded.

"Joe," said Heather quietly, "you didn't ask for this to happen. But it has happened. Nothing else will last if you don't fix it. You know that."

Amy came into the kitchen, wrapped in a dressing gown. Joe smiled at her.

"Can't sleep, honey?"

Amy shrugged. She went to get herself a mug.

"Joe, you can't choose the events that happen to you," said Heather.

"You can only ride 'em," said John. "And I think we've been riding 'em as good as we can."

"Maybe that's not good enough."

"Well, I don't know where we could have done better."

"Where *could* you have done better, Daddy?" Amy looked around from the bench where she was making herself a hot chocolate.

Joe was silent for a moment, then the frustration exploded out of him. "Hell's bells! We had a chance! I had a mandate. In this country you get a mandate like this once in thirty years. Go back over the last hundred years. How many times did it happen? Moments of true generational transition, when the country's got the will to embrace seismic change? I'll tell you. Three." He counted them off on his fingers. "Roosevelt, Johnson—not Kennedy, but Johnson, it took Kennedy's assassination to get Johnson the mandate—and Clinton. I don't count the election after the second Bush as one of them. For all that Barack set out to achieve, it was primarily the people's desire to change the administration, not the country, that put him in power. Three times. And of those three, how many succeeded? One. Roosevelt. Only Roosevelt. Vietnam took it away from Johnson. Clinton, who was so smart at constructing the mandate—it turned out he didn't know how to use it. Lost it in his first year, and what he didn't lose in the first year he gave away to Monica Lewinsky."

"Maybe, at some stage, events are always going to eat into a mandate like that," said Eales.

"No, look at Roosevelt."

"Daddy, it was World War Two that turned Roosevelt into a success." Amy sat down with her mug of chocolate. "Most historians agree that by the late thirties the New Deal wasn't delivering."

"Maybe it wasn't," conceded Joe. If anything, that made things seem worse. "I'm the fourth president in a hundred years with the mandate. This is one of those rare historical moments when this country wants real, fundamental change and is prepared to *do* something about it. And this damn thing is taking it away from me."

"Maybe it's this damn thing that's going to give it back to you," said Heather.

Joe shook his head.

There was silence.

"You know, if you want to look at it historically," said John, "it's not Clinton or Johnson or Roosevelt who are the analogies now. They were, I agree, before this happened. You had the generational mandate for change. That's what we campaigned for and that's what we won. Now it's turned into something different. Joe, with this, I think you've got to look all the way back to Lincoln. What we're facing here is the biggest threat our nation's faced since secession. I honestly don't believe that's an exaggeration. We're going to have to move thirty million people *and* cut back our economy *and* that's if we get a deal with China and the rest of the world that we can live with. Now, if you can lead us through that, if you can keep this country together without some kind of social anarchy breaking out, without the better-off parts of the country tearing themselves away from the parts that are hit hard—not physically, through secession, but in terms of what they're prepared to contribute—if you can do that, then I say, that's a truly great presidency." John paused. "And change will come with that, you bet it will. The mandate's still there, Joe. It's the goal that's changed."

"Do this right, Joe," said Heather, "and we'll still have time. If not in this term, in the next."

Joe glanced at Amy. She nodded. He smiled back at her. But doubtfully. For the first time since he took the oath, Joe Benton seriously didn't know if he was the man for the job. Especially when Eales put the scale of the challenge in those terms.

"What about Olsen and Ball? They're fighting like dogs."

"Let 'em fight," said John.

"That can't be good. I've got to do something about that."

"Joe, there's only one question you need to answer right now." John paused. "Who else would you rather have giving that address from the Oval Office tomorrow evening?"

Joe almost laughed. Plenty of people!

"Who? Mike Gartner?"

"How about Abe Lincoln?"

John smiled. "Maybe Abe Lincoln, I'll give you that. But we're about eight score and ten years too late. Joe, this is about leadership. Don't worry about what the polls say, don't worry about the press. Just do what's right, do what we talked about this afternoon. Do it your way. Lead the American people through this and they'll follow you anywhere. Amy's right. Look at Roosevelt. They would have voted Roosevelt a fifth term if Harry Truman had put wheels on his corpse and run him. Do this, and we'll be able to do in the second term what we don't get done in the first."

Joe leaned back and closed his eyes. It was what those people had been saying to him at the 9/11 dinner tonight. They had elected him to lead. They just wanted him to lead.

Yet it was all turning out so different than the way he had imagined it. And what he was going to do tomorrow, what he had decided he had to do, was the exact opposite of anything that, only a year or even six months earlier, he could have foreseen himself doing. Go back a year and he would have said he couldn't even imagine the circumstances that would bring him to do it.

And what reaction it would bring against him! He could hear the axes being ground in readiness.

He glanced at Amy and smiled wearily.

"You'll do the right thing tomorrow, Daddy. I know you will."

"Honey, you don't even know what I'm going to say."

Amy shrugged. "Mr. Eales is right. Who else would you rather have in the Oval Office?"

Joe gazed at his daughter for a moment. Then he reached across the table and squeezed her hand.

"It's fine, Daddy. You're not Mike Gartner. You'll know what to do."

Joe nodded.

Amy got up with her mug. "Good night."

They watched her go. Joe looked back at Heather and John. "I'm going to turn in."

Heather got up with him.

"See you tomorrow, Chief," said John.

Benton nodded, cocked his finger at Eales, and left.

Monday, September 12

Oval Office, The White House

Jodie Ames, Ben Hoffman, John Eales, Sam Levy, Adam Gehrig and a dozen other aides stood behind the camera, almost spilling out the door. Heather and Amy were watching as well.

The president was calm, composed, but grave.

"My fellow Americans, I wish to speak to you tonight about the future of our nation and of our planet. For me as your president, and for all of us, whatever our private joys and woes, there is nothing more important. I am going to tell you some difficult things. I am going to tell you what we can do about them. In telling you these things, I am going to tell you the absolute and entire truth as I understand it. I hope you will hear me out.

"Over the past months since I became your president, I have received information that shows the changes we have created in our global climate are more severe, more accelerated, and more far-reaching than we have understood before. Although we have accepted for the past thirty years that our world is changing because of our own activities, we have underestimated the pace of change. This is because of a set of environmental processes known as feedback. Scientists have known of these processes for many years, but only now has it become clear how quickly they are operating. The evidence for this is beyond doubt. Tomorrow, I will publicly release the data that show this is the case. It is not a question of whether these processes have progressed further and faster than we thought. They have. The question is what it means for us and what we can do about it.

"We have all come to understand that there will be relocations from threatened areas of our coastal states. Ten years ago, when Relocation was first discussed, those who suggested it were met with disbelief and hostility. Today we accept it. Now we must accept that the relocations we face will be more extensive and more rapid than we had imagined. Tomorrow, I will release detailed estimates of the impact that we face. Let me stress that this is not a burden the United States alone faces. In Asia, in Africa, in Europe, in Australasia, among our neighbors north and south in the Americas, similar effects will be felt. The estimates that I release will cover these areas as well.

"Now, these things will happen. Nothing we can do will stop them. Why? They are effects of things that were done—and not done—ten, twenty, thirty years ago. We signed treaties but did not keep them. We made laws but didn't enforce them. We agreed to long term targets but didn't sign up to the short term goals that would enable us to achieve them. We didn't plan for the worst—instead we hoped for the best. Yet we failed to take steps to make the best happen. I said when I started speaking that I would tell you no lies. The hardest truth, the saddest truth that I must tell you is that for the last ten, twenty, thirty years, you were told lies. You were told we could find a way to cut emissions and still grow our economies at the same rate. You were told new technologies would come onstream and until that happened, we could go on using the old. You were told that voluntary action would be sufficient when regulation was required. You were told, in short, that we had to sacrifice nothing, and yet somehow everything would change. My fellow citizens, I will not tell you lies. I will not tell you that we can continue to grow our economies and yet pay no price. I will tell you the truth. What we must do is going to hurt.

"I have already said that we cannot stop many of the changes to our world that are already happening. Relocations will be bigger than we planned, the impact on our communities will be greater. But that doesn't mean we are powerless. There are things we can do, actions we can take. The fruits of these actions will not be clear for another ten or twenty years. Some of you watching me tonight will not be here to see them. I may not be here to see them. That doesn't mean we should not do them.

"These things will not be painless. For a period of time, we will be sacrificing growth. We will be sacrificing a measure of our prosperity. The sacrifices that we make will be greater than those a previous generation would have had to make. But if we do not make these sacrifices, people of the next generation will have to make them, and the magnitude will be yet greater again. These will not be people you do not know, people whose lives and fate you do not care about. They are your children, your nieces, your nephews. Look around you. Look into their eyes. I will not put that burden on my children. I ask you not to put it on yours.

"Tomorrow, together with the outline of the impact we face, I will release a summary of the measures we must take. I have called these measures the Carbon Plan.

"It is not the United States alone that must take its share of responsibility under the Carbon Plan. The impact is global, the response must be global, and so the plan is global. No one country gains by seeing another country suffer. But we, as Americans, must admit one thing. Of all the lies that were told over the last thirty years, none were greater than those told by the leaders of this country. Of all the leaders who should have taken the initiative, none failed more than our own. And of all the countries that emitted more than their fair share, none did so more than ourselves. Therefore, in acting to bring the ever-escalating cycle of destruction to an end, none must act more vigorously than we. We must stand at the front and expect no one to do what we ourselves will not. We must do it harder, better, and more willingly than anybody else. Our republic has a long and proud tradition of standing for causes that will lead to a better life for all the citizens of the world. We have sacrificed many of our brave young soldiers in many countries for such causes. This is not a war, but it is such a cause, and we are all called upon to make a sacrifice.

"Now, I have to tell you another thing. For the past six months, members of my administration have been in negotiation with representatives of the government of the People's Republic of China in order to reach an agreement about a shared approach to this problem. Although a deal was very close, it was not achieved. I will not go into why this happened nor attempt to apportion blame. However, the terms of the actions that I will release tomorrow in the Carbon Plan are the terms that were negotiated with the government of China. China, like every other country, is threatened by the environmental changes we have collectively unleashed, and as the largest emitter in the world today, it must take a leading role alongside the United States. I call on the government of China to join us in this great endeavor and to fulfill its Carbon Plan responsibilities.

"In order to encourage the government of China to do this, I will tomorrow release a list of trade sanctions that the United States will apply to the People's Republic. They will be applied immediately or, in some cases, as soon as the necessary legislation is passed. These sanctions will be lifted on the day that China signs up to the Carbon Plan. I look forward to that day. I hope, in fact, that day will be tomorrow.

"For other nations, we will provide a period of sixty days for a response to our plan. Countries that do not accept their responsibility by this time will be subject to similar sanctions. I hope none will need to be imposed.

"I want to emphasize something. The trade sanctions we will be applying to China are not aimed at the Chinese people. They are an encouragement to the Chinese government to join us in this necessary endeavor. I know that many Chinese people are as concerned about environmental degradation as we are. The people of China have the same love, hopes and aspirations for their children and children's children as we do for ours. I call on the Chinese government to allow my words tonight to reach the Chinese people complete and unedited, just as I speak them. I call on the Chinese people, as I call on all peoples of the world, to join us at this time.

"My fellow Americans, when you gave me your trust last November I told you that I would dedicate myself to creating a new foundation for our country, a foundation based on health, education, relocation, and jobs. These goals haven't changed. But a new challenge has arisen, a new understanding of the scale of the Relocation that we face, of which I was unaware when I asked for your trust. That doesn't mean I back away from what I promised, it means I seek it all the more purposefully. But before we can lay the new foundation for our country, we must deal once and for all with the monster of emissions that terrorizes our world. We must control it, cage it, master it, and no longer pretend that it doesn't run rampant around us. We must do this once and for all, and we must do it together. This is what the Carbon Plan will do. This now is my overriding goal, and I dedicate myself to achieving it.

"I have had the duty tonight to tell you difficult things. We are at the start of a journey. There will be sacrifices. We will face them together. I see the end of this journey. I see our economy growing again. I see prosperity across the land. I see communities that have been brought together by the great work that we must do, communities that have found in themselves once more the enduring spirit in which our republic was founded. I see the light that will shine upon us as we go forward. At the end of the journey, I do see the new foundation that we seek.

"God bless you all. God bless America. God bless our planet earth and all who inhabit her."

The president was silent. The light on the camera went off.

Still silence.

At that instant, it felt to Joe Benton as if there was a hush not only in this room, this Oval Office, but in the city, in the country, in the entire world outside. His words still hanging, as if corporeal, in the air.

Words, just words, but the words he had spoken, he knew, had changed the world.

He caught a glimpse of Amy, staring at him, eyes wide. But then someone moved in front of her, and a second later, as people came forward from behind the cameras, as the silence was broken, it was as if he could hear the entire world shouting, screaming, howling at what he had done.

Tuesday, September 13
President's Study, The White House

The National Security Council had convened at eleven. Admiral Paul Enderlich, chairman of the Joint Chiefs of Staff, gave a military assessment. At the moment the president's speech began the previous evening, the country's security status had been upgraded from Orange B to Orange A, two steps below full combat readiness. So far there was no evidence of stepped-up activity on the part of the Chinese military. Lou Berkowitz, director of National Intelligence, gave an intelligence assessment. The Chinese government had not responded, either officially or unofficially. Stuart Cohen, CIA director, detailed the information situation in China. Chinese media hadn't yet carried the speech or news of it. Official websites weren't mentioning it, and commercial websites, required to comply with government censorship ever since Google and Microsoft capitulated to the Chinese government's demands in the first decade of the century, weren't taking a chance. The CIA had tracked a number of blogs discussing it, but they were being shut down by the regime's web surveillance operation almost as soon as they appeared. The Agency was pumping the speech into China on its own websites, activating a number of sleeper sites it kept in readiness, but they weren't lasting much longer. News must have been filtering through in one form or another, but the Chinese government was using all the power at its disposal to buy time before it reacted. When it did react, the Chinese people would be presented with Benton's actions not in the way he intended them, but in whatever light the Chinese government chose to cast them.

Everywhere else, things had gone just about as wild as Joe Benton could have imagined.

It was almost disorientating, the chain reactions happening out there over which he had no control. Markets had plunged on the tone of confrontationalism in the president's speech, then plunged further when the documents were released on the White House website and the economic implications of the Carbon Plan became apparent. Rumors were being reported and then denied of Chinese mobilization and the dispatch of American forces to the Pacific and of actual clashes between forces that were, in reality, thousands of miles apart. The Taiwan lobby was demanding an explicit statement that the United States would defend Taiwan from Chinese aggression. Leaders of the Chinese-American community in the United States called on the president to cease what they described as his vilification of China and remove the threat of sanctions. The AFL-CIO condemned the president's action and said it would oppose any sanctions that cost Americans jobs. Every business and trade group in the country was issuing statements.

The U.S. media was divided. Overnight, it seemed, Joe Benton had become the darling of his political enemies on the right. They trumpeted his strong stance and his refusal to be sucked into the quagmire of multilateral negotiations. Simultaneously, he had lost his support in the liberal press, which castigated him for the very same actions. John Eales had the results of overnight polling that showed a similar shift among voters. Politically, Benton was moving into a dangerous position. The solutions he was offering, and particularly the additional government programs he would be proposing over the coming weeks to ease the pain of economic contraction, were going to set the right howling with rage. If he hadn't recaptured the center and the left by then, he'd have no one backing him.

Kay Wilson, Don Bales, Cee Amadi and Val Birley had come in to see him. The movement of opinion mirrored what was happening in the media. Their conclusion was the same as that of Benton and his advisors—the risk was that over the next couple of months the president would get left with no substantial base of support. The president, Kay suggested, needed to speak to the Democratic Caucus, the sooner the better. He needed to launch a lobbying operation that would dwarf anything he had done so far. And he needed to get Angela Chavez, who was well regarded for her work on New Foundation in the spring, prominently involved.

Joe Benton also found time to speak to Marty Montag, the ex-senator whom he regarded, more than anyone, as his political mentor. Marty advised him that all he could do now was hold on while the dust settled. He had set his course and he would have to let the forces it unleashed play themselves out. But when Joe asked him what he thought about the course he had set, Marty's response was evasive. He wasn't privy to the full range of information. Joe pushed him again. He had never held executive power, said Montag, which was hardly an answer.

Few international leaders were prepared to talk with him. Throughout the day, Ben Hoffman's team tried to set up calls. Prime Minister Nakamura of Japan agreed, and Benton spoke with him for twenty minutes. Nakamura wouldn't commit to the Carbon Plan and managed to drop heavy hints about support on the Kurils against Russia. The president told Hoffman to keep trying to get to other leaders. Hugh Ogilvie, at least, would surely be prepared to have a conversation.

The president took the call in his study on the residence floor of the White House. It was six p.m. in Washington, eleven o'clock in London. Bill Price, one of the president's political aides, was listening in to take notes.

"Hugh," said Benton, when the British prime minister came online. "Good to talk with you."

"Joe," said Ogilvie. There was silence. Then Ogilvie laughed briefly. "That was quite a speech you made yesterday. One doesn't quite know where to start."

"I guess it must have come as a shock," replied Benton cautiously.

"Well, it would have been nice to have been . . . I won't say consulted, because it's clear that consultation isn't uppermost in your mind. Let's say it would have been nice to have been warned."

"Would have loved to, Hugh. Just wasn't possible."

"Well, there we are." Ogilvie sighed. "Look, I have to tell you— Secretary Olsen will be getting an official response, of course—but I have to tell you, Joe, I don't think that was the best way to do things. I know you didn't ask me, but I'm going to be blunt."

"I respect your views, Hugh. Tell me why it wasn't the best thing to do."

"Right now you need allies, and you don't keep your allies onside by blindsiding them. I think you've thrown away whatever international goodwill and credibility the United States had managed to recover for itself. After Iraq it took both our countries years to get that back, and with Colombia,

I'm afraid President Shawcross threw a lot of it away again. But I have to say, Joe, now you're looking like the biggest unilateralist of the lot."

"You know I'm not a unilateralist."

"I know you're not," replied Ogilvie. "That's what makes this so depressing. Maybe there's something about being the American president that would turn any person into a unilateralist."

"Just hold on there, Hugh."

"I'm sorry, Joe. But I'm . . . frankly, I'm shocked."

"Well, I'm afraid I just couldn't consult, Hugh, much as I wanted to. The situation didn't allow it. It wouldn't have worked."

"You need allies, Joe. I'm saying this to you as the prime minister of the United Kingdom, which is the best friend the United States has. If I'm saying these things, imagine what everyone else is saying. Have you stopped to think what will happen if you get no support for this from anyone else? What will happen if you end up trying to go it alone?"

Joe Benton shook his head impatiently. He glanced at Bill Price. Price's face was grim.

"Hugh, put yourself in my shoes. Something has to happen here. I've been trying to make it happen but that hasn't worked. Now, what would you have done?"

"I would have used the mechanisms that are available."

"Kyoto? We both agreed the very first time we met Kyoto's a busted process."

"Then set up your own international forum, for God's sake, if nothing else will work. But to come along and lay down the law and say, here it is, here's my Carbon Plan, take it or leave it. Well, I just—"

"That's what we've all been doing for the last forty years. Forums. Channels." Benton was exasperated. "Where's it got us? Into this godawful mess! Have you seen the figures we released today? Have you seen them, Hugh?"

"Not yet. My people are still—"

"Well, you look at them. Look at them! And *then* tell me whether this isn't the right thing to do!"

There was silence.

"Hugh. Listen to me. Much against my own will, it's my honest judgment that this is the only way to get something to actually happen. And

God knows we need that. We can't just keep talking about it. And to your point, maybe that is why American presidents turn unilateralist in office. Maybe you're right. Because everyone will just talk and talk until someone does something, and the only person who can do anything—the only ones with the credibility to do it—seems to be us."

"That's a very U.S.-centric way of looking at the world, if I may say so," replied Ogilvie. "Reminds me of a certain attitude that was common during the days of the British Empire. White man's burden, they used to call it."

"I don't think that's fair, Hugh."

"Granted, the parallel isn't exact. Yet it's not entirely inappropriate."

"Hugh," said Benton solemnly, "my number one, my number one absolute priority, is to deal with this issue. If that's all I do as president, I'll count myself a success. And I'd like to know, what's wrong with that? It has to be dealt with. You look at the figures. Go look at them and come back and tell me something different."

"I'm sure that's true. But my fear, Joe, is that by taking this step, you move yourself further away from achieving what you want. What we all want. After this, it's just going to be all the harder for everyone to come back to the table."

"Maybe you're right. On the other hand, if I didn't do this, I know I'd never succeed. So I guess it's a gamble. It might not work, but it's the only card I can play."

"We differ there," said Ogilvie.

"I guess we do." The president paused. "Hugh, now that I've laid my cards on the table, I need help to make this gamble work."

There was silence. Benton waited. Ogilvie didn't take the cue.

"What are people saying?" asked Benton eventually. "Have you spoken with anyone?"

"Koslowski, Gorodin, Ingelbock, de Silva. Rumain wouldn't talk. I think he wants to work up a full Gallic head of steam before he speaks to anyone."

"Great. What did the others say?"

"They're outraged. They say, even if the measures are sensible, the way you've done it makes it impossible for them to accept."

"Yeah, right." Benton glanced at Bill Price and rolled his eyes. "What about Gorodin? What did he say?"

"The same. Joe, what happens if they all say no? Are you going to apply sanctions to everybody? Are you going to shut down world trade? Do you have any idea what that will do to the global economy?"

"Well, I guess that's one way to deal with emissions," quipped Benton, and it was only half a joke.

"That's funny," said Ogilvie, without a hint of humor in his voice. "You're the ones who'll suffer more than anyone. Everyone else can still trade together even if you cut access to your market."

"Only if no one joins us."

"That's what I'm trying to say!"

Benton knew he needed support. He knew it way better than Ogilvie. That's what this call was about.

"Hugh, I know what effect these sanctions will have. I can send you a whole bunch of models my people have done and not one of them looks pretty. But that's the point. That's how important this is. That's the size of what we're facing. The effects of a global shutdown for a few months—if that's what we have to go through —are only a fraction of what will happen in the longer term if we don't get this thing dealt with. So maybe people will have to have a taste of that. And you know what, if they do, they do. That's okay."

"Maybe it's okay for you."

"We can't think in the short term!" Benton knew what was on Ogilvie's mind. As British prime minister, Ogilvie had discretion over when he called an election, but he couldn't go more than another year now. It was common knowledge that he was intending to run in the spring. The last thing he needed was a global economic recession brought on by an American president with whom he had been notably friendly. "Hugh, that's always been the problem. I will not think in the short term. And if that means I don't get a second term, I don't. If I get this done and the American people throw me out, I don't care. I'll have got it done. And you know, I'm sorry if that affects you. I really am. That's not what I want, Hugh, but this is just too big."

Ogilvie didn't reply.

"I'm sorry, Hugh. I'm really sorry. But I can't fit in with every electoral cycle in the world."

"Of course not," said Ogilvie quietly.

"So what are you going to do? Are you going to come on board?"

"My people haven't had a chance yet to look at the proposals properly," said Ogilvie.

"Fair enough. But they're fair. They're equitable. At the margins, of course, you can always quibble. And the United States will be taking pain. Believe me, we'll be taking pain."

"My people will have to look at them, Joe."

Benton frowned. He needed support early. He needed a critical mass of countries to get behind him so he'd have momentum. The longer things drifted the harder it would be to get anyone else on board.

"We need someone to say yes, Hugh. I need someone to break out of the flock and say yes. I need someone to show leadership. Right now—not in a month's time." Benton waited, listening tensely for Ogilvie's reply. Nothing came. He spoke again. He said it as plainly as he could short of begging. "Hugh, I need someone to be strong on this. This is a moment when the United States needs the United Kingdom. I'm telling it to you straight. Now's the time. We need your support."

There was silence again.

"My people haven't had a chance to look at the proposals yet," said Ogilvie plaintively.

Benton didn't reply.

"Jesus Christ, Joe! It's the way you've done it. Makes it so bloody hard."

After the call, Price left. Benton stayed at his desk, working through a summary of international reaction that Larry Olsen had provided. When he looked up again, Amy was standing in the doorway.

"Hey, honey," he said.

Amy didn't come in.

Benton smiled. "Just got off the phone with the Prime Minister of Britain. I sure hate to see a grown man squirm."

Amy watched him with angry, accusatory eyes. He hadn't seen her since he gave the Carbon Plan speech. She'd had a whole day to brood on it, to talk with people, to hear what they were saying.

"What is it?"

Amy shook her head, almost trembling.

"Amy?"

"What have you *done*?" she said suddenly. "How could you do that? How could you say the things you said last night?"

"Amy, you heard my reasons. I have to do what I believe is best for this country—"

"Best? Best for this country?" demanded Amy. "You're no better than Gartner. You're no better than Bush! You're George W. Bush!"

Joe Benton couldn't quite keep the smile off his face. Amy hadn't even been born when Bush was in office.

"Don't look at me like that! You said you were going to be different, but you do exactly what everyone else does. Once you get your finger on the button, all you can think about is how you can use it."

"What button?"

"What are people going to think? They're going to think what they've always thought about America. We don't listen, we don't care. We make demands and if someone disagrees we nuke the hell out of them."

"Amy, I don't believe we've ever nuked the hell out of anyone because they didn't agree to our demands."

"All right, we attack them, then."

"I haven't said I'm going to attack anyone."

"What about sanctions?"

"Amy, have you read the plan? It's carefully—"

"Sanctions are an attack. And the worst kind of attack, an attack on poor people. Poor people are going to suffer because of your sanctions."

"Not if their governments do the right thing."

"But they won't, will they? They never do. And who is it that suffers? Not the guys in the big mansions. Poor people. And you *know* that, Daddy. It's like you're taking the food out of their mouths with your own hand."

"Amy, do you really think the guys in the mansions would do anything differently if I invited them all over here and asked them to sit down and help me come up with a solution?"

Amy stared at him.

"Do you really? I'm doing this for you and—"

"Don't say that!"

"I'm doing it for you and Greg and every other person who's going to be living on this planet long after I'm gone."

Amy shook her head. "You don't understand."

Joe Benton got up. He started to come toward her. "What don't I understand?"

"You make me ashamed to be an American!"

Benton stopped. "Amy, how can you say that? This should make you proud to be an American. Didn't you hear what I said last night? This country is taking a lead. Finally, this country is living up to its responsibilities and showing the rest of the world how they can as well."

"This country is wielding a big frigging stick and beating the crap out of everyone else!"

Amy turned and headed down the corridor.

"Where are you going?" called the President.

"I'm going back to New York."

"I thought you'd finished in New York."

"Then I'll go back to Stanford."

"Isn't it a little early—"

"I'll go somewhere else! I'll stay with a friend! I don't care. This place makes me feel unclean. I feel like I need to take a shower!"

Benton went to the door. Amy was already across the hall and disappearing into her bedroom. The door slammed.

He hesitated. The phone rang in his study. He stood in the hall. The phone kept ringing. He went to answer it.

Amy was gone within the hour. Joe Benton didn't see her again before she went.

It disturbed him when he found out that she had gone. He had parted angrily with Greg, often, but never with Amy.

Amy would come around, he told himself. She was too smart not to. When she thought about it, she'd understand this was the only way. And yet the way she had gone troubled him deeply, unsettled him, almost more than anything else that had happened as a result of his speech.

The full complement of the National Security Council was in attendance: the president, Angela Chavez, Alan Ball, Larry Olsen, Ben Hoffman, Defense Secretary Jay MacMahon, Treasury Secretary Bob Colvin, Chairman of the Joint Chiefs of Staff Paul Enderlich, National Intelligence Director Lou Berkowitz, Homeland Security Secretary Anne Montgomery, and Counsel to the President Josh Singer. In addition the president had asked for the attendance of Jackie Rubin, Andrea Powers, Commerce Secretary Paul Sellers, Attorney General Erin O'Donnell, CIA Director Stuart Cohen, and Oliver Wu.

Cohen began by giving a summary of the domestic Chinese response. It wasn't until Wednesday that the official Chinese media began to carry reports of the president's speech, presenting it as an act of warmongering in a line of Western aggression going all the way back to the Opium Wars. They had also taken action. Travel of Chinese students to the United States for the fall college semester had been prohibited. An exceptional tax had been slapped on American-affiliated financial service providers, which would affect every bank on Wall Street. And they had announced a more rigorous licensing regime for foreign-language and foreign-owned websites with immediate blocking of those that didn't comply.

Larry Olsen gave an update of the responses of foreign governments to the Carbon Plan. China had called for a UN Security Council session at which they were certain to introduce a resolution opposing it. The only explicitly supportive statements for the plan had come from Lobinas of Colombia and Badur of Pakistan, which carried no weight. Otherwise, there was almost universal condemnation. Even Britain and Japan, normally dependable allies, had described it as unhelpful or unfortunate. The complaints focused on the unilateral approach Benton had chosen to take and his sixty-day deadline. No one, so far, had engaged with the content of the documents or the Carbon Plan's apportionment of emissions cuts. In Olsen's opinion, it was only a matter of time until they did. There were skeptical glances around the table when Olsen said that. He maintained that at some point after the initial outrage leaders would have to engage with the content.

Colvin gave an economic summary. The dollar was down. The markets had come up a little from their lows on the day following the speech, but uncertainty was high and volatility extreme. The Federal Reserve had cut interest rates by a half percent at an emergency meeting and this had helped somewhat. It was too early to identify the effects on the real economy. The first sanctions, for which the president had already signed executive orders, would be implemented on Monday and would affect imports of Chinese steel, cement and other industrial materials. The administration was working with the relevant industries to identify alternative sources of supply, but forward prices for commodities were already sharply higher.

The military assessment from Admiral Enderlich showed no significant activity since the speech on Monday. The domestic intelligence assessment revealed an increase in rhetoric on extremist networks. A similar increase in rhetoric was being seen on international jihadist sites and among left-wing Latin American networks, but there was no evidence of activity on the ground as a result. The country's security status remained at a precautionary Orange A, but this was under daily review and was likely to be downgraded to Orange B if conditions remained unchanged.

After the meeting, the president sat down with Larry Olsen, Alan Ball, John Eales, and Ben Hoffman to talk through the next steps on the diplomatic front. He had also asked Al Graham to come down from New York to join the meeting. Graham was angry about having been left in the dark about the negotiations with the Chinese and had made a vague threat to quit, which Joe Benton had ignored.

The annual opening session of the UN General Assembly was scheduled to take place in two weeks. The United States, like every other country in the world, had a slot for a ten-minute speech in the fortnight-long general debate that followed. The Security Council vote that China was demanding would come before this.

"Do we know when it is yet?" asked Benton.

"Thursday," replied Graham.

"What are they going to ask for?"

"We haven't seen a draft yet."

"It'll be censure," said Olsen. "Demand to return to the Kyoto track. Demand to remove sanctions."

"That's just fine after what they've done," said Benton. "They've acted quicker than us."

"Technically, the Chinese are saying what they've done aren't sanctions. They're internal market reforms."

"What does the WTO have to say about that?"

"I believe the WTO is more concerned about us at the moment," said John Eales.

"The Security Council resolution fails because we veto it," said Olsen. "They know that, we know it. This is all about who isolates whom. They want to show the world no one supports us. At this stage, if we have even one major supporter, that's a win."

"Agreed," said the president. "Who's it going to be?"

"You can forget the EuroCore," said Graham.

"Japan," said Ball. "It's gotta be Japan."

Olsen shook his head. "They want the Kurils."

"So give them the Kurils," said Graham. His attitude toward Larry Olsen was about the same as Alan Ball's.

"That gets Russia pissed," replied Olsen sharply.

"Russia's not voting for us on this anyway."

"We're going to need Russia if we're ever going to get the Chinese to the party," said Benton. "They switch off the gas, we win." He turned to Olsen. "What have you heard from them?"

Larry Olsen shook his head.

"You going there?"

"I'm waiting to hear." In the next week, Olsen was going to meet with as many foreign ministers of as many key potential supporters of the Carbon Plan as he had been able to get to agree to meet with him. His aim was to obtain their support and arrange meetings between their heads of state and President Benton in the coming weeks. A visit with Goncharov, the Russian foreign minister, was number one on his list.

"So who else can we look at?" said Benton. "India? Brazil?"

There was silence.

"Well, I'm not giving in to Japan on the Kurils," said the president. "It's only a vote next week. We veto it. At this stage I'm not going to risk blowing off the Russians."

"The Japanese want whales," said Graham.

"Whales?"

"It's only a vote, as you said. They might do it for whales if they think they'll get us on the Kurils later. They might abstain, at least."

"Then give them the fucking whales," said Eales.

"Hold on a minute!" said Ben Hoffman.

"What?" demanded Eales. "You want to hold onto the whales, Ben, and lose everything else?"

Hoffman frowned. "It's only a vote."

"Offer them whales, Al," said the president. "But nothing on the Kurils. Not a word."

Al Graham nodded. "Also, Nleki wants to see you. He says he has an idea."

Larry Olsen rolled his eyes.

"What's his idea?" asked Eales.

"I don't know." Al Graham looked back at the president. "If you want to avoid us looking isolated, you should see him."

"If we see him," said Olsen, "and it doesn't go anywhere, we just look more isolated than before."

Graham ignored him. "You should see him, Joe. You really should."

The secretary-general had brought James Erikssen, the UN undersecretary for political affairs. Al Graham, had come from New York to sit in on the meeting. Larry Olsen was absent. The secretary of state was in Ukraine, still hoping to arrange a meeting with Foreign Minister Goncharov of Russia.

"I want you to know, Mr. President," said Nleki, "that I applaud your aims. I understand that your desire is to bring an end to the cycle of environmental destructiveness that the world has been in for half a century. And I agree with you, President Benton, that until this time we have not acted sufficiently."

"Thank you, Mr. Secretary," said Benton.

"But I must tell you, sir, that the method is something I have difficulty with. And I speak for a great many member states when I say this. The method turns back years of patient bridge-building by our predecessors, both in my position and yours. I ask you, therefore, President Benton, to think again."

"This was not a decision I took lightly," replied Benton.

"Naturally, Mr. President. I am sure that it caused you much heart-searching."

"It certainly did."

"And I reiterate that I support wholeheartedly your aims. There is no difference between us in that. Indeed, I have been calling for such action from my first day in the secretary-general's post."

That was something of an exaggeration. Nleki's record of environmental action was mixed. Although he had always listed environmental action as a key global priority, he had coupled it with a concern to maintain the Kyoto process as the exclusive forum for discussion and to keep the process under UN control. Compromises had been made in this cause which in retrospect had proved costly.

"You know that you will lose Thursday's vote," said Nleki.

"I thought the outcome of votes wasn't known until they were held," replied the president.

"Mr. President, you will lose it by quite a margin."

"But not unanimously. We'll have support."

The president saw a momentary expression of surprise in the secretary-general's eyes. Either he didn't know something the secretary-general expected him to know, or it was the other way around.

"You'll be isolated. You'll veto the resolution, but it's the isolation that will damage you, Mr. President."

"I'm prepared to risk it."

"How does this help your cause?"

"It doesn't help the cause, Mr. Secretary, but it may be unavoidable. A lot of unavoidable things get done on the way to victory."

"But it's not that it just doesn't help, Mr. President. It damages your chances to get the victory, as you describe it, that you seek."

Benton didn't reply. In the week that had passed since his announcement of the Carbon Plan, the Chinese government had been sitting back from the international stage, letting the rest of the world do its work for it. The formality of a Security Council vote that the U.S. would veto would add fuel to the outrage among those who already thought America was thumbing its nose at the world community, which included pretty much everyone. But on the other hand, how much more outraged could they get? And as for the longer-term implication, Security Council votes had never stopped anyone changing course later on and doing the exact opposite of what they had been advocating, and Joe Benton didn't see why that was going to be different this time around. But it was in the interest of the two men sitting in front of him, both UN officials, to make him think a Security Council vote really mattered.

"I think what the secretary-general is saying, Mr. President," said Erikssen, "is that perhaps now is the time to look at what you have gained and see if there is another way to build on that. Your statement last week, the Carbon Plan you've released, these are powerful things, Mr. President. There is no doubt you have changed the terms of debate. Your plan now is the basis for everything going forward. That's an extraordinary achievement, sir. Your leadership and commitment speak for themselves. Having done that, perhaps, if I may say so, perhaps now is the time to use that recognition, that leadership, that commitment, and channel it back into a process where everybody can engage."

The president glanced at Nleki, then back at the undersecretary. "What exactly does that mean, Mr. Erikssen?"

"If the United States were to come back into the Kyoto process now, with your leadership, sir, I think it's absolutely clear that the process would be utterly rejuvenated. With this commitment from you, others would come on board, others who agree with what you've proposed but, at the moment, can't accept it because they can't be seen to be bullied into it. Reverse the sanctions you've imposed on China, Mr. President, announce that you're going to come back into the Kyoto process under the auspices of the United Nations—but with these clear aims, the ones you outlined in your speech last week, which the secretary-general and I genuinely support—and you could achieve these objectives in a truly collaborative, multilateral, and sustainable manner."

"You think I'd achieve them?"

"Yes, Mr. President, I do. I think you'd also achieve a large number of other things. You'd establish the United States in the kind of leadership role which—if you'll forgive me—is far closer in nature to the way you expressed your thinking about the international role of the United States during your presidential campaign. You could take a great step forward in the way you position the United States to be effective as a leader internationally in the future."

"And you think I'd get what I've set out to get on the question of emissions?"

"I do, sir."

"But if I'll get what I set out to get—which is what's in the Carbon Plan—if other countries are going to do this, why don't they go ahead and do it now?"

"It's the manner, Mr. President."

Joe Benton gazed at Erikssen, a slim man with curly blond hair. Then he turned to the secretary-general.

"Is that also your view, Mr. Secretary?"

"President Benton," said Nleki, "I urge you to avoid this isolating vote. As Mr. Erikssen has said, you've changed the terms of debate. I urge you not to underestimate what that means."

"Take what I've got, you mean, or risk losing it all?"

The secretary-general didn't reply.

"The trouble is, gentlemen, at the moment I have nothing. Only your judgment that I've changed the terms of debate."

"I think that's everybody's judgment, sir," said Erikssen.

"Perhaps. But terms of debate change one way, then the terms of debate change another. As long as it's still just debate, nothing's different."

"Allow me to disagree with you, Mr. President," said Nleki. "What you have done is more powerful than that. Take this step now, bring this back into the Kyoto process, sit down with your partners in the international community with the Carbon Plan as the basis for discussion, and there will be no vote on Thursday."

There was silence.

Benton nodded. "All right. Thank you for your view, gentlemen. I'll think about it."

"Mr. President," said Al Graham, "if I may. I think the mood genuinely is different now. There's a lot to be said for what the secretary-general is suggesting."

"Thank you, Ambassador," said Benton sharply, without looking at him.

At the press conference after the meeting, Benton and Nleki kept things brief. The president said he was looking for any and all ways to work with the global community to implement the Carbon Plan. Nleki said he hoped that the Carbon Plan could form the basis for a genuinely new stage in multilateral discussions under the auspices of the UN.

Afterward, Benton sat down with Graham and Eales and had Larry Olsen patched in on a connection from the embassy in Kiev. He was so angry with Graham after the UN ambassador's remark that he almost told him to get the hell out and go back to New York—on Nleki's plane, if that would make him happy—and he had let Graham know it.

"That's just nonsense," said Olsen when he heard what Nleki had proposed. "Al, I thought you said Nleki had an idea."

"That was his idea," said Graham, not looking at the president.

"Crap!" retorted Olsen. "We met him for that? Where are we on the vote?"

"I think Japan will abstain," said Graham. "We've got Sri Lanka on our side, maybe Norway."

"Norway?"

"I think they heard about the whales."

"And Sri Lanka?" said Benton. "Don't tell me they hunt whales as well."

"No, I think they just don't want to see their island shrink by a third."

"Plus our plan says they cut virtually none of their emissions," said Eales.

That was probably it, thought Benton. "We should have twenty percent of the world's countries on our side on that basis."

"Unfortunately, they don't sit on the Security Council." Graham paused. "Mr. President, really, I don't see why you won't consider what the secretary-general said."

"Here's why we won't consider it," came Olsen's voice out of the speaker. "What we've put out is the bare minimum. We go back into discussion, what will we be talking about? What can we change?"

"Al, I said I would consider it," said Benton quietly.

"Mr. President!"

"It's the way we've done it," said Graham.

"The way we've done it is why it's worked!" said Olsen.

"Everyone's excluded. If we're going to get agreement, everyone has to feel involved."

"Everyone's been involved for forty years, Al, since the very first Kyoto! And where the hell are we?"

"Well, I think there's a case. Mr. President, let's go back into Kyoto now, and maybe you do bring people on board who can't find their way to side with us when we're so unilateralist."

"Go back into Kyoto now," said Olsen, "and everything goes back to just the way it was before."

"Maybe we'll have to give on a couple of things."

"I cannot believe I'm hearing this! Mr. Pres—"

"It might be worth it," said Graham. "It might get us the support we need."

"Mr. President, can I say something, sir?"

"Larry, I know what you're going to say."

"We can't go back! You've come out boldly, assertively, in the *right* cause. Look what's happened. Just by doing that, there's a new sense of urgency."

"More like a sense of crisis."

"Well, it is a sense of crisis, Al. And so it should be. It's a crisis. Mr. President, you've changed the terms of the debate. You sure have. And the reason you have is the boldness you did it with. Who would ever believe anyone would actually come out with a global plan? Who would ever believe anyone would be prepared to use sanctions? Go back on that now, and you lose it. In a week, the terms of the debate will be exactly what they were before. Only now you'll never have the credibility to change them again."

"I disagree," said Graham.

"With which part? That the terms change back or we lose our credibility?"

"That the terms—"

"Like I care! Mr. President, do not go back on this. You have to hold firm." Larry Olsen's voice was urgent, the tone of someone knowing he was far away at a moment when he needed to be right there in the room, looking his president in the eye.

"Joe," said Graham, "no one can change what you've done. Bring it back to the table and no one can ignore it, either."

"Like they're ignoring it now," said Olsen.

"Worse. Because of the way we've done it, they're resisting it." The subtext in Graham's remark was clear. If he had been secretary of state, they would never have reached this point.

Oddly enough, Benton realized, Olsen's subtext was exactly the same.

"Come back to the table now, Joe, and this vote goes away."

"Al," said Olsen, "it's just a frigging vote. What are you scared of? We're going to veto it, and nothing's going to happen."

"It'll show how isolated we are."

"Have you read the papers, Al? Everyone knows that already."

"And while this is going on, the Chinese government sits pretty. Right? They're under no pressure at all, and we're the bad guys."

"Mr. President, don't believe that." Olsen's voice was desperate, reaching across the phone connection in an attempt to get to the president. "Don't believe Wen's under no pressure. I've explained this. The Agency's saying they haven't seen internal repression in China like this for twenty years. That's good. Mr. President, that kind of thing is not a sign of strength on Wen's part."

"I'd like to know what the hell it is a sign of," said Graham, looking at the President and shaking his head impatiently.

Benton's face was grim. It was Olsen, he recalled, who had tried to persuade him that losing fifty billion dollars of business contracts to the Europeans had been some kind of victory.

"Mr. President, the more Wen has to clamp down to keep dissent quiet, the more tension he's trying to suppress. The more hysterical their press gets, the more it shows how worried he is about what he faces internally. That can't go on forever. Something will happen and he'll have to do something horrible. Or he'll make a mistake. Then the world won't be looking at us, it'll be looking at him. Mr. President, it's a game. This is the hard part. We have to wait. He's hoping you crack under the pressure. He's trying to keep his domestic situation under control until you do. We tough it out, at some point he can't continue doing that, and then he's the one who cracks."

"And in the meantime," quipped Graham, "while we're waiting for this miracle to happen, we take a vote against us."

"Hell yes! We take a vote against us."

Benton frowned. It was tempting to think of going back into the Kyoto process now, Carbon Plan in hand, leading from the front. He hated having to do what he had found himself doing. Going back into the process would end this isolation, it would end the chaos that seemed to surround him on every side. It would bring the Democratic Party right back behind him. Maybe he had done enough to unlock the process, like Nleki said. Maybe he'd be more effective now if he did go back in.

Benton glanced at Al Graham, who was watching him.

"Mr. President?" It was Olsen's voice from Kiev. "This vote means nothing. It doesn't tell anyone anything they don't know already. It's the UN. Please. Please, Mr. President, don't do anything! It's just a frigging vote."

Thursday, September 29

Oval Office, The White House

Finally, they had begun calling. Ingelbock, Nakamura, Kumar, de Silva, and a dozen others, all urging him to use the gains he had achieved and turn back to a multilateral approach before the Security Council met. In reply, he asked for their support for the Carbon Plan, yet they all found a way of evading commitment. He had numerous conversations with Hugh Ogilvie. The British leader informed him of conversations he had had with other leaders and urged him to take Nleki's advice. Benton spoke with Alexei Gorodin of Russia, who made pointed remarks about American support for Russian opposition figures. Benton asked directly whether he could count on Gorodin's support by cutting energy exports to China. Gorodin replied that he didn't believe in sanctions as a means of achieving progress. Benton asked him what he did think was the key to making progress. Gorodin laughed. If he knew that, he said, he would have already announced it.

The Security Council vote had gone as expected. The United States, Norway, and Sri Lanka opposed China's resolution of censure. Japan abstained. The U.S. veto came into play. No one internationally or domestically thought any differently afterward than they had before. In practical terms, as Larry Olsen had predicted, the vote made no difference.

At home, restrictions on trade with China were progressively coming into place. Imports of a range of commodities and low value manufactures were now either prohibited or controlled, and exports of critical technologies was restricted. Further sanctions were in the pipeline pending congressional legislation. A coalition had formed in Congress consisting of Republicans and right-leaning Democrats. This would probably be sufficient to achieve passage of the bills but made Benton intensely uncomfortable. It was an unnatural coalition and was unworkable for anything else. Nothing but sanctions bills would progress until this grouping unformed and Benton's true base of support came back together.

Economic stresses resulting from the sanctions were beginning to be felt. The markets remained depressed and jumpy, but the real economy was starting to stutter as well. Export-oriented business groups were talking about losses in volume of thirty to forty percent, anticipating counter-sanctions from the Chinese government. There were reports of layoffs starting in a number of locations. Consumer associations were vocal in predicting price rises and shortages as Chinese goods disappeared from stores. Bob Colvin believed inflation figures would reflect these rises as early as the next month. Manufacturing associations and representatives of businesses oriented toward the home market had initially welcomed the sanctions and said it was high time the United States stopped trading freely with countries that weren't prepared to live up to international obligations, but they were changing their tune now that costs of raw materials were starting to rise. This would add further to inflation and at the extreme could force the Federal Reserve to raise interest rates, adding to the slowdown.

In the days following the vote, governments began announcing that they would be downgrading their representation at the opening session of the General Assembly from head of government to ministerial level. The session had commenced on the now traditional fourth Tuesday of September, the twenty-seventh, and so far all the major leaders had pulled out and sent foreign ministers or other officials in their place. The U.S. slot was on Monday, October 3 and there was talk of a mass walkout from the General Assembly if Benton appeared. None of Benton's advisors thought the president should be put in that position. Joe Benton himself wasn't sure he agreed.

"It'll look like I'm turning tail if I don't go," he said. "You know what? It might be good if the whole world saw their leaders getting up and walking out. Show them what kind of people are in control of their destinies."

"Sir, that would be a disaster," said Jodie Ames.

"Mr. President," said Larry Olsen, "I don't think we should put you out there. I'll go."

"Larry, you're the one who said the Security Council vote didn't matter. And this isn't even a vote."

"There'll be pictures of this. Out there in the real world, no one cares about the Security Council. It's not real. No one recognizes anyone there, it's just a bunch of people sitting around a table. But I'm with Jodie on this.

I think images of you standing up in front of an empty General Assembly, that's something else completely. It'll be bad. People will look at it, and it will say to them . . . America is standing alone."

"Well, we are."

"But we don't want to be."

"It's the image," said Ames. "It'll say more than a million words."

Benton didn't care about the General Assembly meeting one way or the other. If everyone thought it would be better for Larry Olsen to address an empty hall—or a near-empty hall, because surely some people would stay, even if it was only the Pakistanis and Colombians—that was okay with him. It wasn't the idea of standing up there that worried him, or the emptiness of the hall. It was the reality it reflected.

Where was the support? Not one major leader had come out in public and said they would support the Carbon Plan. They hadn't even been prepared to say it in private.

He had given them a deadline of sixty days before sanctions would be applied to their countries as well. A quarter of that period was gone. The more time that passed, the less likely it would be for others to join. If he had to apply sanctions to everyone, foreign competitors would simply step into the places forcibly vacated by U.S. business. Withdrawal of American trade would throw the global economy into recession, but that would be nothing compared with the scale of the downturn that would occur within the United States itself. Benton had told the American people they would have to absorb pain, but it wasn't meant to be pain on this scale, and America wasn't supposed to be absorbing it alone.

Still Larry Olsen was telling him that he had to wait, that he just had to wait and eventually Wen would make a wrong step.

He thought about the empty hall waiting for him, or for Larry Olsen, at the United Nations. Alan Ball, Al Graham and a host of other people were telling him he couldn't afford to keep waiting. If he wanted to go back into Kyoto with authority, he had to do it now. With every additional day that went by, the more it would look as if he was being forced to go back because he couldn't get any support, not because he was choosing to do it. Time was his enemy. If he waited sixty days and went back into Kyoto because no one had joined up to the plan, he'd have no authority at all.

Monday, October 10

Princeton University, New Jersey

The Columbus Day address at Princeton had been scheduled months before. In the circumstances, Benton could have cancelled the speech. Instead, he decided to use it.

He was still waiting on the rest of the world, and the rest of the world was still waiting on him. For four weeks now, there had been a kind of stand-off, no one prepared to make the first move. Yet something had changed, if only subtly. People had begun talking about Kyoto again. In the first days after the Carbon Plan was announced, it seemed that Kyoto was dead and buried, and Joseph Nleki had begged him to come back and resurrect the process. Now ministers in various countries were asking why the Bangkok agenda meeting for the Kyoto 4 round shouldn't go ahead in November as planned. If the United States chose to boycott the round, that shouldn't stop others moving ahead with it. Nleki was becoming openly supportive of that line. In a speech made in São Paulo, he remarked that the only way to overcome the demands of a unilateralist was for multilateralists to continue their work. But the door would never be shut, he said, as if this was some great concession, as if the power balance had now tipped to the other side, and it wasn't up to the United States to return to the table, but up to those still at the table to decide whether the United States could return.

And when he looked at it, Joe Benton couldn't see where his support was going to come from. Pakistan, Colombia and Sri Lanka hardly counted, nor did the impoverished countries of the developing world who had offered their commitment. They were signing up only because the Carbon Plan absolved them of the need to take any action and they stood to lose more from cessation of U.S. aid than from a loss of trade with China. None of the world's leading emitters nor the second tier polluters had joined. Olsen had managed to set up a visit for the president to Tokyo later in the month and claimed the Japanese could well come out in support. But

Benton knew that Olsen was just trying to keep him going. He didn't believe Nakamura would go out on a limb, not with forty percent of Japanese exports going to China, even if he offered support on the Kurils. And he couldn't offer Japan support on the Kurils because of the effect that would have on Russia.

In China, Wen still seemed to be in control, keeping the screws turned on his domestic oppostion. He was waiting, watching as American democracy turned on itself, as its media and its business groups and its unions and its political parties jabbed accusatory fingers and yelled at their president and at each other. He was keeping his head down, doing nothing to remind the world what kind of a regime he headed and whom the rest of the world had chosen to get into bed with, content to stay silent as long as the world viewed America as the villain, seeing how much self-inflicted pain America could bear. If something was going to happen, as Larry Olsen kept saying, if Wen was going to make a mistake, there was no sign of it yet.

The right-wing press, initially so supportive of Benton's action, was backpedaling now, accusing him of taking the country into a trap, saying that America needed to wield a big stick and that this showed a liberal wasn't capable of doing it. But his center-left support hadn't come back and showed no signs of doing so unless he abandoned his position.

He knew what Democrats were saying. Marty Montag, about a week earlier, had come to see him in the White House and told him straight out. He was irresponsible to have launched an initiative like this without lining up support from key allies. And all things being equal, that was right. That's what he would have said himself had he been on the outside looking in. But exactly which allies would have given him support for the plan he put forward? He would have ended up negotiating with them, trying to establish a common position, and pretty soon everyone would have been protecting themselves and their interests and what he would have had would have been another Kyoto, a mini-Kyoto, a pre-Kyoto, with all the problems and constraints of the real one. So he still couldn't see—much as he told Marty that he wanted to—how he could have done other than he did. And maybe he would fail, maybe in a year the U.S. would have to undo the sanctions and come crawling back to the table with its tail between its legs, but that was a risk he felt he had to take, unsavory and humiliating as it would be if it turned out to be true. But it was too early to make that choice, or even think about making it. Way too early. He wasn't even thinking about it.

That's what he said, anyway. But privately his doubts were almost unbearable. The pressure to change tack was enormous. And who was to say he was right to resist? Maybe he wasn't. But until that moment came, until he decided to change tack—if that indeed was what he was going to do— he couldn't show a hint of the doubt that he felt. If people detected that, even the faintest sign of it, the pressure would sweep him away. Right now, people had to believe his determination was unshakable. He was going to use the Columbus Day speech to reinforce that impression.

The auditorium at Princeton seated fifteen hundred. The speech was to be heavily covered, and there were a number of cameras in the hall. About five minutes into the speech, an obviously preplanned, silent walkout began. Students stood up and began to file out. Hundreds of them.

For a short time, Joe Benton kept going. Then he stopped. He wasn't going to give them the victory of walking out while the president of the United States was speaking about the most important issue on the planet.

They weren't in any hurry. Minute after minute it went on. It must have taken another ten minutes until they were nearly all gone. Benton stood at the lectern, face stern, watching them. As the last of the exiting students made their way up the stairs he began to talk off the cuff.

"Remember what you've just seen here today," he said to those who remained in the half-empty hall and to the cameras that were streaming his image. "That's what I'm talking about. That path . . ." he pointed up to one of the doors through which the last students were leaving, "we can all take that path, but it's the path to defeat. That's the door. Anyone else here, anyone want to go through that door? Do it now. I respect your right to do it. Do it now. I'll wait." He paused for a good ten seconds. "I won't blame you, in fact I understand you. That's the easy way. Because if you stay with me, I'm telling you, I'm not taking you down that path." He stopped again. The last of the exiting students were gone. "All right, I'm taking you through a different door. But I can tell you one thing for sure. If enough of us choose to go that way, that easy way, that's where we'll all end up going, whether we want to or not. I can only show you the other door. I can only open it for you. You have to walk there yourselves. Now I trust—I trust—that despite what we have just seen here today, there's still enough good people in this country to make sure we don't end up going down that other way. And those people who *have* gone, I trust that when they see that, they'll come back and come through this door with us. And they'll be welcome. Because it's natural to want to go through the easy door, but I can't tell you that we should. And I know we won't. If I didn't believe that, if I didn't believe that was the kind of country this is, I would never have run for office. I wouldn't be standing here before you today."

He went back to his prepared speech. As he came off the platform, he didn't know whether his response to the walkout would play well or badly. When he saw Jodie Ames's face, he thought it would probably be okay. News streams had cut to the speech as soon as the incident began and commentators were already reporting his handling of it as an exceptional display of presidential poise and steel.

But although he had managed to deal with the walkout, and even turn it to his purpose as a living demonstration of what he was saying in his speech, the episode had shaken him. Right in front of him, he had seen division.

If Joe Benton thought of himself as anything, it was a uniter, not a divider of the American people. Yet he had now seen, in microcosm, the greatest fear that any president can have. He was reminded of what John Eales had said about secession. For the first time, under his stewardship, he feared for the republic.

The second he came off the stage, someone was handing him a phone. It was Larry Olsen, congratulating him on the speech. Determination, leadership, strength. Exactly what was needed in case anyone wondered whether the president still had the stomach for the fight. The message would go not only to the American people, said Olsen, but to the government of China.

Benton realized why Olsen had called. Olsen knew what other people were saying to the president, he knew that Benton's determination to carry on was a day-to-day proposition. He had taken to giving him milestones—just hang on another week, another ten days, until this happens, or that happens. Olsen feared the effect this walkout might have. He was desperate to get in first, before others could have their say.

"Hang in there, sir," said Olsen. "At least until you've been to Japan."

Tuesday, October 18

Air Force One, east of Japan

The briefing book summarized the Japanese position on the Carbon Plan. It covered a range of other issues as well. Benton worked through it carefully. Heather was in the office with him, reading a book.

There was a knock on the door. Jodie Ames came in.

"Sorry to disturb you, sir." Jodie glanced at Heather and smiled briefly. She extended a handheld to the president.

"What is it, Jodie?"

"The Chinese government has just released a statement, sir."

Benton took the handheld. He nodded Jodie toward a chair and looked at the screen.

The government of the People's Republic of China views the unilateral visit of the president of the United States to its region as an aggressive act at this time, coming on the heels of his other actions, and contrary to a spirit of fellowship and common understanding. The actions of the United States government are contrary to respect for the Chinese people and their historical sovereignty. Consequently, the government of the People's Republic of China has decided on the following measures.

First: The visits of representatives of the government of the United States to the province of Taiwan is immediately forbidden without permission of the government of the People's Republic of China.

Second: The export licenses of certain classes of goods from the People's Republic of China to destinations within the United States will be reviewed and will now be subject to suspension and cancellation.

Third: The People's Bank of China will review its currency holdings and dispose of excess dollar reserves.

The people of China are united. The people of China will not bow down to the will of any foreign power, but will resist the imperialist aggression of the United States with every part of its will.

Joe Benton handed the screen to Heather for her to look at.

"What's a unilateral visit?" he said to Jodie Ames.

Ames shrugged.

"See if the communications guys can get hold of Larry and Alan. And come back in on the call."

Ames went out.

Heather passed back the handheld. "What does it mean?"

"I don't know." Benton looked at the screen again. "It's strange. I don't know what it means."

Ames came back. "I'll step out," said Heather, and she picked up her book and left.

Ames sat down. "They'll be on the line shortly."

Benton nodded. "So what do I do?" His first speech of the visit would be at a dinner hosted by the Japanese prime minister. "Do I address this tonight?"

"You could. It's disproportionate . . . It's unfortunate. Actions such as these gratuitously threaten the livelihoods of the Chinese people themselves . . . You wish the Chinese government would step up to its responsibility instead of making threats." Jodie paused. "Or you might not even want to mention it. Don't let it overshadow the visit. They've interfered in a visit to Japan that has nothing to do with them, and we shouldn't let them do that."

"But it's going to overshadow it, right? Whatever we do."

"In the media. I'm not sure Nakamura would thank you for bringing it into his banquet hall."

Benton glanced at the screen of the handheld. What was Wen up to? Why do this now?

Larry Olsen came online.

"Have you seen this release?" asked Benton.

"I'm looking at it right now."

"It's ridiculous. Have they ever claimed they have right of veto over visits in the region? They can't do that, can they?"

"Of course not. This is outrageous and not a single country in the world would think otherwise. It's dumb. Finally Wen's done something dumb."

"Why?"

"I have no idea. Maybe they genuinely feel destabilized by your being in Japan. Maybe they think Japan's going to announce it's signing up. We've been covertly spreading that rumor."

"And Japan's been overtly denying it."

"Maybe that's why they think it's true. Mr. President, I told you, you just had to wait. This is good."

Alan Ball came on. "Mr. President. Did I hear someone say this is good?"

"Al, that was Larry."

"Yeah, who else?"

Benton ignored that. "What do you think?"

"This is going to hurt," said Ball. "Exports, the dollar. The market's going to go crazy."

"They're trying to outsanction us," said Olsen. "Big deal. They're prohibiting exports of stuff we were going to prohibit importing anyway."

"They're going to sell down the dollar."

"Really? Who's buying?"

"Larry, that's a little glib," said Benton.

"They've just turned themselves into an aggressor in the eyes of everyone else in the world. That's worth paying a price for."

"They must realize what they've done."

"They may not."

"They're not stupid."

"They're thinking about other things. Mr. President, this is exactly what we've been waiting for."

"We've had reports of arrests overnight," said Ball. "More than we've seen recently. The Chinese press this morning is crazy. It'll all be in the daily briefing. Your visit's being reported like it's some kind of invasion."

"Are American citizens in danger?"

"No, not as far as we know."

"Okay." Benton was silent for a moment. "What do they want? They want me to turn around and not land in Japan?"

"No," said Olsen. "They know they have no right to demand that and you'd never do it. That's the whole point. They're not asking you to do something. They're saying, because you've *done* something, here's what we're going to do. It's a pretext."

"Mr. President," said Ball, "look at the first point. No more visits to Taiwan."

"I don't understand that," said Benton. "That's gratuitous. How can they forbid us going to Taiwan?"

"They claim it as their sovereign territory."

"Have we got any visits planned?"

"We send people there all the time. We have a trade delegation going in a couple of weeks."

"Exactly," said Olsen. "Sir, this is the structure of what we've got— you've done this, a visit to Japan, therefore we prohibit you sending anyone to Taiwan. You send someone to Taiwan, and . . ."

"And what?" said the president.

There was silence.

"You think they're trying to set up a pretext to invade?" Benton looked up at Ames. She was watching him intently.

"That's exactly what they've done. The question is why. Why now? Mr. President, something's going on over there. What we're seeing are the external signs. Maybe your visit's precipitated it. For some reason, they need to start banging the nationalist drum. They need to look tough. Whatever we're doing, it's working. We need to sit tight and keep going as we are."

"Invading Taiwan might not be an option they want to exercise," said Ball. "They might just be putting a pretext out there in case they decide to. It might be all they want to do is clamp down on some of their opposition people—make a few more arrests, which is what we're seeing—and they'll sit back and review things then. Could be that if they do that, they'll feel secure enough to sit down with us and do a deal on the Carbon Plan. We should take it back into Kyoto now. That'll give us more support, and it'll be easier for the Chinese to join us."

"Easier for them to hide," said Olsen. "Look, the whole point here is something inside the regime has changed, and it's changed because of what we're doing."

"You think there's been a shift in control?" said Benton. "You think it's not Wen anymore?"

"I don't know. Whatever it is, this is the start. We've got them into the open. We're into phase two. This is where they blink, and we get on top."

"Jesus Christ," muttered Ball.

"Alan," said Benton, "I want a security update twice daily. If there's any danger to American citizens, I want them out."

"Yes, sir."

"I don't want them hostage to whatever game Wen's playing. All right. What else do we do?"

"As I said, now's the time to take this back into—"

"We make a statement about this thing," said Olsen. "That's it. We make a dignified statement and let them keep digging their own hole."

"Oh, for God's sake!" said Ball. "Let's seize the opportunity to take this back into Kyoto."

"We're not taking it back anywhere! Now's not the time to turn chicken. A statement. That's it."

"The president has a speech tonight at the state dinner with Nakamura," said Ames.

"I wouldn't say anything there," said Olsen. "You drag Nakamura in and he's not going to thank you. We should release a statement separately."

"Jodie?"

"I agree."

"Mr. President—"

"Alan, right now, for the moment, let's see where this goes. I'm prepared to do that. I'm going to make a statement, and then let's see what happens."

"But, sir—"

"Alan, that's what I'm going to do. I'll keep other options open."

They crafted a statement. At last, it was a chance to paint the United States as victim rather than aggressor, and getting on a high horse would blow the opportunity. The tone was understated, more bemused than outraged.

But it was just a statement, thought Benton, after Ames had gone out to polish the wording. Statements were just statements. It was the reaction they created that mattered.

He wondered if Larry Olsen was right. He had come too far now not to wait a little longer and find out. Maybe Wen had made a serious mistake, or at least had been forced to sacrifice a degree of international support for the sake of something he had to do internally. Or maybe not. If not, what was Wen expecting *him* to do? What he had just done, or something different?

Either way, the pressure on him was about to get even greater. Every sign of deterioration in the situation led to a fresh wave of panic.

The statement was released two hours later. Jodie Ames read it aloud to the journalists on the plane, and it was then streamed to the agencies.

They landed at Narita. It was seven in the morning in Tokyo, six p.m. in New York. The dollar had slid eleven percent. The Dow Jones had plummeted eight percent in the last hour of trading, giving it its biggest one-day fall since 2013, when nuclear war between India and Pakistan seemed imminent.

Friday, October 21

Situation Room, The White House

The Chinese government had reacted to the president's statement by issuing a response asserting that the province of Taiwan was an inseparable part of the People's Republic of China. They had also cut air links between the mainland and Taipei and reiterated the demand for a suspension of official U.S. visits. Internally, the crackdown had intensified. The democratic and environmental oppositions were being vilified in the press, and people were being exhorted to inform on anyone suspected of opposition activity. The CIA estimated that upward of five thousand opposition figures had now been arrested and a large number of businesses forcibly closed. A selective shutdown of exports to the U.S. was under way.

"The Chinese government is offering compensation in the way of wages to the factory workers affected," said Stu Cohen, briefing the National Security Council meeting. "The one thing they don't want is popular unrest because of the unemployment this will cause."

"How long can they sustain that?" asked the president.

Cohen shook his head. "They've already said they'll sell down their foreign currency reserves."

"Who's got renminbi to pay them?" said Olsen.

"No one," replied Bob Colvin.

"So what do they do?" asked Angela Chavez. "Print money?"

Colvin shrugged. "They could if they have to. Eventually the inflationary effects would be unbearable, but they could do it for a while."

"Stu?" said the president, "what about U.S. interests?"

"We've got reports of disturbances outside factories doing business with us and a number of attacks on American-owned or affiliated businesses." Cohen consulted his handheld. "A branch of Citibank had its windows smashed, similarly a McDonald's and some other franchises. There have also been crowds outside residential compounds that are known to house Americans in Shanghai and Guangdong."

"Anyone hurt?" asked the president.

"Not yet. The authorities appear to be keeping it under control. It's rent-a-crowd activity."

Benton glanced at Olsen.

"I had Ambassador Liu in my office yesterday and issued a formal protest. I'll have him in again today."

"Have we had any disturbances here?" The president directed the question to Anne Montgomery, secretary of homeland security.

"Not to our knowledge, sir. Some agitation among the usual suspects. We've had reports of an increased level of racist abuse."

"I want to know about that. I'm going to issue a statement condemning any kind of violence against law-abiding people in our communities."

Montgomery nodded. "I've ordered additional security outside Chinese diplomatic missions and other likely targets."

"What about American missions overseas?"

Olsen shook his head. "We've had some demonstrations, but those have been going on since we issued the Carbon Plan."

Benton turned back to Cohen.

"Internally in China," said the CIA director, "we're seeing a full-scale crackdown, supported by the media, which are completely caught up in the fervor. Dissident activity on the web has been almost entirely absent for the past week. Activists who aren't in jail by now are probably on the run. We're still not sure whether the extent of the reaction is a genuine response to unrest we've been trying to stimulate or whether elements in the party are using the atmosphere of external crisis to take care of matters at home. Foreign Minister Chou, by the way, hasn't been seen in public for ten days. Premier Zhai has also had a very low profile. Ding's featuring. He's made a number of widely covered speeches and it looks like Wen's letting him make the running."

Benton tried to process everything he had been told. "How much danger do we think American citizens are in?"

"My sense, Mr. President," said Cohen, "at the moment, it's entirely up to the authorities. They're driving it. They've turned it on, they can turn it off. But that could change. Once they unleash the tiger, anything can happen. We saw that repeatedly in 2013 and fourteen. The Chengdu incident started as a rent-a-crowd demonstration, and there were twenty-eight American deaths."

"Once this kind of thing starts, there's always the risk that things get out of hand," said Lou Berkowitz.

Benton was silent. "All right," he said eventually. "Militarily, what's the story?"

Mr. President, we're seeing a moderate buildup of forces in Fujian province," replied Admiral Enderlich. "That's the province opposite Taiwan, where they'd likely launch an attack."

"They know we'd know about that, right?"

"Absolutely," said Enderlich. "They want us to know it's happening."

"Anything else?"

"We've got fleet movements out of Zhejiang, Jiangsu, Hainan. Technically, they're not yet in breach of the Manila Understanding, but it wouldn't take much more. They've stepped up air patrols and are violating Taiwanese airspace, but that's pretty normal."

"Isn't that a breach of the understanding?"

"It is, but it's nothing new. They've never kept to the terms on air flights."

"What are the Taiwanese doing?"

"They're on full alert."

"What are they doing about the air patrols?"

"Just watching them go by. Like us. We've increased our patrols, strictly sticking to international airspace. We haven't made any other moves yet." Enderlich paused. "The Pacific Fleet is about two days away. The third air wing is on standby to go out to Guam."

"Do we know what the Taiwanese government wants?" asked the president.

"President Tan wants to talk to you," said Olsen. "At this stage, they're looking for a public statement of support. Something in excess of the Taiwan Relations Act."

"You mean they're looking for us to commit to defend them," said Angela Chavez.

"Probably. They want something that guarantees them militarily."

Chavez glanced at the president.

"I think I should announce a visit this week," said Larry Olsen.

Joe Benton looked at him. "The purpose being . . . ?"

"The purpose being to demonstrate to the Chinese government that we won't accept illegal ultimatums about Taiwan."

"Don't we have a trade visit coming up in a couple of weeks?"

"We need to show more than that."

"That's exactly what they want us to do," said Alan Ball.

"Right. They issue a challenge, we come right back and call their bluff."

"So we send you," said the president. "What do they do next?"

"I don't know what they do next."

"Well, that's a problem, don't you think?" said Ball.

"I bet *they* don't know what they do next."

"So we both step off into the unknown. That's great."

"There's a principle here, Alan! It's a principle of sovereignty. You've got the Chinese dictating to sovereign governments—"

"They don't accept the Taiwanese government as sovereign, we all know that. They want Taiwan back. When they're ready, the Manila Understanding will be out the window."

"Unless we prevent it."

"Then let's not give them a pretext."

"They don't need us to give them a pretext. They make their own. The president takes a trip to Japan and it's a pretext. Mr. President, the only way you stop this is if you hit back at every single stage."

"Larry," said Benton quietly, "I'm not escalating this thing over a visit. We've got a trade visit in two weeks. That's good enough."

Olsen shook his head. "Next they'll be blocking Taiwan's ports."

"That's enough," said Benton. "This thing's getting out of hand."

"We could take the Pacific Fleet a day's sail closer without breaching the Manila Understanding," said Enderlich.

Benton glanced at him for a second, then turned away.

"If they sell down their dollar reserves in a hurry, there'll be chaos," said Bob Colvin. "It'll kill anyone who's holding dollars or U.S. government bonds."

"You said before no one would buy them," said Ball.

"Not for renminbi. No one's holding Chinese currency. It doesn't help them financially, but if they want to do it just to hurt us, they'll sell the dollar for anything they can get. It'll hurt them as well, but they might figure it'll hurt us more. They sell down the dollar, our bonds are worthless. We'll be paying a premium of ten, fifteen percent to finance our deficit. Could be more. Could be we won't be able to sell our bonds at all."

"But they haven't started yet?" asked the president.

Colvin shook his head. "Not as far as we're aware."

"Let's park that." Benton could deal with only so many things at a time. The markets were in panic and had been since the Chinese statement three days earlier. He had a meeting set up later in the day with Colvin and Henry Schulz, chairman of the Federal Reserve, to go through the options.

"Mr. President," said Olsen, "everything they do is designed to make you back down. That should be clear by now. That poses a question: Why? Why do they need you to back down now? Even if we don't have the answer, the conclusion is obvious. If they're so desperate for us to back down, we need to keep going."

"To where?" demanded Ball.

"To where *they* back down."

"What if they don't?"

"They will."

"Why?" asked the president.

"Because someone always blinks. We have to show that we won't be the one. In the Cuban Missile Crisis, who blinked? Who turned the ships around? Khrushchev. That's the last time two superpowers really looked each other in the eye."

"Mr. President," said Ball, "Cuba was in our sphere of influence. Taiwan's in theirs. There is a point to back down. And a way. Once they go too far, once their demands are too much, you then have the rest of the world on your side. That's the point where you back away."

"And you think we're there now?"

"Nowhere near!" said Olsen. "Mr. President, they will back down. The key to this is their internal politics. This no longer has anything to do with us. Once they've achieved what they want internally, they'll climb down."

"You mean once they've achieved their crackdown?"

Olsen nodded.

"I think the secretary's got a point, sir," said Stuart Cohen.

Joe Benton felt ill. The idea that the Chinese government had magnified the crisis so as to launch a wave of repression against opposition to the regime, and the idea that he had to sit by and allow that to continue until it was done—even hope that it got done—filled him with revulsion.

"Let them finish that," said Olsen. "Then they'll be much more reasonable."

"And they'll sign up to the Carbon Plan?"

"We have to be hard on Taiwan."

"Larry, it's not about Taiwan!" Benton struggled to contain his exasperation. "It's about the Carbon Plan."

"They're linked."

"They're not."

"Mr. President, we have to show them there's a line on Taiwan. In the meantime, we keep building support for the plan. The two things go together."

They didn't, not in Joe Benton's mind. He closed his eyes for a moment. When he opened them again, he avoided looking in Olsen's direction.

"Here's what I want to do," he said. "First, we issue a warning to all American citizens to leave the People's Republic."

"But Mr. President, that's thousands of—"

"I don't care, Stu. I want our people out. I want that weapon out of their hands. Second, I'll talk to President Tan. I'm not going to commit to anything beyond what's in the Taiwan Relations Act. I want that to be absolutely clear to everyone here. But I will talk to President Tan. Third, we issue a statement condemning the arrest and detention of legitimate opposition in China. And fourth, let's see if this is starting to make a difference with anyone else. Larry, you keep saying when Wen does something dumb, that's when we get support. Well, let's see if you're right. Ben for a start, try to set me up a conversation with Gorodin. Let's see if he's prepared to consider shutting off the lights in Beijing."

Hoffman nodded.

"We're not being hard enough," muttered Olsen.

"Larry, this is as hard as it's going to get."

Sunday, October 23

Situation Room, The White House

China was now in breach of the Manila Understanding, which limited the number of troops in Fujian province to one hundred thousand and prohibited Chinese aircraft carriers from the Taiwan Strait and an exclusion zone of fifty kilometers around the island. Protests had been sent. The Taiwanese government had appealed publicly for the immediate stationing of U.S. troops on its territory. The Chinese government had publicly stated that it would regard this as an act of war.

"We can have three brigades of the 82nd Airborne in Taiwan inside of two days," said Enderlich. The Pacific Fleet had moved closer to the island and the third air wing was in transit to Guam.

"I wasn't asked to authorize that," said the president.

"I did," said Jay MacMahon. "Mr. President, if we're considering any kind of action, we need sufficient force in place."

"The staff has three plans, Mr. President," said Enderlich, "and I'd like to go through them with you."

"Plans for what?"

"Plans for defending Taiwan. First, we have a preemptive option."

"Wait." Benton looked at Enderlich imperatively. "The government of the United States has never committed itself to the military defense of Taiwan. That's clear. And I made that clear again. President Tan knows it."

"We've always had plans," said MacMahon.

"This administration is not going to war over Taiwan. Period."

"What, then, do you propose to do, Mr. President?" asked Admiral Enderlich. "Every clause of the Manila Understanding has been breached."

The president opened his mouth to speak, then stopped, shook his head. "I'm not going to war over Taiwan. What happens if I do? Say we stop them. What do they do next?"

"There is no next," said Larry Olsen. "Superpowers never fight each other directly. They fight by proxy."

Alan Ball shook his head. "China's been looking for a chance to flex its military power for years."

"And Taiwan's the proxy. That's why by moving to defend it, we bring this to an end. That's it. Nothing else they can do. They have to back down."

"And we'll be there for years," said Ball. "Mr. President, Nleki has said he's prepared to send an emissary to talks between Taipei and Beijing."

"That gives it away right there. Once you start talking, you concede there's something to talk about. Mr. President, Taiwan's a crucial ally of this country. If China swallows Taiwan, it'll leave our credibility in tatters."

"At some stage, China has always been going to get Taiwan back," said Ball. "Everyone knows that. Implicitly, the Manila Understanding was based on that recognition. A genuinely sovereign state doesn't need something like the Manila Understanding to protect it."

"Sir," said Enderlich, "we need to do something. We're already in a standoff. Our boys are flying alongside Chinese planes ten times a day, every day of the week. All it takes is one pilot to fly a little too close to another and we've got an incident."

"The tinder's dry," said MacMahon. "Right now it only needs a spark."

There was silence.

"Jay," said Benton eventually. "Tell the government of Taiwan that we won't be sending troops."

"Sir," said MacMahon, "with respect, I think that's something you should tell President Tan yourself."

"I will. I'll call him this morning."

"It's a mistake," said Olsen. "China won't go to war. They're pushing. If you don't send the troops, *then* they go to war. Then they invade."

"That's your judgment," said Ball.

"Of course it's a judgment."

"If they get Taiwan, do they come back to the table on the Carbon Plan?" said Ben Hoffman.

"Ben," replied Olsen, "by that argument, you give them Taiwan to get them in on the plan. I take a different view. If they get Taiwan, they feel so confident they become even more intransigent."

"But I might be right."

"Are you feeling lucky? If we're going to sacrifice Taiwan to find out, why didn't we do that back in Olso and save ourselves all this trouble?"

"Good question," muttered Ball.

"I'll tell you why. Because if we give on something, they'll come back to us on something else. They will keep taking. True, the harder we are, the harder they'll push, so right now it feels uncomfortable. But if we keep going, at some point they'll stop. They will blink. If we're still standing, if we're still pushing back hard at that point, we win."

"That's absolutely wrong," said Ball. "This is way too public now. It's in their media, it's all over their domestic scene. They have to win on something or they're discredited at home. And one thing the party will not accept is to lose face at home. We have to give them something."

"So you give them this?" demanded Olsen. "Because they've set themselves up domestically, we have to make sure they get it? That's the greatest argument for appeasement I've ever heard!"

"It's the reality."

"It's fucking outrageous! I'm sorry, that is not an argument! That's not a reason to give them Taiwan."

Benton broke in. "For the hundredth time, this is not about Taiwan!"

"With respect, sir, it is!" Olsen gazed at him. "Mr. President, I know the linkage pains you, but it's there. They've created that linkage. The way to carbon is via Taiwan. And I'm telling you straight, Mr. President, right now you're the only person in the world who refuses to accept it."

There was a hush in the room. Benton knew that every eye was on him. He took a deep breath. Maybe Olsen was right. Maybe he couldn't keep resisting it anymore.

"Then explain it to me," he said quietly. "If we do nothing, what do they do? Do they take Taiwan, or do they keep talking?"

"They take it," said Olsen.

"They take it," said Enderlich, and Jay MacMahon nodded his head.

The president looked at Alan Ball.

"It's possible," he said reluctantly. "They're talking themselves into a corner."

"They engineer an incident," said Stu Cohen. "Easy to do. Then they move."

Enderlich nodded. "That's probably how they'll do it."

"All right," said the president. "Say they do. What then? Do they turn around and agree to the Carbon Plan?"

"Why should they?" said Olsen. "We've just let them take Taiwain. What credibility do we have?"

"The United States government has never stated outright that it wouldn't let them take Taiwan."

"With respect, sir, I believe that's a subtlety that might be lost on your average Chinese citizen in the tsunami of triumphalist nationalism that will swamp China if they take Taiwan."

"Then that lets them back down on carbon, doesn't it?" said the president. "There's our linkage. And at this stage, having watched China invade Taiwan, the rest of the international community is on our side."

"Are they?" said Jay MacMahon. "Mr. President, I don't see too many countries coming out in support of Taiwan right now. Frankly, I don't see too many of them who even give a damn."

"But they won't condone force."

"Even if they don't, what are they going to do?" Olsen shook his head, almost in amusement. "The EuroCore? Taiwan's gone, Mr. President. Fait accompli. What are they going to do now? Boycott Chinese business? Can anyone here really see them doing that? If we let them do this, the Chinese get away with it. They will get away with it with impunity, and the last thing they'll do then is sit down with us to sign up to the Carbon Plan."

"Alan?" said the president.

Ball frowned. He thought for a moment before he spoke. "It depends, deep down, whether they really think they need to sign up to the plan. If they think they can keep holding out and force us to take bigger cuts, then I think they will. No matter what happens."

"See?" demanded Olsen. "Even Alan agrees!"

"But that's what it's always been about, hasn't it?" retorted Ball. "Do they really think they need to act on emissions? If they do, then this is a way for them to get something that helps them come to the table. It's a way of giving something to their base so they create the space in which they can do something painful, something, remember, that threatens the very legitimacy of the regime. But if they can get this, then maybe they can do it."

"And if they *don't* believe they really need to cut emissions?" asked the president.

"Then they get something for nothing," said Larry Olsen.

"Alan?"

Ball shrugged. "I guess they do."

Joe Benton stared at the dark varnished wood of the table. "I wish I knew what they were thinking," he murmured.

"Mr. President?" It was Oliver Wu, who had been silent throughout the session. "Sir, I'm not sure if it's quite as straightforward as this."

Benton looked up at him. Straightforward? That was an odd way of putting it.

"I think we're giving the Chinese leadership too much credit for having a single coherent approach. Taiwan is simple for them. If they can get it, they'll take it. There's not a single Chinese leader who isn't committed to getting the island back. But there are big differences among them on how much risk they'd take to get it back. On the one hand, you have some generals who'd invade this afternoon if it was up to them. On the other hand, you have people like Hu and Xuan who wouldn't put at risk even a fraction of China's economic stability for the sake of it."

"Surely someone's driving this now?"

"Yes, to the extent that this is a serious attempt to recover Taiwan—and remember, we haven't seen any real action take place. This might all be saber rattling for domestic consumption, or some kind of opportunistic attempt to see how far they can go. But the leadership isn't going to be sitting around a table like this, all the leadership, and agreeing that first we do this, then this, then this, then we get Taiwan, then we do this, and this, and this on the Carbon Plan. If they're able to get agreement on what to do about Taiwan, that in itself is a huge achievement, and it's probably taking all their attention. Beyond that . . . don't assume there's a game plan. Anything can happen."

"And they'd risk that, to get Taiwan?"

"Definitely. China prides itself on its antiquity. They waited ninety-nine years to get back Hong Kong, but they got it in the end. It's only eighty-five years since they lost Taiwan. To them, that's like yesterday. It's the blink of an eye."

Benton looked at Olsen. "Dr. Wu seems to be saying there's no linkage, Larry."

"No, sir," said Wu quickly. "That's not exactly what I'm saying. The linkage is that the disruption over the Carbon Plan has put them in a position where maybe they think they've got the opportunity to get Taiwan, or maybe they feel they have to get it to shore themselves up, and that's what they're focused on. My point is, it's probably opportunistic. I doubt they have a plan that says what happens next. More likely, what happens next depends on who comes out on top once whatever happens over Taiwan has happened."

"If Oliver's right," said Olsen, "and if we assume whoever's pushing the hard line on Taiwan would also push a hard line on the Carbon Plan, then our best bet is to make things tough over Taiwan so that person loses credibility."

"Mr. Secretary," said Wu, "with respect, taking a hard line on one thing doesn't necessarily imply that the same person would take a hard line on something else. And on the other hand, if things start to look tough over Taiwan, that person may move to shore up his position and crack down internally even harder while he still can, which means, if he succeeds, there's even less domestic pressure to push him toward the Carbon Plan. Or we could see a scenario where the tensions build until the party splits into its factions and you get something approaching a civil war, which means you've got no one to negotiate with until that's resolved, and that could be years. In China, that's a real possibility."

Benton frowned. He tried to find a simple way through the maze that confronted him. This wasn't about Taiwan, it was about carbon. Taiwan had become opportunistically entangled with it. But it was about the future of the planet. He wasn't going to sacrifice that over a part of China that, one way or another, was always going to be recovered by the Chinese. Yet defending Taiwan might be the best thing he could do to safeguard the future of the planet. Maybe it really was his most important bargaining chip. Resist now, trade later. But how Congress, how the American public would react to armed intervention in Taiwan, that was another thing he didn't know. The media was already divided along predictable lines, some demanding vigorous action, some warning against yet another American involvement in someone else's backyard. He remembered the hall in Princeton, the sense of division that he had felt descending on the union. In the last weeks, he had asked an awful lot from the American people. He had asked them to follow him into a period of pain now in order to prevent greater pain later. He didn't know what would happen if he had to add even more.

Yet if Wu was right, it was impossible to say what effect the loss of Taiwan would have on China's position on the Carbon Plan. And if that was right, then the only thing he could predict was the effect it would have on America's position. And that wouldn't be good. If Taiwan was forcibly taken, it would result in a massive loss of U.S. credibility.

On the other hand, it would show China as an aggressor, and possibly make other leaders less likely to support them.

But the United States would look weak. And why ally yourself with a weakened power?

He was conscious of everyone waiting, watching him.

He looked at Enderlich. "Take me through your plans on Taiwan, Admiral."

Enderlich nodded.

"That's not a commitment, Admiral Enderlich. I just want to see them."

Wednesday, October 26

Situation Room, The White House

Overnight, there had been a near miss between a Chinese and American plane over the South China Sea. Something had then malfunctioned on the American aircraft and the pilot had been forced to eject. The Chinese media portrayed it as some kind of victory. A Chinese government spokesman asserted that if hostilities broke out between China and the United States, they wouldn't be restricted to East Asia.

In the Situation Room, the president puzzled over the wording. "What exactly does that mean, do you think?"

"Could be they're meaning to attack us on Guam, sir," said Enderlich. "It's certainly within range for their aircraft." He smiled. "Bring it on."

"What about Hawaii?"

"Ditto. Alaska's different, they could do better in Alaska, but what are they going to achieve? Blow up a bunch of icebergs."

"What about the continental United States?"

Enderlich shook his head. "As far as we're aware there's no naval activity within range. It's been a long-standing understanding that we would react strongly if the Chinese put vessels in a threatening posture. There's only one way they could hit us here, Mr. President."

"What about knocking out our satellites?"

"We'd take out theirs. And we have plenty of redundancy in the system. Ever since that little show they put on when they destroyed that satellite in '07, we've built that in. They'd have to knock out fifty."

"What if they did?"

Enderlich shrugged. "They know the Shawcross doctrine. They take out enough satellites to blind us, we nuke 'em."

The president looked at the wording of the Chinese statement again. "So you're saying there's only one way?"

"That would be just as bad for them," said Larry Olsen. "They may be crazy, but they're not that crazy."

"One warhead lands here, they get a hundred back," said Enderlich. "They know that."

"What if a hundred land here?"

"They still get a hundred back."

"They're rational," said Olsen. "They believe they can absorb more pain than us, which is true, but if the pain is total destruction, that doesn't matter, does it?"

"Mutually assured destruction," said Enderlich. "Kept us safe through the Cold War, and at their height the Soviets had five times the number of warheads the Chinese have got pointed at us now."

"Let's not make the mistake of fighting the last war," said Alan Ball.

"Where's the difference?"

"Different protagonists, Admiral. The Soviet Union had proven itself when the Cold War began. The Chinese haven't. They've been trying to show they're a military superpower for years. They're looking for an opportunity."

"And you think nuking us is the opportunity they want?" Olsen rolled his eyes. "Who's going to be left alive on their side to see it, Alan?"

"They might not think we'd hit back."

"They'd be wrong."

"Sure. They could be. Hitler was. That's why he invaded Poland, and look what happened to him."

Enderlich looked at Ball with a smile that was almost condescending. "I thought you didn't want to fight the last war, Dr. Ball."

"I'm just saying—"

"Mr. President," said Olsen. "They're rational. Right? This is ridiculous."

"They hit us," said Enderlich, "that's the ball game. We know it. They know it. This stuff about taking it out of East Asia, that's talk."

"All of this is talk," said Olsen. "Look at this near miss. Why make a noise about it? Mr. President, they're not *doing* anything. Why haven't they attacked Taiwan already? You're standing firm, that's why."

"They have to attack, though, don't they?" said Benton. "They're as mobilized as they can be without actually moving. They've crossed every limit. They can't go back without losing face domestically."

"That's why I suggest we put the preemptive plan into action," said Enderlich.

"I'm suggesting something else," said Benton. "They need a way back. Let's give them one. We've lost sight of what this is about. It's not about Taiwan, it's about carbon. Remember? They've forgotten it, just like everyone else has. It's time to remind them."

"What do you have in mind?" asked Alan Ball.

"We come out and say Taiwan's open to negotiation. Larry, before you start, hear me out. I issue a public statement. I say we're sure some kind of arrangement can work. We're prepared to work with the Chinese government on that—but only after we get agreement on the Carbon Plan. There's a linkage, right? You said it yourself. Well, I'm going to turn it around. Taiwan doesn't lead to carbon—carbon leads to Taiwan."

"You sure that's a way out for them?" said Olsen skeptically.

"Why not? They can present it any way they like internally. They don't even have to mention the Carbon Plan as part of the deal in their press. They can show it as us climbing down. I don't care about that. I don't mind giving them a cheap victory, if that's what it's going to take."

Jay MacMahon shook his head. "So we're betraying Taiwan?"

"Call it a betrayal if you like, Jay. I'd call it something else. Taiwan's been in a situation of limbo since 1949. It's an anomaly, this entity which we kind of do recognize but kind of don't. The United States has never guaranteed it. At some point, this was always going to need to be resolved, and the fact that we've never committed to a Taiwanese state suggests that it was always going to be resolved by reversion to China. Well, if that was always going to happen, let's get something back for it. I'll talk to President Tan again. We'll help in whatever way we can to smooth the transition. We can use Hong Kong as a model."

"Yeah. That worked," muttered Olsen. "Mr. President, this is a hell of a change in policy."

"It's a hell of a different world we're living in, Larry. It's a different one than the one I thought I was living in when I took office."

There was silence.

"Umm . . . Mr. President?" It was Oliver Wu. "What you said, that only works if they see the whole picture, if they accept the way you're trying to connect the issues."

"That's exactly what I'm doing."

"I guess so. But they might not accept that."

"I'm not sure I know what you mean, but . . . so they reject it. So what? What's the downside?"

"The downside is you make it worse. What you're doing is, you're implicitly recognizing they have a right to Taiwan, but now you're dictating to them when they can have it. If they choose to interpret it like that, it's more Western colonial imposition. It's an insult."

"It's a way out."

"It can also be seen as an insult."

The president looked around. There was an exasperated, confused shaking of heads.

"Mr. President," said Olsen, "all I can say is, if we do this, we're the ones who are blinking. We're the ones backing down. And we don't need to. What we're doing is working."

"They're not moving their forces, sir," said MacMahon. "I agree with Larry."

"Maybe they're still preparing," said Ball.

Enderlich shook his head. "They're ready. We know their numbers."

"We need to stand firm," said Olsen. "Keep our forces in position, ready to fight. If we're ready to fight, we won't have to."

"And what if we have to fight?" said Benton.

"Then we will," said MacMahon.

The president nodded. "I've had the statement drawn up."

Ben Hoffman got up and handed out a set of papers.

"What is this?" said Olsen. "Who have you been consulting?" He started to read his copy. "You're really going to put this out?"

"They need a way out and this is going to give it to them without any bloodshed," said Benton.

"Except the bloodshed when they take over twenty-six million people on Taiwan," muttered MacMahon.

"Who said there'll be bloodshed?"

"They're not exactly best friends, Beijing and Taipei."

"Well, frankly, I'll take my chances with that. Any day of the week, I'll trade whatever happens there for the welfare of millions of Americans whose lives are going to be destroyed if we can't get agreement on Carbon."

"And what if—"

"I've said this is it!" Benton slammed the table. "There are a thousand what-ifs. I've decided this is what I'm going to do. I'm going to call President Tan and let him know, and then Jodie's putting this statement out. Now I want you all to look at it and tell me if you think we need to change anything."

"I just think this is the biggest mistake we can make," said Larry Olsen.

"Noted." Joe Benton looked around at the others to see if they had anything to add. "Okay. I know you'll all do your best to support it."

Three hours later, the statement was issued. Overnight, an American F-42 was blown out of the sky over the South China Sea. The Chinese authorities claimed the plane had entered Chinese airspace and failed to turn back after repeated warnings. They described it as aggression amounting to an act of war.

No one knew whether that was Beijing's response to Benton's statement or the lucky shot of a trigger-happy pilot.

Thursday, October 27

Family Residence, The White House

Joe Benton sat on the edge of the bed. He was haggard, exhausted. He felt as if he hadn't slept in a month. He stared at the floor, at his feet in their blue slippers.

He could feel himself being dragged into war. It seemed inexorable. It was like a nightmare, a closed, stifling nightmare world of briefings and intelligence and speculation and escalating incidents with the Chinese that somehow he couldn't bring to an end. What did they want? No matter what he did, what he said, they wouldn't stop. UN Secretary-General Nleki had offered to mediate, but China refused to recognize the right of the UN to involve itself in events concerning Taiwan. The Chinese had said they would boycott a Security Council debate that was scheduled for Friday. At home, everywhere Benton looked, there was division and acrimony. In Congress, in the press, among his own advisors. On Capitol Hill, there was talk of a Democrat-backed resolution urging restraint on the president and a Republican-backed resolution demanding defense of Taiwan. Half the media seemed to be consumed by war lust, as if Taiwan was the fifty-first state. The other half excoriated him for even having troops in the region.

His presidency wasn't supposed to be like this. It was supposed to be about setting policy and getting legislation sponsored and cajoling congressmen and all the stuff he'd seen from the other end of Pennsylvania Avenue for so many years. It was supposed to be about dealing in a civilized fashion with civilized leaders from other countries. It wasn't meant to be about launching an attack on China.

He couldn't come to grips with it, how he had got to this point. It was so hard to step outside it and understand. Where had he gone wrong? Had he gone wrong? Maybe he had been too much influenced by Larry Olsen. Olsen and Ball, he understood from John Eales, were barely on speaking terms outside meetings. They were barely on speaking terms in meetings, either. If he hadn't invited Olsen into his administration, he felt, he wouldn't be in this position. He would still be talking with the Chinese, with everybody, in some kind of Kyoto preparatory process. And everyone would still be temporizing. At what point would he have concluded that he had to do something radical? If it was coming to a clash now, then at some point it would always have had to come to a clash. Or would it? Maybe a more skillful president would have handled it better. Might have skirted this abyss that was opening at his feet.

A series of foreign leaders had been on the phone to him over the last two days, urging him to withdraw American forces from East Asia and promising him they were speaking to the Chinese government and asking them to pull back their forces as well. That was another thing that was making him wonder. Maybe they were right and he was wrong. Maybe he'd lost his judgment, lost his bearings over the past weeks. He continued to question whether he was up to the job. A few times, he had wondered whether he should resign. That would leave Angela Chavez in charge. Would Angela do a better job? He had put her on the ticket largely for the Latino vote, but she was shrewd and competent. Yet these foreign leaders who were talking to him, telling him to withdraw, they were the same leaders who had refused to take his calls after he announced the Carbon Plan. And still they slipped and slithered when he asked for a commitment. It wasn't the content they disputed, they said, it was the manner in which he had presented it. Well, one thing Joe Benton knew for certain, the Carbon Plan was right. That was about the last thing he knew absolutely, the one thing he could hold onto while everything else seemed to be spiralling crazily away. So how could he back down now if he couldn't get the commitment of any other leader? How much more desperate did things need to be before they'd understand?

But he would have to launch an attack. That was what was going to happen. He knew it.

Heather watched him. "Joe?" she said.

He looked around at her.

"Honey, are you okay?"

The president shrugged. The burden felt heavy. Too heavy.

"Is there anything you could have done differently?"

So many things. "It's ironic. Everyone used to think there'd be wars over resources. Remember? Everyone used to say, the oil's going to run out, we'll end up fighting China for it. We should have realized, the clash wasn't going to be over the resources, but over the emissions."

"Are we going to fight them?" asked Heather quietly.

Benton was silent.

"Are you going to Congress?"

"Erin doesn't think I need to. Not yet. There's ambiguity in the wording of the War Powers Act, and anyway, the executive has never accepted Congress's rights under the bill. They were supposed to clear it up after Iraq, remember? But they never got around to it."

"Shawcross got approval for Colombia, didn't he?"

"Doesn't mean I have to now, not for what we're planning."

Heather nodded. "Can I ask what that is?"

Benton heaved a troubled sigh. "Something limited. It's not a war. A strike, something aimed at a military target. A runway, a hangar. We're not looking for casualties. I've hauled back hard on MacMahon and Enderlich, but we have to do something. Our forces are being attacked in international airspace. There are incidents every few hours now. One man's dead, another three are missing. We can't let that go unanswered."

"What about the UN?"

"We need to deal with this with force. On this, I'm on Enderlich's side."

Heather nodded. "So we attack. What happens then?"

"One all. They back down, so do we." The president's voice was despondent as he said it.

Heather's face was grim. "What if they don't?"

"We scuffle. It draws to some kind of close. They make a noise about having protected their homeland. We make noise about having prevented aggression against Taiwan. Both sides get to slant it as a win."

"Don't they attack Taiwan?"

"It doesn't look like it." Joe Benton frowned. "I really don't know what's going on inside their heads. They've had days. They've waited so long, our troops are just about as close as they can be without physically hanging out in downtown Taipei. It doesn't look like they want to invade."

"Yet they want to mess with us?"

Benton shrugged. "It's crazy."

"What if we get bogged down? Like a Vietnam? Like an Iraq?"

"You can't get tied down against a country like China. You just skirmish. Going all out is too horrible for anyone to contemplate." Benton paused. "There'll be more loss of life somewhere along the line, Heather. We've got to be prepared for that. But I think the American people will accept it if our forces are being attacked. And they are being attacked, genuinely."

Heather shook her head. "It seems pointless."

"I agree." Benton sighed deeply again. "Well, I guess it's not pointless if it allows us to come back and make something happen. It won't be in vain if we get them signed up to the plan. When this little scuffle is over we come back, offer them Taiwan again in response to them doing the deal on emissions. By then, hopefully, when other leaders have seen how far this has gone and how determined we are, that'll be enough. Maybe we just have to be prepared to go to the brink to make them see it. I'm talking to Gorodin again tonight. If we can get Gorodin on board, that's the difference. Turn off the lights in China and it's over. He just needs to see this is really a matter of life or death for us. For all of us. Maybe our action is going to make them all see that. I don't know. Maybe this is what it takes."

Heather frowned, deeply disturbed. "You've decided, then?"

"I'm going to try to get one more message to Wen."

"Will he take a call?"

"No. I'll have to use another channel. I keep thinking about Kennedy and Khrushchev during the missile crisis. That's seventy years ago, but we have exactly the same problem. Communication."

Heather looked at him in alarm. "There isn't a nuclear risk here, is there?"

"It'll be conventional. They know the kind of retaliation we'd launch. Complete devastation. That's the doctrine, and they know it."

"Is that what would really happen?"

Benton shook his head wearily. "Only if I'm disabled. I have sixty minutes to decide on how much and how quickly we retaliate. Otherwise, there is an automatic, all-out response. But they don't know that. They think it's predetermined, all or nothing. One strike, ten strikes, a hundred, we respond the same. Massive, overpowering."

"But we don't?" said Heather. "Not necessarily?"

"Not necessarily, but that's not what we say. You'd have to be a hell of gambler to test it."

F. William Knight looked ill. Thinner than the last time Joe Benton had seen him. He was gaunt, his eyes haunted.

He listened to what the president had to say. Ben Hoffman and John Eales watched him closely. It was possible that Knight would refuse to go through with it. It was possible he felt too resentful toward the president, who seemed to have precipitated this crisis.

But they knew no one who had a better chance of getting to Wen.

"Tell me if you're prepared to go," said the president.

"I haven't seen President Wen since . . ." Knight cleared his throat.

"Since he refused to see you last time?"

Knight nodded.

"But it's still possible for you to let him know you want to see him?"

"I think so."

"How do you do that, by the way?"

"There's a number," replied Knight.

"You call a number?"

"That's right. I call a number and I leave a message."

"You're kidding," said Ben Hoffman.

Knight cleared his throat.

"Maybe I should try that," said the president. "Get around Ben here."

"What if he's changed it?" asked Hoffman.

"No," said Knight. "Very few people have this number."

"I don't suppose I could have it?" asked the president, only half jokingly.

Knight cleared his throat. "I'll try, Mr. President. I can't tell you whether he'll see me."

"We'll put a plane at your disposal," said Hoffman.

"I've got my own."

"Let me give you an idea of the message you'll be carrying," said Benton.

Knight looked at him, coolly, without a trace of emotion on his drawn features.

"I'll be saying to President Wen that the door is open for him. The emissions deal on the table is exactly the deal his people agreed before Ding turned up in Oslo. If he pulls his troops back—if he goes back to the Manila Understanding—and if he announces China will go with the Carbon Plan, we pull our troops back as well, and we *will* sit down and talk about Taiwan with a view to resolving the issue."

"I'm sorry, Mr. President," said Knight. "What does that mean, resolving the issue? If you don't mind telling me."

The president took a deep breath. "It means we'll agree to the restoration of Chinese sovereignty to the island."

"The sovereignty of the People's Republic," said Hoffman.

Knight cleared his throat. "What if he says no?"

"You bring that message back to me."

"No, does your message tell him what will happen if he says no? Is it some kind of ultimatum?"

The president looked at Eales.

"We want to focus on how we can solve this crisis," said Eales, "not on what happens if we can't. We're giving him an offer, a way to resolve this without bloodshed."

"If he wants to get Taiwan back," said the president, "this is the way to do it. He won't get it through aggression. You can tell him that, if he asks what I said. Is he likely to ask?"

Knight nodded.

"Then tell him that. If he wants Taiwan, there is a way, but not by force. The United States can't let that happen."

Knight cleared his throat. "If you'll excuse me, sir, it sounds like you're holding him to ransom."

"How so?"

"Well, you say he can have Taiwan, but he can have it only if he does something he doesn't want to do."

"Mr. Knight, China has to be part of the Carbon Plan. None of us on the planet is immune from this. This isn't about Taiwan. President Wen has to sign up whatever happens with that. But what I'm saying is, okay, the People's Republic does have a legitimate historic issue over Taiwan, and having to do what we have to do on carbon is an extraordinarily difficult thing, it's also a historic thing, so if we can come to some kind of agreement to allow a smooth and peaceful integration of Taiwan . . . if that helps him get his people on board with the Carbon Plan, okay, we'll help him out. But the Carbon Plan's the primary issue. Taiwan's a sideshow."

"Not for him."

"It is for us. And that's why we're prepared to be flexible on this. But there's no room for flexibility over the Carbon Plan. The Carbon Plan's core."

There was silence.

"All right," said Knight.

"You'll take the message?"

"I'll try."

Joe Benton picked up an envelope from his desk. Inside was a letter he had written in his own hand.

F. William Knight took it. A car drove him to Reagan, where his plane was waiting. For the next thirteen hours, he was in the air to Beijing.

For the next thirteen hours, Joe Benton was in meetings. The Joint Chiefs presented their plans, starting with a limited strike on the airbase in Guangxi province from which had come the plane that shot down an American pilot two days previously. They presented targets for additional strikes, should they prove necessary. There were three levels of escalation illustrated on maps in the situation room. The Joint Chiefs also talked through plans for defending Taiwan, should the president choose to order it. Joe Benton wondered whether an identical meeting was taking place somewhere in Beijing. He wondered what the maps there were showing.

During those thirteen hours, Chinese and American fighters in international airspace came closer than a hundred meters on eighteen separate occasions. A Chrysler showroom was burned in Zhejiang province, and the windows of a string of Bank of America offices were smashed. An exchange of shellfire broke out between a shore battery and a Chinese destroyer off the northern coast of Taiwan, killing eleven Taiwanese soldiers and wounding thirty-four.

Sunday, October 30

Oval Office, The White House

Benton waited impatiently for Knight to arrive. He knew by now that the banker had seen President Wen. He knew that he was carrying a letter that Wen had given him. He also knew that over the last twenty-four hours, the incidents and provocations around Taiwan and China's southern territorial borders had continued to intensify, and the pressure building on him to take action was almost unbearable. By luck, there had been no further U.S. casualties. Had another American died, he wouldn't have been able to hold off, even with Knight on his way back.

Knight was ushered in. Hoffman, Olsen, Ball, Eales, Cohen and MacMahon were waiting in the Oval Office along with the president.

Hoffman introduced the banker to Cohen and MacMahon.

"You saw President Wen," said the president when the formalities were done.

"Yes, sir." Knight took an envelope out of his pocket. "He asked me to give you this."

Benton took the envelope. Then he stopped. "What was he like?"

"President Wen said very little to me." Knight cleared his throat. "He took your letter and read it. Then he told me when to come back, and he had this letter ready."

"He didn't say anything else?"

"He said that you should take it seriously. What he says in his letter."

Benton frowned. Of course he would take it seriously. "He didn't say anything else to you?"

"No, sir."

The president nodded. "And . . . how did he seem?"

Knight didn't answer immediately. In private, with people he trusted, even on serious occasions, Wen Guojie was an expansive character, almost uproarious. Knight could hardly remember a conversation with him that hadn't included a string of jokes. There had been no jokes this time, not one. Not a smile. Wen's handshake at the end of their meeting had been dry, clasping. As if Wen had been trying to impress something upon him, something desperately grave, desperately important, that words alone couldn't capture. Maybe it was that handshake that unsettled the banker more than anything else. Knight had been through dark, difficult days with Wen back in 2013, but he had never seen him like this. Wen was under intense pressure. Knight even wondered about the extent to which he was still in control.

"Quiet, Mr. President," said Knight.

"That's all? Quiet?"

"Troubled. Not the Wen Goujie I know."

Benton looked at him thoughtfully, then he nodded. He took the envelope to his desk.

"Shall I go, sir?" said Knight.

"No, stay while I look at this, if you wouldn't mind." The president waved toward a space on the sofa next to Ben Hoffman. Ben moved to make room.

The president slit open the envelope and took out the sheet of paper inside. Like his own note, it was handwritten.

He read it. Then he looked up. "Mr. Knight," he said quietly, "thank you for everything you've done. I don't believe I will be requiring your services any further at this time."

Knight stared at him. "Thank you, sir," he muttered hoarsely.

Ben Hoffman got up and took Knight out.

The president read over the note again.

To His Excellency Joseph Emerson Benton, President of the United States of America:

The government of the People's Republic of China will not tolerate the interference of the United States or any other foreign government in its internal affairs. The province of Taiwan is an integral part of the nation of China since time immemorial. It is time to bring its anomalous situation to an end. The full normalization of the gover-

nance of the province of Taiwan is not dependent on the resolution of any other matter, nor is it in the gift of the leader of any country or a matter for external negotiation.

I urge you therefore to withdraw your forces from the region and allow our two nations to resume the friendship they have labored so hard to build in recent years. In times gone, hostile actions by foreign governments were tolerated by governments of China and led to many years of subjugation. The government of the People's Republic will never adopt this attitude. Do not make the mistake of thinking that the armed forces of the People's Republic are intimidated by the army of the United States. Do not think your country will be safe because it is distant. Any hostile action by the forces of the United States on the sacred territory of the Chinese people will be met by a terrible response that will shake your nation to its foundations. Pay heed to this warning. If you do not, you alone will bear the responsibility for the result.

I urge you to withdraw your forces immediately and end the crisis that you have created in a region of the world that is far from your own country.

Wen Goujie
President of the People's Republic of China

Benton handed the letter to Stuart Cohen, who was nearest, and he watched as Cohen read it and then passed it on. There was no note of conciliation in the Chinese president's words, thought Benton, not even a hint. Not even an intimation that Wen would sign up to the Carbon Plan once Taiwan was recovered. If Wen had said that, at least, there might have been a glimmer of hope, even though Benton had demanded that the sequence should be the reverse. But there was nothing on which to hang any expectation.

"Mr. President, did you really think you were going to get anything different?" asked Olsen when he had read it.

Benton didn't reply.

Jay MacMahon was left holding it. "It's bombastic," he said. "You can hardly take it seriously."

"He's expecting you to back down," said Olsen. "At every stage, sir, he's expected you to back down. He's had a week to invade Taiwan if he was really prepared to fight for it, and he still hasn't done it. We're at the end now. This is where it's been heading for the last year. Now's the time to show we've got the courage to go all the way. One strike, Mr. President, and everything changes. What will he have left then? Nothing. Nothing but empty threats."

"All we need is the go-ahead," said MacMahon.

Olsen took back the letter and scanned it. "A terrible response that will shake your nation to its foundations," he said contemptuously. "What the hell's that supposed to mean?"

MacMahon shrugged. "They don't have a plane or a naval vessel within a thousand miles of us."

Alan Ball's face was grim. He didn't say a word.

"Sounds like President Wen's been reading his own press," said Cohen.

Jay MacMahon laughed.

The president took back the letter, read it again. It was bombastic, as MacMahon had said. A ridiculous, almost schoolboyish response to the serious and constructive message he had sent with Knight.

"He just doesn't get it," said Benton. "I don't know what else I've got to do. I don't know how much plainer I can give him the message. He just doesn't seem to get it."

"He will soon," said Larry Olsen.

Monday, October 31, 2033

The scope of the initial strike had widened. By now incidents had taken place that could be traced to four separate airbases and a naval base. All of them would be attacked, with the intention to target installations that would be unmanned at two a.m. local time, the time designated for the action. The attack would be carried out by eight Lance cruise missiles launched from submarines in international water off the Chinese coast.

The previous night—a crisp Monday morning over the South China Sea—an incident had occurred that could only be described as a dogfight without shots. Thirty-eight aircrafts were involved. One Chinese plane went down for causes that were unclear. The Chinese media were informed that it had been fired on by two American planes. A U.S. Air Force spokesman immediately denied the claim. In retaliation, the northern batteries of Taiwan's coastal defense came under prolonged bombardment from a Chinese naval group.

On Monday morning, the president received a final briefing from the Joint Chiefs. The heads of naval and air force intelligence reported that no Chinese vessels were in striking distance of the continental United States for the Ying, the Chinese cruise missile. To get the U.S. cruise-firing submarines in position, Enderlich needed approval by midday.

Joe Benton spoke to Secretary-General Nleki, who had nothing to offer but a despairing plea for calm and dialogue. He then spoke to Hugh Ogilvie, informing the British prime minister of the upcoming action and asking for his support. He gave the same message to Prime Minister Nakamura in Japan. He also spoke with Gorodin again, hoping that a last-minute declaration of support from Russia might bring China to the table. But he didn't trust that he could reveal to Gorodin the imminence of military action, and the Russian president, unaware of what was about to happen, remained equivocal.

At eleven forty-five, Admiral Enderlich came to the Oval Office. President Benton gave the order.

Then there was nothing to do but wait. The address that he would give after the firing was already written. In the Oval Office, technicians arrived to set up for the broadcast. Benton left the office. He found Ewen MacMaster as he went down a corridor in the West Wing, and he pulled him into the Cabinet Room to talk. Education. He asked Ewen what was happening. It felt as if he hadn't talked about stuff like that in months, years. This was what he really cared about. And yet it was surreal, like some kind of dream. In the South China Sea, three submarines were positioning themselves for a cruise launch on China. Ewen, like every other staffer, knew something was likely to happen, even if he didn't know what and he didn't know that the order had already been given. The president found it hard to focus. He let MacMaster go.

He went up to the residence floor and had lunch with Heather. Soup and salad. He had no appetite. Heather didn't know he had just given the order, but she guessed. She didn't say anything. He tried to read, kept glancing at his watch. The time crept toward two o'clock. Finally it got there. He watched the hand move, the final twitch.

He looked up. Heather was watching him.

"We've just fired."

She nodded.

They didn't say anything after that. Fifteen minutes later, he got a call from Enderlich, confirming the attack had taken place. Sunrise over southern China would be in about three hours. Shortly after that, the first satellite images would be analyzed, and they'd have a good idea of the degree of success.

The president called Jodie Ames and told her he was coming down.

He stood up. Heather stood as well. She stopped him, looked in his eyes, and kissed him. Then she took his arm, and they went down together.

The moment Ames put down the phone, she had put out an alert. Web stream controllers had ten minutes to get ready. As he took his seat behind the desk in the Oval Office, Joe Benton knew that all over the United States, all over the world, announcers were interrupting their programs, and in another minute they would carry his image from the camera positioned on the other side of his desk.

He glanced at Jodie. She nodded. Then he glanced at Heather.

"We're ready, sir," said Jodie.

He looked at the camera, set his face.

"Okay, Mr. President."

The light on the camera went on. He began.

"My fellow Americans. Although I speak to you today as your president, I speak also to the people of China as the leader of a friendly nation who wants nothing more than our mutual goodwill and prosperity. I speak to all the people of the world as an American president who wants nothing more than to work with you, your leaders, to achieve a better world for us all.

"It is my grave duty to announce that in the past hour United States forces have been in action against a number of facilities attaching to the armed forces of the People's Republic of China. We have been forced to this measure by the series of unprovoked attacks over the past week by the army of the People's Republic against both United States forces in international airspace and against Taiwanese targets, a number of which have resulted in fatalities, and by the failure of dialogue to achieve a cessation of this activity. I emphasize that this is not a declaration of war by the United States on the People's Republic of China, nor does a state of war exist between us. This carefully selected set of defensive actions was designed only to protect United States service personnel from attacks in international territory. Every care has been taken to avoid casualties, whether civilian or military, on the Chinese side, and I have confidence that our soldiers have achieved this aim. I ask now that the Chinese government . . ."

At the edge of his field of vision, something caught Joe Benton's eye. He tried to keep looking at the camera, but couldn't avoid glancing aside for an instant. A man in uniform, someone Benton didn't recognize, had come into the room and a conversation was going on between him and Jodie Ames. A very agitated conversation.

"I ask that the Chinese government withdraw its forces from their positions threatening Taiwan in compliance with the terms of the Manila Understanding . . ."

He looked again. Jodie Ames was frantically whirling one hand, telling him to finish up, while trying physically to hold back the uniformed man with the other.

"I ask that they withdraw their forces from Taiwan," said Benton, cutting to the key messages of his statement and trying to maintain the same steady, measured tone despite what was happening beyond the camera, "and sign up to the Carbon Plan that the United States has proposed. There is a peaceful way forward for all of us. God bless America. God bless China."

He looked up. The uniformed man was already coming around the desk. "Cut it!" yelled Jodie. "Cut the feed!"

The soldier got to him and grabbed his elbow.

"Come with me, sir, please!"

"What is this?"

"*Now, sir!*" The soldier was literally dragging him up from behind the desk. Another half dozen uniformed men poured in through the door from the Rose Garden. The president was being hustled out. He looked for Heather. She was surrounded by soldiers as well. His mind raced. What was going on? Why were these soldiers coming for him?

He was outside now. A helicopter stood on the lawn with its rotors turning. He tried to stop, pulling back against the two marines who were propelling him toward it.

"What's the hell's going on here?" he shouted. "Who are you?"

"Lieutenant Rivers, sir!" snapped the man who had first come into the office. "Duty officer, Alpha Unit!"

Alpha Unit, thought Benton. Alpha Unit . . . That was the unit tasked with ensuring his safety if the United States came under attack.

He looked for Heather.

"*Sir!* Please keep moving, sir! We've got to get you airborne!"

The strike had hit the San Francisco Bay area. Joe Benton didn't find this out until he was aboard Air Force One. He sought Heather's eyes.

The Bay area. Stanford. Amy.

But there was no time for that, not for the president. Already on board were Alan Ball, Admiral Enderlich and a half dozen cabinet members. The secretary of state was supposed to be with the presidential group in an Alpha event, but he wasn't on the plane when the president arrived and the rules were clear: the plane took off as soon as the president was aboard. The engines were already running.

Enderlich grabbed the briefcase with the nuclear codes from Benton's military aide, and he and another senior officer took the president and Alan Ball straight into a room off the communications hub, which doubled as a situation room. As the plane was taking off, they began to give him the details as they knew them. A device had exploded over the Bay area at 2:28 p.m. eastern time. The center of the strike zone appeared to be two miles west of Palo Alto. Satellite pictures were obscured by the dust storm the detonation had raised and seismic records were still being analyzed. It was too soon to know the size of the device or the extent of the damage.

"Two twenty-eight?" said the president, struggling to get his head clear. "How does that . . . ?"

Flight time from eastern China to the West Coast for an ICBM is fifteen to twenty minutes," said Enderlich.

"So it's Chinese?"

"That's our working assumption."

"Do we know that?"

"What other poss—"

"Do we *know* that?" demanded the president.

"We didn't identify it before it hit, sir. We're going over our scans. We'll track the route and then we'll know."

"Have they acknowledged responsibility?"

"Not yet, sir."

There was a knock on the door. An officer came in. He handed a piece of paper to the admiral. Enderlich studied it.

"Order China targeting," said Enderlich, and the officer nodded and left. Enderlich turned to Benton. "Mr. President, we have it launching from a base in Hunan province at two twelve p.m. eastern time."

Benton put his head in his hands. He could hear the hum of the plane's engines. He remembered what F. William Knight had said about President Wen. Take it seriously, Wen had said. The bombastic words of the Chinese president. Take it seriously. But who could have imagined?

"What's being done on the ground?" he murmured.

"Alpha Plan is in place, sir. The vice president is being bunkered. Director of the CIA, secretary of defense, and cabinet members are with her. The Speaker of the House is being bunkered at a separate location."

"No, Admiral. I mean on the *ground*. In California."

"Nuclear Emergency Plan, sir."

"What does that mean?" demanded Benton, looking up at him. "Right now. What's being done?"

"Assessment. Satellite initially. Other information will be coming in via reconnaissance drones once the dust clears to provide adequate visibility. We'll have personnel moving in from the periphery of the zone as radiation levels allow. Mr. President, I know your thoughts are with the victims, but I have to ask you to think about something else. We're waiting on your decision for action, whether we launch full-scale retaliation or a limited strike."

The president stared at him.

"Sir?"

Joe Benton felt cold. The reverberating thrum of the plane engines seemed to grind right through to his marrow.

"Sir, you have one hour from the strike time to override the general attack response. The code has now been transmitted to all relevant facilities to target them on China. If they do not receive your override in . . . it's thirty-one minutes now, the system will assume you're dead and we're going to wipe China off the map."

Enderlich put the codes briefcase on the table and snapped it open.

Benton looked at Alan Ball. Ball closed his eyes, slowly shaking his head.

"What happens in a full-scale strike?" asked the president. He must have been told, he knew, but his mind had gone blank.

"Strike on every known nuclear and nuclear-ready facility and all previously known locations of mobile launchers," replied the admiral. "Also on major nonnuclear military facilities. One way or another, this will affect most major population centers. Certain offshore and unidentified nuclear assets will survive the attack, and we should expect that they will attempt to respond. In the case of China, we anticipate twenty to forty warheads of various sizes will be launched at the continental United States. Not all will reach their destinations."

"What other choices do I have?"

"There are three choices, Mr. President. Apart from the full-scale response, there's a limited response and a single strike. In the case of China, the single strike could be Beijing, Shanghai, or we could target a secondary city."

Joe Benton felt ill. The room was small, the air stifling.

"Or nothing?"

"In principle, it is possible for you to stand down all facilities. But I strongly recommend against that, Mr. President. We have no deterrent if we are not prepared to use it." Enderlich waited for a reply. "Sir?"

"I heard you. I also heard you when you told me a couple of days ago they'd never try something like this."

"I repeat, Mr. President, we have no deterrent if you do not use it."

"Is there any evidence they're planning other attacks?"

"Not yet."

"We wouldn't exactly expect them to notify us," said the officer with Enderlich.

Benton dropped his head again, trying to get it straight in his mind. Did he need to launch a retaliatory strike? Would that stop the aggression or escalate it? What if it escalated? What was the next step? How would he stop it?

He was aware of time passing, the seconds spinning away.

Suddenly he felt extraordinarily isolated from the outside world. He was in a small, closed room on an airplane. He was being told things. How did he know any of this was really happening? All he knew was what Enderlich was telling him. Suddenly he thought, how did he know it wasn't a coup? Why wasn't Larry Olsen here? How did he know this wasn't some kind of coup by Olsen and the military?

"Show me the pictures," he said suddenly.

Enderlich looked at him, not understanding.

"You said you've got satellite pictures of the strike zone."

"Mr. President, we really don't have time to—"

"Show me! Right now, Admiral."

Enderlich stared at the president for a moment, then he glanced at the other officer and nodded. The officer went out and closed the door behind him. As they waited there was silence. Benton's face was taut. He glanced at Alan Ball. When that door opened again, he thought, he would know. Either someone would come back with a handful of pictures or a squad of marines.

The door opened. Two officers came in. One of them gave a handheld to Admiral Enderlich.

Enderlich put it down in front of the President. "These are satellite images. That's the Bay area, two twenty-seven. Everything's okay." He tapped on the handheld. "There it is, two twenty-nine."

The picture spoke for itself. A disk-shaped smudge had appeared over the base of the fingerlike projection of the San Francisco peninsula.

Enderlich tapped. "Two thirty."

The cloud was bigger.

Enderlich tapped again. "Two thirty-five."

The cloud was elongating into an oval, now reaching out over the bay.

Benton glanced at Alan Ball, who had been looking at the screen over his shoulder. Ball's face was a mixture of awful misery and fear. He had just seen a nightmare come to life, a vision of the apocalypse. A mushroom cloud over an American city.

"We need a decision, sir." Enderlich looked at his watch. "We have twenty-three minutes."

The president turned to Enderlich. "What do you recommend, Admiral?"

To Benton's surprise, the admiral didn't recommend the all-out strike. "Limited response, sir."

"What does that mean, exactly?"

"It's targeted on known active nuclear sites. The message it sends is that we're only concerned to extinguish the enemy's nuclear capability for our own self-defense, but we do not aim for their destruction nor the eradication of their conventional military capability."

"In China," said one of the other officers, "we would estimate an immediate one hundred to one hundred twenty million casualties from the blasts and an equal number again over the first month from burns and other injuries."

Benton stared. "That's the *limited* strike?"

"Yes, sir. The collateral damage is a function of the Chinese military policy of locating nuclear facilities in proximity to population centers. It's a risk they've always run, and they're aware of it. If they did the same to us, we would take blast and first-month casalties of no more than fifteen to twenty million."

The president looked at Alan Ball. Ball slumped in a chair. His face said it all, the crumpled, helpless expression of a man who wished he wasn't there.

"I can't kill two hundred million people," murmured Benton disbelievingly.

"Mr. President," said Admiral Enderlich, "we need a decision. We have to act."

Suddenly Joe Benton was reminded of Whitefish, the first day of the siege, when he had been asked to authorize an assault. The sense of responsibility that had struck him so strongly, the doubt. The way he had put off the decision.

"If we don't act, sir, we have no deterrant. We become vulnerable to every other nuclear power."

There was no comparison with Whitefish, he knew. It was incongruous to think about it, even for an instant. There was no comparison at all.

"Mr. President. I repeat, we have no deterrant if we don't act."

Joe Benton turned back to the admiral.

"Sir, we need a decision."

"Launch a single strike," said Benton quietly.

"A single strike, sir? Are you certain?"

Joe Benton nodded. He didn't know if he could bring himself physically to say it again.

"That leaves the enemy with its nuclear capability intact."

"I realize that, Admiral."

"That puts us behind them in the game. They've already launched a single strike. Doctrine says we hit back harder."

Doctrine says, thought Benton.

"You always hit back harder."

"*Always?*" demanded Benton sharply. "There is no always. When has this happened before? Your doctrine is theory, Admiral."

"Mr. President, I think you should consider your responsibility as commander in chief to safeguard—"

"When I want a lecture about my responsibility, Admiral, I'll let you know! Understand me? Launch a single strike!"

Admiral Enderlich clenched his jaw. Benton could see his muscles working.

"Where, sir?" he said eventually. "Shanghai? We know that two of President Wen's children live in Shanghai, but we would assume by now they'd be bunkered."

The implication of the admiral's words hit Benton like a blow. He almost physically threw up.

"Sir?"

"Not Shanghai. And not Beijing. Somewhere smaller."

"We have a series of secondary targets." The admiral slid the open briefcase toward the president.

One of the other officers began typing on a handheld.

"Your right thumb, sir," said the admiral, pointing at the briefcase.

The president pressed his thumb on a pad inside the case. The device beeped.

"Now your right eye."

The president picked up the iris scanner that was in the case and put it to his eye. The device beeped again.

A set of codes came up on the screen, red numbers.

"Your thumb again, sir."

The president swiped his thumb, and all but one of the numbers disappeared.

"And again, sir."

Benton swiped once more. The device beeped again, and then the number disappeared. The screen was blank.

"What's happened?"

"The code's gone out," said the Admiral.

"For a single strike?"

"I'll be giving that order in a moment."

Benton looked at him suspiciously.

"If you'll sign, sir," said the admiral coldly. Beside him, the officer who had been typing was pointing his handheld at the briefcase, and a page was coming out of a printer in the case.

"The paper's more distinctive than the paper for a dollar bill," said the admiral. "If anyone ever wants to verify, it could only come from one printer." He pulled out the page and handed it to the president.

Benton read the page. It was an order for an immediate nuclear strike on a secondary city in China.

"Sign, sir, if you will."

Benton signed.

Enderlich picked it up. "Thank you, Mr. President." The admiral turned to leave the room.

"Admiral," said the president, "do you know what city will be targeted?"

Enderlich stopped at the door. "Not at present, sir. There's a rotating roster. I'll have you informed."

Joe Benton nodded. He felt numb. "I guess it doesn't really matter."

He had been taken to a bunker complex in South Dakota. He recorded an address to be streamed to the nation. He said that a grave attack had been launched by China on the soil of the United States. He said that all efforts were being made to get help to those who had been hit. He said the response of the United States had been swift and decisive, proportionate and firm, aiming to demonstrate the determination and power of the United States, keep the country safe, and prevent further escalation. Stopping short of issuing a formal declaration of war on China, he called on the Chinese government to desist from further attacks or risk severe punishment, and to immediately declare adherence to the global Carbon Plan. He said nothing about Taiwan. The Chinese government could have it if they wanted it. Had Larry Olsen been with him, he knew, he would have had to fight him over that, but he wasn't going to sacrifice one more American life, military or civilian, for the sake of Taiwanese independence. Finally, he called on all world leaders and the community of nations to confirm their acceptance of the Carbon Plan and join with the United States at this time of crisis.

Jodie Ames, who was with him, had persuaded him not to do it live, and he was glad she had. It took him four attempts to get the address right, to get enough sense of leadership and hope into his voice, not to appear as hollow and stricken as he really felt.

In the situation room in the bunker complex, Admiral Enderlich and his staff were taking reports and debating the next action to take. Their only answer seemed to be a bigger, harder response if there was any indication that the Chinese were going to hit them again.

Greg was known to have been safe in New York, and had been bunkered. There was no information on Amy, not even for the president. Heather was desperate for news. She sat in front of a screen watching reports on the news sites being streamed into the bunker.

Tuesday–Wednesday, November 1–2

South Dakota

The situation room was a frenzy of activity but somehow there was nothing for him to do. He felt almost redundant. Every hour through the night there was a briefing, yet hard information about what was happening on the ground didn't seem to increase appreciably from one briefing to the next. He made calls, and more calls. He spoke with Mary Okoro, the governor of California, who knew only what she was being told by the Federal Emergency Response Authority. He already had that information direct from Lou Katz, the Authority's director. He spoke to other governors. The National Guard had been mobilized throughout the country, but disturbances had been few. He spoke to Angela Chavez and Jay MacMahon. Larry Olsen was apparently close to D.C. in a bunker to which communication had failed. This was the first time the Alpha Plan had been put to the test in real life, Enderlich said, so inevitably there were going to be glitches. No one seemed to know whether the Chinese government would be able to reach Olsen if they wanted to. Benton wondered whether they would be able to reach him here in this bunker and demanded that Enderlich find out.

The estimate was that the warhead had been approximately one megaton in size. Heather sat constantly watching the news streams in the bunker, but the only solid information the streams had was from the Emergency Response Authority. Otherwise, they were filling time mostly with speculation by reporters far from the scene and analysts giving their views on what the president ought to do or criticizing a relief response of which they could know absolutely nothing. The satellite photographs released to the agencies showed a flare-shaped smear of dust over northern California, being blown in the direction of Sacramento, which had been evacuated. Lou Katz, who was designated under the Alpha Plan to direct operations from a bunker in Ohio, was ubiquitous on the streams. One site after another showed footage of him announcing that emergency teams equipped with protective gear were entering the strike zone. The president imagined people all over the country, all over the world, restlessly seeking information, and seeing only Katz's jowly face with the same hunted expression saying the same words over and over again. Katz told the president he had reports of hospitals in San Francisco and San Jose choking with burned survivors. That was something the agencies weren't being told. It was chaos in those cities. Those who could, had fled, including many of the doctors and nurses from the hospitals at which survivors were arriving. The electromagnetic pulse from the strike had disrupted computer and communication systems throughout the Bay Area, which added to the mayhem, although it also meant that no unofficial reports were coming out of the area. Yet some news streams were now starting to carry acounts purporting to be from witnesses in the periphery of the strike zone. Under the powers of the Nuclear Emergency Plan, Katz had the power to shut down sites carrying unauthorized reports but he hadn't taken that step. A blackout on major new streams, he believed, would just throw the country into even greater panic. But it was only a matter of time before unofficial reporting got out of hand unless they could counter it with better information. A one-megaton device, Benton was told, would blast everything flat in a radius of five miles and burn anything to a cinder that was within twice that distance from the strike. So far, the only reliable reports were coming to Katz's headquarters from no closer than fifteen miles from the strike zone in Palo Alto.

"To tell you the truth," said Katz, "no one seems to know how fast it's safe to move in there. We're just trying to get enough radiation suits for people to use. If you'll excuse the French, sir, it's a fucking nightmare."

"Weren't we prepared?" demanded the president.

"For this, sir?"

Katz's tone said it all, the sheer overwhelming magnitude of what he was trying to deal with. Benton nodded. How could they have been prepared for this? How could anyone be?

"It's a hell of mess, Mr. President. I just hope whoever dies in there dies quick."

Joe Benton closed his eyes. He had had exactly the same thought.

He came back and Heather looked up at him. "The situation's still very confused," he said.

He went into the situation room. They had satellite pictures of China. The U.S. strike had targeted Changsha in south central China, a city of eight million people. A dust cloud smeared the image, like the one that hung over San Francisco Bay.

There had been no response from the Chinese government. As news of the U.S. retaliation came out, governments around the world were condemning both attacks. Hugh Ogilvie got through to Benton. He just kept saying they had to stop this. They had to stop it. Benton asked him to try to talk with the Chinese government, try to get a message to them, tell Wen that he stood by the statement he had made from the bunker. There was a way out of this. Ogilvie said he had tried, and he couldn't find anyone senior to take a call. Benton assumed they were bunkered, just like him. Then it occurred to him that he didn't know who was in charge in China. Who was calling the shots? There was no way of knowing that it wasn't Ding, or some other hardliner, or the army that was now in power.

Ogilvie said he didn't know either.

Between briefings, he sat with Heather and stared grimly at the screen. His thoughts veered wildly. At one moment he'd be thinking about Amy, numb with disbelief, like any father, like thousands of other fathers who had a child at Stanford or somewhere else in the Bay area when the strike hit. And then suddenly he'd be the president again, and he found himself wondering how he'd got to this position, what he'd done wrong along the way, if he'd done anything wrong. He must have done something wrong if he had brought a nuclear strike down on his own people, the first president in history to have achieved that distinction. There must have been a misjudgment. Maybe he had backed Wen too much into a corner, given him no room to wriggle out. Maybe he had misread the signals. But who would think Wen would *do* it? No one thought anyone would ever do it. If India and Pakistan had managed to keep their fingers off their respective buttons for thirty years, surely anyone could. And what should he do now? If he had made a misjudgment already—he and all his advisors—what was to stop him making a misjudgment again? Should he keep waiting for a Chinese response? Shouldn't he preempt it? Where was Larry Olsen when he needed him? Still out of communication. Alan Ball seemed to be having some kind of breakdown. He was surrounded by military, military advice. He had absolutely no idea what the government in Beijing was doing. Should he try to contact Wen? But Wen hadn't tried to contact him, and Ogilvie, who was trying to mediate, still hadn't been able to get through to the Chinese leader. But by sitting here like this, waiting, he was allowing the other side to make the running. That wasn't what the doctrine said he was supposed to do. But the doctrine was pure theory. But then what was he supposed to do? Make another statement? Announce that he was . . . what? Backing down? Or should he go ahead and nuke the hell out of them, like Enderlich wanted? And then he would glance at Heather again, and all he could think about was Amy.

Heather had said hardly anything. Hadn't eaten. Just kept watching the news streams, hungry for information, any information, looking up at him each time he came back from a briefing with Enderlich, and then, when he had nothing more to offer, looking away again.

He hugged her, and they held each other, and then she turned back to the stream.

There was a pair of pundits on the screen. They were discussing what was going to happen next. One argued that the U.S. should have hit back harder. One argued it shouldn't have hit back at all. The first one responded that an all-out Chinese strike was now inevitable. "So we're all about to die?" asked the anchor.

"I believe so, yes," replied the pundit smugly, as if it gave him some kind of satisfaction.

Joe Benton wanted to scream. Could nothing get these people off the screen? Why weren't they at home with their families?

Waiting. For what? Was he at war? Nothing seemed to be happening, nothing real. Just briefings and more briefings. Armed soldiers were everywhere in the bunker. Above him, outside, up there, the United States was in lockdown. Forces in every ocean and every airspace were ready. It was like a trigger. Under his finger. He didn't know himself what would make him pull it.

He was exhausted, he felt hollowed out with a tiredness beyond reason. It seemed like days ago, weeks ago, that he had issued his statement in this bunker. A statement. Another statement. What was the point? All he ever seemed to do was issue statements. And now five million people were dead, or maybe ten million, or maybe more, people who had been alive thirty-six hours ago. Who could even start to comprehend it? And how many more would be dead before he issued his next statement?

There was a room for him with a bed. People were telling him to get some sleep. He needed sleep, he knew that. He lay down, closed his eyes: Thoughts of Amy. Restlessness, agitation. Maybe he slept for a minute. More thoughts. Disoriented. He hoped everyone in there died quick. The last time he had seen Amy, she had run out on him. The only time she'd ever done that. Amy. Maybe she was alive. Could the whole thing be concocted? Could it be a coup? You could doctor pictures. You could prepare web streams and make them look as if they were live. Chavez would know only what she was told as well. What about Lou Katz? But you could fool him too, if you were sufficiently prepared. Or he could be in on it. So could Chavez. So could everyone.

He sat up. *Was he going mad?*

In the other room, he found Heather watching a screen. What time was it? Here in the bunker, it could be day, it could be night. He stood staring at the screen. The news stream was showing some kind of vox pop on the streets. Cameras were out in various cities. People were shaking their heads, some searching for words, some almost incoherent with anger. One woman in Boston, tearstained, shocked, cried at the camera, "Where's our president? How do we know he's even alive?"

The words hit him like a slap. Like a splash of cold water to the face.

There was a knock. Enderlich came in. He looked grave.

"What is it?" asked the president.

Enderlich glanced meaningfully at Heather.

Benton had no patience for that. "Admiral, what is it?"

"Mr. President . . ." Enderlich hesitated, glanced again at Heather. "Mr. President, it appears the Chinese military has responded."

The president stared at the chairman of the Joint Chiefs. "How?"

"The United States has come under a second nuclear attack, sir."

413

Heather gasped. Benton continued to stare at Enderlich.

"Kansas, sir. The town of Junction City was the strike point."

Junction City, Kansas? Benton had never heard of it.

"At this stage we have little information, sir. We're estimating a population of up to a quarter million in the critical radius."

"Do we have missile silos in the area?"

"No, sir. We're assuming the missile came down early. The continued trajectory of the flight path would target it close to Miami. Alternatively, if it went off course, it was probably heading for one of the population centers on the East Coast. Possibly Washington. Mr. President, we're facing a clear escalation. We have to counterattack with serious force."

Joe Benton said the first thing that came into his head. "What if it didn't come down early on its flight path?"

"There's a military facility outside Junction City but it's a small conventional base. Never had a nuclear role. The Chinese wouldn't even know about it. There would be hundreds of bases like that in China we wouldn't know about."

"Then why would they attack it?"

"Mr. President, I just said, they didn't."

"But, Admiral, they just did." Maybe he wasn't thinking straight— Benton was aware that was possible, more than possible—but why assume the strike had been an error? Why not assume it had taken place as intended, and look for the message in that? "What did you say exactly, Admiral? Was the trajectory targeted on Miami, or close to Miami?"

"Mr. President, we've had a lucky escape on this and right now we need to take every ounce of luck we can get. If that missile didn't come down early we'd be talking about a place a whole lot bigger than Junction City. We need to launch a serious counterpunch. A single strike is no longer enough." The Admiral put the briefcase on the sofa beside the president and snapped it open.

Heather stared at it with revulsion.

"Sir? Your thumb?"

Joe Benton didn't move. He gazed at Enderlich. *Could* this be a coup? Could it be an attempt to get him to launch a major strike to create the conditions for the military to take over. Led by who? Jay MacMahon? Larry Olsen? In the meetings over the last few days Olsen and Enderlich had been saying pretty much the same things. And Olsen wasn't here, even though he was meant to be. Where was he? Maybe he was up there, on top, orchestrating things.

"Sir?" Enderlich pointed at the briefcase. "We have to act. They're escalating."

"Put it away."

"We have to respond."

"What if they're de-escalating? They attack the Bay area. They kill, how many? Three million? We respond and kill the same. Or more. Then they attack Junction City. It's a de-escalation, Admiral. Isn't that obvious?"

"It's an error, sir. A lucky escape. We have to take our chance—"

"What if they're looking for a way out?"

"What if the next missile is already on its way?"

Benton stared at the admiral. Suddenly the bunker seemed unbearable. Benton felt utterly cut off from reality, dependent on information filtered through to him by people he didn't know, didn't trust, didn't understand.

The woman's face on the vox pop flashed into his mind. Tearstained. Shocked. Her voice. "Where's our president? How do we know he's even alive?"

"Get me out of here," he said suddenly.

"What?"

"Get me back to Washington."

"Sir, I can't do that. Remember what your position is."

"Your commander in chief. I said get me back to Washington."

"Sir, Alpha Plan requires—"

"I don't give a damn about Alpha Plan. I'm giving you an order. Get me back to Washington!"

"Mr. President, we have complete airspace shutdown over the United States. Any plane up there gets shot out of the sky."

"Then you'll inform whoever's going to shoot me out of the sky that they're not going to do it."

"No, sir."

"Yes, sir."

"No, sir. It is my responsibility to secure the person of the president in case of mortal danger to his person and I will do that, sir, whether you or anyone around you . . ."

Benton walked out of the room. Outside, he found one of the armed military detail that seemed to be everywhere in the bunker.

"Give me your gun," he said.

The marine looked at him in surprise.

"Give me your gun, soldier." The president pulled the pistol out of the marine's holster. He turned around. Admiral Enderlich was in the doorway behind him.

"Mr. President—"

Joe Benton raised the gun and put its muzzle against the admiral's temple.

"So help me, Admiral, if I have to, I'll blow your brains out. I'm your commander in chief. Admiral Enderlich, in front of this soldier as witness, I'm giving you a direct order. Get me back to Washington."

Enderlich didn't move. Half a dozen soldiers had gathered now, all staring, including Rivers, the lieutenant who had pulled the president out of the Oval Office at the start of the evacuation.

"Lieutenant," said the admiral calmly, "have your men disarm the president."

Benton threw a glance at Rivers. "Stay where you are, Lieutenant."

"Disarm him, Lieutenant."

"As your commander in chief, I'm ordering you to stay where you are." Benton watched the lieutenant for a moment, then turned back to Enderlich, his gun still raised to the other man's head. "Now, I don't know what's going on here, but I know one thing. At a time like this, the president of the United States shouldn't be hiding down at the bottom of a bunker. If this country is under attack, then I'm going to be out there to face it. So if you don't want to do what your commander in chief is ordering you to do, Admiral Enderlich, I'm going to have you put under arrest."

"Lieutenant," said the Admiral, speaking slowly and emphatically, "please have your men disarm President Benton."

"All right, have it your way," said Benton. "Lieutenant, arrest Admiral Enderlich."

Lieutenant Rivers drew his gun. He glanced from one man to the other. Then he stepped forward and raised his pistol.

"Lieutenant!" roared the Admiral "I *order* you—"

"Step back, Mr. President," said Rivers, eyes trained on the admiral, his pistol aimed at his head. "I'll handle this now."

"*Lieutenant!*"

"I'm sorry, Admiral Enderlich. The president's right. At a time like this, a commander in chief shouldn't be at the bottom of a bunker. He should be with his men."

Wednesday, November 2

The White House

The first thing he did was to go out on the south lawn and speak with the White House in camera shot behind him. Heather was on one side of him, and Angela Chavez on the other, and around them were his cabinet secretaries. They had been given the choice to stay bunkered or come back, and they were all there.

The message was short. He started by telling the American people that they had just lived through terrible days, but that he was here, he was at his post, and he was doing everything he could to make sure they would never see such days again. Then he said: "This part is for President Wen of the People's Republic of China. I have a message for you, President Wen. The United States government is here. The United States government is open for business. And in the United States government, the buck stops with me. So if you don't like what the United States government is saying, leave innocent people alone. Hit *me* with your bombs." He spread his arms. "Right here. I'm waiting. And when you're ready to sign up to the Carbon Plan, it's the same address." He pointed to the White House behind him. "I'll be right in there, ready to hear from you, one way or the other." He paused, gazing at the camera. "President Wen, I'm not going anywhere."

Back inside, he gave orders for the evacuation of the Washington area. Only essential military staff would be asked to stay. Then he went to the situation room where he gathered the National Security Council and the other service chiefs. He had brought Enderlich back with him on Air Force One and decided to include him in the discussion, even though the admiral was technically under arrest. Larry Olsen was there. He had been bunkered in Virginia, as the president had been told, and there had been a communications failure.

"Mr. President," said Jay MacMahon, "you've made your point. Quite magnificently. We should now move you out of Washington to safety."

Joe Benton looked at him incredulously. "Jay, I didn't just say that. This is where I'm staying. Every six hours, the American people are going to see me in front of this White House to know that's exactly where I am."

MacMahon glanced at Enderlich. "But sir—"

"I'm not taking discussion on this. Now, let's have a full briefing. Let's get everyone up to speed."

Lou Katz gave a summary of conditions in the Bay area and Kansas and the relief operations that were under way. Satellite imaging showed the extent of the devastation at the centers of both strike zones. Rescue teams had moved in until they ceased to find survivors, which left them some miles short of the strike zone in both areas.

Joe Benton couldn't keep himself from asking the question. "Stanford?"

Lou Katz shook his head. "That's gone, sir." He almost whispered it. "Would have been gone in seconds."

Some of the people at the table gazed at the president, others looked away.

Benton was silent. He frowned, then nodded slightly to himself.

"General Steiffel," he said, turning to Dan Steiffel, head of army intelligence who was coordinating information from the theater. "What can you tell us?"

Steiffel reported that Chinese forces had moved on Taiwan and were encountering resistance, supported by the U.S. Pacific Fleet and the Grant and Franklin carrier groups, which had been in action since the previous day.

"Who ordered that?" demanded Benton.

"I did," said MacMahon. "I was told you were not in contact, sir."

"Who told you that?"

"That was my information, Mr. President."

Benton gazed at him, then turned back to Steiffel. "Give me the details."

"As of zero nine hundred we've flown four hundred thirty-seven sorties and have inflicted substantial losses on the enemy."

"Our losses?"

"Twelve F-42s and five B-3 bombers, sir. The destroyer USS *Cable* is lightly damaged. The destroyer USS *Morley Kade* is reported sinking and assistance is being rendered."

"Sinking?"

"We don't have an estimate of casualties yet."

"What's the crew complement?"

"Three hundred twenty-three crew and officers at full strength, Mr. President."

"Are Chinese forces on the island?"

"Yes, sir. PRC forces have landed in strength in four places along the west and northeast coasts and we have reports of advance units on the outskirts of Taipei."

"Sounds to me like Taiwan's gone," said the president.

"Not necessarily, sir." Steiffel went on to report what was happening on the mainland. There were reports of uprisings in Shanghai, Guangzhou, Hong Kong, Dalian and the central provincial capitals of Lanzhou and Chongqing, all being opposed by government troops. From Nanjing there were reports of an army division going over to the opposition and a battle taking place on the streets.

"Mr. President," said MacMahon, "if we can sit this out a little longer, the Chinese regime might fall. We could help that process. We have forces in the region. Let's deploy away from Taiwan and toward the mainland."

"You want to invade China?" demanded Alan Ball, who had recovered some of his presence since the return to Washington, but still had the look of an utterly shell-shocked man.

"I don't want to invade China. I'm saying a little targeted assistance might help some of these uprisings to succeed."

"What exactly are these uprisings?" said Benton. "General Steiffel? Can you be more specific? Are these demonstrations? Are they riots? Are they genuine insurrections?"

"It varies," said Steiffel. "Our intelligence isn't perfect."

"So some of these might just be demonstrations?"

"For the moment, Mr. President. But the force the government is exerting is likely to make them worse."

"Or end them," said Ball.

"Mr. President," said MacMahon, "I think we could be seeing the end of the regime."

"Let's say you're right, Jay. What happens next?"

"Well . . ." MacMahon was puzzled. "They're gone."

"I think what the president is asking," said Larry Olsen, "is who do we negotiate with?"

"And who has control of a nuclear arsenal that has attacked the United States twice within the last seventy-two hours," said Benton pointedly.

"We combine it with a knockout attack on their nuclear capability," said General Anderson, chief of the army staff. "We disrupt command and control."

"And kill half a billion people."

"We didn't ask to start this."

"General, if we do that, some of their weapons will be fired automatically. Isn't that true?"

Anderson didn't respond. The president looked at Enderlich.

"Yes, sir," said Enderlich. "That's true."

Joe Benton nodded. "Gentlemen," he said to the Joint Chiefs. "You all need to understand something. This is not a war for regime change in the People's Republic of China."

"But it's an extraordinary opportunity," said Jay MacMahon. "If we can get—"

"No, Jay, that's where you're wrong. We need a strong government in China. This is a war about carbon. Not about Taiwan, not about the Chinese nuclear capability, not about regime change. Carbon. It's about the future of our people, the American people, and what kind of life they're going to live. We need a government in Beijing we can talk to which can cut emissions. We don't need chaos in China. How long will it take them to sort themselves out if we help foment some kind of revolution? Two years? Five years?"

"A generation," said Olsen.

"A generation," said the president. "If that happens, we lose this war. Do you understand? We don't win, no matter how many people we kill, no matter how many nuclear weapons we destroy. We lose."

"Mr. President," said Jay MacMahon quietly, "what do you want?"

"I want the Chinese government to remain in power. I want it to come out of this situation prepared to do what it has to do over emissions and to be capable of doing it. Otherwise, all of this, everything we've suffered, has been in vain. And we'll probably end up suffering it again."

There was silence. The president looked at Olsen, who bore nearly as much responsibility for what had happened—right or wrong—as he did. Larry Olsen met his gaze and nodded.

"Here's what we're going to do," said Benton. "Admiral Enderlich, you will start immediately to withdraw all U.S. forces from the Taiwan region. And any covert support we're giving to opposition groups on the mainland stops, right now. Have we been providing covert support?"

Complicitous glances were exchanged around the table.

"It stops. Now. Larry, I want you to make sure that President Wen, or whoever the hell's in charge over there, knows we're doing this. Make sure they know we're withdrawing from Taiwan and we won't interfere in internal affairs on the mainland. And tell him we're not going to retaliate for their second nuclear strike for another twenty-four hours." Benton looked at his watch. "Say until midnight our time tomorrow. If he publicly pledges support for the Carbon Plan by midnight our time tomorrow, we won't retaliate."

"And if he doesn't?"

"We will. It's an ultimatum. He does what he has to do, he signs up to the Carbon Plan, or we hit him. I've done it once, I can do it again. His choice."

Olsen nodded.

"And in the meantime," said Enderlich, "we sit here waiting for them to throw whatever they've got at us."

"Don't worry, Admiral," said Benton. "If they do blow us all to hell, our response will do the same to them, won't it? That ought to make you happy."

The admiral gazed resentfully at the president. Benton thought of putting the handcuffs back on him.

"I just think of those people," said Jay MacMahon. "The people the Chinese government is going to repress. And the people of Taiwan. We're betraying them all. We could bring this regime down, but instead we're betraying them all." MacMahon paused, gazing directly at the president. "It makes me sick."

"Mr. MacMahon," said Benton, "you are relieved of your duties." He looked around the table. "With immediate effect I am assuming the duties of secretary of defense."

MacMahon stood up and walked out.

"Anyone else?" Benton waited a moment. "All right. Admiral Enderlich, you remain under arrest. General Anderson, I appoint you acting chairman of the Joint Chiefs of Staff. You have your orders."

"Yes, sir."

"Go and execute them."

Thursday, November 3
The White House

Armored vehicles were on the White House lawns. The White House itself was full of soldiers. Anti-blast nets were draped across the windows. A further Chinese strike was possible, and whoever had stayed in Washington knew they were the likely target. Troops patrolled the streets to prevent looting in the evacuated city. There were scares. Reports of possible incoming missiles that failed to materialize. Whenever there was a loud noise, someone would jump.

By two in the morning, Taipei had fallen. Chinese news agencies had announced the reunification of the province of Taiwan with the motherland.

But by now Joe Benton had started getting calls. They began a few hours after his statement on the White House lawn. Maybe it was the sight of him literally putting his own life on the line that did it, maybe it was the realization of the sheer, unimaginable horror of what had actually happened. First Ogilvie, then Nakamura called. When Ingelbock of Germany rang to announce his support, Benton knew the balance was really shifting. Sometime after the Chinese announced the fall of Taipei, Prime Minister Kumar of India came on the line. He apologized for the lateness of the call but said he thought the president would still be awake. Benton listened to him promise that India would sign up to the plan.

At seven in the morning he heard Alexei Gorodin's voice. "Please make certain that President Wen knows," he said after Gorodin had told him Russia would join.

Still no word had come from anyone in authority in Beijing.

Shortly after eight a.m. Larry Olsen called to request that the president come down to the situation room. The military chiefs were waiting when he got there.

"I have a verbal message from Minister Ding," said Olsen.

The president looked at him expectantly.

"He said the government of the People's Republic understands that the United States requires retaliation for the nuclear strike on Kansas, and that his government will therefore accept a strike on a tertiary target in China. He's given me four alternatives."

"What did he say about the Carbon Plan?"

"Nothing. That was his message, Mr. President. We are free to launch a retaliatory strike on one of these targets and there will be no response."

The president stared at him.

"When do they want us to hit them?" asked General Anderson.

"Today."

"Have you got the list of targets?"

Olsen pulled a piece of paper out of his pocket and handed it to Anderson. The general studied it.

"Bob," said Steiffel, "I'm not so sure this is a good idea. We hit them, it makes them look like the victim again."

"How can they be the victim?" said Anderson. "They attacked us. This is a retaliation."

"But if we don't retaliate the second time, we keep the moral high ground. Strategically, that's more significant than a strike on some godforsaken town."

"Dan's right," said another of the generals. "That's what they want. They want to be able to say, the United States launched the last attack, and *we* were the ones who held back."

Anderson shook his head. "You have to understand the way they think. They'd demand retaliation, so they think we will. They think if we don't have a retaliation, we'll always be wanting it. It's important we do this for their sake. They need it to feel safe."

"Sir," said a colonel who was one of Steiffel's senior aides, "I would also say, unless we do retaliate, it'll look like we backed down and were too scared to stop them taking Taiwan. That sends a bad message to other states that might be tempted to attack us."

"Exactly," said Anderson.

Steiffel frowned. "I don't know. That might be right, but . . . they asked us for this. That means we're giving them what they want. It doesn't smell right. We should think about it."

"We're doing it!" said Anderson.

"No, we're not." Joe Benton had listened in disbelief. "I am not going to kill another million, or two million, or whatever-it-is million people just because someone tells me I can." He looked at the Joint Chiefs in revulsion. "Listen to what you're saying!"

They were silent.

The president turned to Olsen. "Thank Ding for his kind offer. Tell him our deadline stands. They have until midnight eastern time to sign up to the Carbon Plan. If they don't do it, we will launch retaliation, and we'll be the ones to choose what it is. And it's Wen himself who has to say they sign up. In public, in Chinese, and on a website that's unrestricted in China."

Olsen nodded.

"And in the meantime, get on the phone to every foreign minister in every country that's signed up and get them calling whoever they can find in Beijing to tell them they'll join us in sanctions if China doesn't come on board."

"And if they don't, Mr. President?" said Anderson. "You've told them we'll retaliate. We'll have to do it. What do you have in mind?"

Benton gazed at him. "I'll cross that bridge when I have to."

He found Heather in the middle of the day. Her eyes were empty, grief-stricken. No uncertainty remained, not the slightest shred of hope to cling to. Joe knew he was lucky right now to have so many demands to occupy his time.

The hours seemed to fly by, filled with meetings and briefings and decisions he had to make to drive the emergency relief effort. The midnight deadline loomed closer. Benton was acutely aware that Ding's message hadn't mentioned the Carbon Plan. What if Wen didn't sign up? What if he just said, effectively, come on, hit me? China would suffer deeply if it tried to go it alone for any length of time with the whole world applying sanctions, but maybe Wen thought, when it came to it, the sanctions would never be applied. And maybe he thought Benton wouldn't launch any retaliation. Or maybe he didn't care. China survives. Whatever happens, China survives. Maybe Wen thought that somehow all of this would actually be good for the party's hold on power. So maybe that's what he was going to do, like he had done all along, at every step, call anything that looked even remotely like an American bluff. Benton couldn't bear to think about it. It was too horrible to imagine.

At nine p.m. he was in the Oval Office. Ball, Hoffman, Eales and another half dozen people were with him. Olsen arrived. They discussed the outlook. All afternoon, the Joint Chiefs had been pressuring Benton to authorize specific action in the event that Wen didn't sign up. He hadn't been able to bring himself to look at their plans, as if just considering them might make the nightmare come true.

Now he had to.

At ten o'clock Jodie Ames interrupted them. There had been an announcement across the Chinese media that President Wen would be speaking from Taipei at ten thirty in the morning local time, ten thirty p.m. in Washington.

At ten thirty, the Oval Office was crowded. The screen showed Wen at a lectern in front of an enormous crowd of civilians. He was waiting for applause to stop. Benton wondered how many people they must have shipped to Taipei to get that response.

Then Wen began speaking.

The web stream carried an official translation. In the Oval Office they listened to Wen's words in Mandarin and Oliver Wu translated.

Wen began by formally announcing the reintegration of the province of Taiwain into the People's Republic. There was prolonged applause, and Wen stood there, beaming, and clapping in response as it went on. When the applause died down, he eulogized the Chinese military that had carried out the conquest. He could hardly get through a couple of sentences without more applause breaking out. He launched into a history of the loss of Taiwan and came back to the theme of its glorious recovery. The motherland was reunited. The great imperialist wound on the body of the Chinese people was healed.

Wen kept going on that theme. He kept stopping for applause. In the Oval Office, the group listened in somber silence. Only Wen's triumphant voice, and Oliver Wu's following it a moment behind, were audible.

"This is like watching Hitler dance his jig in Paris," murmured Olsen, and he shook his head in disgust.

Still Wen talked. Applause kept stopping him. He was eulogizing the party now, its determination, its iron will to recover every last piece of alienated Chinese territory. On and on he went about it. The speech seemed to be going on forever.

Benton looked at a clock. The Chinese president had been talking for almost an hour.

He had demanded a public statement. It had to come soon. If it was going to come, it had to come soon.

Wen kept going. Only the party could have harnessed the will of the Chinese people in this way. Only the party could have led the people to the dawn of this glorious day.

"Now the party will show that it can lead the whole world. China will show what must be done to reduce the emissions of carbon gases. As we know, President Benton of the United States has put forward a plan which, in reality, is a plan that came from the government of the People's Republic of China. Now I think President Benton has learned that China is not told what it should do, but chooses what it will do. We choose to launch the plan that President Benton announced, and we call on him to join us and ensure that the United States of America fulfills the responsibilities that the plan entails."

Wen stopped. More applause broke out. It was almost hysterical.

In the Oval Office, there was stunned silence.

"What the hell was that?" said Larry Olsen.

Joe Benton shook his head in disbelief. "I think that was President Wen saying yes."

Monday, November 7
Capitol Hill, Washington, D.C.

There was no handshaking, no smiles, as Joe Benton made his way onto the Senate floor. The faces that watched him were grave. He walked quickly and silently to the rostrum.

He had struggled long and hard with what he would say. Whether the words were right, or not, he didn't yet know. First the joint session of Congress, then the world, then history would judge.

All of Congress waited for the president to speak.

"A little more than a year ago today," he began, "the people of this great nation paid me the highest honor it is in their gift to pay. They asked me to be their president and lead our nation for the coming four years. I knew then what we all know, that leadership involves hard choices, hard times. A week ago today began the hardest time that I, and any of us, can imagine."

He paused. The moment he had first heard about the strike on the Bay area was alive in his mind, as it was, for each person in his or her individual way, in the mind of every man and woman listening.

"I stand before you, I think, as a president who bears the gravest burden a president has ever borne. Two nuclear strikes on our country. Millions of our fellow citizens dead. The number isn't yet known, perhaps never will be fully known. But whether one has died, or one million, the pain for the victim's loved ones is the same. I share the grief of every relative, every friend, every acquaintance of one of the many who died or lies injured today. I share the grief of every father and mother. My daughter was among the victims. Her name was Amy Wallcott Benton, and she was twenty-three."

He stopped again, felt the emotion welling up inside him. He knew, if he didn't go on, the tears would begin to run. Yet he didn't know if he could go on.

In the Senate chamber, many were in tears now.

"I also grieve . . ." He stopped, frowned hard, then drew breath. "I also grieve for the many Chinese men, women, children who have died. I made a decision to strike back once we had been struck. I will relive that decision for as long as I live. Perhaps, in years to come, historians will decide whether I was right. Whether I could have done otherwise.

"When life is suddenly taken away, we seek a reason. We want to be able to say our loved one did not die in vain. Like any bereaved father, I want to say this. Can we? My fellow Americans, history will judge on this as well. But already there is one thing we can say. Out of this catastrophe has come a new path forward. China, and the rest of the world, has agreed to play its part in the Carbon Plan. The knowledge of this is more than a mere glimmer of hope. It is a moment of salvation for our planet, it is the guarantee for our children, and our children's children, and their children beyond. Today our wounds are fresh, our pain is raw. Let this knowledge be a balm, however small, however insufficient, that will grow more soothing with time. They did not die in vain. Only if we fail to carry through the work that lies ahead of us, will this be so.

"There is work ahead. There will be difficulties, there will be challenges. But when we get beyond these—and we will get beyond them, we will overcome the obstacles that today seem so great—our world will be a better place, and we can be secure that we have made it safe for the generations to follow.

"Our first priority, today, is to help the survivors and the families of those who are gone, and we are doing this to the utmost of our ability. Many private citizens have made important contributions to this effort, and in their vast response we are seeing the spirit of our republic at it finest. In addition, as we do this, preparations for the programs and legislation to put the Carbon Plan in place are under way. After what has happened, this will be more difficult than we expected. We will have to try harder, we will have to sacrifice more. But we can do it, and we will do it. Rest assured that I and every member of my administration will spare no effort, no resource, no ounce of our energy, no moment of our time, no attempt that is humanly possible to bring our nation through this. This is not the moment to dwell on the details. In the weeks to come, I will be putting these before you.

"I will also be asking Congress to hold an investigation into my administration's handling of the recent crisis. If there was any misjudgment or negligence that ought to exclude me or anyone else from office, I want this to be known and the appropriate action taken, even if it involves myself. Especially if it involves myself. Last week, on the White House lawn, I said the buck stops with me. And so it does.

"But now, as I said, is not the time to dwell on the details. I believe that our republic, and the nations of our planet, have the potential to emerge from this crisis, and from the shared endeavor of the Carbon Plan, a better place. Surely if we have learned one thing from the past week, it is that our capacity to destroy when we are divided is great, but our capacity to build when we are united is even greater. Out of the ashes of the fires that burned, I sense arising a great spirit of hope and fellowship across our nation and across our world. Let this truly be a turning point for the community of nations, let us capture this spirit and hold fast to it always as we go forward. From our shared endeavor we will emerge a more humane world, a more understanding world, a more friendly world. I know that nowhere will this spirit reign more truly than in these United States of America, for it is the very spirit in which our republic was founded so long ago. By helping each other, we help ourselves. By giving opportunity to others, we create opportunity for ourselves. By welcoming into our communities those who have been displaced, we make our communities stronger for all who live within them. These communities, my friends, will be the monument to those who gave their lives. A year ago, I asked you to build with me a new foundation. Tonight, I ask you again. Let us build it well. Let us build it strong. Let us build it worthy of those who are no longer with us.

"God bless America. God bless every nation on earth. God bless the great and shared endeavor on which, this day, we all embark."

On the ride back to the White House, Heather stared out the window. The November night was rainy. The drops clustered on the glass, streamed back in the wind.

"Heather," he said softly.

She didn't turn.

"Heather, what I said back there, I believe it. There is a spirit of hope now. If we harness it, this country can do great things, all the things we always talked about and more." He hesitated. "It doesn't bring her back. But at least it means it wasn't in vain, doesn't it?"

Heather shrugged, still staring at the night.

"I don't know if it had to happen like this. Maybe . . ." Joe Benton frowned. He had gone through every step, every step, and he would, he knew, until his dying day. A horrible suspicion was beginning to form, deep within him, that it had always been the case that something like this would have to happen. That only a massive catastrophe would shock the world out of the delusion that half measures and half steps would be enough and that the problem would be solved tomorrow, if not today, without any price to be paid. Maybe it had always been inevitable that some agonizing convulsion would be needed to galvanize the will to do what should have been done—and could have been done—so much more easily, and less painfully, ten, twenty, thirty years before. And maybe it had always been the case that this catastrophe would have to be something that human beings inflicted on each other, since all the catastrophes that nature so abundantly inflicted seemed not to be enough. And yet it was almost unbearable to think that this was true, that despite all the science, the evidence, the analysis and the projections that the most sophisticated computers could produce, in the end it would take the crudest, most primitive argument—death, millions and millions of needless deaths—to make this happen. It shook his faith in humanity. It made him wonder whether human beings had ever made any progress at all, whether, deep down, they weren't still just tribes of cave men clubbing each other into the mud.

"I don't know. Maybe we can make a better world out of this. That's what we have to do, Heather. That's what Amy would have wanted."

He watched her. He wished he knew better how to comfort her. He wished he knew better how to fill the great emptiness that Amy's death had left within himself.

He laid his hand lightly on her arm.

Heather turned.

"You know what the thing is?" she said.

"What is it?"

"We don't even have her body. There's nothing left of her. Nothing at all."